BOOK ONE OF
THE REBEL EMPIRE DUOLOGY

EMPIRE
OF
BLOOD

Olivia Cornwell

EMPIRE OF BLOOD
Copyright 2020 © by Olivia Cornwell

ISBN: 978-1-953185-00-6

To the Master Storyteller
The firstfruits of the stories You've given me to tell.

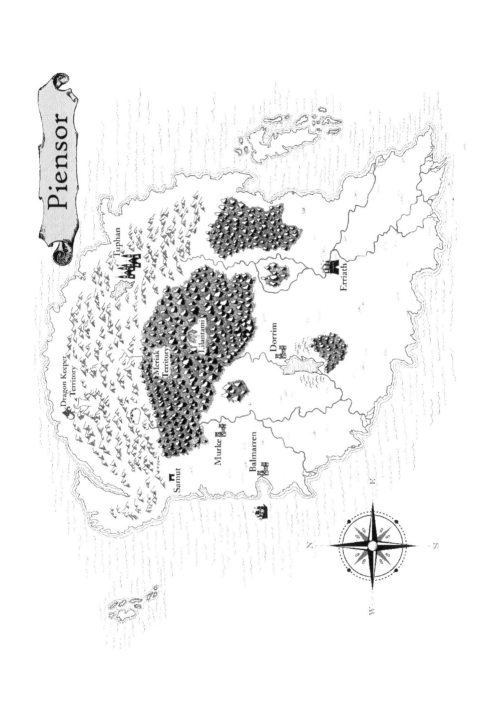

TABLE OF CONTENTS

1
COPING MECHANISMS

The day the Bean blew up, Lilly punched a kid named Dante who thought he was funny.

One of those things was something Chicago had never seen before. The other was something Lilly Faine had done before.

But to be fair, she didn't usually *plan* it.

"This one." Amber leaned over the cafeteria table, holding her phone out. "I ordered it last night."

Lilly examined the image of the cerulean gown. "You're gonna look smoking hot."

"I know." Amber preened. "Have you decided what you're wearing?"

Lilly took a chip from the bag. "I found a maroon dress online this morning. I'll order it tonight." She grinned. "The neckline may or may not make the chaperones have a fit."

"Oooh." Amber's perfectly trimmed brows waggled. "I'm almost jealous."

Lilly snorted. "Oh, like yours is within the guidelines." She leaned forward to whisper, "Has Jeremy asked you yet?"

"No." Amber pouted. She eyed Lilly almost cautiously. Or slyly. Lilly wasn't sure. "I thought I'd ask Gabe."

Sly. Definitely sly. Lilly grimaced. "Why? He's a dork and

wouldn't realize you'd asked him until, like, tonight, and then I'd have to deal with him." Lilly scanned the cafeteria. "Ask Dante."

"You don't like Dante."

"I *tolerate* Dante," Lilly corrected, tucking her red hair behind her ear. "But he's kinda cute, and he's been watching us since you pulled out your phone."

Amber cast a glance at the neighboring table. Lilly smirked as Dante's gaze quickly shifted to his food; his buddies looked from him to the girls. Lilly rolled her eyes. Super subtle. "Show me your dress again. We'll send it to him—"

"Lilly!"

Amber looked up from her phone faster than Lilly did. Lilly barely gave her brother a second glance. "What?"

"Where is your phone?" Gabriel waved his own cell phone in her face. "I've been trying to find you."

"It's right here." Lilly dug in her bookbag. "Why didn't you call—oh."

"You have problems," Amber said, peering at the dead-battery symbol on Lilly's phone. "That's, what, fourth time this week?"

Lilly glared and looked back up at Gabriel. Her annoyance faded. His expression was something deeper. "What's wrong?"

"Dad called."

"He *called*? Why? Is everything..." She stopped. "Oh, it's today." Her brother's humorless mood made sense now. Lilly bit her lip and stood. "Okay. Okay, let me grab my stuff—"

"Leaving?" A boy with sandy hair spun Lilly around and kissed her. "What's wrong?" He searched her face. Lilly patted her boyfriend's arm absently.

"Nothing," she said. "Family stuff. Amber, show Nick your dress. He'll get Dante to ask you to the dance."

Gabriel blinked. "You don't like—"

"I *tolerate* Dante." Lilly glowered. "I am doing a good deed and making sure my best friend is not dateless."

"So, you're sticking her with a guy you don't even like?"

Amber groaned. Lilly smacked Gabriel's shoulder. "Not the time, Gabe. Dad, remember?"

Nick glanced at Gabriel, then Lilly. "Oh, today's when... your mom. Right." His words brought Lilly's focus back. Her lunch twisted nervously in her stomach. If he was *calling*, it was pretty bad.

"He might just be lonely today." Lilly kissed her boyfriend. "I'll probably be back before next period." She followed Gabriel to the cafeteria doors.

"Or he's just crazy."

Lilly froze. Gabriel slowed too, and Lilly ignored the warning in his eyes. She turned to face Dante's table. A few of the guys at the table lost their snickering grins. Nick, who'd started to sit down beside Amber, slowly rose again. Amber watched, her eyes bouncing between Dante, Lilly and Gabriel.

Lilly took a careful breath. "What did you say?"

Dante looked at her. He wasn't anything impressive, just a little taller than she was. He wore reading glasses, which he took off and set on top of his political history book. He pivoted in his chair. His T-shirt was some graphic logo of a hipster band Lilly didn't know, but "Desdemona's Kybosh" sounded as stupid as Dante was, so it was fitting.

"Or he's just crazy," Dante repeated. "You know, talking about a magical world and a homicidal king. I'm kind of surprised it hasn't gotten him locked up already."

Lilly's fingers curled into fists. She started forward, but Gabriel grabbed her arm.

"Leave it," he said. "He's not worth it." Gabriel's grip was too tight as he pulled her away, and his glare bored into Dante's. A second passed, and Gabriel turned his back. Lilly forced herself to follow. Dante wasn't worth the detention. Her father told her time and again to ignore the words, ignore the rumors. He did, Gabriel did. Why couldn't she?

"Not going to stick up for your old man, Gabe?" Dante jeered. "I have to know: Where he comes from, are there insane asylums, or do they just have dragons?"

"Shut up, Dante," Nick snapped. A few kids looked up from nearby tables. "It was years ago and doesn't matter now."

Lilly clenched her teeth. *Just keep walking.*

"What?" Dante said. "Not every day you hear about somebody who thinks he's from another world. I've heard the stories, same as you. He's pretty much straight out of Dungeons and Dragons."

"That was *fifteen years* ago," Amber fired back. "Just drop it."

Lilly took a breath. Keep walking. Keep—

"But nobody actually knows *what* happened. Is there really an evil king after him?" Dante asked, loud enough for the whole cafeteria to hear. "I heard he just made it up to cover up how his wife really died—"

Gabriel's grip faltered. Lilly wrenched free and strode back, a tidal wave of fury. She wasn't sure how fast she moved. Only that her upper body twisted, uncoiled, and her fist cracked against Dante's nose before he could move. The pain reverberated back through her hand and arm. Her fingers throbbed with a satisfying sting.

Tables erupted in shouts of alarm. Dante's tablemates scrambled back as he tumbled out of his chair.

"Say it again, and I'll pound you into the floor," Lilly snarled, shoving the chair out from between her and the boy. "You don't know what happened, so shut up."

Dante scrambled to get to his feet. His nose bled, and his eyes watered. He glared at Lilly. "I'll say what I want. Your dad's crazy, and it seems to run in the family—"

Lilly swung again. Dante brought his arm up to catch her blow or strike back, but before it could land Nick grabbed her arm, pushing himself between them. Gabriel had done the same, his arms hooked around Dante's to hold him back.

"Babe, take it easy," Nick grunted as Lilly squirmed.

"What in heaven's name?" A teacher rushed up, with two more and the principal in tow. Her eyes scanned Lilly, Gabriel, Nick, and a bloody Dante.

The principal sighed. "Lilly Faine, how many times—"

"As many as it takes to get it through people's heads." She hadn't meant to snap at the principal. The words came in a rush and she didn't care to stop them. "My father *isn't* crazy, and he had *nothing* to do with how my mom died." She glared at Dante, who glared right back and jerked against Gabriel. Lilly's brother snarled and wrenched Dante back, slamming him into a chair and blocking his path. Gabriel's brown hair—the same shade as their father's—fell in his face, giving him a wild, almost rabid look, his hazel eyes going dark. Lilly's anger faltered at the sight.

Before Dante could stand, one of the teachers hurried to examine his nose. Lilly kept glaring, her body pulsing with a ferocity that needed quenching. She only vaguely heard Gabriel explain to the principal about their father's phone call and the altercation. Nick watched her, worried.

"Babe?"

"I'm fine," she ground out. She pulled free of him. Nick let her.

"She broke it!" Dante whined.

"Good," Lilly hissed.

"Miss Faine!" a teacher scolded.

The principal rubbed his temples. "Gabriel, if your father needs you both, you may go." He looked at Lilly. "There will be suspension, Miss Faine. I will be calling your father to discuss this further." He gave her a stony look. "This is one time too many."

Lilly tried not to notice Gabriel's dismayed look. If their father heard about it today, of all days...

"We'll be back," Gabriel promised, pulling her away. "I'm sorry, sir."

I'm not. Lilly ignored the silent eyes that watched her like she was a freak show.

"Want me to come with?" Nick followed them partway, passing Lilly her bookbag.

"No," she said dully. "I won't be long."

Nick grabbed her hand and waited until she looked up at him. "Tell me if there's anything I can do. I can bring dinner. That Thai place he likes, and lemon-lime ice cream for you."

Lilly forced a smile and kissed him. "Thanks. I'll see you later. And you'd better have ice cream tonight."

She pulled away from Gabriel as soon as they left the school. "I'm not going to apologize."

"I didn't ask you to."

"He deserved it."

"I know."

"I made him bleed."

"Yeah."

There was silence as they walked. Silence as they waited for the traffic lights to change.

Gabriel sighed. "How do you do it?"

"Do what?"

"How do you... I don't know." Gabriel looked away, frustrated. "How do you find the strength to stand up to people like him?"

Lilly looked at him, tilting her head. She considered the question, then shrugged. "I dunno. I just... it just happens. Like I can't stand sitting still or letting him have the last word."

Gabriel smirked. Lilly shifted her backpack. "Why? You looking for lessons?"

"No, no." Gabriel started across the street. He shook his head. "I don't know. Nevermind."

She stuffed her hands into her coat pockets when the silence stretched. "None of it's true, right?"

"Did those words just come out of your mouth?"

Lilly smacked Gabriel's shoulder. He veered away and almost ran into a lamppost. "Of course it's not true."

Lilly hunched her shoulders as the wind picked up. "Just... Dad never talks about what happened. He talks about everything else about her except that."

Gabriel's breath puffed white clouds. "It's probably not something he wants to talk about." He pulled her into a side-hug. Lilly leaned into him.

"I worry too," Gabriel murmured. "But Dad's fine. He's not crazy."

"How would *you* explain the stories, then?"

"Coping mechanism?" Gabriel shrugged, pulling away. "Like how you need ungodly amounts of tea just to start your day." He sprinted to avoid her. "The stories might be a side effect of whatever happened that day. Something to avoid dealing with the real thing." Gabriel's smile slipped. "I do think that there were other people involved, though."

"Like an actual murderer?"

He shrugged evasively. "All I know is that the details are vague, and Dad won't talk about it. Like it scared him. Or someone did something to make him this way. News reports just say we were all at the Bean, and fresh out of Scotland, when it happened." His brows twitched. "And nobody's done a thing about it since."

Lilly nodded. Details *were* vague, and nobody seemed to know what had happened that day, not even eyewitnesses. Only that it was weird, and their father wouldn't stop speaking in Gaelic. Or something like it. His wife's body in his arms, two crying babies beside them.

And far too much blood.

After that, there were a lot of police, and Tilas Faine had been taken under the wing of Nathaniel and his wife, a cop and a substitute teacher. They helped him and his two infant kids get settled in Chicago, and life went on from there. The world slowly forgot that day, and told Tilas to forget it too. Told him his stories were just impossible.

But Gabriel's tone in his last sentence...

It's just leftover anger at Dante. He's just in a mood. Lilly shivered as they walked to Millennium Park. The winter sun provided little warmth, and Lilly huddled next to Gabriel. "He'll be okay, won't he? Someday?"

"Of course," Gabriel said, his voice the usual big-brother tone. "We just need to be there for him on days like this."

They reached the park, cold and rather bare. Even in winter their father worked the gardens, keeping things neat and clean. Some days he would simply pick up trash. The smallest of chores was reason enough for him to go, even if there were others who could do it just as well. It was *his* park, in a way; a space that meant almost as much to him as his own children.

"I did try to ignore him," Lilly blurted. "But then he brought Mom into it."

"I know," Gabriel said. "I would've punched him too." The tone of Gabriel's voice was dark again. Something Lilly didn't often hear. Unsure, she forced a smile.

"I'd pay to see that. I've never seen you punch anybody."

Gabriel smiled faintly. "You always beat me to it."

They reached the top of the steps. The Bean stood a few yards off, surrounded by people even on this cold day. The snow hadn't fallen yet, but the weather promised it soon.

"There he is." Gabriel pointed. Lilly smiled and waved as they approached. A middle-aged man with graying brown hair stood beside a metal cart full of tools and a dangling trash bag. He lifted a hand in greeting. That was their father's way. Tilas Faine rarely waved. It was always a simple lift of the hand, but it still made you feel noticed and welcomed.

"Hey Dad." Lilly hugged him. She inhaled the scent of his coat. It smelled like outdoors and grass clippings and dirt, life and exercise and all the seasons at once. It calmed her. It always did.

"Hello, my darling." Tilas held her close, then Gabriel. "I am sorry to pull you from school. I don't think I can spend the day alone." He drew a slow, heavy breath. "Come, sit."

Gabriel and Lilly exchanged glances before following him to a bench. They had a clear view of the Bean, though they couldn't see what was going on under it. They took a seat on either side of him.

"There is so much I need to tell you..." He went quiet, as if looking for the right words.

Here we go. Lilly forced an uneasy smile. "Are you okay, Dad?"

Her voice seemed to rouse him from his trance. He blinked and took a breath. "I'm sorry..." He smiled. "How is school? Gabriel, you had a test today?"

"Yeah." Gabriel nodded with a smile. "I feel pretty confident about it."

"Good!" Their father's voice strengthened, happy. "Then we will celebrate."

Gabriel ducked his head. "We don't have to—"

"No." Tilas clapped Gabriel's knee. "I have not taken proper interest in your schooling, and it is time I do." He winked at Lilly. "Tests are a milestone, are they not?" Tilas smiled at Gabriel. "On my honor, I will not embarrass you."

Gabriel rolled his eyes, cheeks flushed. Tilas chuckled and looked at Lilly. His brown eyes fixed on hers, and his smile started to fall. Lilly tried not to shrink back.

Crap—

"You are angry."

"Not with you!" Lilly said quickly. "Just... other stuff."

Her father's brows furrowed. "What happened?"

Gabriel was watching her. Lilly chewed her lip. "I... might have gotten into a fight."

"She punched Dante," Gabriel supplied. Lilly glared at him.

"You know what, Gabe—"

"*Lilly,*" Tilas sighed, disappointed.

"Dante's a disrespectful jerk," Lilly grumbled. "He was making fun of you."

"And have you ever known me to strike a man who mocks me?"

Lilly slouched in her seat, only to have her father nudge her upright again. "No..."

"Have you ever known me to engage with someone who does not know what he speaks of?"

"No..."

"My Fire." Tilas tilted her head to look at him. "Having the last word is not always a battle you must pick. Let people say what they will. I know the truth, and that is enough. I know you and your brother are under my roof, safe, fed, healthy, and clothed. That is enough for me. Fighting with this... *smartphone* is the only battle I care to wage."

Lilly smirked. "I told you we could get you a simpler one."

"Ahh, but then how would I be able to see my daughter's photographs of her winter formal?" Tilas winked. "I also quite enjoy carrying a whole library in my pocket."

Gabriel laughed. Lilly leaned against her father. "Are you angry?"

"No..." Tilas said carefully. "But I expect you to apologize to this boy."

She moaned. Tilas chuckled. "Swallowing pride is part of being human, my dear." He looked ahead at the Bean, at the people moving around it. The lighthearted mood vanished, turning gray again as Tilas lapsed back into silence for a moment.

"Do you remember when I took you both to the aquarium here? You were only ten, and Gabriel eleven."

Lilly blinked. "Yeah. It was disgustingly hot outside, and Gabe wanted to swim with the turtles."

"Oh, but you talking to the clownfish was the highlight."

Lilly glared at her brother.

Tilas nodded. "Do you remember what you both told me it was like?"

Lilly frowned. What they'd said it was like? How were they supposed to remember that from seven years ago?

"We said it was like another world," Gabriel said. "Like Atlantis."

"Just so," Tilas agreed. "Another world…"

Lilly glanced at Gabriel, who shrugged. She looked at Tilas. "Dad, let's go home. We can talk there." *Not here. Not in the open where people will see—*

"You were not born here," Tilas blurted. His vaguely Scottish accent was more noticeable, as if releasing this knowledge released that too.

Lilly nodded. "We were born in Scotland, right?"

"No, that is what you have been told," Tilas said. "You were not born in this *world.*"

Silence, then Gabriel ventured to ask, "Where?"

Lilly frowned. They had heard this kind of thing before, but today felt different. Their father was preparing to say more this time.

"A world different from this one," Tilas said. "Allare…" His voice dipped, almost tender. Longing. "In Allare, you both were born in the country of Piensor." He looked at his children. First Gabriel, then Lilly. "It is a world where magic runs like blood through veins."

Or he's just crazy. Dante's words stung, but the way her dad was talking… Lilly shot a warning look at Gabriel. Her brother looked back at Tilas. "Dad, we have papers that say where we're from. I was born in the hospital, and Mom had Lilly at home."

"Words." Tilas shook his head. "They were made up by Nathaniel when we arrived. I wanted to give you both a life without fear, without… oddity. We created a normal beginning for you both. A hospital here, a house here."

Well that was new. Lilly frowned. Their father had been doing well, not talking about these impossible stories of magic or whatever, except on days like today. The day it all happened. Then the stories would come, and there was no telling what they would be about. Except they were strange and vivid and just... impossible.

And as far as Lilly knew, Nathaniel—a *cop*—wasn't into making forgeries.

Tilas gave a slight nod. "He explained to authorities here that the originals had been stolen from us, when your mother..." Tilas's jaw clenched.

There it is. Lilly took one of his hands in hers. His calloused fingers relaxed. "Why don't we get something to eat, Dad? You can tell us back home." *Get him home, get food. Maybe he won't be... like this.*

"No, I must say it here." Tilas shook his head, stroking her hand with his thumb. "It's here that it all happened."

Lilly frowned at the huge silver structure before them, its mirrored surface smudged by thousands of fingers. Tourists took pictures next to it and under it, walking in and out of it as if through a gateway. "What happened here? Mom dying?" Lilly bit her lip. "Daddy... we know. We've seen the reports."

Tilas, silent, took something from his pocket. A necklace, a circular amulet just a little bigger than a ping-pong ball. It had a metal back and jagged glass edges, like the top had been broken. Tangled in the silver chain was a piece of broken glass with similar jagged edges, dull on the surface but still sharp. He gave the amulet to Lilly and the glass shard to Gabriel.

Lilly blinked. The amulet tingled in her hand, like pins and needles. It looked old, scuffed and dull. She glanced at Gabriel, who examined the glass closely. Did it tingle for him too?

"We left our world the day the soldiers came. I thought we would be safe... that *it* would be safe, in another world. They would never follow us." Tilas's voice was tight. His frequent pauses made Lilly anxious. His stories weren't usually this emotionally charged. Lilly's insides twisted at the thought of her father's mind slipping for real. Why did he believe so hard in these stories that just couldn't be true, or even possible?

Tilas looked at the Bean, his brown eyes sad and moist. "I've made many mistakes, but the one I regret is not protecting her..."

He needs to get out of here. Lilly looked up at Gabriel, mouthing her concern. Gabriel nodded slightly and stood.

"Dad, let's get you home. This place is upsetting you," Gabriel coaxed gently. "You can tell us everything there. We'll get takeout. Nick offered to get Thai, and—"

Tilas grabbed Gabriel's arm. He gave a surprised yelp and jerked back. Lilly jumped. "Dad?"

Tilas didn't answer. He stood slowly, his eyes locked on the Bean as if he were in a trance. He was trembling.

Startled cries from the Bean made her turn. Tourists scuttled out from under it, their eyes filled with fear. Four men in dark clothes stepped out from under the structure. Some of the tourists took pictures. All four carried swords or daggers, like characters straight out of a medieval fair. They didn't look happy.

Lilly stood, slipping the amulet into her pocket.

"Stay close to me," Tilas murmured. "Do not run."

One of the medieval warriors turned their way. He looked Tilas up and down as if trying to place him. His black hair was as greasy as his smug, triumphant sneer.

"Tilas Faine?" he finally asked. The other three men watched, then their eyes were drawn to the nervous civilians nearby, to the buildings and cars. To the flash of smartphone cameras.

Tilas gazed at the man, his eyes distant, as if he were trying to recall some memory.

"Zal Ira, isn't it?" Tilas finally responded, his voice a wary kind of calm. "You were only a student."

The man scowled. He looked at Gabriel, then Lilly, and back to Tilas, as if searching for the resemblance. Lilly glared at him when his eyes came back to her, and Zal grinned.

"These yours?" He motioned to Gabriel and Lilly. "Where's the wife?" His voice held the same not-quite-Scottish flavor as Tilas's, but rougher.

"What do you want, Zal?" Tilas asked.

"In time," Zal said, his posture casual. He enjoyed having the advantage. "My first order of business is meeting your precious family." His eyes scanned the park. "Where is your lovely wife, Faine?"

"Hollyn is dead." Tilas's voice strained. "She was killed, an arrow in her back. It caught her before she made it through, and she died here."

Lilly stared at her father. His eyes clouded with grief. She looked at Gabriel. He was watching their father, slack-jawed. They'd suspected foul play, but to hear it from their father's lips...

"Pity. The children will do."

Tilas visibly stiffened. "You will not touch them."

"I'll do what I like," Zal said. "It makes it easier to get what I want. I've spent a long time looking for you."

Zal spread his arms out to either side. Afternoon shadows rippled on the cement and leached from the trees, the lampposts, the Bean. They snaked toward Zal to make four pools of darkness.

"Have your children seen magic, Tilas?" Zal asked. Lilly gaped as four *things* rose from the ground. Shapeless at first, but then taking different forms: Jagged spikes along one spine, a hunched-over humanoid figure with scythes for hands on another. They were silent, facing Tilas and his children. Their faces had no eyes, but Lilly's stomach twisted uneasily. They still *saw* her. Ready to attack the second she moved.

Bystanders shouted in alarm, scrambling away. Some took off running, others dialed 911. The stupid ones still held up their smartphone cameras. Zal's men focused on Tilas.

Zal, however, seemed hardly concerned as he surveyed the creatures around him. One lifted a long, horse-like head to him. Zal flicked his wrist at Tilas and his children.

The shadow monsters sprang forward. Lilly flinched back, and Gabriel pulled her to his chest to shield her. She couldn't tear her eyes from the living shadows as they surged forward, snarling like rabid beasts. Their bodies... tangible, but they molded into each other and broke away instead of bumping against each other.

Then her father's hands exploded into literal flames. Lilly's yell of alarm was covered by the shrieks of the monsters as the fire plowed through them. All four dissolved into nothing. Zal cursed.

Two more shadow monsters rose up on either side of Lilly and Gabriel. Lilly shouted and smacked the one nearest her. Her hand passed through its shoulders and chest. The creature was cold. Cold and empty.

The monster stood on two legs like a human, about her height, without eyes or facial features. It silently held out a hand to her. Lilly shrank back against her brother, only to find the second monster offering a hand to him.

"They will protect you," Tilas said. "These are mine."

"Yours?" Lilly squeaked. "Dad, what the actual h—"

"Lilly," Tilas cut her off. His expression softened. "My Fire, do as I tell you."

"Got a few novices, eh?" Zal laughed. "Haven't you taught them anything?"

"That life is no longer ours," Tilas said, turning to him. His shoulders, once bowed, had pulled back. He stood taller, more solid.

"Then you won't mind giving me that amulet."

Tilas's body was rigid. Fire licked up his arms again. Lilly reached out and touched one. It was warm, but not burning. Tilas squeezed her hand gently before pushing it away. "I gave up everything to keep it out of his hands, and that will not change."

Zal shrugged. More shadow monsters rose up around Zal and charged like demonic monkeys, their elongated arms lined with curved spikes. Whips of darkness sprouted from the ground before Tilas, cutting through the air inches from the shadow beasts. The monsters squealed and jumped back.

Gabriel's yelp of alarm made Lilly whirl. He stood enveloped in a sheath of darkness, like a suit of armor. He lifted a hand in front of him, flexing his fingers. The shadows covered each digit. "Ohhhh man."

A sharp, cold darkness touched Lilly from behind. It penetrated her coat and clothes until she was surrounded. Her vision darkened.

"Dad!" Lilly snapped.

Tilas didn't answer. The fire slid down his arms and into the palms of his hands, swirling and growing, angry, hot. He swung his arms like a pitcher and threw two balls of fire into the new cluster of shadow monsters, just as they dodged the shadow whips.

Zal gestured with a hand. Lilly flinched as the wind picked up, blowing her hair back and deflecting the fire into the trees. They exploded, lighting up like giant tiki torches. An electrical pole sparked and popped.

The shadow monsters kept coming. Tilas swept his arms wide, and *lightning* erupted at his feet, ripping through the air. It skewered the monsters into oblivion.

"Leave my children alone," Tilas snarled. It was a vicious, feral sound. A tone that warned he wouldn't care if he got blood on his hands.

One of the strangers swiped at the air. More lightning darted across Tilas's bolt, halting its approach with a crack that made Lilly's hair stand on end. Tilas didn't stop, throwing three more balls of fire one after the other. Water shot up out of the concrete like a wall. The fire struck it and sizzled out.

Two of Zal's men stepped forward, shadow monsters rising up by their sides before rushing for Lilly and Gabriel. Tilas twisted around, more fire pulsing bigger in his hands, and a lightning bolt stabbed his side, throwing him back.

"Dad!" Lilly screamed, a second before the shadow armor pivoted her body to swing her fisted hand into a shadow monster. Lilly gaped as the monster bowled into three others that approached. She and Gabriel stared at each other.

"That wasn't me," Lilly said, spitting her hair from her mouth.

"It wasn't?"

"This thing did it. It used me." She couldn't help a shiver of discomfort. She flapped her arm. The shadows followed it.

Zal scowled. "We're wasting time. Get them!"

Piercing sirens halted the fight. Bright blue and red light flashed as police cars rushed up close to the Bean. Zal and his men turned, most of them going for their swords.

Tilas groaned, gripping his metal cart for support. The police rushed up, guns drawn, but no one fired. The confusion on their faces was enough explanation. Who was the enemy?

Lilly's eyes scanned desperately for Nathaniel before she remembered he was on vacation. Her dismay turned to relief. She wasn't sure the cops would be able to contain whatever was going on here.

"What is this?" Zal frowned.

"This world's military," Tilas grunted, struggling to his feet. "Of a sort."

"They look ridiculous."

"I do not disagree."

Zal rolled his shoulders. "They are a nuisance, at any rate."

Tilas lunged forward with a yell as Zal swept a hand at the cops. Fire hurtled toward the officers, and they scrambled to find cover.

Darkness whirled up and channeled the fire away from the cops.

Right into the Bean.

The explosion rocked the park and threw Lilly and Gabriel backward. Lilly hit the ground without her shadow armor, and the thick smoke turned to darkness.

2

GONE

The world wouldn't stop ringing. And everything hurt.

Lilly coughed on dusty air as she rolled, shaking, to her hands and knees. Her skull throbbed, and she gingerly touched the source, grimacing when her hand came away bloody.

Someone yelled. Her father?

A figure materialized in front of her. Lilly scrambled to get up, but the figure was faster. Human hands grabbed her arms, pinning them to her sides. Lilly writhed, her hair falling in her face. "Dad!"

Tilas shouted back, and the wind picked up. It scooped the haze into the air, pushing it into Chicago's skyline. Lilly blinked her vision clear, and her heart dropped in horror.

The Bean was destroyed, with only the two ends left standing, like two halves of an eggshell. Its pieces lay scattered everywhere, jagged and melting. Arms of rebar and other supportive materials stuck out from inside the two ends like jagged ribs.

Some police lay motionless on the ground, while others picked themselves up or crept out from whatever cover they'd found. A cop car was on fire.

One of Zal's men pushed to his feet. Zal himself had remained standing, shadows wisping around him. His second man stood with his sword to Gabriel's throat.

Gabriel held her gaze, his hair in his eyes as he willed a silent question to her: *Are you alright?*

Lilly nodded once and scanned the park until she found her father.

Tilas stood among the remains of his gardening cart, eyes dark with a fire Lilly had never seen. Her friends often commented that her own brown eyes got dark like that, but this was different. It made her father look... younger, less like the quiet gardener she knew.

He looked like a warrior.

"Reckless as ever," Zal panted. He wiped blood from his lip. "Now take a good look around and reconsider your choice."

The ferocity didn't last long when Tilas finally found his children. His breathing heaved, and the warrior-look disappeared into one of defeat. Fear.

"Let them go," he gasped. "This isn't about them."

"It is now." Zal stalked toward Tilas. "Where is the amulet? Your precious children won't be spared unless you give me what I want."

"Leave him alone!" Lilly screamed.

Zal waved a hand at Lilly. "We'll start with her."

A cold, sharp blade kissed Lilly's throat. She whimpered as it sank into her skin. She stomped on her captor's foot, but his boot was too stiff. Lilly pinched her lips against a cry of pain.

"No!" Tilas cried. "Leave her alone!" He started for her, but a shadow monster pounced on him, wrapping elongated limbs around him. It held him back and anchored him in place. Tilas roared, writhing, and fire blazed for a second before the monster butted its faceless head into Tilas's skull. His legs buckled, but he remained standing. The fire faded out and died.

The blade dug in. Lilly flinched and yelped, but there was

nowhere to go. She couldn't move without making it worse.

"Enough, enough!" Tilas screamed. "I'll give it to you!"

Zal held up his hand. The blade stopped moving, but didn't go away. Lilly froze, her eyes locked on her father, begging him to rescue her.

Normally, she preferred to do her own saving. But this was so far out of her wheelhouse. This was... it was impossible.

"Where is it, Faine?" Zal crooned. "Tell me, and this will all be over."

"My daughter," Tilas forced out. "I gave it to her."

Zal turned his eyes on Lilly. He opened his mouth to speak, but a cop beat him to it.

"Stand down!" he shouted, gun raised. "Lower your weapons!"

Zal looked at the officer, frowning. Lilly willed the man to stay back.

"This doesn't concern you, general," Zal told him.

"I said stand down!" the cop shouted. "Put your weapons down!"

Zal rolled his eyes. "Search the girl."

Lilly stiffened as the knife withdrew and her captor gripped her arm. His free hand searched her coat, fumbling with the zipper.

"Don't touch her!" Gabriel roared, writhing.

"Gabriel, no!" Tilas strained against the shadow monster. Lilly screamed as a flash of light struck Gabriel's side. Her brother crumpled, groaning. His coat smoked, but he wasn't dead. He jerked and yelped when his captor poked him with the toe of his boot.

A gunshot ripped through the air. Everyone froze.

Lilly stared, horrified as Gabriel's captor collapsed, lifeless. Gabriel pushed himself away from the man, eyes huge and face pale as he clutched his side. Bile rose in Lilly's throat.

"Put your weapons down!" an officer ordered. "On your knees!"

Tilas whipped around to the police. "Get out of here! Go—" He choked, a tendril of shadow around his throat like a noose. Lilly writhed against her captor as her father clawed at the shadows. Zal and his remaining man threw bolts of lightning into the crowd of officers. The cops ran for cover, but some were struck and went down. Unlike Gabriel, they stopped moving.

Gabriel staggered toward their father. He yanked uselessly at the shadows binding Tilas. A shadow monster appeared at Gabriel's side, ignoring his cry of alarm and helping tear away the shadows. Once freed, Tilas shoved Gabriel behind him and threw his own bolts of lightning to cut off Zal's. The shadow monster who'd helped free Tilas busied itself with fighting off more of the dark, creeping tendrils.

Before her captor could find her jeans pocket, Lilly twisted in his grip and jerked her elbow free to jab into his throat. He gagged and let go, staggering back. He recovered fast, however, and lunged for her, his knife aimed at her heart. Lilly dove aside, her blood pounding and her instincts telling her to move, to fight even without the shadow armor. That familiar voice that said "don't stay down."

Another gunshot. Lilly ducked, and a weight crashed against her, knocking her flat.

Gabriel's scream reached her over those of the crowd. Lilly winced when she moved, and pain throbbed in her forearm. Her captor cried out as she shoved him away. His blade slid out of her arm, but she barely noticed. Lilly stared at the man clutching a bullet wound in his side. More gunshots.

"Fall back!" Zal roared. He conjured a slew of shadow monsters to draw away their fire. "Take them all!"

Zal's last man grabbed Lilly from behind, seeming to materialize from nowhere. His arm wrapped around her as smoky shadows rose up around them. Zal latched onto Gabriel's coat collar.

"No!" Tilas choked out a yell as Zal grabbed hold of him too. "Leave them!"

"Dad!" Lilly writhed, shadows wrapping around her again. But this time they blocked out the flashing police lights, and the shouts and gunshots. The alarmed cries of Zal's fallen companion were smothered. Gabriel, Tilas, and Zal disappeared.

Sheer cold penetrated her winter coat, empty and dangerous. It was a cold *inside* her body, not outside. Like her soul was touched with it. The sensation pulled at her and made her skin crawl. It choked out her scream as the world went dark.

And then it was over. The shadows drifted away like fog. Lilly sucked in air, her eyesight blinded by the whiteness of snow.

Lilly froze.

Snow.

There had been no snow in Chicago. Not even a dusting. Lilly looked down at the white flakes and thin, crusty ice beneath, then at Tilas. Gabriel stared too, wide-eyed.

"Dad?" Lilly said, her voice tight. She took in the rest of their surroundings. The Chicago skyline was gone. The Bean was gone. The gardens, the cars, the cops. All gone. Everything had been replaced with a new city that looked straight out of the same medieval era Zal had come from. It smelled of wood and stone and smoke, and something coppery that made Lilly's stomach churn, though she wasn't sure what it was.

Men and women rushing by yelped in alarm and jumped back. Nearly all of them bore weapons and had on some light armor.

More yelling in the distance was getting closer.

"Dark weavers!" one woman yelled. "Find the sevenths!"

Zal cursed. He thrust Tilas and Gabriel from him. "Rebel vermin. We need to move." He wheeled on Lilly. "I'll make this quick."

"No..." Tilas tried to move. The blade returned to Lilly's neck. Gabriel froze when two ghoulish shadow monsters prowled to him and Tilas. They looked alien, crawling on long, grasshopper-like legs. Tilas swore.

"Don't touch me," Lilly spat, glaring at Zal.

Zal's smile was sickly sweet as he drew closer. Lilly's heart pounded as his finger tucked under her chin, lifting her face to his.

"She's got your eyes, Tilas." Zal grinned. He bent down until he and Lilly were at eye level. "Now, be a good lass, and don't struggle. Or do." Zal straightened. "It will be fun either way."

Lilly spat in his face. Zal twitched and backhanded her, his other hand searching her pockets. Her head spun.

Tilas's hands exploded into flames, and the fire swirled toward Zal. Lilly yelped and flinched back against her captor. Zal swore, jumping back. Lightning surged from his hands, cutting through the fire like paper and striking Tilas. Lilly screamed.

Tilas cried out, and the flames died. He sank to his hands and knees, gasping and clutching his wounded side.

"Stop it! Don't hurt him!" Lilly begged. She blinked hard, fighting tears. Gabriel's glare was murderous.

Zal tsked, drawing a knife. "Perhaps, Tilas, you need a reminder that your children are very much expendable."

Lilly's scream of panic died in her throat as Zal hurled the knife.

Gabriel screamed. Lilly stared in horror as her brother doubled over, a blade in his arm. He looked shocked, and winced as he felt for the knife. Lilly strained against her captor, and grimaced at the blade's edge. Blood trickled down her throat, staining her shirt.

This couldn't be happening. This had to be some awful, messed up nightmare. Maybe she'd really gone at it with Dante and been knocked out. Or maybe the cafeteria food was just that bad. She wanted to believe the latter. Dante was a wimp.

"That was a warning." Zal looked at Tilas, who struggled to rise, crawling halfway to Gabriel before sinking down, groaning. The shadow monsters guarding them only watched, unaffected.

Lilly's body shook, her breath catching. The people who'd called the warning at the start hadn't moved, unsure either where to help or how. They could only watch warily. The shouting was getting closer.

"Zal, we have to *go*," Lilly's captor snapped. "Enough games."

"We will," Zal said, reaching for Lilly again. "I want that amulet in my hands before we go presenting our prize to Lord Rothar—"

A shrill bird call pierced the air. It sounded too sharp to be real, and Zal froze, eyes darting around the city. The shouting was closer now. His expression darkened.

Green vines shot out of the ground and snapped around Zal's legs, yanking him down before wrapping around him. Zal quickly burned them to ash. He swore, his eyes darting around.

"Where are you, seventh?" he roared, getting back up. "Face me!"

Lilly's captor gagged in her ear. His grip loosened, and she jerked away out of reach. The man went down, a vine around his neck, and more anchoring him to the ground. But he too burned them, snarling as he wrenched the vines off.

Gabriel pulled the knife from his shoulder with a sharp cry. Pressing a hand to the wound, he ran to Tilas. "Dad!" He smacked Tilas's cheek. "Hey, stay with me!"

Lilly ran for them. An arrow whizzed past her. She ducked and heard a scream from her captor. She tried not to look at the arrow in his foot.

"Where is it?" Zal shrieked, burning more vines. An arrow nearly sliced his calf.

"I would suggest you stop burning those."

Lilly twisted around. A lady with plaited blonde hair stood in the open, a narrow street at her back. She held an arrow drawn taut in a bow, aimed at Zal's heart. Her brows knitted darkly behind the soft gray fletching of the arrow. The fletching matched her eyes. "Get away from them."

"You're the seventh?" Zal looked the woman up and down. "Will you scream if I burn your earth magic?"

"She won't."

A young man stepped into view beside the archeress. He looked weakened, but firm, his dirty-blond hair plastered to his forehead. It made the scar on his face stand out, stretching from his forehead to his right ear. His fingers sparked with lightning even as more vines cracked through the street around him. "But you will, if you lay one hand on her."

"We have the best of the rebellion surrounding you, all ready to fire at a single command," the woman said, her voice strong, though not harsh. "This is our city."

Lilly glimpsed more people drawing close: most in varying amounts of armor, against others in full armor. The ones already there shouted to them and raised their weapons. It was madness and chaos Lilly didn't understand, and her heart thundered in a terrified race against something unknown and powerful.

"Magic outranks arrows or blades," Zal said. He swept his arm upward, and fire sped across the ground straight toward the woman and the scarred magician boy. The boy's vines dropped, and a surge of water roared around the corner at a sweep of his arms. It split around the pair and met the attack head-on, drowning it out.

A second rush of water bore down on Zal himself, but the man swept it aside, the wind picking up speed and shattering glass as it shoved the water through them. He snarled, turning to Tilas, who was on his feet, arms outstretched.

"The gods damn you, Faine," Zal snarled. A quick hand motion, and lightning arced down at Tilas.

"They already have," Tilas grunted, countering with a slice of darkness, pulled from the people-shadows. It shot out of the ground like a spike.

Zal swept his arms around in a complex pattern. A literal tornado of lightning roared in *Lilly's* direction. Her mind screamed at her to run, to *move*.

But something empty, dark, and *cold* held her to the ground like roots. Lilly jerked, anchored by those dark tendrils, like so many hands had reached up from hell. She heard Gabriel scream, then her father. Shadows were wisping around him.

Lilly flinched, covering her head, as the tornado flew toward her. The next second she was flying back, hitting the ground as a scream rent the air.

She fought to regain her breath, grimacing as she moved her aching limbs. Her clothes weren't burned, she wasn't zapped to a crisp. How had she—

"Dad!" Gabriel cried, staggering to him. Lilly sat up, her body aching. *No, no, no—*

Tilas lay between Lilly and Zal. His body trailed smoke, and his skin was streaked with black. His coat smoldered with charred, ragged holes.

Lilly stumbled over to them. Their father barely stirred. Lilly grabbed for a pulse. Panic filled her mind. What was she supposed to do now? What did those emergency classes say? Look for a pulse, then CPR? "Dad, stay with us!"

Zal's partner stopped him from approaching Lilly. "Zal, leave it! They have more sevenths coming. Leave them all and let's *go*."

An arrow whistled through the air. One of the shadow monsters with the grasshopper legs sprang into its path and snatched it out of the air. Zal laughed, shoving his companion away. "You've got spirit, lady. Didn't know the rebels had you."

Vines shot up from the ground again, barring Zal from Lilly. The scarred boy's hands and body visibly trembled, but his gray eyes were fire and wrath.

The fighters got closer. Lilly tried to block it all out. "Gabe, he's not breathing—*Gabriel!*" Lilly grabbed for her brother's sleeve as he dashed past, their father's knife in his hand, cutting through the vines. The scarred boy yelped, staggering. Ahead, shadows were surrounding Zal and his partner. "Gabriel, no!"

Gabriel lunged at Zal, knife raised. Zal ducked and grabbed Gabriel's knife arm. He twisted, forcing Gabriel to his knees, and looked at Lilly. No sneer on his lips, only frustration and malice. "If you want your brother, bring the amulet to Erriath."

"Fall back!" the woman yelled to the approaching fighters. "Don't touch them!" Before she could ready another arrow, the shadows covered all three of the men before her. Lilly, her hands fumbling for her father's pulse, could only stare as they all disappeared like wisps of smoke. The vines lashed at air, too late.

Gabriel was gone.

3
A WHOLE NEW WORLD

Lilly stared at the spot, hardly breathing. This had to be a nightmare. She would wake up and be in her apartment with her dad and her brother. Everybody would be safe, and none of *this* would be real.

Tilas groaned, his breath rattling, startling her back to the present. His eyes fluttered, and he coughed. Lilly grasped his hand and tried not to look at the blood and charred flesh. "It's gonna be okay, Dad; we'll get an ambulance, just hold on."

Footsteps set off Lilly's nerves and she spun around, hands clenched into fists. The woman lifted her hands. Lilly glimpsed a braided maroon cord around her wrist. "I want to help. We need to get out of the open."

Tilas coughed again. Lilly didn't have time to be suspicious. Her father didn't have time. She looked around, trying to take in the buildings, the fighting that had come uncomfortably close, flashing between streets. Fighters wearing light armor held back soldiers in full battle gear, shielding her from the rush of a war she didn't understand. "Where did they take my brother?" Lilly dragged her attention back to the archeress.

"I don't know," the woman said, her voice soft, sad.

"It doesn't matter now. They're gone, and we need to go. This place is about to become a bloodbath." The boy with the vines limped over, but stopped partway and leaned against a wall for support. His sides heaved for air, and he looked ready to pass out. "Is he alive?"

"Only just." The woman frowned at him. "We can't move him, Jek. He might not make the trip."

"Well he's not going to survive out here, either." The boy staggered forward. He waved off the woman's support when he tripped over his own feet.

"What's going on?" Lilly snapped. "Who are you people?" She tried not to look at the disrupted snow. At the blood stains. Her blood. Gabriel's blood. Her father's blood.

"Those are questions to ask when we aren't about to die," the boy said. "You and I will carry your father. Aderyn will cover us." His gray eyes met Lilly's. "The rebels are holding the soldiers off as long as they can, but we need to get to the safe house. So breathe, get up, and walk."

Lilly took a breath and nodded. She and the boy grabbed her father's arms, pulling him upright. Tilas moaned, his cry weak and small. Lilly nearly buckled under his weight.

"Jek, you can't carry him all that way," Aderyn protested.

"Just start moving," Jek panted.

They moved away from the fighting. Tilas was half-conscious, his legs noodly and nearly useless.

"Hang on, Dad," Lilly gasped. "We'll get you help."

They walked between squished homes and shops made of simple cut stone and wood. Doors were closed to them, and no light came from windows. But for the battle growling around her, Lilly would have thought the place deserted.

Sweat beaded down her face despite the cold. She saw more

bodies as they walked. Some looked ordinary: light leather armor, simple clothes. Others wore polished metal armor, now stained with blood and the grime of the city. A three-headed winged snake was emblazoned on the metal armor. Amethyst eyes glared at Lilly, vicious and deadly even when their wearers were cold.

"What happened here?" Lilly asked. She forced her eyes from the corpses whose faces started resembling her father's.

"War," Jek said. His face was dangerously pale, and his steps were shaky. "Almost there."

Bodies followed them, as if marking their path. A thousand questions rattled around Lilly's head, but she didn't have enough breath to ask them.

They turned a corner, where men stood guard by a building that looked like a hotel. They whirled, swords drawn. Above them, a maroon banner rippled lightly. Five stars were in its center, encircled by leafy vines and three golden lilies.

"Weapons down!" Jek barked, authority strengthening his voice. "A healer, *now!*"

Two men dashed inside, and three others hurried forward. Jek moved to let one take his place, and as soon as he stepped away his legs nearly gave out. Aderyn caught him, and this time Jek didn't refuse her help.

"Miss." A second man approached Lilly. She looked at him warily, but moved to let him take her father inside. The third man assisted Aderyn with Jek as Lilly followed her father. The door closed behind her, surrounding her with warmth. The smell of sweat and unwashed bodies hit her next, and she grimaced.

People were yelling. A man and a woman hovered around Tilas where he'd been laid on a long table. Jek was put in a chair, slumped over. The same maroon banner had been draped over the banisters of the upstairs railing, tattered and stained.

"Dad!" Lilly rushed forward. The man turned to block her path.

"Don't," Aderyn intercepted. "He's her father."

The man stepped back. "There isn't anything we can do... the damage to his body is too severe."

The words struck Lilly like a punch to the gut. "Wh-what?" She could just see Tilas's chest rise and fall in too-short breaths. "No. No, he can't—he has to live! Where's a hospital?"

"This is one," the man said softly. "Or the best we can make. The proper one is still imperial-held, and they would kill him in an instant."

Lilly pushed past to Tilas's side. She shook him gently. "Dad, stay awake. Please. Come on." Her heart pounded, blood roaring with the adrenaline and fear. Nothing was making sense. She needed him to make sense of it all.

Tilas grimaced as pain shuddered through his body. "Gabriel..."

"He's fine, Dad," Lilly said, hating the lie the second it came out. "Stay awake for me. Talk to me."

Tilas's eyelids lifted again. "The amulet—" He winced and coughed. Blood speckled his chin.

"I've got it. It's in my pocket." Lilly looked at the people standing around. "There has to be something we can do! He can't die!"

Aderyn shook her head. Tears shone in her eyes. A cold fist closed over Lilly's heart. Her breathing hitched in panic. "No, no, there's got to be something—"

Tilas coughed, the fit lasting too long. He grimaced, his hand reaching. "Lilly."

Lilly turned back to him, taking his hand. "I'm right here, Dad."

For a minute, Tilas's eyes were focused, gazing at her. "My Fire..."

His weak smile was replaced with a grimace, his body arching as the pain came back. Lilly choked on a breath. "Dad—"

"Don't let him find it," Tilas gasped, desperation lacing his voice. His grip tightened. "Don't let him use it—" More coughs wracked his body. Lilly tried to steady him. Tilas groaned, his voice dropping to a whisper. "Stone... The Meriak..."

"Don't try to talk," Lilly soothed. Tilas's hold on her hand started to soften. Lilly gripped his tighter. "Dad, no! Stay with me! You have to stay with me! Y-you need to stay awake. Gabriel's coming! He-he'll know what to do. I take it back, you need to keep talking!"

Someone laid a hand on her shoulder. Lilly shrugged it away. "Just stay awake." She didn't feel a pulse, but she could see Tilas's short, ragged breaths. "Tell me the stories you used to tell us," she begged, squeezing his hand back. "Tell me what you meant back in Chicago. Were Gabe and I born here?"

Tilas seemed roused by her touch and voice. He struggled to keep his eyes on Lilly's. The brown was dull and glassy. "You and Gabriel... in Murke—" Pain coursed through him again, taking his breath away and destroying his focus.

"Dad, no!" Lilly gripped his hand when it went slack, and his chest didn't rise like it should have. "Daddy, please!"

The scream ripped through her, tearing her heart, squeezing her lungs until she had no more air, no more of anything, as she watched her father's life slip away in a final breath, his eyes gazing at the rafters.

Lilly shook her father, panic overtaking her. She begged him to come back, to wait until Gabriel came back. Gabriel needed to be here too. He couldn't leave without saying goodbye. He couldn't *leave.*

The tears came hot and unceasing. Lilly doubled over as the sobs choked out her breaths. Someone touched her again. Lilly let Aderyn hold her tight as she cried and sank to the floor. The icy fist squeezed her heart.

She was frozen, her eyes on her father's hand, dangling where it had fallen from her grasp. The blackened veins under his skin were ugly, like Zal's monsters were still there, poisoning him. Stealing his life.

Gone. Her father was gone. The man who'd gotten her up in the mornings on school days. Helped her with her homework—or struggled with her. Held her and cried with her when she had her first ugly breakup. Taught her to defend herself when she kept getting into fights at school.

Her father, the man who'd been there for everything. Who hadn't gotten angry with her for punching Dante. The man who had loved her and Gabriel more than life itself, and sacrificed all of himself so they would be happy.

But he was gone, like her mother. Taken by forces she didn't understand, didn't know. Lilly choked on another sob.

A door opened, and a rush of cold air made Lilly shiver and brought her focus back. Voices spoke, but Aderyn's arms didn't move. Lilly didn't move either.

Floorboards creaked. "Aderyn?"

A new voice. A man with auburn curls and a bit of scruffy ginger stubble. His eyes were mismatched, one green and one gray; they looked at Tilas, then Lilly, then Aderyn. His expression morphed to one of understanding. Behind him, men with swords and light armor stood silently watching.

"There wasn't anything we could do... Kedmir, there were dark weavers, and—" Aderyn's voice cracked and cut off.

Lilly shuddered. She watched as the man approached the table and gently closed Tilas's eyes.

"What happened?" Kedmir asked, addressing Aderyn and Jek. Lilly took a shaking breath, grateful she wasn't called on.

"We found them in the city," Jek said, his voice soft. "Dark weavers, led by Zal Ira."

Kedmir cursed, checking himself halfway through with a glance at Lilly and Aderyn. "Why was that roach here? Our reports didn't say anything about him."

"He seemed to have his own objectives," Jek said. He started to say more when a coughing fit doubled him over. Kedmir's frustration instantly turned into concern.

"What happened to you?" Kedmir knelt by him.

Jek waved his hand. "I'm fine. I need to gather the weavers." He stood, but one step sent him to the floor. Aderyn cried out in alarm, and Kedmir caught him. Jek's body shook with the effort just to stand. Lilly glimpsed a braided maroon cord on Jek's wrist, just like Aderyn's.

"You're not going anywhere," Kedmir said, putting him back in the chair, holding him there when Jek tried to push back. "That's an order."

Jek hesitated, but sat back, scowling at the floor.

"Okay." Lilly reluctantly extricated herself from Aderyn's arms after a too-long silence. She needed answers. She wiped her tears, trying not to look at her father's body, her chest still constricted. "Who are you people? Who were those men with the superpowers?" She forced her breathing to steady. She needed her mind to focus on one thing at a time: *Find out where I am, and where Gabriel is. Those two things, Lilly. You can do that. Just focus on Gabe. Don't think about Dad...* She swallowed hard. *Don't. Don't.*

"Those men were imperials," Jek said. His voice was ragged and exhausted, but he didn't look hurt. "Dark magic weavers."

"Magic?" Lilly frowned. "That's not real."

"Then how would you explain what you witnessed back there?" Jek nodded to Tilas. "How would you explain what your father could do?"

"A world different from this one. Where magic runs like blood through veins." Tilas's voice whispered through her mind. As if he were still there, trying to help her understand in the midst of the madness.

"Oh, gosh," Lilly breathed. "His stories, they were all true." She ran her hand through her hair, guilt piercing her already-aching heart. *And I never believed him...*

She was in another world. A world with magic. A world her father had once lived in.

"No, nonono." Lilly stepped back. "This can't be real. That world isn't supposed to be real. Allare or Piensor and everything else he talked about. They're not real—"

"Piensor is real. It is where you stand now," Jek said softly. "Breathe. You've felt the snow, smelled the wood and stone of the city, heard the steel of swords, aye?" He watched her, patient. "And you saw the magic. Your father's and mine."

She forced herself to stare at Jek, not her father's lightning-scarred body. She didn't want to believe it. Nothing she'd seen should have been real. Just stories made up to help cope with traumatic events. Just stories her father stopped telling when people threatened to take his children away because he was crazy.

But she *had* smelled the wood, the stone. *Heard* the swords. It was so different from the exhaust and 24/7 traffic of Chicago, yet somehow this place felt... not as alien as she thought it should.

Lilly blew out a breath. "Alright, we'll put a pin in that. Now where the *hell* is Erriath? That's where Zal took Gabe." Her hand went to her pocket. "He wants the amulet. I have it. I can give it to them and get Gabe back. That's what he said."

Jek shared a glance with Kedmir. "We can't do anything until it's time to march. It's at least a week's journey away." He gave Lilly a look. "And you are in no condition to go anywhere right now."

Lilly crossed her arms. "And when do you 'march'?"

He started to speak, but Aderyn cut in.

"Let's move away from here," she said, her voice gentle, though firm. "We'll get you something to eat, and clean you up. This has been a lot to process."

"I want to bury him first," Lilly said, looking at her father. Her insides twisted as two men gently laid a sheet over the body, concealing Tilas's face.

"We will bury him when the city has been secured," Kedmir promised. "What's your name?"

Lilly took a slow, deep breath. "Lilly Faine. Yours?"

"Kedmir Annor," Kedmir said. "That's my little brother, Jek, and our friend, Aderyn Scalestride." He motioned to them in turn before stepping back to the door.

"I'll take a few men out to make sure the north side is clear, and find Rune." He pointed at Jek. "Make sure he *rests*."

"The weavers—"

"Ghiana can manage them for now. I'll give her her orders," Kedmir interrupted. "You're no use to us when you can barely stand. Zal is a nasty hit for anyone to take." He pinned his brother with a hard stare, challenging him to argue. Jek looked ready to take him up on it, but nodded, his lips pursed. Kedmir turned away and left with his men.

Aderyn stepped toward a door. Lilly turned to follow, but as she did the room swayed, and her vision blurred. "Whoa."

Jek pushed up from his seat and steadied her. "You're hurt."

"There." Aderyn flew back to them. She lifted Lilly's arm. Lilly yelped and pulled back, the movement triggering a sharp pain. Her hand was streaked with little rivers of blood. She noticed a puddle of blood staining the floor beside her. She'd assumed it was someone else's. Her head pounded where she'd hit the pavement.

Aderyn herded her into the kitchen. There was no fire, but it was clean and tidy, and smelled of meaty foods.

"Take off the coat," Aderyn instructed.

Lilly obeyed. She winced as it scraped over the wound, and once it was off, she remembered: one of Zal's men, in Chicago. His dagger slid into her arm after he was shot.

"So, why are you fighting?" Lilly asked, drawing her own mind from the physical and emotional pain as Aderyn set to work. She inhaled. Her muscles were too tense. "Or who?"

"Emperor Yovak," Jek said. He knelt by the wide fireplace, his movement slow and unsteady. "We fight to free our country, and the countries beyond, from his rule."

"Did he do something bad?"

"He takes more power and control than he ought, and abuses it," Jek replied, not looking at the girls, "all in the name of openness and unification." He moved back from the hearth, where a fire pulsed strong. Lilly hadn't even seen him touch a match.

He smiled when her brows furrowed. "Magic," he said simply, and held up his palm. Fire flicked once, a little flash.

"Can you do the magic my dad did?" Lilly asked. "Those... shadow monsters?" The faceless beings seemed to peep in the shadows of the room, and Lilly shivered.

Jek shook his head. "No. What your father and Zal Ira can do is a dark magic. Something learned, not something one is born with."

"Why is that dark?"

"Because it pulls open a place inside you that your Maker did not intend to be opened." Jek looked at the fire. "If you are born with magic, that place was always open and filled. But otherwise..." He shrugged. "You open a place that was never meant to be."

"My dad wouldn't do that," Lilly protested. "He's not... evil. He wouldn't do that."

"Regardless, it is what he possessed."

Lilly glowered at him. Then flinched when Aderyn started to dab at the slice across her throat. She took a slow breath. "Fine, then what can *your* magic do? What are those vines?"

"I am seventh in a family of eight," Jek said. "Seventh born, male or female, are always born with magic, but not the sort of magic that is considered the norm."

"Meaning...?"

"I whisper to the green and growing things." Jek winked. "You didn't see their full effect, but earth magic is the only kind that can truly defeat shadow magic."

"No more talk of this," Aderyn said suddenly. She pulled away from washing the wound on Lilly's head. "We'll find you a fresh shirt and a room for the night."

Lilly barely looked at her bandaged arm, ignoring the ache. "What will Yovak do to my brother?"

Jek hesitated. "I don't know..."

"Then speculate." Lilly barely refrained from snapping. Aderyn sighed, her suggestion going unheeded.

"It depends on why Zal was after your father in the first place."

"He kept demanding my dad give him this." Lilly dug into her pocket with her good arm and pulled the amulet out. It tingled against her palm. She tossed it to Jek, and he caught it easily, frowning at it as he turned it over in his hand.

"Did he tell you anything about it?"

"No, only that it was obvious Zal shouldn't get his hands on it." Lilly shrugged. "Do you know what it is? Why does it tingle when I touch it?"

Jek shook his head. "I don't—what?" He looked up sharply.

"It tingles. Like when your limb gets a needly feeling after being numb. Don't you feel it?"

Jek frowned thoughtfully. "It could be magic-based. Magical items, or the elements created by weavers, feel different in the hands of someone who doesn't have magic." He handed it back. "Whatever it is, your father was probably right to keep it hidden."

"It's my only way to get Gabriel back," Lilly protested.

"But if you hand it over, then there's nothing keeping your brother alive," Jek said. "It sounds cruel, but it's the truth. Yovak will keep Gabriel alive as long as you have it."

Lilly bit her lip, but nodded reluctantly. She slipped the amulet back in her pocket.

Aderyn looked at Jek with a slight smile. "Are you done?"

Jek smirked, almost guiltily. "Yes."

"Good, now go find her some spare clothes." She turned to Lilly. "We'll get you a hot meal and a room to yourself to rest."

"I'm not hungry, but thank you," Lilly said. She looked at Jek. "Thanks, Jek."

A ghost of a smile crossed his lips, and he nodded before getting up stiffly and leaving.

Lilly watched Aderyn clean up the kitchen. Her stomach grumbled despite her refusal of food, but she wasn't sure she could eat without being sick. She wasn't sure her cafeteria lunch would stay down.

Her stomach flipped at the thought. Her friends were probably out of school by now. Nick would be worried sick. They would have heard about the Bean blowing up, the freaky magicians assaulting the police, then disappearing without a trace.

She smirked inwardly. Dante would at least be so far discredited that when she got home, he wouldn't dare say another word. If he was smart, he'd avoid her altogether.

"Lilly?" Aderyn looked at her. "Are you alright?"

Lilly stared at the fire. "Everybody back home is gonna be worried. I don't even know how we got here in the first place, or how to get back."

"The Annors will help in any way they can," Aderyn comforted. "So will I. I know what it's like, to come from a different world."

Lilly looked up at her, startled.

"I don't think from your world," Aderyn amended. "I can't go back to mine, but we will help you find a way back to yours. Magic didn't bring me here, but it did bring you. So... perhaps it can take you back."

But what would she and Gabriel say when they got back? They'd sound as crazy as their father. People would call it a defense mechanism against the trauma of their father's death. Despite the many witnesses in the park... eventually they'd be labeled unstable.

What would Nick think? That his girlfriend had finally snapped?

No. He wouldn't. Well, maybe, but he wouldn't leave her over it. Right?

Aderyn had just finished cleaning up when another man stepped into the kitchen. He was short, but his limbs were gangly, like he hadn't quite grown into his adult body even though he looked to be in his forties.

"Unvar." Aderyn sounded surprised. "Is everything alright?"

"Everything is fine," the man assured her. "Rune and Kedmir are still out, and we're receiving favorable reports." He held up a bundle of cloth. "I'm to give this to you? I found Jek nearly passed out on his way here, so I sent him to bed before his brothers caught him." Unvar smiled, amused.

"Thank you, Unvar." Aderyn took the clothes from him. Unvar's eyes landed on Lilly.

"May I be of any assistance?" he asked.

"No, thank you," Aderyn said. "We've just finished."

"Thanks for the clothes," Lilly said.

Unvar smiled, inclined his head, and left. Aderyn found a spare room on the second floor of the repurposed tavern, and left Lilly to change. She also left a small jar of ointment she could use if the pain in her arm became too much.

The tunic was a bit big, not made for the smaller frame of a woman, but it was warm and clean. The pants were a little big too, but Lilly grabbed the belt from her own jeans. The fabric scraped against her skin, and she paced the room, high-stepping to adjust to it.

The bed was stiff, but Lilly didn't care. Her adrenaline was gone. Exhaustion anchored her to the mattress. Not even the sounds of yelling outside would bother her.

She was nearly asleep when she realized: Jek had never told her what Yovak might do to Gabriel.

Sleep didn't come easily after that. The tears, however, did.

4

SOMEONE TO CALL FRIEND

Gabriel's wounded shoulder hit rock-hard ground when the greasy-haired man pushed him away. Gabriel groaned and tried to find his footing in the thin layer of snow. Blood mixed with the snow on his fingers, leaving them wet and slippery. He took a shaking breath. He was bleeding. A lot.

He watched as the man summoned and sent a small shadow-thing toward the wide double doors of a huge stone castle.

Gabriel gaped at the structure. It stood tall and proud, at least four stories high. Glass windows peered outward, all closed against the winter air. A wide courtyard surrounded it, hemmed in by stone walls. Where was he now?

"What if he doesn't want the boy, Zal?" the second man grunted. He was on the ground too, clutching his leg.

"He's the son of Tilas. Rothar will take him." Zal glanced at Gabriel.

"The plan was to bring Tilas and the amulet, not his spawn," the man snapped.

Gabriel grunted, trying to sit up. The world tipped a little. "What do you want with my dad?"

"It's not like Tilas would have been much use anyway. He was half-dead—"

Gabriel lunged at Zal. It caught the man off guard and sent him to the ground, but Zal's fist struck Gabriel's shoulder. Pain exploded where it had been strangely numb before. Gabriel cried out and flinched back, curling around the wound.

The doors of the castle burst open. Several people strode out. Gabriel groaned, but he couldn't move. He hurt too much.

Someone touched him. Gabriel flinched back, pain flaring in his side and shoulder. He yelped, but darkness numbed his body. Whoever touched him was gentle. If they spoke, Gabriel didn't hear.

When Gabriel awoke, something heavy weighed him down, soft and warm.

The dull pounding in his head made him grimace. He reached his right hand up, and his arm throbbed a little. Gabriel tensed, but there was no pain. He frowned at his arm, flexing it and straightening it. Nothing. A slight tingle that was already fading.

Gabriel sat up. The room was large and warm. Curtains over the large windows dimmed the sunlight, though some squeezed in around the edges. A fire crackled quietly against the wall opposite the bed. It smelled woodsy, and Gabriel inhaled a noseful of it.

In the far corner, he noticed a desk, a table, a large, sturdy wardrobe, and a door. A second door stood a few yards away. On the desk was a small bag, and on the table was a book.

"Okay..." Gabriel loosed a breath. "Don't freak out. We don't need to panic yet."

Carefully, Gabriel looked himself over. He wore a shirt that wasn't his, and pants that weren't either. Both felt infinitely softer than his own clothes. Cleaner, too, given that he'd shoved on day-old jeans and a questionably clean shirt before school. He slipped his other hand under his shirt to feel for a wound.

His skin was smooth and whole. Untouched. Further inspection revealed not a single scar. And the places on his body he was sure had been hit by *lightning* were spotless. No sign of any damage. Not even scarring.

"Okay." Gabriel lowered his shirt. "Maybe we can panic a little bit."

I haven't, like... died, have I?

He ventured on bare feet to the nearest window and pushed the heavy curtain aside to peek out. The view looked down on the same courtyard he had been taken to, and over the wall hemming the castle in was a huge and sprawling city. Gabriel's gaze jumped to the nearby, flat-roofed buildings. He glimpsed a few figures standing on one, moving about, hanging up swaths of sheets. Beyond the city walls, Gabriel glimpsed a river.

"Whoa..."

A door opened. Gabriel spun around, backing up to the table with the book. It was a hardcover, so it was a weapon. Better than nothing, even if it hurt his soul to use a book as a bludgeon.

Instead of Zal, a man with a startling shock of red hair entered. It was gray in some places, and refused to be tamed. The man had a tired, patient expression, and he stopped short when he saw Gabriel standing. Behind him, a skinny young man in a matching gray shirt and pants halted, eyes wide. And his ears!

They were pointed. Elf ears.

No way.

"It's alright," the red-haired man said, easing closer. Gabriel stepped back.

"Don't," he snapped, holding up the book. "Who are you?"

The man stopped, watching Gabriel like he was a wild animal poised to flee at any moment. "My name is Raul. The castle physician." He held up his hands to prove they were empty. "I'm not going to hurt you."

Gabriel didn't lower the book. "Where am I? Where's my sister and my dad?"

Raul's brows furrowed. "You are the only one we rescued."

Gabriel sifted through his memories. "So they're just... they're back in that city?"

"I'm afraid I don't understand. If you'll just sit down—"

"I said stay back!" Gabriel backed up again, his shoulder bumping into the wardrobe. He almost tripped. "What do you mean rescued? Where am I?" He looked at the gray-clad man, who stood by the wall, watching silently.

"You're safe," Raul tried again. He didn't move. "You are in Erriath, in the castle."

"Where's Erriath?"

"It is the capital of Piensor. A little southeast of where the rebel weavers took you."

"Rebel what?"

"Weavers. Magic users." Raul moved to the desk and the bag. "They took you and your family hostage, but only you were brought here to Erriath."

"Why?"

"I do not know." Raul shook his head. "You arrived, and you and the rebel were at blows. We only just managed to separate the pair of you."

Gabriel frowned. His mind still felt foggy, but memories were falling back into place. The attack at the Bean, the weird medieval city...

"I may be able to supply any answers he needs, Raul."

Gabriel whirled, bumping into the wardrobe again. He moved to put the bed between himself and the door as another man stepped inside. He leaned heavily on a glossy dark-wood cane, though he looked younger than Raul by several years. He was tall, and a bit too pale to be healthy. His black hair was pulled away from his face, revealing pointed ears.

"My lord." Raul bowed to him. The gray-clad man bowed deeply, holding it a very long time.

The newcomer's sharp eyes watched Gabriel, calm and at ease. "You will not be hurt here, my boy, but I recommend you sit down. Your wounds are healed, but you are still weak. Not even magic can return blood lost, and it is important to rest and let your body do that for itself."

"What did you do to me?" Gabriel asked, hoping his voice didn't shake. "I was... I was stabbed. And electrocuted."

"We summoned a weaver to heal your injuries," the elf said. He watched Gabriel carefully. "Are you the son of Tilas Faine?"

"Who's asking?"

The elf, resting both hands on his cane, leaned his weight off his left leg. "I am Seiryu Rothar. Your father and I are close friends."

Gabriel pursed his lips, considered. "My father never talked about you."

"Didn't he? Well... perhaps he's still angry with me." Seiryu Rothar smiled, though it was sad and a little bitter. "We did not part on good terms."

"Why not?"

Seiryu approached the chair by the table. "We—"

When he was nearly to the chair, Seiryu's leg gave out. He lurched forward, and Raul was at his side faster than Gabriel first thought the man could move. Seiryu coughed. And the fit didn't stop.

"Easy, my lord," Raul said, lowering Seiryu to the floor. The elf had one hand pressed against his chest, the coughing hard enough to shake his body. "Seiryu, breathe!" Raul looked at his silent assistant and barked a command. The elf sprang into action, darting to the bag on the desk. The man snatched up a silver flask, and Raul took it from him.

Gabriel inched closer to the door. He watched as Seiryu's fit eventually slowed, and only sometimes interrupted his heavy breathing.

"Breathe." Raul's tone was stern, but gentler. He knelt by Seiryu, one hand on his shoulder. "That's it, breathe..."

After one final cough, Seiryu looked at Gabriel with a weak smile. "My apologies... had I known this would happen I would have waited for a better time to make a first impression."

"Are you okay?" Gabriel asked, rooted in place.

Seiryu nodded, taking another ragged breath—he sounded like a man just pulled from the depths of the earth—and let Raul help him into the chair. The physician propped the cane against the table and handed Seiryu the flask.

"Enough for one dose. Drink it all."

Seiryu grimaced, but didn't argue.

"My lot in life," Seiryu said, catching Gabriel's stare. "An illness no healer can cure. Not even our most qualified." He gave Raul a grateful look and passed the flask back.

"It sounds pretty bad."

"Would you believe me if I told you this is not the worst?" Seiryu smirked. "But I will be alright in a moment."

"Why would my dad be angry with you?" As far as Gabriel knew, his father was rarely angry with anyone. If he was, he did a stellar job of hiding it.

"We disagreed," Seiryu said, wincing as he shifted in his seat. "He and I studied and researched a wide variety of subjects together. He believed he had found a way to travel to other worlds. I thought it was foolish and too reckless to risk, and we argued about his intention to proceed with trials."

Gabriel's mind whirred as he tried to put the pieces together. There wasn't any harm in talking, was there? As long as he kept his distance. He was closest to the door if he needed to run. "But he did it anyway."

"I can only assume as much. I never saw him again after we fought."

"But why would he take us?" Gabriel frowned. "He said... he said my mom was killed. An arrow in her back."

Seiryu's lips parted in shock. "I'm so sorry... I had no idea..."

Raul looked from one to the other. "Tilas's family lived in Murke, didn't they?"

"Aye. He must have returned home."

"Where's Murke?" Gabriel cocked his head. "Was that where Zal took us?"

Seiryu nodded. "If Zal managed to follow your father to whatever world he had traveled to, Murke is where Zal would start his search for the remnants of the magic." His expression turned thoughtful. "Even fifteen years later..."

Gabriel ran a hand through his brown hair. "My dad knew him. Zal. Knew him by name."

"Your father tutored many dark magic weavers," Seiryu said. "Zal turned traitor against the crown, joining those who tried to rebel against Emperor Yovak's rule when he was still king. We think Zal used his experience here to bring you directly to the castle, instead of walking you through the city, which would have been his death sentence."

"There were other people there. Two of them, but others fighting," Gabriel said. "The man used..." Gabriel paused. Magic? It still felt impossible. But before he could confirm, another thought nagged at his mind. "If they were rebels too, why would they fight Zal? He called them rebels."

Seiryu frowned. "As to that, I'm not sure... perhaps Zal Ira defected from them too. He is a man who prefers to look out for his own gains."

Gabriel chewed his lip. "So... magic is real."

"A world different from this one, where magic runs like blood through veins."

"Magic is very real." Seiryu held up his hand. A small flicker of lightning sputtered on his palm. Gabriel caught himself flinching, then edged closer to see. The sparks disappeared, and Seiryu reached for his cane. "But let us walk. We can converse better with exercise."

Raul stared at him. "You need to rest—"

"Walking helps the medicine to work." Seiryu waved the physician's words away. Raul looked skeptical, but he didn't argue. Seiryu looked at Gabriel. "Is it safe for him to walk for a bit?"

Raul paused. "Bah, fine. Just bring him back. I don't want him doing anything strenuous." He motioned to Gabriel. "The markings on your shoulder. They are a tattoo, yes? It was undamaged in your fight, but I wanted to be sure they were something you were aware of."

It took Gabriel a second. "Oh, yeah. That's a tattoo. An otter."

"An ot-tur?" Seiryu lifted a brow.

"A furry animal that swims a lot. My sister picked it out. That's the last time I let her dare me to do anything."

Seiryu laughed. "Already, your sister sounds much like your father. But come, we will let Raul attend to his other duties."

Gabriel hesitated. Seiryu smiled gently.

"We mean you no harm, Gabriel," he said. "If at any point you feel uncomfortable, you are free to go."

Gabriel looked at Raul, but the physician was employed in packing his medical bag. He looked at Seiryu again, chewing on the inside of his cheek. This man had answers, and Gabriel found himself craving them. He could always play along if things turned suspicious. He could mark exits as he walked.

"Lead the way."

The castle was mostly stone and wood. To stave off the chill, the walls bore thick tapestries with tiny woven details throughout.

Servants in simple clothes, trimmed in a dark amethyst color, passed them and bowed quickly to Seiryu. Other servants, dressed in the same gray uniform as Raul's assistant, ducked their heads in a bow before hurrying on after Seiryu and Gabriel had passed. The gray-clothed ones were both human and elf. They had pointed ears, though if Gabriel hadn't noticed this, they would have looked human. Once or twice he glimpsed their eyes. Beautiful eyes, soft blue or green or brown, but all had pupils surrounded by tendrils of gold.

Seiryu paid no attention to any of them.

"Why are they dressed different?" Gabriel ventured. "The elves and humans in gray."

"They are half-elves, not elves," Seiryu said, his voice a touch sharper. He smiled stiffly in apology. "They are half-elves—born of human and elf unions."

"Why are they and some humans in gray? Raul's assistant was too."

"They are slaves."

Gabriel's brows furrowed. "You keep slaves? Why?"

"The ones working in the castle are working off a debt," Seiryu said, casual and unconcerned. "Do not trouble yourself. They are treated well and fairly."

Gabriel frowned but let the silence push the topic away. He had bigger things to worry about.

"They're still back in Murke, my dad and sister," Gabriel said. "My dad's hurt."

"We are doing all we can," Seiryu said. His limp was more pronounced, but he walked with confidence. "And I wouldn't worry about your father. His magic has the power to heal wounds. He is not so easily beaten down."

This only eased Gabriel's mind a little. "Can't your magic do that too?"

"No. His magic is different from mine." Seiryu took them down a wide hall, where the windows stood tall and let in the cold winter light. "I was born with magic, as most elves are. Tilas's magic comes through learning it. Summoning it, if you will." He caught Gabriel's skeptical look and chuckled. "You are not so much a believer as your father."

"I grew up in a world where magic isn't real," Gabriel said. "It's just in stories. Fiction."

"I think you will find that any world holds a small degree of magic, in some shape or form."

"So, what can your magic do?"

"Any type of magic can use the four elements: fire, water, air, and lightning," Seiryu said. "If you are born with magic, as I was, you are limited to simply those four."

"Not earth? That's usually the fourth in my world."

"A small group may be born with that fifth," Seiryu conceded. "If you are seventh born, then you can also use that magic, in addition to the other four."

"But Dad learned magic."

"Yes. Learned magic—or dark magic—has more capabilities." He looked at Gabriel. "You saw its power when Zal Ira brought you here, or perhaps you saw the creatures of shadow. Itzals, is their proper name."

Gabriel suppressed a shudder. "Yeah, I did."

They stopped by a window, and Seiryu leaned against the sill, keeping all the weight off his bad leg. Gabriel stood a few feet away. If Seiryu noticed, he didn't comment.

"Are you sure you're okay?" Gabriel glanced at the elf's leg.

"I'll be alright." Seiryu adjusted his perched position. "Dark magic can also heal wounds." He nodded to Gabriel's shoulder. "Such as yours and, temporarily, mine."

"Can't you learn it too?"

"I already have magic," Seiryu said. "You cannot have both at once. Except by... unorthodox means."

"And that means what?"

"When your father was here, I discovered a way to obtain learned magic. A way to circumvent magic's rules, in a sense. An amulet that hosts the magic when the body cannot." Seiryu waved a hand, searching for the right words. "An artificial channel, I suppose."

Gabriel started. "My dad had it. He gave it to my sister, Lilly, right before everything happened. She has it now."

"Does she?" Seiryu looked thoughtful.

"And a piece of glass. My dad gave it to me when he gave Lilly the amulet." Gabriel hurried on. He reached for his pocket but stopped. "My other clothes! Are they still here?"

Seiryu looked almost relieved. "I believe they were stored in your room."

Gabriel crossed his arms. "But why did my dad have it?"

"In the heat of our argument, we forgot he had the amulet in his possession. He had been helping me in my research." Seiryu stood again. "A simple mistake, but it has cost me..."

"So, if we rescue Dad and Lilly, you'll have it back." Gabriel turned, walking backward. "We have to go back for them. I have to go—"

"Slow down." Seiryu held up his hand. "It is safer for you to remain here in Erriath. We have already sent others to help them escape, and we have a contact within the rebel ranks that I have informed of this event. He will be watching out for them."

Gabriel considered this. "Why doesn't Dad use his magic to escape with Lilly? Like Zal did?"

"Because it is possible that the rebels have them separated. They are savages, but they are not stupid enough to underestimate a dark weaver. Keeping your sister separate from your father will keep him docile."

"Then what can we do?" Gabriel ran his hands through his hair.

"Calm yourself." Seiryu gripped Gabriel's shoulder, stopping him in his tracks. He met Gabriel's eyes. "We are doing all we can."

"What can *I* do?" Gabriel pressed, shrugging him off. "I couldn't help them. I..." He swallowed. "I can't fight here, and I don't want to be so useless. I don't want to just sit around while people hold my family hostage. What will they do to them?" He found himself hoping Seiryu would reassure him. Tell him they wouldn't hurt either of them.

"I don't know," Seiryu said instead. "Tilas is clever in his own right, and he will know not to aggravate them. If your sister is anything like him, she will too."

Gabriel paled. There was no way his sister would be able to keep a low profile. Especially not now. "Seiryu—err, Lord Rothar... I need to help them. Give me a sword and tell me which direction they're in."

"Do you know how to use one?"

"Well... no," Gabriel admitted. "But I can learn."

"I'm sure you can," Seiryu said placatingly. "But until you do, it isn't safe for you to go off to war, especially on your own. We do not send new soldiers to the field until we know they can properly and safely wield a blade for their own survival." He watched Gabriel, thoughtful. "However, a sword will not be enough against magic... the rebels aren't without their weavers."

"What are you saying?" Gabriel looked at him suspiciously.

"You could, if you wanted, learn magic," Seiryu said. "Just as your father did, and just as the emperor himself. You would have abilities beyond even my own." He smiled. "We can provide you tutors who worked alongside Tilas himself."

Magic. The idea sent tingles through Gabriel, but they stopped just shy of the word "yes."

His mind replayed the magic that flew through the Chicago air. The magic that burned the park, that hurt his father and *killed* policemen.

"My dad never used it until now," Gabriel said. "He never once told us he had magic, and I've never seen it before. He didn't like it whenever we'd see somebody do magic that was more than sleight of hand." He looked at Seiryu, suddenly wary. "Something that felt... darker. Like what I saw."

Seiryu only nodded. "Your father did have his reservations about dark magic. Once you learn it, you cannot undo it. That in itself takes getting used to." Seiryu brushed his fingers against the polished knob on top of his cane. "But, he learned to use it for good. Some dark weavers relish the power it gives them—Zal Ira, for example—and they will do unspeakable, sadistic things. But your father was far from them. He used his magic to raise a healing empire."

Gabriel frowned. His father had *definitely* never told them that. It sounded like something his father would do, but why wouldn't he have said *anything* about any of it?

"I don't know." Gabriel shook his head. "Can't I just use a sword?"

"Of course. I cannot, in good conscience, let you go gallivanting off as soon as you would like, but with practice and time, perhaps."

"I just want to protect my sister," Gabriel said.

Seiryu nodded. "Perhaps... may I take the liberty of offering you books on magic? So you can read for yourself that it is not so wicked as you feel it is?"

"I didn't say—"

"You do not have to say." Seiryu winked.

Gabriel frowned at him. "I guess... can you bring me books on the other kinds of magic too? If I'm gonna be stuck here, I want to know what I'm up against."

"I will have a selection brought up from my own library." Seiryu began walking. "Come, I will return you to your room. Raul will expect us both to rest."

"Seiryu, there you are!"

Gabriel and Seiryu both turned. A young lady glided toward them, perhaps Lilly's age. She wore a lavender dress that flattered every curve, and her dark brown hair fell in curls over her shoulders, framing dark brown eyes. A choker of diamonds glittered at her throat.

Dang. Gabriel tried not to stare. She, too, had elf ears. She smelled like springtime. Lovely and refreshing.

Trailing behind her was a young man about the same age. He wore light armor, a sword at his hip. Somehow the look didn't fit him. His pale green eyes sparked with too much youth and mischief for a soldier, his dirty-blond hair too unruly. His ears weren't pointed.

Seiryu bowed low to the girl. "Highness."

Gabriel hurried to follow suit. The girl stopped before them and looked at Gabriel.

"Hello!" Her smile was bright and warm. "Entya did well with you."

"Who?" Gabriel looked at Seiryu.

"The dark weaver who healed your wounds."

"I'm Odalys," she said, not at all annoyed by Gabriel's interruption.

"Gabriel Faine." Gabriel offered his hand.

"Odalys, daughter of Emperor Yovak," Seiryu added, a teasing note to his voice.

Gabriel's eyes widened and he bowed. "I'm sorry, Your Highness."

Odalys glared at Seiryu. "Oh, don't. Only servants and people in the city call me that."

"Sorry." Gabriel ducked his head. He looked at the soldier. "Who are you?"

"Oh!" Odalys turned before the soldier could speak. "I have something for you."

She waved the soldier forward, and he obeyed. His eyes slipped to Seiryu once, then back to Gabriel.

"Found it outside," the young man said, holding a long knife out to Gabriel handle-first.

He recognized it immediately. Images flashed of his father using it to remove big weeds or dead flowers, or nights spent sharpening the blade. It had been a part of his father as long as Gabriel could remember.

It was a beautiful piece, more a work of art than a gardening tool. Gabriel took the knife and ran his finger over the flat of the blade before looking up at Odalys. "Thank you."

She smiled. "It's not much, but I know if I were in a strange place, I'd want something familiar to hold on to."

"Yeah." Gabriel smiled. "Thanks. I guess it's not so much a gardening tool like I thought."

"I don't believe Annor was assigned to your guard, Highness," Seiryu said. His eyes scrutinized the soldier. The young man didn't meet his gaze.

"Oh, he isn't," Odalys said lightly. "Tesmir was called to the courtyard when everything happened. He found the knife."

"Thanks," Gabriel addressed Tesmir too.

The young soldier's eyes flicked to his, a moment of caution there, but he smiled slightly and bowed.

"Do you want a tour of the castle?" Odalys piped up, her voice cheery and eager.

"I was just going to return Gabriel to his room," Seiryu intercepted. "He needs a little more rest."

Odalys looked at Gabriel. "After that?"

"Sure." Gabriel grinned. "I'd like that." It would help keep him busy. Keep him from flying off and doing something reckless.

Is this what Lilly feels like all the time?

"Oh, Seir," Odalys said before turning away. "Father wants you. He says it's about the Gold Mark."

After parting ways with the princess, Gabriel followed Seiryu back through the halls and stopped at his door.

"Here is where I leave you," Seiryu said. "I'm afraid I must attend to business, but you may summon a servant at any time. They will serve you, or fetch Raul if you need him."

"Thanks." Gabriel laid a hand on the doorknob. "What's the Gold Mark?"

"Ah, do not trouble yourself with it." Seiryu shook his head. "A network of rebel weavers have wormed their way into Erriath, and have started some form of underground activity. They cause more mischief and inconvenience than real harm, but we are working to dig them out before it can evolve. As far as reports go, they have a great deal of seventh weavers. Earth magic."

"Would they know anything about where the other rebels have Dad and Lilly?"

"I don't know," Seiryu sighed. "But once we catch one, we will learn. As advisor to the emperor, I will be in the thick of it, so I will provide you information when I can." He shooed Gabriel off. "Now go rest."

Gabriel started to obey but stopped again. "Lord Rothar?"

Seiryu turned. Gabriel made himself look Seiryu in the eyes.

"Were the rebels the ones who killed my mom?" He held Seiryu's gaze. "Dad said she was shot in the back... we lost her fifteen years ago. Did that happen here?"

Seiryu's features drooped. "Fifteen years ago was the first rebel uprising against Emperor Yovak. He was king then, and newly crowned, wresting control from the oppressive war lords that exploited the land and people. The rebels had fought alongside Yovak then, winning back their country.

"But they wanted to rule themselves—which is what brought them under the war lords in the first place—and they, led by Ranson Annor, were not satisfied with a king. They fought to dismantle the structure the emperor raised for their benefit. We uprooted the rebellion before it had a chance to grow and spread, but that battle took place in Murke..."

Seiryu hesitated, then took a slow breath. "Your family resided in Murke, not here in Erriath. Your father and I argued the day the battle took place, and he left. But it was at the time of the skirmish..." Seiryu shifted his weight. "I don't know why he would have tested his magic theory with your family in tow, but it is possible the rebels attacked without warning, and he sought to get your family to safety."

Gabriel's blood went cold. "They... they just shot my mom? For no reason?"

"I wish I could provide you answers. The rebels are not kind. They are greedy, and will do anything to get what they want." Seiryu's voice sounded tired. "But we will not have history repeat itself. We will rescue your father and sister, I promise."

Gabriel nodded and let Seiryu leave this time. He started inside his room but paused in the open door. Sleep was the last thing on his mind. He wasn't tired.

He tossed Tilas's knife onto the bed and left the room again. He needed to walk, to think.

He retraced the path he and Seiryu had taken. The halls were still empty, and Gabriel's bare feet made no sound over the wood floor. It did little for his growing anxiety. He was safe, but his father and Lilly? In the hands of murderers, imprisoned, maybe hurt.

Seiryu seemed to be forthcoming with answers, but there was still so much Gabriel wanted to know. Guilt pricked him. He felt as if he didn't know his father anymore. And he felt... he didn't know.

Gabriel took a slow, shaky breath as he leaned against a window, looking down at the city that stretched below. He would figure things out. He had to. He'd find Lilly and their dad and get them all home. He could only imagine what their friends were going through as newsreels reported some whacked-out standoff at the Bean.

Despite himself, Gabriel smirked.

In your face, Dante.

"Gabriel?"

The familiar voice jerked Gabriel back to the present. He turned to find Odalys standing before him once more. Alone this time.

"Hi." Gabriel eyed her. "How did you know I was here?"

Odalys smiled primly, joining him. "You're not *resting*."

"Can't." Gabriel shrugged. "There's just too much to think about."

The princess looked at him. "About your father?"

"Him, all of this." Gabriel motioned to the city, the castle. "Magic."

Odalys smiled. Little ribbons of water slid around her, spiraling up to create a liquid tiara over her head. Gabriel stared.

"Come on." The water dissolved into a fine mist. Odalys pushed away from the window and took his hand. "Let me show you around the castle. I know the routes to avoid Seiryu and Raul."

Gabriel kept staring. Then he smiled, and he followed her.

5

GRAVESIDE VOW

Morning sunshine warmed Lilly's cheek, rousing her from cozy unconsciousness. She scowled, eyes closed, and burrowed under the blanket. She thought she heard her alarm, and snaked a hand out to hit snooze. Five more minutes.

Her hand flailed at empty air. She grumbled. Where was her nightstand?

Something cold and wet touched her hand. Lilly squealed and jerked her hand back. Not her alarm.

A dog. How did a dog get in her room!? She mentally listed the dogs in the apartment building on their floor. Only two, both small and fluffy. Lilly peeked out.

The dog was neither small nor fluffy. A rottweiler, big, muscled, and panting in her face. It cocked its head to one side, panted again.

Lilly frowned, squinting at it, then at the room. It was bare, save for the bed and a small table with a basin and pitcher by the window, and smelled... weird. Not the usual smells of the apartment complex. This smell was fresh, rough, and deep with something alive.

It was also cold. Lilly squirmed deeper under the blankets.

Not her room. The memories filed in unbidden: the Bean exploding, magic flying at the police, Chicago disappearing, replaced with a city in another world. A room in a tavern-turned-war-headquarters.

Her father, dead. Gabriel, kidnapped.

Lilly's throat tightened. Tears pricked her eyes, and she couldn't stop them. The memories replayed over and over. Gabriel's cry of pain. Zal's magic intended to kill her. Tilas stepping in its path.

Her father was gone. Forever. She wouldn't find him waiting up in the night for her when she came back from a late shopping trip or a date. She wouldn't help him work the stove to make eggs, or watch Gabriel help him plan next year's flower beds. She wouldn't see his smile, or hear his voice, his laugh.

Lilly pursed her lips, but her chin quivered, and she curled in on herself. She needed him. She couldn't do this without him. She needed to know what he knew, to hear the stories again. To beg him to tell her every single one, to fill her with them. And then she needed to tell him she believed him.

The guilt crashed into her. She'd never believed him. She had thought he was crazy sometimes, just like stupid Dante. Now she knew better, but she'd never told him.

I'm sorry, Dad. Lilly sucked in a breath, but the tears still came. A sob escaped her. *I'm sorry*—A cold nose touched her arm. Lilly recoiled with a yelp and a gasp, swiping at her tears. The sharp motion sent pain throbbing down her injured arm, and she cursed.

The rottweiler was still there, watching her with knowing eyes. Lilly took a deep breath and squinted at it.

You don't have time for this. Gabriel's still alive. Dad would want you to focus on that.

The dog whined softly, put one paw on the bed, then thought better of it. A small smile crossed Lilly's lips, and she scratched the dog behind its ears with her good arm. It pressed close to the mattress, its long tail wagging in contentment. Lilly blinked at it, then at the dog. No... definitely a rottweiler. Just with a tail. It looked a little more cuddly that way.

"Beron!" a voice hissed outside her room. Lilly looked up as an auburn head of curls peeked in around her door. The gray and green eyes flicked up to her. "I'm so sorry. He's not supposed to be up here—"

"It's alright." Lilly gave the dog a final head-scratch and sat up, hugging the blankets around her. "You're Kedmir, right?"

Kedmir nodded. He waved to the dog. "And you've met Beron." He leaned against the doorframe. "How's the arm?"

"Hurts. And it's really cold in here."

"Aye, it's not the most solid place." Kedmir glanced around the room, then back at her. "Are you hungry? There are eggs and bacon left over. We captured the barracks and found a full supply of food. It will help warm you."

"Thanks." Lilly smiled. "Is... everything alright, out there?" She didn't hear anything now. No swords, or yelling.

"We won," Kedmir said. "You arrived just as we turned the tide. We've been routing the last of the imperials." He shooed Beron out of the room. "Come on, before someone else gets the idea. The others are all still out sweeping the city for imperial stragglers, but they'll be back soon."

Lilly grinned. "Is there tea?"

"There will be, if you wish it," Kedmir laughed.

Lilly followed him down creaky stairs. The main room was nearly empty. A couple of tables hosted one or two men, most slumped over in sleep. Her eyes traveled to one particular table. It was empty.

Of course, they'd have to move him.

The air down here smelled stuffier, with sweat and that coppery smell. Lilly wrinkled her nose.

"What is that smell?" She sniffed again. "Metallic. Not swords."

Kedmir glanced back. His warm smile had faded. "Unfortunately, war washes streets and soil in blood. Some days, I wish I could still smell it. Then I'd know I hadn't gotten used to it."

Lilly halted on the last stair. Blood? Her gut flipped. She'd known blood had a smell. But this meant there had to be a lot of it...

The fire was out in the kitchen, smoldering embers left behind. Kedmir knelt down and worked at it while he gave Lilly directions to the tea. She sniffed it. The smell was soothing, similar to chamomile, but a little sweeter, with a trace of orange.

Kedmir took longer to build the fire than Jek had, without magic, but they soon had a kettle of water over the flame.

"How is any of this possible?" Lilly asked after a long stretch of silence. "All of those stories my dad told us... they were just supposed to be stories. They weren't supposed to be this." She looked all around. "None of this should be possible!"

"The world doesn't often work under our ideas of 'should be.'" Kedmir positioned another log on the fire. He sat on the floor instead of a chair, legs splayed out before him. His fingers played with a braided maroon cord around his wrist. "I find it helps if you approach everything as possible until proven otherwise. Before I met Aderyn, before I glimpsed her world, I didn't think other worlds were possible either."

"You saw her world?"

"I was in it, for a few minutes." Kedmir smiled sadly. "It was probably the stupidest thing I could have done at the time, but since then... I'm not so much a skeptic anymore."

"Why were you in it?"

"Hoping to find her kin." Kedmir glanced at the door. "All she had was destroyed, her home, her family, and she was thrown into our world. The portal wouldn't let her go back, but it let me through."

"Aderyn said magic didn't bring her here."

Kedmir shrugged. "Maybe not. We don't really know. Aderyn has never been a supporter of any kind of magic." He looked at Lilly. "But either way, my point is that the world usually isn't without its mysteries, without its 'impossibilities.'"

"I watched my dad use magic," Lilly mumbled. "For fifteen years, I'd never once seen anything like it. He was like... like a fighter out there." She smiled bitterly. "I'm just not sure what to believe anymore."

"Believe your father. Believe what he has told you."

"I don't know if I remember all of it..."

"You will," Kedmir encouraged. "Just give it time."

Soon the smell of the tea wafted through the building. Lilly eventually found her way from the chair to the floor beside Kedmir, and Beron never left her side. The pressure in her chest slowly eased as she stroked him. He leaned into her hand as she scratched behind his ears. When she reached his belly, the dog dropped and rolled over, one hind leg kicking the air.

Lilly laughed. It felt strange, almost wrong, but it helped. It kept her mind off the pain that lurked like a wild animal, caged and cornered and needing to lash out.

"What are those?" she asked suddenly. When Kedmir looked up at her, she pointed to his wrist. "Jek and Aderyn have them too, but nobody else."

"A reminder," Kedmir said. "A reminder of what we lost before, and what we stand to lose if we don't win this war." He tugged at it absentmindedly. "It's the color of our country. The color of strength." He smiled. "My brothers and I wear them, and Aderyn. Our own personal message to ourselves when the night brings more than just sleep."

"Like your flag?"

"We wanted something to unify the rebels. My brothers didn't want us looking like ragged, disgruntled farmers. If we wanted to be taken seriously, we needed to look the part." Kedmir shrugged. "A Piensoran flag could have done the job, but we wanted something that set us apart. Our new flag partly represents an old country. We fight for a new one. The maroon, for the country we love. The stars are part of my family's own crest."

"The vines?"

"Earth magic. The lilies aren't supposed to be gold, but the magic they can do..." He spun his bracelet around his wrist. "Well, we took some creative liberties, just to let Yovak know he doesn't scare us, and he should be the one who is afraid."

When the tea was ready, Kedmir replaced the kettle with a pan of eggs and bacon, seasoning them with unfamiliar spices. They smelled rich and earthy, and soon Lilly's stomach was growling.

The kitchen door opened. "I don't think I gave orders for an assault on food stores."

A mountain of a man stood in the doorway, his arms crossed and his lips smiling. He looked strong enough to tear the door off its hinges, but his posture was relaxed, even with a sword belted at his side. His dark brown hair, a color that matched his eyes, was tied in a knot at the back of his head.

Beron barked at the man, his tail wagging faster. The large man bestowed a fond smile on him before looking at Beron's human friends. "I believe the chairs are free for the taking."

Kedmir shrugged. The stranger's smile softened when he looked back at Lilly. "How are you feeling?"

"I'm..." Lilly shrugged. "Sorry, who are you?"

"I'm Rune." He waved at Kedmir. "His brother."

"Oh." Lilly smiled. "I'm Lilly." She looked at the two men. "Who's older?"

"I am," Rune said. "But Kedmir fusses like he's the elder."

Kedmir huffed as he leaned toward the food, turning the bacon. "I wouldn't if you'd just get some sleep. You and Isilmere both."

Rune waved him off and approached the fire to observe the food sizzling in the pan. "Jek and Aderyn still asleep?"

"Aderyn was up with the dawn, as usual. Jek is still sleeping."

"Good." Rune nodded to Lilly's arm. "How is your wound?"

"Hurts," Lilly said. "Is Jek alright?"

"He will be fine," Rune said, as Kedmir took the food from the pan. "His magic took a heavy toll, but he has endured worse." He took a seat by the fire, warming his hands. His maroon bracelet hung on his left wrist. "I understand that your father lived here? Aderyn told me what happened."

Lilly fought back the rising emotion. "My dad told stories, and people told my brother and me they weren't true, but..." She waved her hand around. "I guess they are." She looked at Kedmir. *Approach everything as possible.*

Rune sat back, thoughtful. "Your father's name?"

"Tilas Faine." Before, it had seemed like an unusual name, but now it made sense. Now even her father's long garden knife, always so impractical-looking, made sense.

Rune's brows furrowed. "Tilas Faine..."

Lilly's heart skipped. "Did you know him?"

"I was only a boy, but I knew of him." Rune nodded slowly, thoughtful. "He was a good friend of our father." Rune looked at Kedmir. "In the early days of the first rebellion. Father and Mother had the Faines over for dinner; we were allowed to eat in the parlor."

It was Kedmir's brows that furrowed next. Rune went on. "They had two young children—"

"They had a baby girl!" Kedmir exclaimed. "I'd gotten so excited because of her red hair. And they had a boy, and he didn't let us touch her until Tilas told him it was alright."

"Gabriel!" Lilly blurted. "That sounds exactly like something he'd do." She couldn't breathe. A laugh escaped her. "You were excited to hold me?"

"We're a family of eight brothers. A girl was a new creature entirely," Kedmir chuckled. "You were so small, still wrapped in a blanket. I had to sit if I wanted to hold you, and your brother would sit right by you."

Lilly blinked back tears. Here were two people who *knew* her, knew her whole family. Their families had been close. She had been held by these men as a baby. It should have sounded weird. Her friends would have thought so, but it wasn't. Lilly's heart lightened just a little.

"I don't remember seeing him often," Kedmir said. "His wife and children a few times but never him, except once or twice."

"Isilmere might know more," Rune told her. "He is the eldest, and worked more closely with our father, and possibly yours."

"Is he here?"

"He is in Balmarren. A port city to the west. He commands our men from there."

"Can we go there?" Lilly asked. "If he knew my dad, maybe he knows why Yovak wants the amulet."

"It's possible." Rune nodded. "We will be returning to Balmarren in a few days, but we have one more place to go." He looked at Lilly. "It may interest you to come with us. The half-elf we are going to see was involved in the first rebellion too, so he may have known Tilas."

"Half-elf?" Lilly's eyes went wide. "They're real? So elves are real, too?"

Rune laughed. "Of course, lass. And you will get to see them up close in Lilantami." He winked.

Lilly considered this. "And then we'll rescue my brother?"

Rune nodded. "After Lilantami, we march on Erriath, and we will do all we can to rescue your brother."

Lilly chewed her lip. "What if they hurt him?"

"You have that amulet," Kedmir said. "Yovak expects you to make the first move. Bring an army to his doorstep, instead of going alone and unprotected. If your brother is smart, he'll keep his head down."

Lilly wanted to argue; she wanted to protest and demand they rescue Gabriel first thing. But if Yovak wanted the amulet, he would keep Gabriel alive, and make her come to him, alone and reckless and unprepared.

She wouldn't play that game. She had the advantage, and the ball was in her court.

"When do we leave?" Lilly asked, pushing her hair back.

"Today," Rune said. "I need to give Unvar his orders, and after we bury our dead—and theirs—we will go."

Kedmir scowled. "Let the imperials bury their own dead, Rune. Isilmere wouldn't waste time on it."

"I am not Isilmere," Rune said. "We bury the soldiers as well."

The burials were quiet. With the ground frozen through, Jek and a couple of his magic weavers used their powers to soften it.

Rune had said no to a mass grave for the imperials. There had been argument, but being more experienced and having more authority, he won out. The people of Murke refused to see the imperials buried in their city's cemetery, unless the imperial was a citizen. So, outside the city, a fair distance away, there were more holes for nameless imperial bodies.

Lilly stood in the Murke cemetery that hugged the city wall, her back to the sharp, cold air. Aderyn and Kedmir stood with her, as a few rebels lowered Tilas into the grave. Lilly clenched her jaw against the fear that squeezed her. But the tears slipped out anyway, silent.

I'm sorry I couldn't save you, Dad... Her gut twisted with each shovelful of dirt. *But I'll save Gabriel. I'll get him back, and I'll make sure they all pay for what they've done.*

This final thought struck a hammer blow with the last shovelful of dirt, filling the grave and trapping her words under it like a vow. They lit something inside her. A fire that burned hot.

Lilly had found a place in the cemetery for two graves. One full, and one empty. Kedmir helped her carve two names into a board, which she stuck into the dirt between the graves, both piled with stones to mark their places.

Two names, and she made the same promise to each.

Hollyn Faine, shot in the back with an arrow.

Tilas Faine, murdered over a broken piece of jewelry.

She would find the people who had ripped her family apart.

And I'll make them all pay.

6
THE GHOST OF WINTER NIGHT

It didn't take long for Lilly to realize that sneakers and travel across snowy ground made a bad combination. Her borrowed clothes were warmer than her own, but they hadn't found boots that fit her well enough for walking long distances. Horses wouldn't get them far through the forest, so everyone traveled on foot and carried their own gear.

Their party consisted of Rune, Kedmir, Jek, Aderyn, and Lilly. No one spoke. And after crossing the river that backed Murke, the only sound came from the crunching of the snow and dry, dormant undergrowth of the forest. The trees harbored no birdsong in their naked branches, and only reached up and out to fracture the view of the cold white sky.

Lilly strained for any sound other than her own footsteps and breathing, but all that answered were the others' footfalls, and the sharp intake of air that filled her lungs to bursting. It was heavy with cold and a foreign energy all its own.

Jek would creep ahead, silent as a ghost, then slink back to Rune to report. Lilly tried to imitate him, but she seemed to find every twig and crunchy ice patch known to man. Kedmir and Aderyn tried to help. While it was doubtful soldiers would be in the woods at this season, they didn't want to take any risks.

Two nights into their journey, Lilly was trying not to toss and turn too much, to avoid waking Aderyn. It was constantly cold, and her arm still throbbed, but her mind still buzzed with unanswered questions. What was the amulet for? Why did Yovak want it so badly he'd searched for Tilas for fifteen years?

After she forced the questions to quiet, memories took their place. Lilly scrambled to think of anything but that day. She knew she wouldn't be able to sleep at all otherwise. Nor would there be sweet dreams. The first night of their journey had found her crying out mid-nightmare, with Aderyn's arms around her.

Not happening again. Lilly's fingers slid up her arm and pressed against her wound, letting the pain fill her mind instead, until tears pricked her eyes.

A chilly midnight breeze brushed through the tent flaps. Lilly shivered and groaned, pushing blankets away to get up. Aderyn stirred in her sleep as Lilly moved. "Stupid tent—"

A hand clamped over her mouth, stifling her cry, and a hard knee dug into her gut, pinning her back down. All air left her. A cold blade touched her throat, and fear rose in Lilly's chest. She barely dared to breathe. Above her was a man. His face was shadowed by his hood, his figure silhouetted by the dim glow of the fire that leaked into the tent.

"I'm sorry," he whispered. The dagger trembled. He hesitated.

Lilly didn't. She swung her fist and it connected with his head. The man grunted, losing his balance. Lilly shoved him back. "Deryn!"

Movement out of the corner of her eye. The assassin saw it too, and pulled away from Lilly, pivoting in place. Metal clanged and something small hit Lilly's thigh. The dagger. She grabbed it.

Aderyn stood tall in the tent, her sword at the attacker's neck. The man didn't move, his eyes on Aderyn.

Lilly touched her own neck. No blood.

"Drop your weapons," Aderyn addressed the assassin. "I don't want to kill you."

"Nor I you." The assassin's tone was flat and unworried. "Drop your sword. The emperor sent me for only one life tonight."

"It is one he shall not have." Aderyn didn't move. A shiver passed down Lilly's spine. "Why were you—"

The tent flap shuffled again. The assassin tried to move, but Rune was faster, his large frame blocking escape. He grabbed the man and put a small knife to *his* throat. The assassin struggled without effect. Aderyn's sword lowered to the assassin's midsection.

"Now what business does the emperor's attack dog have here?" Rune asked. "It's improper to enter a lady's tent uninvited." He pulled the assassin out of the tent. Aderyn and Lilly followed. Lilly's eyes never left the assassin, but he didn't fight back. Yet.

The fire still crackled in the late night air. A body lay beside it, with Jek kneeling over it.

"Kedmir!" Aderyn cried out in alarm. Lilly's heart dropped.

No.

Jek looked up. "He's just unconscious."

Aderyn whirled on the assassin, her sword at his chest now. "What have you done?"

The assassin said nothing. Even in the dim firelight, Lilly could see that he was young, in his mid-twenties. His eyes were dark and angry. He was also a great deal shorter than Rune.

"What have you *done?*" Aderyn's voice rose. She pressed the sword point to the assassin's chest.

"Aderyn, stop," Rune said sharply, guiding the assassin back. The stranger watched Aderyn and her sword. Aderyn drilled a final glare into him before moving toward Kedmir and Jek. Lilly wished Rune's dog were here. But Rune had left Beron behind in Murke. The dog would have barked at any imperial it saw. Despite Rune's hold on her would-be murderer, Lilly felt exposed standing near them by herself.

"It's just a sleeping drug. Give it an hour." The assassin glanced at Rune. "If you're going to kill me, do it."

"I'm not a savage," Rune said.

The man smiled. Lilly shuddered. "I know."

The assassin twisted and slashed at Rune's chest with a new dagger that seemed to appear out of thin air. Rune staggered back to avoid it. The assassin lunged for Lilly.

Two green vines shot up between them and slammed into the assassin, throwing him across the camp. Lilly stared, gasping as her heart thundered in her ears. The stranger groaned, struggling to his feet. Before Rune could reach him, the assassin fled.

Rune swore and rushed after him. "Jek!"

"I'm sorry!" Jek shouted back, getting up to follow. The girls were left alone.

"Aderyn?" Lilly whispered.

"I'm here." Aderyn looked up from examining Kedmir. "Come and sit."

Lilly sat slowly, eyes on the darkness where the weakened fire didn't reach. She looked down at the assassin's dagger. The blade was long and slender, and the handle was a dull black metal, to ward off light's reflection.

Lilly closed her eyes, reminding her body to breathe. She was safe. Alive. Not dead. Definitely not dead. She wasn't entirely sure how she wasn't dead, but her strong heartbeat confirmed it.

She looked back out beyond the camp. "They'll be okay, right?"

"I'm sure they will." Aderyn looked at Kedmir, the firelight casting weird shadows over her worried face. She had already tended the wound, and though Lilly could see him breathing, the stillness unnerved her. She reached down, dangling her fingers just in front of his face, feeling for the warm puff of life.

"Kedmir said he entered your world," Lilly said, covering the silence. "What happened?"

Aderyn's fingers stalled over her double-check of Kedmir's bandage. The woman's lips pursed. She didn't speak, and Lilly ducked her head. "Sorry... just trying to avoid the quiet."

Aderyn still said nothing as she took a seat by the fire. Her gray eyes flickered in the light, deep and far away. Lilly tucked her knees under her chin, shrouding herself in her cloak.

"I did not see it," Aderyn said softly. "I heard a great roar. A dragon—" Her words cut off. Lilly watched her as she fed a stick to the flames.

"It killed my family, and something pulled me here." Aderyn scanned the area, but no Annor or assassin emerged. "And so here I have been."

Lilly's throat felt dry. "I'm sorry."

Aderyn gave only a small nod. When she smiled, it didn't reach her gray eyes, where a grief too fresh still lingered. "You thought quickly, in the tent."

"He hesitated," Lilly said. "I figured it was my move."

Rune returned a few minutes later, looking frustrated. "He escaped. Jek is still out looking." He knelt by Kedmir. "How is he?"

"Still asleep. I found where the drug may have been administered. It's deep, but it didn't break any major veins," Aderyn said. "Is there any way to wake him?"

Rune shook his head. "We can only wait."

Lilly rubbed her arms, glancing at the shadows nervously.

Jek hadn't returned when Kedmir awoke an hour later, just like the assassin had predicted. Rune soothed his brother's frustration at being caught off guard.

"I should have been more watchful." Kedmir accepted the water from his brother. "He snuck up from behind and I didn't hear a thing."

"That tends to be an assassin's skill."

Kedmir glared.

Lilly took a slow breath. "Why would he try to kill me?"

"I don't know." Rune shook his head. "The Ghost has never been known to kill women."

"The Ghost? That's his name?"

"It is a name people call him," Kedmir said. "The Ghost, or the Emperor's Attack Dog."

Lilly's hand strayed to her throat again. "Charming."

"He helps the emperor keep the nobles and other politicians under control when they start to grow discontented or disobedient," Rune said. "If he does not kill, he reminds them of the emperor's power. Yovak removed many of the war lords' leaders, but some swore fealty. The Ghost keeps them from grumbling."

"How did he know where I was?"

"I expect he was summoned after Gabriel was taken," Rune said.

"Zal or some other weaver might have brought him to Murke with dark magic. He must have followed us out here."

Lilly shuddered. "But why does the emperor want me dead? I have the amulet." She looked at Rune, fear gripping her. "If I'm not useful to him anymore, does that mean Gabriel is...?"

"We can't know for sure," Rune said. "It's possible Yovak still has use for him. He will wait until he gets a report from his assassin. If he knows you're still alive, Gabriel is likely still alive too."

Lilly's heart felt like ice. "What else do we know about the Ghost?" She looked at the Annor men when they didn't answer. "If I'm going to have a target on my back, I want to know who I'm up against."

Kedmir's eyes tracked Rune as his brother put a pan over the fire to heat leftovers from supper. He spoke first. "Only what we've told you. He's been more of a story, rumors and whispered fears. He's made it difficult for us to convince higher-ups to join us."

Rune frowned at the fire. "If he's smart, he won't come back tonight."

Lilly squeezed her eyes shut, sucking in a long, slow breath. *Could really use you here, Dad.*

Footsteps made Lilly's heart skip a beat. She twisted sharply as Rune and Kedmir stood, weapons drawn.

"It's me!" Jek's hands flew up. "It's me!"

But he wasn't alone.

Behind him a thin wisp of a girl squealed and ducked back. She peeked out with wide, nervous eyes, clutching a cloak five times too big for her. It was wrapped around her at least twice.

"Easy," Jek said again. "It's alright."

Rune sheathed his sword. "Who is this?"

"This is Tae," Jek said. He looked at the girl. "These are my brothers, Rune and Kedmir, and that's Aderyn and Lilly." Jek reached down for her hand, and the little girl let him draw her closer to the camp.

Lilly and Kedmir exchanged bewildered looks. Aderyn stepped forward to help Tae to a spot by the fire.

"Where did you find her?" Rune frowned, watching the little girl. Tae's eyes didn't meet his.

"Wandering the forest." Jek pointed behind him.

"My friend went hunting," Tae explained. "Mordir. He said he'd come back, but he never did... and I got worried and went to look for him. And I got lost..."

Lilly looked toward the dark. Who would be hunting at this time of night?

"Are you alright?" Jek's voice drew Lilly's attention. He watched her.

"I'm fine," Lilly said.

"You, Ked?"

"My pride is more wounded."

Jek smirked. "Well, you did need to be taken down a few rungs."

"Who are you?" Tae watched them with wide eyes that were blue in the firelight, tinged with slivers of gold. Peeking out from under the girl's thin blonde hair were small, pointed, elf-like ears.

"Rebels." Rune winked at her, taking his seat again. "Where were you and your friend coming from?"

"Lady Rothar's house," Tae said, watching Aderyn's actions. "Way back by Murke."

Everyone but Lilly stared at her. Tae blushed and hunched over.

"Who's that?" Lilly ventured.

"Eeris Rothar," Kedmir said. "Sister to the emperor's advisor. And a menace to any man she fancies, married or not."

"Kedmir." Rune's tone hardened, and Kedmir fell silent.

"You were a servant?" Jek asked Tae.

Tae nodded, then stopped. "Well, a slave, but not anymore. Mordir said so."

"He freed you?" Aderyn passed Tae a plate of reheated dinner.

"Yes ma'am. Because of the war, the city isn't safe anymore, so Lady Rothar was going to stay in the capital with Lord Rothar." Tae paused to eat, shoveling the food down like she hadn't eaten in days.

Lilly frowned. "I've heard that name. Zal said it."

Rune nodded. "Seiryu Rothar. An elf, like Yovak. He aids the emperor in politics and other matters, though he's cunning enough to be a military general. Those who favor the empire say Lord Rothar is a generous man."

"Mordir was there to make sure rebels didn't hurt Lady Rothar until she left," Tae said, finishing the food in record time. "But he talked to me." She tugged the cloak closer to herself. "He asked if I wanted to leave forever, and he promised to come back when everybody was gone." She smiled softer now. "And he did. He gave me my name, too. I told him I didn't have one, so he said he would give me one, 'cause names help you to know who you are."

Lilly smiled. "How old are you?"

Tae frowned at this. "Paetr says I'm..." She looked at her fingers, each digit moving as she worked out the math in her head. "Fifteen."

"*Fifteen?*" Lilly gaped. The girl looked barely more than ten or eleven.

Tae giggled. "Mordir said it like that too."

"Who is Paetr?" Kedmir asked.

"Another friend. But he had to go to the capital too." Tae looked at Rune. "Is Mordir coming?"

Rune frowned, hesitating. Kedmir leaned forward to look around Aderyn at Tae. "Where was he taking you?"

"A city of people like me," Tae said. "He said I would be safe there." She looked down at her hands. "Even though I don't know anybody there."

"You're a half-elf?" Lilly glanced at Tae's ear, just peeking out. Tae nodded.

"Surely you have family there," Rune suggested.

Tae only shrugged and picked at the fraying edge of the cloak. "I was with Lady Rothar since I was a little baby, Paetr said. He never says it out loud, nobody does, not when I'm around, but sometimes I eavesdrop." Her thin shoulders sagged. "They think Lady Rothar had a man to her house, and then she had me."

Realization settled into the group. Anger passed over Jek's face. Aderyn hugged Tae close. Tae leaned into it, though a little stiffly.

"Others say my parents didn't want me," Tae said. "Paetr says not to listen to them, but..." Tae's voice quivered. "He won't tell me if they're wrong."

Anger boiled through Lilly's veins. But Rune's warning look stilled her tongue, and Lilly directed her fury into the fire instead, glaring.

"So, your friend was taking you to the half-elves?" Kedmir prompted.

"Yes." Tae smiled a little. "He said I would find people there who did want me."

"Well, we're headed there ourselves," Kedmir said. "You can come with us."

Tae looked back. "Really?" She looked at Aderyn and Rune next. Rune smiled. "Of course. Your friend had the right idea. The half-elves will take good care of you."

"Will Mordir come with us?"

Rune hesitated now. Lilly and Jek shared a wary look.

"I don't want to go if he's not coming," Tae said, her voice steadier. "He's all alone too." Her eyes brightened. "Did you see him out there? He has dark eyes and dark brown hair, and a scar on his left arm, but he doesn't like to talk about it. He doesn't talk very much, really... But he is kind."

When he's not murdering people. Lilly saw Rune give her another look, and closed her mouth, returning to her stare-down with the fire. Her glare softened. *Or he was murdered like I could have been...*

"Tae..." Rune said, carefully. "He may not be coming back."

All eyes were on Rune now. Aderyn looked at him, startled. Kedmir's eyes flicked from man to girl. Rune's expression was hard to read. He struggled for his next words. How did someone break the news to a little girl that one of her only friends was a killer?

"Why not?" Tae's voice wavered.

"There was an assassin in our camp tonight," Rune said. "Do you know what that is?"

Tae nodded, her face paling.

"He tried to kill me," Lilly said. Tae's head snapped to Lilly, eyes huge. Aderyn took her hand.

"The assassin escaped into the forest," Rune said. "We followed him, and that's how Jek found you. If your friend was out hunting... he may have seen the assassin. And if the assassin didn't want to be seen..."

Tears sprang into Tae's eyes. "No. He's too smart. He knows how to fight, and he has lots of knives. He would scare away the assassin."

"Even the best fighters lose," Rune said. "How long ago did your friend go hunting?"

"Right before supper. The sun was about to set."

Hours. Either her friend had been killed, or her friend was the killer.

"I'm sorry, Tae." Rune's voice was gentle enough to cradle the wind. "There's not enough game in these woods to hunt that long, especially not in the dark like this."

"M-maybe he's just hurt." Tae's voice shook.

"Assassins don't leave most people hurt, Tae," Kedmir said quietly.

Tae shook her head vehemently. "No. No. He said he would come back. He told me to wait. He promised." Tae looked at Aderyn desperately, tears flowing. "He promised."

Aderyn opened her mouth to speak, but no words came, no reassurance. She pulled Tae into a hug. The girl let her, the tears coming faster.

"Take her to bed," Rune said, pained.

Lilly watched Aderyn take Tae into her tent. When the flap had closed, she turned. "The *heck*, Rune?"

"What else are we to tell her?" Rune said. "That her friend, who has been kind to her, tried to kill you?" He shook his head. "Whether he is or isn't an assassin, she won't be seeing him again. Letting her hope is cruel."

No one said anything. Lilly heard muffled sobs from the tent. She wasn't keen on going to bed now. Rune urged Kedmir and Jek both to get some sleep, while he took the last watch. He and Lilly sat by the fire as Tae's crying faded, leaving only the crackle of the fire to spark sound out of the silence.

7
NOT LIKE THE NOVELS

"Wait, I don't understand." Odalys held up a hand, halting Gabriel in his speech. Gabriel's last word hung awkwardly in the air.

"Understand what?"

Odalys scrunched up her nose—a common expression during these kinds of conversations—and peered at him like she *still* wasn't sure he wasn't just pulling her leg.

"How can people," she said slowly, "fit inside a flat square— that's not a box—and perform as if they were on stage?"

"It was recorded somewhere else," Gabriel said. "They shoot in all kinds of locations—"

"They go shooting? What do they hunt?"

"No, no." Gabriel tried not to laugh—he'd learned that lesson before. "With cameras. There's no actual shooting, unless it's with a prop, and that's usually fake."

Odalys frowned. "But how do they get them into the box? It must be exhausting traveling from box to box."

"They record the people on sets, a kind of stage, or in a real-life location." Gabriel pulled a plush cushion over and hugged it to his middle. "They don't go in any boxes. The camera crew records everything on the cameras, so they turn it into video."

"Vih-dee-oh."

"Yeah. And that video—recording—is what the television shows."

Odalys sat back, considering this. "So the people aren't ever there."

"Nope. They're probably at their own mansions watching the same movie." Gabriel grinned. "Your turn."

It was a game they'd started almost the first day of meeting. They took turns, each picking something from their respective worlds and describing it. Four days later, they had yet to run out of things to describe.

"Alright..." Odalys' fingers had twin water snakes slipping around them, yet she never got wet. Gabriel stared at them, entranced. It was... magical, obviously, but so much more. Alive, and something he knew could be powerful. But here in this sitting room, it looked as gentle as the princess herself.

Odalys caught him looking and smiled. "We have our own performers. They use magic to tell stories."

Gabriel's eyes widened. "You do?"

"They're on a big stage instead of boxes. Usually it's only normal weavers, but sometimes they have a dark weaver or even a seventh on the stage." The princess' eyes glittered. "That's when it's most beautiful."

Gabriel shifted, unease creeping into his good mood. "The dark magic isn't... scary?"

"Well, sometimes, when a villain is using it, but that's just an act." Odalys shrugged. "Heroes use it too, and then it's not scary. They make it look so pretty."

Gabriel wasn't sure how that was possible. He'd seen it, and there was no way anybody could make it look tame, let alone *pretty*. Reading the books Seiryu had sent him didn't help much. It didn't seem right. He still remembered the way the shadows moved, how ruthless the magic was, hungry for destruction. Zal's sadistic grin as he wielded it.

"Have you been to one?" Gabriel asked, mentally shrugging the unease away.

"A few, usually with Seiryu. Father's too busy, and my baby brother's birth was hard, so my mother's recuperating. But she used to go with us sometimes." Odalys flicked both water snakes into the air, letting them swirl around each other.

"Congrats." Gabriel grinned. "When was he born?"

"Just a couple days before you came, actually." Odalys beamed. "His name is Khaiel, but we call him Kai for short." Another flick of her hand, and the water snakes dissolved into a fine mist. Gabriel blinked as it settled over him.

"But now that Eeris is here, she can take us to one if you want," Odalys went on.

Gabriel grinned. "That would be cool... who's Eeris?"

"What plot are you two scheming against my poor sister?"

Gabriel looked up at Seiryu, who stood in the doorway of the sitting room, amused.

"Gabriel wants to see the magic performances," Odalys informed him.

"Indeed a sight to behold." Seiryu nodded sagely, still smiling. "One, I think, any visitor should see at least once."

"Do you think Eeris would take us?"

"I do not think you will find it hard to convince her. She's been restless since she got here," Seiryu chuckled. "Has your research piqued your interest, Gabriel?"

Gabriel bit his lip. This was a topic he hadn't wanted to broach yet, so he shrugged noncommittally. "It just sounds really cool to see."

The elf didn't seem to notice his evasiveness. "Well, I will inform Eeris of your wishes. But right now, I believe you two have lessons to go to."

"Oh no." Gabriel scrambled up. "I forgot!"

"Go on. I will see the princess to her own tutors."

Odalys whined, but Gabriel was already up and to the door. He stopped beside Seiryu. "Any word on Dad and Lilly?"

"None yet," Seiryu said. "This will take time, Gabriel. It's a fragile situation. We don't know the rebels' plan for them, so we don't want to spook them into doing something rash."

Gabriel bit back a protest. "It's been almost a week—"

"I know." Seiryu's hand settled comfortingly on Gabriel's shoulder. "All reports pass through me before they go to the emperor, and when I know more, I will bring you word, I promise." He nudged Gabriel into the hall. "Now go on."

Swallowing another argument, Gabriel hurried on. He promptly collided with a gray-uniformed man in his mid-twenties.

"I'm so sorry!" The young man bowed deeply. "I'm so sorry, Master Faine—"

Gabriel flushed. "Don't—" He groaned. "Seleen, what did I say?"

The young man ducked his head. "...Sir."

Shortly after receiving a clean bill of health from Raul, Gabriel had been given an attendant. A slave, Seleen. Gabriel balked, but slaves were the norm. He'd seen enough of them to know they appeared... not necessarily happy, but not afraid. Not really. Though Seiryu and Odalys tended to ignore them, Gabriel was polite, which usually startled the slaves, both parties awkwardly removing themselves from the situation.

So Gabriel was stuck with Seleen. Seleen was human, and always alert and ready to respond to Gabriel's needs. He wasn't any good at conversation, though, and often forgot Gabriel's request to call him "sir" and not "Master Faine."

Gabriel, however, couldn't help but feel awkward. Seleen followed him almost everywhere, and Gabriel quickly learned to tell him when to stay put.

Like now.

"Um." Gabriel inched around Seleen. "Just... wait outside my room, okay? I've gotta go train. I appreciate it, but you really don't have to follow me everywhere."

Seleen hesitated, then bowed. "Yes, sir."

Gabriel bolted for the castle's front doors. Out in the courtyard stood a young soldier, huddled in a cloak against the crisp air of a dying winter.

"I am so sorry," Gabriel panted. "I was talking to Odalys and lost track of time."

Tesmir Annor shrugged, a half-grin on his face. "She makes a lot of people forget the time. Come on, or else I'll have to fight sitting down due to frozen legs, and humiliate you by still beating you."

Gabriel rolled his eyes and followed Tesmir out of the castle walls. He had yet to explore the city, but Odalys had promised to take him soon. The buildings they passed were simple wood and stone, but Gabriel craved to see more.

There were three huge barracks in Erriath. This one flanked the northwestern wall of the city. There were men on the flat rooftops, standing with crossbows or traditional bows and arrows. Gabriel was thrilled. One more thing he wanted to learn. But first— swords.

Tesmir had been selected to help him train. The emperor's top commander, unhappy at being saddled with a person of zero experience, picked the man he apparently could do without.

Tesmir seemed neither pleased nor annoyed. Just a soldier obeying an order.

He was fun to spar with, and a good teacher. They'd had three lessons so far, and Gabriel had yet to walk away without a bruise or two, but that didn't stop him. He didn't stay down. He tried to think of the bruises as signs of progress.

They hadn't talked much since they started, but Tesmir was sociable without being chatty, and Gabriel liked that about him. Being so close in age balanced their teacher-student relationship with a nice friendship, and helped Gabriel feel less isolated.

Gabriel glanced at Tesmir as the young man selected their swords. "Tesmir?"

"Mm?"

"A few days ago," he started, slowly, "I was talking to Seiryu—I mean, Lord Rothar. He told me about the first rebellion."

"The one Emperor Yovak started?"

"The other one."

Tesmir was still for a fraction of a second before striding ahead to claim a sparring ring. "What about it?"

This was a question he had been hesitant to ask, but curiosity was getting the better of him.

"He said it was led by somebody called Ranson Annor." Gabriel picked up his sword. "Are you and he related?"

Tesmir hesitated, as if weighing his words.

"He was my father." The soldier shrugged. "But he died when I was a baby, so I don't remember anything about him."

They exchanged a few blows, Tesmir giving Gabriel critique or praise as needed. Gabriel felt his insides stir with adrenaline. He loved the feeling. Loved the sound of metal striking metal, the hiss as they broke away.

"So he was a rebel, but you're an imperial."

"Yes." Tesmir swung fast, and Gabriel couldn't deflect it in time. The blow smacked his bicep, stinging. Tesmir pointed his sword at him. "Focus."

Gabriel settled into position. "You don't believe in what he did?"

"No." Tesmir swung again, and this time Gabriel caught the attack and shoved Tesmir to the side. "My brothers do, but I don't. That's why I came here."

"How many brothers?"

"Seven." Tesmir parried Gabriel's thrust. "I'm the youngest."

"And I thought one sister was enough."

Tesmir laughed, breathless. "I'd take one sister over seven traitor brothers any day."

Gabriel paused. "I'm sorry."

"Don't be; they made their choice." Tesmir shrugged as he circled Gabriel. "If they want their lives to end in the noose, I can't stop them."

"Haven't you tried talking to them?"

"I did, and it got me here." Tesmir lunged in attack, sending Gabriel scrambling to defend himself. He barely got away without another hit.

Gabriel's brows furrowed. "They kicked you out?"

"They made it clear I was not welcome."

A flicker of anger sparked in Gabriel. "Why are they rebelling now? Wouldn't that first defeat have convinced them? Why are they still after power?"

"Same as before, I guess." Tesmir shrugged. "They don't want a king. But what they fail to realize"—Tesmir blocked Gabriel's next thrust, just barely—"is that he's trying to keep this country from dying. It's going to take sacrifices to bring it back to life, like close supervision of trade, or raising taxes. He's done the same for Luminne and Raijan. All of Allare has prospered under his hand."

"He conquered them?"

"I suppose, but they have their own problems, and they were also content to live under them." Tesmir thrust forward, and Gabriel's sword hissed sharply against his. Gabriel grinned, breathless, at the successful parry. Tesmir smiled back. "Good. Now again."

The two exchanged blows without speaking for a while. Gabriel had been clumsy when he first started, but the exercise and adrenaline had sharpened his focus. He wasn't near Tesmir's level, not even close, but he didn't mind. Learning was half the fun.

"Break, a break!" Tesmir cried, shoving Gabriel's last attack away. "I need a breather."

Gabriel's blade swung lazily at his side. "Come on. A little longer."

"Gabe, I'm exhausted as it is without you begging for every inch of lessons." Tesmir flapped his hand at Gabriel. "You're insane. We can go another round in a minute."

Gabriel followed Tesmir to the ring's edge. They quenched their thirst to the sound of other soldiers sparring.

"So," Gabriel broke the silence after a long swig. "Your brothers want to rule?"

"They don't want to be ruled." Tesmir's expression was indifferent, closed off. He wiped his mouth. "I didn't ask what they planned to do if they won. I don't know how they expect to win, anyway."

Gabriel frowned but drank in silence. Inside, his anger boiled a little hotter.

This world was so unlike the ones he'd read about in novels. He loved fantasy, especially if it had magic, but this... this wasn't it.

This was too despairing. Rebels tearing their own families apart, causing destruction, because they thought a man who saved the country was hoarding power?

Gabriel tried to give the rebels the benefit of the doubt, but then he thought of his father, and Lilly. The rebels held them prisoner. Good guys didn't keep innocent people hostage like that, as leverage or ransom.

The betrayal of this revelation stung. Gabriel gripped his sword tighter. Maybe once he rescued his family, he would help restore order. This was his father's world, wasn't it? This was Gabriel's world, to an extent. He couldn't just leave it to wither under war. His father wouldn't. He'd probably be ready to fight once he and Lilly were free.

Tesmir's fist lightly punched Gabriel's shoulder, shaking him from his thoughts. "You ready for another round?"

"Let's go." Gabriel hefted his sword. "Sorry, got lost in thought."

The young soldier cocked his head. "Don't worry about me. I've come to terms with it, and that's that. My brothers will learn soon enough."

"Don't you miss them?" Gabriel circled Tesmir.

Tesmir seemed to consider the question. "Sometimes... but I miss my bed most. Now strike first, and keep yourself guarded."

Gabriel did, and *almost* landed a hit. Tesmir parried, and Gabriel sidestepped.

"What about the network I've heard about?" Gabriel asked. "The Gold Mark? Seiryu said they're causing trouble in the city."

Tesmir narrowed his eyes, taking a step back. "You're asking a lot of questions today."

"I wanna know what I'm up against. What my family is up against."

Tesmir considered after taking a swing at Gabriel's leg—Gabriel deflected the blow. "I don't know much... they don't do any real lasting damage. Take military supplies, free prisoners. Some rumors say they smuggle fugitives around—"

"Oi, Annor, you gonna keep the soft green to yourself?" A coarse laugh called across the ring. Gabriel paused and looked over. Two soldiers stood watching.

"Soft green?" Gabriel panted, looking at his instructor.

Tesmir rolled his eyes. "New trainees." He waved the soldiers off. "Leave him alone. He's not ready for your dragon-skulled brawn."

The soldiers didn't seem at all offended by this. The taller one smiled. "You telling him stories to give him bad dreams?"

"He asked about the Gold Mark."

"Ahh." The taller soldier sauntered over. "They'll be done away with soon enough, not to worry."

"I heard their leader is a seventh," the shorter soldier added. "A woman."

Tesmir rolled his eyes. "Sure, and I'm a Meriak's uncle."

"S'true! Heard Koranos talk about it. That spy they've got with the rebels gave us a name: Jinnet."

For a split second, Gabriel thought Tesmir flinched. But when he looked over, his friend stood relaxed and annoyed. "You two gossip more than the servants."

"You're one to talk." The taller soldier scoffed. "Never seen you so conversational."

Gabriel stepped up to Tesmir's defense. "I started it. I wanted to know more."

"We have training to do," Tesmir said gruffly. "Go spread rumors elsewhere."

"Aw, come on, Annor. Let us in on this." He nodded at Gabriel.

"Bet you three silver pieces the soft green can't hold up to us."

It took Tesmir's expression a minute to relax. "By himself? Of course not." He glanced at Gabriel with a grin. "But, with me..."

"Two-on-two?" The shorter soldier drew his sword. "I accept those odds. I can take you anyday, Annor. I beat you once in Murke."

"Yes. *Once.*"

Gabriel looked at the three bantering soldiers. "I'm not sure I'm ready for any of this."

"Stick close," Tesmir said. He thumped his fist against Gabriel's chest. "I'll even let you keep the silver. Show them you're no soft green."

Gabriel looked at the two soldiers, who watched him eagerly. With a smile, he stepped back to follow Tesmir, their opponents claiming the other end of the ring. The sight drew the attention of others training around them. He could just imagine them whispering: the new kid thinks he can take on two trained men?

Probably not, but Gabriel wasn't going to chicken out now. Not in front of other grown men. Not when *Lilly* wouldn't have. And what better way to learn? Not all battles would be one-on-one. His enemies wouldn't play fair.

Thinking optimistically, Gabriel figured he'd stand a fair chance with Tesmir by his side.

He failed to bargain with his high chance of failure, and having to explain the large welts and bruises to Raul. He basked in his success, however, of giving a goose egg to the shorter man just before he was laid out on his back.

8

ROOM UNDER THE WALL

Lilly felt the warmth of the sun penetrate the girls' tent. She moaned in protest, burying herself in the furs.

Someone poked Lilly's cheek. She rolled over. "Go away."

"Rune says to get up, and that if you don't stop being so stubborn in the morning he'll come get you himself." Tae poked again.

Lilly swatted at her and missed. "Let him come, if he thinks he's brave enough."

"But this is the girls' tent."

"Then he will have to be very brave. Five more minutes." Lilly burrowed deeper into her blankets.

Tae moved. "I'll go ask."

"Nooo, Tae—" Lilly rolled over to stop her, but the girl was already gone. Lilly huffed and pulled the blanket back over her head. Why did she have to live with such early risers?

"Lilly!" Rune's voice came right next to her, outside the tent. Lilly yelped and recoiled from the canvas. She heard Tae and Kedmir laughing. "Get up. We're wasting daylight!"

Lilly groaned. "Fine! Fine."

Outside, Jek and Kedmir packed away the camp. Aderyn looked up from the fire and smiled, then said to Rune, "She would have gotten up eventually."

"So I've been told these past two days," Rune grunted. "And it has yet to happen *eventually*."

Lilly stuck her tongue out at him and drowsily accepted a plate of food from Aderyn.

The Ghost had disappeared like a whisper. Lilly still caught herself glancing around at any sudden movement or sound, though it had been several days since the attack. Her senses were on fire, and it was exhausting.

But not quite as exhausting as keeping track of Tae.

Tae's newfound freedom had given her wings. She flitted from tree to tree, peering into the thick clusters of pine needles, or squinting into the sky. Occasionally her wandering would stir up a creature with pale yellow fur akin to a rabbit but with the tail of a squirrel, and it would bolt away.

"A hornoss," Jek told Lilly. "Not much meat on them, but they make good pets."

When Tae wasn't exploring every log and divot, Lilly would catch her gazing into the forest, as if searching. Searching for the friend who wouldn't come back. The friend who'd left her behind. Then Lilly would glimpse tears on Tae's cheeks. She didn't talk much. Kept her head down, eyes on her worn-out shoes.

When they were within a few miles of the half-elf city, Rune put an end to the free-ranging. Aderyn kept the girl's hand in hers. Everyone became quiet.

The half-elf city, Lilantami, was just ahead, but Rune took them away from the gates, keeping their distance. A nearly frozen river barred their path as they approached the city from a different side, and a flat, rail-less bridge straddled it. Lilly kept as close to the middle as she could.

"What happens if they agree to help?" she asked.

"Then we send for troops in Murke and strike from without," Rune said, his voice low as they crept through the last of the forest. "And the prince will muster the half-elves to join the attack inside the city."

"Prince? Not the king?"

"To half-elves, it is the same thing," Rune said.

"And if he doesn't help?"

"There's no reason he wouldn't," Kedmir said. "Yovak has oppressed his people harder than anyone, simply for who they are. Nearly cutting off their access to the world outside the forest, enslaving them. He forces them to manufacture weapons and other supplies for Yovak's armies. Wouldn't you jump at the chance to free your people?"

"Imperials will be everywhere." Jek frowned at Rune. "One wrong move and any of them could recognize us. You and Ked especially. Lilantami's not going to be busy enough to disguise us."

"We don't have a choice," Rune said. "We need the half-elves' help, and it's high time they received their freedom."

Once inside, Rune said, they would all go in pairs. Lilly was to go in with Jek, and Aderyn with Rune, and Kedmir with Tae. That had been Lilly's suggestion: each pair a man and a woman. A lady on Rune's arm would make him a little less suspicious. Kedmir teased that the pair could take down the imperials by themselves. Aderyn blushed.

Lilly felt a tingle in her spine, and not from the amulet resting under her shirt. Battle... she'd be in the middle of another fight, with swords and yelling, and that revolting coppery stench of blood.

Would she be expected to fight? Or hide with Tae someplace safe, far away from it all? Lilly touched the dagger at her hip. Jek had helped her secure it safely to her side, but she had no idea how to use it.

The forest ended and left a swath of bare frozen earth between them and a tall, white-stone wall. The stone was worn smooth, with patches of moss in places, giving the city an abandoned appearance. The wall stretched far to the right and left, with a little door just ahead. It was too quiet. Lilly had expected to hear the sounds of city life. If she hadn't known better, she would have thought Lilantami uninhabited.

Two imperial soldiers stood on the wall above the door, but they appeared distracted. They turned their faces toward the city often, watching whatever caught their eye. After concealing their swords, Rune and Aderyn went first, hurrying across the clearing before the imperials turned back.

Kedmir and Tae went next, barely making it across before one of the guards looked back out. Lilly ducked instinctively as Kedmir swept Tae close, clamping a hand over her mouth. No one moved for a good minute, glancing across the clearing at each other.

"Watch your skirts," Jek whispered, shifting. Lilly scowled, gathering two fistfuls of the cloak Aderyn had fashioned into a skirt to conceal her pants. Before they left Murke, Lilly *had* tried a dress, but she'd shucked it within a couple hours. She wasn't sure how Aderyn pulled off even *fighting* in one and making it look effortless.

Lilly needed some kind of disguise, or soldiers within the city would notice something was off. Women wearing trousers wasn't altogether uncommon, but Rune didn't want to take any chances. They needed in and through the city with as little attention as possible.

They hurried across the clearing when the guards' backs were turned, and Lilly's skirt held fast. When they had made it safely across, Jek hunched over the door, producing a lockpick. Lilly controlled her panting, glancing overhead. No soldiers looked down.

A soft click made them all wince. Jek paused, listening, then opened the door. It swung inward, creaking a little. Rune ushered the girls in first, then his brothers. Jek locked the door behind them.

It was dark for all of two seconds before light flooded the room. Lilly squinted at a short figure holding a lantern. A boy, no older than twelve, stared at them with wide, terrified eyes. Pointed ears poked out from his blackish hair. His lips parted.

Kedmir shot forward faster than Aderyn and Rune could whisper reassurance. He grabbed the boy, clamping a hand to his mouth. Aderyn caught the lantern before the boy dropped it. Lilly pulled Tae close when the girl clutched her hand.

"Shh, shh," Kedmir whispered as the boy struggled, his cries muffled. "It's alright, we're not going to hurt you."

The boy trembled, his eyes jumping to each person in the room. Lilly offered a smile and a wave. The boy slowly stopped struggling.

"We're here to help," Kedmir went on, his hand not moving. "We're not imperial soldiers. Do you understand?"

The boy nodded, whimpering.

"You're alright," Kedmir said. "We can't let the soldiers know we're here. It's a secret." He smiled. "You can keep a secret, right?"

Lilly smiled at the boy when he nodded, his expression curious, though he eyed Rune warily.

"I'm going to let you go," Kedmir said. "Do you promise not to yell or make any noise?"

The boy nodded again. Kedmir let him go, stepping back to block the door. The boy wiped his mouth, looking at them all.

"Are you rebels?"

"Would you yell if we were?" Rune winked.

"No sir," the boy said quickly. "My father says the rebels are good. The Annors started them, and he knows them. They're good people."

Rune knelt before the boy. "What if I told you three of them stand in this room?"

The boy's jaw dropped. He looked at them all, trying to pick out the three. "Which ones?"

Rune chuckled. "I am one." He turned and motioned to Kedmir and Jek. "And so are they."

The boy stared, awed. Lilly exchanged amused smiles with Aderyn.

"Have you come to free us?" The boy looked at Rune again, eyes hopeful.

"We've come to try." Rune ruffled his hair. "What's your name, lad? And why are you in here?"

"I'm Notanan. I play in here sometimes." The boy shrugged. "Papa says to stay out of the way so the soldiers don't put me to work like him and Momma." He looked at Tae. "You're a half-elf too. How'd you get outside?"

Tae only nodded, watching the boy with wide eyes, as if he were as new a thing as the hornoss. Rune drew Notanan's attention back to him. "Do the soldiers know about this entrance?"

"Yes, sir."

Rune rubbed his eyes, his shoulders sagging. He looked exhausted.

"I can get my father," Notanan offered. "He told me he was captain of the guard before the first rebellion. Now he just helps Prince Seymour."

Rune's jaw worked, barely disguising his anger. He took a moment to collect himself before speaking. "Notanan, we need to get to the palace to see Prince Seymour. Can you tell your father we're here?"

The boy nodded. "He's helping the workers haul in wood for cutting, but I can make him come without anybody knowing."

"Go," Rune said. "Take your lantern and only speak if spoken to."

"Yes, sir." Notanan saluted.

He took the lantern back from Aderyn before disappearing down a hall outside the room, leaving them in the dark. It was only a moment before Jek found candles in a cupboard, and a snap of magic lit the wicks. It gave them enough light to see each other by.

The room was barely large enough for all of them. A table and three chairs had been squished into a corner, where Aderyn and Tae now sat. Rune stood at the door Notanan had exited through, and Jek took a post near the one they had used.

They remained silent. Lilly paced the room, adrenaline still buzzing through her. What would happen if they were caught? They wouldn't make it to the cover of the forest before being arrested, or killed.

She hugged her arms to her chest. Tilas's pained expression flashed in her mind's eye. The groans as the pain spasmed through his body and slowly took his life. Dying hurt. She wasn't ready for that.

The room felt too close, too crowded. She needed air. Needed to clear her mind of her father's damaged body, the hot, burned smell—

"Lilly!"

She gasped, choking on the breath. For a split second, her father stood before her, his eyes boring into hers. Her breathing hitched. "Dad."

"Lilly." The voice wasn't Tilas's. Jek stood before her now, gripping her arms so tightly it hurt. It took her a second to focus on his eyes, then on the scar, and then back on his eyes.

She gasped. "Sorry. I..." Her voice froze. Her chest constricted as the monster prowled out of its corner. She took a deep breath. The others were watching them. "I'm fine. I'm fine." She pulled out of his grip.

Was she okay? She looked at her hands. She'd washed the blood off, but in the dim room she thought she could still see the stains.

Then the door opened.

Jek withdrew from her and slipped just behind the door while his brothers reached for their swords. Lilly ducked back with Aderyn and Tae, forcing her breathing to hold steady. Her fingers closed around the assassin's dagger.

A half-elf slipped inside. He was smartly dressed, and though his back was bowed, his bearing commanded respect. His long dark hair was tied back neatly. He wore a long tunic, reaching to his knees. His shirt and pants were faded.

He took in the room and locked eyes with Rune. "Which one are you?"

"Rune Annor. Are you captain of the guard?" Rune didn't move.

"Once. I am Havan." Havan crossed his arms, looking at each person in the room, including Jek, who'd been hidden in shadow. Lilly touched the cloak-skirt, suddenly glad for it. The fewer questions were asked, the faster they could get someplace secure.

Rune straightened. He even smiled. "Havan. That name I know."

The former captain sighed. "You're all fools."

"We couldn't risk sending word."

"I know," Havan said. "Hide your packs and *all* weapons here and come with me. We'll have a better chance of getting through this city alive if we don't give them anything to stab you with."

9

PRINCE SEYMOUR

The sneaking got a lot harder.

Lilly crept along the outskirts of Lilantami with Jek, sometimes forgetting to breathe, and sometimes breathing too fast. The buildings surrounding them were tall and quite wide, like an apartment complex, and constructed of stone and wood. All were in a state of disrepair—shutters chipped or missing, and doors completely gone. These had been replaced by hanging rugs or other fabric, some hardly thick enough to keep out the winter chill.

Moss decorated the buildings, giving the city a ruined look. The streets were all grass, now pale and dead.

It was unnervingly empty... quiet and still.

Lilly saw no adults. Occasionally she glimpsed half-elf children who quickly disappeared indoors, nearly startling her into a heart attack.

The rest of their party had split up again. Havan walked with Kedmir and Tae, for if anything went wrong, he could ignite more chaos accompanied by a titan rebel warrior or a seventh weaver than by a man with a little girl.

"Where is everyone?" Lilly whispered. Jek didn't answer until he finished scouting around their next turn.

"Put to work, most likely," he said. "They're probably deeper within the city, where the shops are."

Lilly glanced up at a window. Darkened, lifeless.

The city, its atmosphere and its people were a surrendered, broken gray.

"How could someone do this?" Lilly murmured. "The emperor's just... made them slaves? Leaving their children alone at home?"

"To the elves, half-elves are little better than cattle," Jek said, eyes ahead. "Human and elf relations are forbidden, and offspring are a disgrace."

"So he makes them all slaves because they're not pure-blooded one way or the other?"

"On the premise that they aided the first rebellion, yes. After Yovak and the first rebels overthrew the war lords, Yovak's reign began to... grow suspect. He acted on behalf of unity, but Piensor suffered. His overseas campaigns started then, and taxes rose higher, and soldiers were quartered and caused trouble. My father and Seymour went to Yovak to speak with him, to confront him."

Jek peered around another corner, his eyes taking in every detail. "They went with only peace in mind, to broker a better structure for Piensor. But they were turned away without seeing Yovak. Lord Rothar accused them of treason, and attempting to take power for themselves."

"And Seymour was implicated with the rebels."

"He helped them start the first rebellion. What else could they do, when they'd been turned away?" Jek's gaze strayed to the buildings, silently watching. "I just didn't think it was this bad..."

"Have you guys tried going to the emperor again?"

"It was discussed, but Isilmere didn't think it was worth our time. Yovak has more power now. Why would he listen—"

Jek wrenched back, grabbing Lilly's arm and pulling her with him before she stepped around the corner. Lilly's heart screeched to a halt, and her breath choked out. She stood frozen against the wall, her pulse throbbing under Jek's grip.

Then, voices. *Adult* voices.

"You're supposed to be supervising the wood loaders, Havan." It was a man's voice, so arrogant that Lilly imagined him with a puffed-out chest as he strutted around.

"My son called me away." Havan's voice next, still strong. Defiant. "I was on my way back when I thought I would check on the other children in the area."

"Were you given permission to leave?"

"There was no foreman there. He had gone to review Prince Seymour's reports after the prince departed for the day. I did not plan to be gone long—"

"If you weren't given permission, you should have kept your filthy hide where you were told," the new voice growled. "You'll be written up, Havan. And I *think* this'll be your third one, won't it? I do wonder what the general will do..."

Silence. Lilly looked up at Jek. He stood still as the stone at their backs, head inclined toward the voice. Brows furrowed in... rage.

Lilly twisted from his grip and grabbed his arm instead, squeezing.

Havan spoke again. His voice slightly less authoritative. "Apologies, sir... but if I may ask... aren't *you* supposed to be at the city gates? I do believe that's where the *general* assigned you."

Lilly winced, expecting to hear a slap echo through the silent city.

Instead she heard choking. Jek's eyes lit up with fury. He started to move. Lilly squeezed his arm tighter and lightly punched his middle. He flinched back.

"Don't," she hissed.

"I would be very careful how you speak to me, *Captain*," the imperial said. "I am your superior, and I am very capable of making sure you know your place. Your precious wife and boy are expendable."

Lilly's heart nearly imploded at the word. Expendable. Lilly and Gabriel had been expendable when Zal attacked. To intimidate a father into submission.

Innocent people. Expendable to the empire if the mood struck.

The choking ceased and was replaced with coughing and gasping. The stranger's voice trailed away.

"I like patrolling places nobody expects," he said. "I find such *interesting* things when people don't know they're being watched."

Havan's breaths evened out, and Jek pulled out of Lilly's grasp and rounded the corner.

"Havan," he breathed.

Lilly followed, her heart twisting in sync with her stomach at the sight of Havan on his knees, head bowed.

Havan's head snapped up, and he relaxed. "I'm fine." He stood. "Your brother and little friend are fine. I sent them down another way." Havan pointed. "I must leave you all to find your own way. With Dazan prowling around... be very careful."

"Who is he?" Lilly whispered.

"No one you want to meet."

"We'll be careful." Jek took Lilly's hand. He pulled her down a narrow alley, circling toward the city wall, giving Dazan a wide berth.

Traveling too close to the wall, they nearly fell upon a cluster of soldiers. They ducked inside an empty house, hiding in shadows until the soldiers passed by.

Lilly's heart never stopped hammering.

Next came the tricky part. They had to forge deeper into Lilantami. That meant stone-paved streets, shops, and people. And more imperials.

Jek avoided streets whenever possible. They circled around the backsides of empty shops, retracing their route whenever they heard voices.

Turning a corner, Jek and Lilly dodged into an empty shop, ducking under the windows as a procession of half-elves were marched by, bearing crates or sacks, escorted by imperial soldiers. Sunken features, skinny bodies, exhaustion written into every line and breath.

The soldiers watched them closely, keeping them marching at a pace Lilly feared they couldn't hold for long. Hands rested on sword hilts or whips. Lilly's blood boiled hot with wrath. The half-elves never raised their eyes to them. Never said a word.

Lilantami was no better than a ghost town, full of abused ghosts living in fear of the demons in their midst.

When the procession's shuffling steps had faded away, leaving the street in silence again, Jek motioned to Lilly to rise. She took slow breaths, forcing herself to walk. She could do nothing for these people now.

Finally, Jek turned off the paved streets, and their footsteps crunched softly over dormant grass. Here, apartment buildings abutted a bare, spindly hedge surrounding a humble garden. In it stood the tallest, thickest tree Lilly had ever seen.

White stone was grafted into the wood, thickest on the first two floors. Looking higher, Lilly spied the white stone reinforcing wooden balconies. Lilly craned her neck back to see boughs stretching into a network of branches like so many interlocking fingers. The tree looked strong and healthy, and had accepted the stone as part of itself.

"Whoa."

"One of the greatest mysteries and wonders of the world. Some say that on dragonback, you can see it rising higher than any other tree." Jek smiled a little. "Just wait until you see the inside."

Lilly stared. "Dragons are *real*?"

"Come on."

They crossed the garden and reached a side door. Jek crouched down to pick the lock.

It swung back on its own, and he lunged backward, knocking into Lilly.

"Get in," Rune hissed, grabbing his brother's arm and yanking him inside. Lilly darted after them.

They stood in a brightly lit kitchen, from the same stone as the palace. There were four aisles of counterspace and wide metal basins with waterspouts, and a rack of utensils, pots, and pans on a far wall. Along one wall was an army of cookstoves.

A small group of half-elves glanced at them nervously as they resumed their work. Aderyn stood at the other end by a hallway leading out.

"Where are Kedmir and Tae?" Lilly asked when her eyes had taken it all in.

"Likely on their way—"

A timid little knock on the door caused Lilly to jump back. Before Rune could open it, a half-elf woman with graying hair and crisp, neat clothes shooed him aside. Her clothes were similar in style to Havan's, but her belted tunic flowed from the waist like a skirt. Like Havan's, the colors had faded. Dying like the city.

"Move, you mountain of a rebel. If it's some little soul looking for a scrap, I don't want you scaring them off." The woman plucked a small parcel from a basket and opened the door.

"Corelle," Rune muttered. "As imperious as ever."

Lilly fought a smile.

"Hello, dear." Corelle's voice transformed into something motherly and tender.

"Hello." Tae's voice seized Lilly's heart for a second. "Can... can I come in? And my friend? We're supposed to be meeting—"

Rune gingerly nudged past Corelle. "Tae, get inside. Where is Kedmir—Ked, get out here. What were you thinking, hiding and letting her stay in the open?"

"I thought she would be better received than me!"

"What in the Creator's name are you all doing here?" Corelle surveyed them all when the door closed behind them. "Sneaking around like thieves, trying to break in." She glared at Jek, who ducked his head.

"Corelle, you remember Kedmir and Jek—"

"Oh, yes, I remember. But I didn't ask who they were." The half-elf woman crossed her arms.

"Captain Havan brought us," Tae said. "But he was stopped, and we had to go alone."

"Havan? He sent you?"

"We're here to see Seymour," Rune said.

Corelle's lips pursed. "Well, I'll take you the rest of the way. No soldiers in here, so no more sneaking around."

"No imperials here?" Kedmir asked.

"Used to be," Corelle said, leading them down the hall. She smiled as Tae bounded to Aderyn's side. "But when Prince Seymour's son was born, Lady Aelynn was anxious for his safety, and her health suffered. The prince haggled for the soldiers to remain outside the palace. By a stroke of mercy Yovak allowed it.

Seymour is permitted to take part in organizing the work in the city, so he's down among those imperials enough that they feel they can spy on him without skulking in his home."

Corelle led them along narrow, winding corridors to a wide hall with a high ceiling. It was made of a half-circle of white stone, with a thick tree root high above that cut through the middle of the ceiling, like a single rib. It forked around a pair of thick wood doors, where two half-elf guards were posted. Little lantern orbs hung from the root, their shutters ranging from yellow to white.

Across from the palace's front doors, at the other end of the main hall, stood another pair of doors, carved with the image of a man and a woman. On either side of these were stairs that ascended and curved around the edge of the tree's trunk. Next to the stairs were smaller corridors. They had emerged from the left corridor.

"This way," she said, heading for the right staircase.

Lilly paused by a little window to gaze at the view of the city sprawled below. Above, she watched imperials make their rounds, supervising the half-elves in their work. They stood out cold and unnatural in the earthy, humble appearance of Lilantami.

Lilly stopped again when she reached the top. Glossy, colored murals had been painted on the stone wall to the left. One depicted a man and a woman. The woman was an elf, tall and slender, but the man was human. He knelt before the elf-lady, kissing her hand. It was the same couple depicted on the doors downstairs.

She walked on, noting the two people represented in different scenes: sharing a kiss, hiding in the treetops from elves *and* humans, building a home in the forest. Sometimes there were additional characters, and often the murals were done in different artistic styles, as if many people had contributed to the collection.

"Their history, told in pictures," Jek murmured close to her ear.

"What happened?"

"Human diplomats came to the elves, and one of their guards fell in love with an elven diplomat's daughter."

"Yikes."

Jek chuckled. "Somewhere in this place there are murals of them meeting in secret. One depicts them meeting disguised as servants. That one was my favorite."

"You've been here before?"

"Aye, as a child."

They followed Corelle and the others down another hall made all of stone, with murals on either side, to a wide door where two half-elves stood guard. They stiffened as Corelle approached.

"They're here to see the prince." Her voice was clipped and carried the same air of authority as Havan's. The guards stepped aside. Corelle waved Lilly and her friends through.

They entered a spacious sitting room with four tall windows looking out at a balcony along the wooden wall, which offered an even higher view of the city. The floor was covered in thick, brick-colored rugs, and tapestries with intricately embroidered knots and swirls in shining colors hung on the three stone walls.

There were shelves carved into the walls, holding some books but mainly odd trinkets of wood or silver. More books lay scattered on a small round table in the corner.

In the middle of the room was an assortment of couches. The woodwork looked beautifully smooth and glossy even from a distance. The room smelled warm, and Lilly spied a bowl on a metal stand sitting on the table. Candlelight pulsed within the stand, heating the water in the bowl. It gave off a pleasant peppermint fragrance.

A half-elf looked up from a sheaf of papers, startled. "Corelle?"

"Visitors, my prince." Corelle dipped into a curtsy. "Come back to torment me once more."

Kedmir laughed.

The prince stood up from the couch. He was tall. His brown hair fell nearly to his waist and was tied back. His face was strong and firm, with an element of gentleness. His eyes, blue with the same gold slivers as Havan and Tae, were warm and fatherly and told Lilly she was already welcomed. Protected.

It made her heart squeeze just a little.

His smile for Rune was no less warm as he stepped forward to meet him.

"What on this green earth are you all doing here?" He embraced Rune. "We've been hearing rumors of the fighting."

"We are all well," Rune said, grinning. "It's good to see you again, Seymour."

Seymour stepped back and looked at them all. "As good as it is to see you... it's not safe here, not for rebels."

"Rebel business is why we've come," Rune said quietly. "Is this room a private enough place to talk?"

"Aye, but let us talk while you eat. I can't imagine the journey here was pleasant."

Lilly's hand rose unbidden to her throat, and the motion caught Seymour's eye. "And who are these?"

Rune turned. "This is Lilly Faine, Aderyn Scalestride, and Tae. Isilmere wrote of Aderyn, I believe, several months ago."

"So he did." Seymour turned to her and bowed. "An honor, Seera Scalestride."

Aderyn looked startled at the formality. Seymour smiled. "Isilmere says that in your world you are a knight. You are a brave woman to stay amidst the conflict."

Lilly's jaw dropped. Suddenly, Aderyn's first appearance made sense: The firm, unafraid stance when she faced Zal. She wasn't just a soft-spoken lady. Aderyn was a real *knight*.

Gabriel's going to flip out.

Aderyn's blush deepened, and she curtsied, standing a little straighter. "Thank you, sir." She smiled at the Annors. "I couldn't leave my friends to fight alone. Not if I could help them."

Seymour turned to Tae next. "And what is your story, my dear?"

Tae leaned a little closer into Aderyn, shy. "I'm a half-elf, sir. I was a slave in Murke, but I escaped."

Seymour nodded, his smile fading. "Well, I am glad to know that is no longer your life. You could not have found finer people to travel with."

Tae smiled shyly and nodded.

Seymour at last turned to Lilly. "And how did you come by this hardy group of fellows, my dear?"

Lilly managed an awkward curtsy with her cloak-skirt. "I kind of showed up in the middle of their battlefield."

"Lilly joined us in Murke during the skirmish," Rune said. "She comes from another world, like Aderyn."

"But not the same one," Lilly added. "It's complicated."

"We hoped you might have known her father," Rune said.

Seymour frowned. "This too sounds like a discussion best had over a meal." He moved to the door. "Thank you, Corelle. If you would, please see that rooms are prepared?"

Corelle curtsied. Seymour beckoned to the others. "Come. I will have refreshments brought while we talk." When everyone had been seated, Seymour took his place and looked at Lilly. "What was your father's name?"

Lilly fidgeted anxiously in her seat. Why did it sound so

ridiculous now? "Tilas Faine. But he—and my brother and me—disappeared from this world fifteen years ago."

Seymour frowned thoughtfully. "What happened that brought you back?"

"People with dark magic," Lilly said. "They said the emperor was looking for my dad, and for this." She pulled out the amulet and set it on the table. She felt a lump in her throat, and swallowed hard. "They killed my father over it, and kidnapped my brother."

Do not cry. Pull it together.

"I'm so sorry." Seymour's voice was gentle, saddened.

"Me too."

There was a brief interruption as food was brought in. It was hot and delicious, nothing like camping. The main dish was a vegetable soup, with chunky vegetables that still crunched. There was dried fruit—of which Kedmir couldn't get enough—that tasted as sweet as candy.

As Seymour sat in thoughtful silence while his guests ate, Lilly ventured to speak again. "He was friends with Rune's father, and Rune and his brothers knew me and my brother when we were little. My father might've been a rebel then." Lilly paused for breath. "I don't remember the stories, so I don't know much else about him." She bit off the words she wanted to say: *I don't feel like I know him at all anymore.*

Seymour at last nodded slowly. "I didn't know him well, but I met him a couple times. Tilas was a spirited man. A little overconfident but with a good heart, and a great love for his family and country. Last I'd heard, he was a spy in Yovak's court. He already had a friendship with Seiryu Rothar from previous years."

"Seiryu?" Kedmir blinked. "Not Yovak?"

"Not to my knowledge. But I never knew him well, only what

Ranson told me."

Lilly drank all of this information in. "He was a spy? For the rebels?"

"From what I remember. Though I don't know what would drive him to another world." Seymour smiled gently. "I'm afraid I cannot tell you anything more, or anything about that trinket there."

Lilly tried to sift through the new information. Why was there still so much she didn't know? It was thrilling to learn each new piece of the puzzle—her father had been a *spy*—but there were so many unknowns. It was infuriating.

Seiryu Rothar. Not Yovak. It made little difference. Lilly would deal with them both one way or another.

Rune cleared his throat. "Seymour, we've come here for the rebellion, just as our father did. To ask you for your help again."

Seymour's expression fell, and betrayed the depth of his exhaustion. A kind of exhaustion that saw no sleep, only fear and suffering. Lilly's heart ached for him.

"I wish we could help you, but I can do nothing even for my own people," Seymour said heavily. "Before you and your brothers came to us, Yovak took my infant daughter from me when his forces captured our city." Seymour paused, as if he struggled to speak. "He holds her as leverage against me still. I cannot risk her safety, or my son's."

His eyes closed briefly. "My people are suffering here. We are enslaved and treated as animals, worked to exhaustion. Yovak took half of my people to Erriath, where they work in the fields. We are not even permitted to train. If we try to help you, Yovak will give the order to slaughter the half-elves in Erriath." Seymour's eyes clouded with pain. "And my daughter."

Rune's lips parted in shock. "I'm so sorry," he murmured. "I didn't know…"

Seymour leaned back. "I'm afraid all we can do is offer you supplies for the journey back." His smile was weak, sad. "It may be best for you to leave in the morning. The higher-ranking soldiers and weavers have no qualms about entering my home unannounced."

Rune nodded. "Thank you for putting us up for the night. We will leave at dawn."

Lilly couldn't help but slump. She'd hoped for at least twenty-four hours without travel. Maybe a chance not to rise before the sun.

"Are there baths?" She felt bad about asking, but the question escaped before she could stop it. Her sanity was slipping, and a bath was essential for its recovery.

Seymour's laugh reminded Lilly of her father. Her heart ached again. "Aye, baths are certainly included. As many as you need."

Corelle returned to escort them to their rooms, and to baths. Aderyn went to assist Tae, and Lilly was left to her own bathing room. The square-shaped bath made of smooth, polished stone stood in the center. Three steps led up to the wide edge, and three steps led down into it.

Corelle left a collection of oils and soaps for her to choose from. Most of them smelled something like mint, but spicier. Lilly liked it. She poured a few drops of scented oil into the water before sinking into the hot bath with a moan.

The emptiness and silence of the room allowed her mind to wander over memories of the past few days. The yelling, and the smell of burned flesh—

The sorrow crashed down harder than ever. Lilly sucked in a sob and scrubbed her hair, trying to focus on that; not the image of her father's lifeless, damaged body, Gabriel's cry of pain, or her own throat-ripping scream of grief like the one threatening to explode now.

Her breath heaved and her hands shook, despite all attempts to steady them. The sob escaped this time. Lilly clamped her hand over her mouth and took sharp, shaking breaths. The images wouldn't leave her mind. She shivered, the water suddenly cold, and shut her eyes tight, but Zal's smug sneer, as he kicked Tilas over, exploded in her mind. Her father's cries of pain echoed in her head.

Before she could rethink it, Lilly fully submerged, eyes shut tight, and *screamed*. Bubbles rushed out of her, the water drowning the scream in silence. Lilly's cry choked into a sob, and soapy water flooded in.

She jerked back to the surface, coughing and spitting as water sloshed over the edges of the bath. She rubbed her stinging eyes and let her lungs breathe again. She didn't feel as coiled, but she didn't feel much better. She needed to hit something. Over and over.

A knock at the door made her jump and silenced her whimpering. Lilly sagged with relief and cleared her throat. "Yeah?"

"Are you doing alright, love?" Corelle's voice was muffled through the door.

"Yeah... yeah, I'm fine. I'm almost done." Lilly took a shaky breath and pushed her hair back. "I'm fine."

"Do you need more hot water?"

"No, thank you." Lilly leaned her head against the lip of the tub and closed her eyes, her voice somehow steady. "I'm really fine."

"If you need anything, ring for a servant to fetch me. I'll be right up."

Lilly thanked her and continued to scrub her body of travel grime, inspecting each fingernail before getting out. She tugged on the clothes Corelle had set out for her, black with gold stars embroidered on the hems. They were the same style worn by the half-elf woman; warm but loose and comfortable. Her sneakers were still there—her other clothes had been taken to be washed and mended—but a pair of sturdy boots stood next to them.

She pulled on the snug, warm boots and ventured out onto the balcony connected to the room she would share with Aderyn and Tae. It looked down on the garden, which was brightly lit by lanterns.

She heard childish, happy *laughter*.

10
FEAR INTO COURAGE

Lilly found her way downstairs and into the garden through a pair of thick doors. These were opened by a half-elf woman who nodded to her before resuming her guard post.

Outside, Lilly followed the squealing laughter deeper into the gardens. Lanterns like the ones in the main hall were strung in the bare trees, marking one of the faded paths as the sun dipped below the trees. It ended in a little round clearing, where an empty fountain stood. Its centerpiece was a sleeping dragon, curled up tight on its pedestal, neck arched back, snout to the air.

The clearing was filled with boys and girls of all ages, hair in wild and careless disarray, clothes torn, faces dirty, all smiling. Some ran to and fro, some clustered in groups. Several sat around a little fire, stuffing their mouths with food.

It felt too loud in a city otherwise so quiet and gloomy, but Lilly couldn't help a smile. The warmth and love were bright and full here. A pocket of gold.

Corelle stood at the edge of the cheerful chaos, watching closely. She hugged a shawl around herself, and smiled as Lilly approached.

"Ahh, that bath did you good."

Lilly grinned. "It was *amazing*. Thank you."

Corelle nodded, returning her gaze to the children. "Most of the time, these wee things are left to fend for themselves until the imperials think they're old enough to work without being a nuisance. So they come here." She smiled sadly. "We feed them a meal, or tend to sickness and injury, until the day's labor is done, and their parents are released. It's a place to just be a child."

Lilly watched the children. They seemed unaware that their families were working just to see another day.

Corelle jerked her chin out. "Your friends are over there. Leave me to my supervising that brat of a young princeling—Tarkas! What did I tell you?"

A boy not much older than twelve, with brown hair falling in his face, sheepishly climbed down the fountain dragon's neck. Notanan, who had been standing nearby, bolted away. Tarkas ran after him.

Leaving Corelle to her muttering, Lilly walked around the edge of the space. "Hi."

Jek smiled at her. He wore half-elf clothes too: khaki pants and a dark red tunic with black embroidery that made him look pale.

Beside him, Tae watched the children play. Her clothes were green with blue embroidery. Her hair, still wet, had been braided with a matching ribbon.

Lilly poked Tae's shoulder. "Not going to join in?"

Tae rocked on the balls of her newly booted feet. She chewed her lip, then shook her head.

Lilly frowned, glancing at Jek. He watched Tae, his gray eyes softening.

"This is something I've always loved about the half-elves," Jek said. "They take care of each other, and they're all a family here." He looked down at Tae. "And they don't care where they come from, or who they come from."

Tae continued to bite her lip. Jek motioned to the shrieking children. "Lots of half-elves here were born just like you, Tae. They weren't wanted, kept tucked away so no questions would be asked." He crouched down by her. "But did you know there's not one child here without a family?"

"Really?" Tae looked at him.

"Half-elves don't let orphans stay orphans," Jek said. "They find them a family, and they love them like they were their own. I haven't seen anybody without a family yet, so it must be true." He smiled at the scene before them. "This only proves it."

Lilly smiled. Tae fidgeted with her fingers. "Even if they were like me?"

"*Exactly* like you." Jek turned her around to face the kids again. One little girl ran, crying, to Corelle. The woman knelt down, wrapping her arms around the child, and another half-elf hurried over. Within a minute, the little girl was smiling again, a small bandage on her arm, and running back into the fray.

Lilly grinned at the tiny smile that grew on Tae's face. Jek nudged her forward. "It's not safe for you to stay here now, but someday. And nobody is without a family here, just like nobody is without a name." He glanced at Lilly. "Family helps you to know who you are, too. And you will find one who will love you with everything they have."

Tae nodded, tears in her blue and gold eyes. She flung her arms around him, nearly knocking him over. Lilly grabbed Jek's flailing arm as he steadied himself. He hugged Tae back and whispered in her ear. Tae hugged him tighter.

Finally, Jek pulled away. "Go on."

Tae scampered forward. Notanan's face lit up when he recognized her, and he pulled her over to his friends by the empty fountain. She was swallowed into their midst like an old friend. Tarkas pulled her up on the fountain's edge and began showing her how to balance around it.

Lilly looked at Jek. His eyes had taken on a faraway look. "How did you know that? That there aren't any orphans here?"

Jek took his time answering. "I don't know for sure. But I've never seen a child without a home here. When our parents died in the first rebellion, my brothers and I tried to survive the first winter on our own. But it was just too cold, so we sought help from Seymour, and he took us into his own home." He laughed softly. "Eight boys, only two old enough to go to work, and they took us all. We learned then that everyone had a place to call home."

He looked at Lilly. "Even those who think home is gone for good."

The words struck close. How many nights had Lilly spent wondering if she could go home? How she and Gabriel could replicate what Zal Ira had done? She wasn't sure, and that scared her. But she clung to the hope that there *was* a way home. Somehow.

The children started a train around the fountain, balancing on the edge, arms spread out like wings. Wings that flailed in a panic as water burst from the fountain dragon's muzzle, spraying high before flicking to each child. They ran shrieking and laughing, except for Tae, who stood in the spray with her arms raised.

Lilly smirked. "Huh, didn't think that fountain worked."

"Must have had a bit of water left in it." Jek grinned, watching the magic chase Notanan and Tarkas around like a liquid lasso.

"That night we found Tae, what she said... I've felt alone like that too," Jek said. "I don't want her to spend as long as I did wondering if there was anybody like me."

"Like you?"

"When you're a child with magic, it's new and confusing. Without parents to explain what it is, you start feeling like you're the only one. At least for a while." Jek watched Notanan burst through a water ribbon, laughing as it drenched him. "I wanted Tae to go forward without worrying that she would be abandoned again—"

"Alright, all of you clear out!"

Jek's magic dropped to the earth with a splash. Half-elf children fled in all directions as a man stepped out of the shadows, his features contorted in anger and... glee? Lilly's gut curled, and she felt uncomfortably naked without her dagger.

She recognized the voice, too. Dazan's superior arrogance. He stood like he owned the place, but he wasn't dressed like a soldier. He wore dark clothes like Zal's, along with black metal armguards. In the fading light, Lilly glimpsed the emperor's three-headed snake on each.

Tarkas bolted for the palace, and Corelle swept him inside. Tae stood alone, staring in fear at the dark weaver in their midst.

"Who was it?" he barked. "Which one of you used magic?"

The half-elves who remained were frozen in place. Dazan turned, eyeing each of them. He stopped at Jek and Lilly. "Don't think I recognize you."

"It's a big city," Jek said. "There are a lot of us."

The dark weaver snapped his fingers. Lilly stifled a yelp as fire flickered in their faces. But the fire simply hung suspended in the air. Tae sidestepped slowly, then darted for the palace. Dazan didn't move.

"You're not half-elves." He frowned darkly. "How did you two get in here? I don't remember any record of humans entering the city."

The words "you were busy bullying others" *almost* slipped from Lilly's lips.

Shadows writhed up around her and Jek. Lilly recoiled, but the magic grabbed her wrist, curled around her arm, and slid its cold, dark emptiness around her, pinning her limbs behind her. Jek wrenched against the magic holding him, his eyes alight with wrathful fire.

Dazan grinned as they struggled. "Go ahead and fight, weaver. See where that gets you, when I've caught you using magic without a license."

Jek snarled. "Weavers don't need licenses."

Dazan's smile turned wicked. "They do here."

"He is my guest, and under my roof, Dazan," Seymour's voice boomed behind them. Lilly twisted as the prince strode into the light, Havan right behind him.

The dark weaver turned, unafraid. "You're harboring humans now, Seymour?" he sneered. "I don't think the emperor will approve of that."

"That is not your concern," Seymour said. "Emperor Yovak gave permission for all those under my roof to be in my care, not under your authority."

"Not when they're humans who enter without permission." Dazan crossed his arms. His black metal armband glinted in the lantern light. "So I don't think you really have any authority here now. You should have reported it."

Lilly didn't dare move. The magic shifted against her skin, the cold penetrating her clothes. Jek watched Dazan, his face contorted in anger.

Seymour glanced at them. "I will discuss it with General Amisa. I believe she is your superior, is she not?"

Dazan's smug expression morphed into a scowl. "Amisa is busy. I am conducting my own patrols—"

"In my home?" Seymour interrupted. "With all due respect, Dazan, I will speak to your general. I'm sure we can settle this. My guests will be departing tomorrow, and they will not leave the palace until then." Seymour looked at Lilly and Jek. "I'm sorry you've taken issue with children's games, but visitors do not know our laws these days and cannot be expected to obey what they do not know."

Dazan glared at Seymour. "Fine. If you will come with me, then, *Prince*."

He flicked his hand, and the dark magic dissolved. Lilly shuddered and stepped backward. Jek remained rooted in place, staring down Dazan.

Seymour offered a slight bow and followed Dazan. Havan turned to Lilly and Jek and pointed to the palace.

"Get inside," he said. "And stay there." And he turned to follow Seymour.

Jek didn't move, so Lilly pulled him on. She didn't look back until she had pushed Jek into the foyer. Right into Kedmir.

"What happened?" Kedmir blurted, looking from Lilly to Jek. "Jek?"

"A mistake," Jek growled. He stalked past Kedmir, but his brother grabbed his arm.

"No," Kedmir snapped. "You don't get to walk off. What happened? Where did Seymour and Havan go? One minute he and Rune were talking and then Corelle came storming in about a dark weaver, and Tae's in tears—"

"I said it was a mistake!" Jek wrenched free. "I was careless. It won't happen again!"

Rune's towering figure appeared in the dim room. "Any more yelling and you'll bring more than a dark weaver to Seymour's doorstep."

Jek didn't answer. Lilly stood by the door, watching the three brothers. For a few minutes, all she could hear was her own hard breathing.

"Upstairs," Rune said, quiet. "I want a report. We may need to leave sooner than the dawn."

Jek walked off without a word. Lilly watched him disappear, her fingers scrunching her long tunic.

Lilly didn't see the Annors for the rest of the night. She kept to her room with Aderyn and Tae, and tried to calm her heart. It still beat a mile a minute and every sudden sound made her jump. It was the assassin all over again. It was Zal all over the again. The cold sensation hadn't left her skin. Her insides.

Seymour and Havan didn't come back until dark. Seymour summoned Rune, Jek, and Lilly to his study.

"They only know about you two," Seymour said, nodding to Jek and Lilly. "Jek, they do not know you are a seventh."

"Will we be leaving tonight?" Rune asked.

"No," Seymour said slowly. "But you should leave before the sun rises, when the soldiers and weavers are lethargic. I've paid the fines for Jek and Lilly—"

Lilly started. "Fines?"

Seymour nodded. "Visitors must pay to enter. The payment has appeased General Amisa, and the situation brought her attention to Dazan's leaving his post." Seymour actually *smirked*. "We are fortunate that her foul mood was turned toward her subordinate."

Jek's eyes were on the floor. "I'm sorry. I wasn't thinking."

"You have nothing to apologize for," Seymour said. "You did nothing wrong."

"We cost you money—"

"Money that would have gone to the empire anyway," Seymour said. "What matters is you are both safe, and that is all I ask."

They were dismissed to their rooms, but Lilly couldn't sleep. The moonlight webbed through the branches outside the bedroom window, casting jagged shadows on the floor. Lilly bit her lip and turned her back to them, squished against Tae and teetering on the edge of the bed. She didn't need to be so afraid of shadows. They wouldn't hurt her. She was being a baby.

Am I though? I saw monsters appear out of shadows. They can hurt people in a second. Lilly smushed her face into the pillow. She just wanted sleep. She just wanted to find Gabriel. No more stupid soldiers, no more stupid dark magic.

With a huff, Lilly sat up, carefully easing herself away from Tae. She stuffed her feet into her shoes.

"Lilly?" Aderyn's sleepy voice floated through the darkness.

"Gotta use the bathroom," Lilly said.

Lilly sneaked into the hall and took a slow, deep breath. It was colder there, but the brisk air cleared her head. She wandered down the corridor. The lantern orbs still burned dimly, their light gleaming off the murals. Lilly ran her fingers over a scene where the elf woman and human man stood under an arbor, inches away from a kiss. The stone was cold and smooth, but the colors were soft, gentle. Romantic.

Lilly halted where the murals ended, before a set of stairs. She looked back the way she'd come, suddenly aware that she was lost.

The door before her stood open, and a long staircase led upward.

Curiosity winning over, Lilly ascended. Lantern orbs hung in niches there too, but there were no windows. At intervals she found landings, with other doors leading to various floors of the palace.

By the time she reached the top, Lilly was breathing a little harder. She listened for a second before easing the last door open. Cold air struck her face, making her gasp and shudder. It penetrated even her thick nightgown. The outside was dark and still, save for the breeze.

No, not totally dark. There was firelight pulsing steadily. Lilly peeked around the door to see a brazier, and the fire inside it going strong. The door opened on a large balcony suspended among the tree's branches.

Standing by the railing was a dark silhouette. Lilly ventured out, shivering as she approached the fire's warmth. "Hi?"

The person started, turning. The light illuminated Jek's features, and Lilly relaxed. She offered a smile. "Sorry."

Jek blinked, as if trying to process. He turned fully and joined her by the brazier. "What brings you up here? How'd you even find it?"

"Honestly couldn't tell you. I couldn't sleep, so I wandered around looking at the murals and found the stairs."

Jek hummed, impressed. Lilly watched his face. "Couldn't sleep either?"

"No..." His hand dipped *into* the fire. Lilly gasped in alarm, but Jek didn't cry out. He played his fingers over the flames.

His breath shuddered out. "I'm sorry for putting you and Tae in danger. I wasn't thinking. I didn't know that weaver would be watching."

"There is a little girl in this palace right now who would still be believing she was unwanted if you hadn't said anything." Lilly reached out before she could stop herself, and turned Jek's face to hers. "You wanted to make her happy. You wanted to make those other children happy. That's nothing to be sorry about."

Jek smiled faintly. He looked up into the tree boughs. A second later, a slender green vine lowered between him and Lilly. She stared as a single red flower, a lily, blossomed, ignorant of the weather around it.

"It's beautiful." Lilly touched the flower. It tingled under her fingertips.

Jek carefully plucked the flower. A tiny wince flashed across his face but disappeared as he offered it to her. "A seventh weaver's signature mark. Comitza lilies, or fire lilies. The pollen that comes from them is the only thing that can effectively combat dark magic. It pushes the dark magic down, deep into its host, so it goes dormant for a little while."

Lilly shivered. "Those shadow monsters."

"Those are called itzals. Seventh magic can counter them too. So... if Dazan had found out tonight, things would have been even worse. Dark weavers have no love for people like me." He let the vine bear two more flowers, gazing at them with a kind of reverence. "I can only use them where there is soil, or in a tree."

"So, anywhere but in the middle of an ocean."

"Sometimes." Jek smiled a little. "Cities with stone roads are a challenge. I have to search deeper for the soil. And it comes at a cost. It's a part of us, so it's also alive. Whatever damage is done to the vines or the flowers, we feel it too."

Lilly swallowed. "That day in Murke. Zal hurt you, when you protected us."

"I should have done more." Jek spoke quietly. "I'm sorry."

"Thank you for trying," Lilly whispered.

Jek nodded once, letting the conversation fall for a minute before adding, "It can also heal plants of disease, cleansing them, if you will, but that's not terribly useful in a war."

"Ahh, so you have a green thumb." Lilly grinned. "Can you grow things for other people too?"

"I can," Jek said. "It's helped us through a few rough winters." He frowned darkly at the fire. "After the first rebellion, Yovak required all seventh born to be registered. They were made to report to the nearest barracks, and many of us were made to tend the fields, to help them heal and grow."

"Did you at least get paid?"

A bitter smile. "We got to eat another day, if that's what you mean. Some of us were willing to help. Yovak's goal, to heal the farmland, is a worthy one."

"But instead of asking, he forced you." It was Lilly's turn to scowl at the fire. "Like a slave."

Jek nodded. "I didn't have to go to work in the fields until a year or two after my magic manifested, when I learned to control it." He shrugged. "We had no chains or collars, but some days we might as well have. Another seventh took me under her wing until I could stand on my own against arrogant overseers." He smiled. "She even tried to get me to run away and start our own little rebel group."

"Why didn't you?"

"There were people in Murke who needed me." Jek shrugged again. "But it worked out. That seventh came back with a rebel root lodged in Yovak's own lair. She's been our eyes and ears. But it was good practice for me, learning to control my magic."

They were silent, both trying to keep warm, neither willing to go inside where only sleepless beds awaited.

"I wish I could have done more, too," Lilly said at last. "In

Murke. I couldn't fight back, I couldn't do *anything*."

"They were a force you couldn't have prepared for."

"But my dad and Gabriel tried anyway." Lilly looked up at him. "And what did I do? Nothing. I didn't give them the stupid amulet like they wanted. I'm the reason my dad's dead."

Jek moved fast. He grabbed her shoulders, making her look at him. She stiffened and tried to push him away, glaring, but the look in his eyes made her pause.

"Don't ever say that," he said. "You know that's not true. They would have taken all of you captive, or they would have killed you. *You* are not the cause. It is *not* your fault, do you understand?"

"But maybe my dad wouldn't be dead." Lilly fought back the sob, pushing him away this time. "Maybe he'd be alive, and I would have him and Gabe with me, and ask my dad all of these questions I still have, questions I don't think I'll ever get answered." Lilly laughed bitterly. "I'm in a world that I never believed existed, and I was born in it. And I didn't believe him when he needed me to."

Jek was silent for a long time, his face half-shadowed. "Your father had a reason for what he did. It was one he was willing to die for. More than that, you and your brother were something he was willing to die for. Whether or not you believed him. That's just... it's what fathers do."

Lilly looked away. The view from the balcony stretched far over the city all the way to the outer wall, where she could see the firelight of the sentries. "I still should have done something." Lilly took a slow breath. "I don't want to feel helpless. I know you and the others will protect me, but if I'm going to be stuck here, I don't want to be a defenseless damsel, or freeze up in front of every scary thing." She looked at him. "I want to be able to protect myself next time. Fight back."

"We could probably arrange something," Jek said carefully. He drew two daggers and offered one to her, hilt first. "I can show you a few defensive techniques right here."

"In the dark, in an insanely high tree?" Lilly smirked. "One of us will end up sleeping in a hospital instead of our own bed. How did you even sneak two daggers in?"

Jek laughed and beckoned her away from the brazier. The fire burned brighter when they moved away. "When I found out I had magic, I was terrified I would hurt someone with it. Sometimes I did." He spoke as he helped Lilly position her feet correctly.

"You have a pretty good handle on it now," Lilly said, looking at the fire and the lilies.

"I was seven then," Jek said. "A child who still had occasional tantrums."

"Lies. Jek Annor doesn't have tantrums."

Jek laughed again, and the sound put Lilly at ease. He walked her through a few moves, slow and easy. Lilly was clumsy, especially in her nightgown; but Jek was patient, and soon her performance became smoother, more fluid and swift. The dagger began to feel comfortable in her hand. Her body responded to the motions as if she had been made for this. Maybe she had.

After nearly an hour of practice, Jek stepped back. "You learn fast."

Lilly grinned, pleasure warming her. "You're not a bad teacher." She shrugged. "I picked my own fights with bullies at school. I know a little bit. And Dad taught me to defend myself."

"Ahh, so you're one step ahead already." Jek received his dagger from her. "Remember, real fights won't be slow. You'll need to think and act fast. Sometimes not in that order."

"I usually don't do that order."

Jek laughed. "Well, sometimes it pays to think before you act." He extended a hand toward the warmth of the fire. "Even when you're up against something that scares you."

Lilly joined him. "You said you were afraid of your magic. How did you overcome it?"

"My brothers. I was more terrified of myself than of the king who killed my parents. But my brothers weren't afraid. They saw in me their brother, not a monster." He put his hand into the fire. It danced through his fingers, a handshake between friends. "They taught me not to let my fear control it.

"Magic can be finicky. It responds to our thoughts, our feelings. If we leave both to their own devices, they can make a worse enemy than anyone you could face. My brothers taught me that I can be bigger than my fear. I can either use it, or let it use me." He lifted his hand from the fire and looked at her. "Turn fear into courage, and you can do a lot that others won't."

Lilly turned to face the view of the world below. She would rescue Gabriel, and make Yovak and Seiryu take them home. Next time, she would be ready.

"Does this not sleeping thing ever improve, or are we stuck with it for life?"

A tiny smile twitched at Jek's lips. "We can only hope it gets better."

Lilly took a long, slow breath, savoring the cold air. Air that had known her once before.

"It's sure pretty here..." She stopped and squinted. "Late-night hunting party?" She pointed toward the wall. Jek frowned and followed her gaze to the cluster of lights. They flickered at the edge of the city, moving further in, toward the palace.

Jek's fire went out in a whoosh.

11

FLIGHT AND FIGHT

Lilly blinked in the darkness. A rush of cold swept in to fill the space. Jek's voice came low and solemn. "We need to find Rune and Seymour *now*."

"What's out there?"

"I don't know. Hopefully nothing."

Lilly scrambled after him down the stairs inside. She caught up with his longer strides halfway down the hall to their rooms when Rune appeared ahead.

"Rune—"

"We know," Rune said, cutting Lilly off. "Go wake the girls and get dressed. Jek, wait for them and take them to the kitchens. Kedmir is already there."

"What's going on?"

"The imperial soldiers got it in their heads that Seymour's guests are rebels," Rune growled. "Havan's runner says they'll be here any minute, and they won't be knocking."

Jek shifted. "Rune, I'm sorry—"

"It's not your fault." Rune strode past them. "Do as I've said."

Lilly took off down the hall, her heart thundering in her ears. What if they couldn't get out in time? Surely the soldiers would know of the back doors and have a guard posted.

Lilly pounced on Aderyn first, shaking her shoulder. "Deryn, wake up!"

Aderyn was up in a heartbeat, almost knocking heads with Lilly. "What's going on?"

"Soldiers. Gotta go. Get Tae up while I get dressed."

Aderyn was instantly on her feet, rousing Tae and collecting their things. Lilly snatched up the amulet after shoving herself into the clothes she'd borrowed in Murke, and hopped around forcing her feet into her boots. She left the room to find Jek standing uneasily at the door.

"Quietly," Jek whispered as Aderyn and Tae emerged. "We don't know if any soldiers are here. We're leaving the way we came."

Lilly crept close to Jek. He kept to the muraled walls, pausing at corners to listen. Lilly forced her breathing to slow down, measuring each inhale and exhale until she could think without panicking.

They found their way to the dark, cold kitchen. Lilly drew in her breath at the sight of a shadowy figure near their exit. It looked up.

"All's clear." Kedmir's voice broke the silent space. "But we need to move now. Rune's already outside."

"Won't they suspect we escaped this way?" Lilly whispered.

"Hopefully not until we're long gone."

Outside on the ground, the air was less chilly. In the dark, without the lanterns, the gardens looked almost skeletal. A winter graveyard.

Kedmir led the way to the hedge of bushes, where Rune was waiting for them. They struggled through the shrubs, as Lilly and Jek had done before, avoiding the direct route.

They walked through the dark city in heavy silence. Lilly shivered. So many more places for prying eyes to see them. For dark weavers to skulk in ambush.

But there was no ambush. No soldier stopped them or sounded an alarm. The city wall, with its familiar door, loomed just ahead.

There were four new guards on duty, standing with weapons drawn.

Lilly breathed in, counted to three.

No more time to be scared.

Before the boys could move, she snatched a bottle from a doorway and flung it down the street.

Rune swore as the glass shattered, the sound bouncing off the walls. The guards all hurried toward the sound. Lilly and the others bolted across the narrow street into the wall and the hunter's room. Once they were all inside, Kedmir shut the door behind them. The room went dark.

"You are an idiot," Jek hissed. "But I'm impressed."

Collecting their gear took no time at all, and Rune shepherded them through the second door and out of the city.

"We don't stop until we're far from here," he said. "They may send search parties out when they don't find us in the city."

Lilly shivered in the open cold, and clenched her teeth together to keep them from chattering. They hurried over the wide bridge and into the snowy forest.

Lilly was the last to cross the bridge. Just as she stepped off it, a figure with dark clothes and a hooded face rushed at her from the forest a few yards from the others. She jumped aside, and her attacker followed, a dark-bladed knife in his hand.

The Ghost was back.

"Lilly!" Jek cried. She ducked to avoid the Ghost's swing and slashed at his arm. The assassin pulled away, lunging again. Lilly scrambled back toward the middle of the bridge.

A sharp pain sliced into her thigh. She cried out, losing her footing and tumbling dangerously close to the edge. She hissed, grimacing as she touched the gash. Her vision blurred, and the world around her seemed to wobble. "What—"

Another figure intercepted the Ghost, both men tumbling to the ground. Soldiers shouted from the city.

Jek grappled with the Ghost, struggling to stay on top. Lilly swayed, trying to stand. She opened her mouth to speak, but the world went fuzzy again, and then there were four of Jek and the assassin.

Kedmir grabbed her before she pitched over the edge. "Jek, come on!"

Lilly looked back. Soldiers were running across the clearing. Jek and the Ghost were too close to the bridge's edge. The assassin landed a blow on Jek's ribs, making him double over. Lilly felt Kedmir haul her away. Her legs didn't work. She clung to Kedmir, but even her arms failed her. Jek twisted away from the Ghost's knife, causing it to miss his heart by inches. Vines exploded from the earth, throwing up hard chunks of dirt and blocking the soldiers' path.

Lilly's vision began to fade. She needed to stand, needed to stay awake. She tried to scream as the assassin slashed across Jek's middle and they collided, teetering on the edge of the bridge.

Then, her vision went dark.

Everything felt heavy. Sluggish. Her blood was leaden, holding her down.

Lilly drew a deep breath, stirring. Her limbs obeyed slowly. She cracked open her eyelids, squinting at the backlit ceiling of a tent.

"Lilly?" Aderyn leaned over her. Worry and exhaustion marked her features.

Then everything clicked.

"Jek!" Lilly flew upright, the lead in her veins gone. Aderyn tried to push her back down.

"Easy, easy," she said. "Jek's fine. Everyone is."

"But the assassin. The soldiers—"

"Gone," Aderyn said. "We lost them in the forest last night. It was too dark for them to follow, and Jek's magic held them back to give us a head start. The dark weavers were too busy at the palace."

"Last... night?" Lilly frowned. "What time is it?"

"Afternoon," Aderyn said. "I bandaged your leg. The cut wasn't deep, but it might be sore."

Lilly sat up in spite of it. "What happened to the Ghost?"

"Jek pushed him off. The river's frozen, so he didn't drown, but it gave us time to get away, and probably distracted the soldiers." Aderyn stood. "Come on. Let's see if you can walk before we start packing up."

Outside, Tae hugged Lilly so tight she could barely breathe. The boys were just as relieved, though Jek could only manage a tired smile.

With their camp packed, they set off, Rune taking the lead. Jek peeled off to cover their tracks, but no one followed them.

Lilly's leg throbbed and burned as she walked. Every limp made her gasp, but she didn't complain. Jek looked worse off, pale and panting heavily.

Tense silence controlled the party for the remainder of their journey back to Murke. No one slept well, tempers were fragile. Jek snapped at his brothers when they tried to persuade him to sleep, and Aderyn even snapped at Kedmir, which made everybody nervous. Aderyn rarely snapped at anyone. Lilly had given up hope of ever getting a full night's rest again. The wound in her leg still burned and bled from the constant motion. They had to stop frequently to change her bandage.

They'd narrowly escaped arrest and probably execution, and Lilly wasn't sure she liked that feeling at all. She was still rattled, and adrenaline pumped through her senses like caffeine.

With their luck, Lilly expected Murke to be in flames, yet it still stood as they emerged from the forest. The rebel banner had replaced the flag of the empire. Lilly let out a sigh, and her body slumped with relief. They were safe.

In the city, Unvar met them at the door of the tavern-turned-headquarters. "We were starting to worry. We didn't receive any word." He frowned. "Will they help us?"

"No," Rune said. "Prince Seymour is unable to send us aid for the time being. Our arrival was noticed, and we had to flee the same night we arrived."

"We could have used his help, Rune."

"I know that," Rune snapped. Lilly stiffened as Unvar took a couple steps back. "I'm well aware that without them our forces will be stretched at Erriath. I didn't go there to catch up!" His voice rose. Tae sidled behind Lilly with a squeak. Unvar glared at Rune for a second, then looked away.

"What news here?" Rune asked him.

"All is well," Unvar said, his voice strained, holding back anger. "You've received a message from Arialina."

Rune's expression softened immediately as he took the proffered letter. "Thank you." He looked back at Unvar. "We will rest tonight, and head for Balmarren in the morning."

Lilly's shoulders sagged. "More walking?"

Rune smiled tiredly. "No, lass. Tomorrow we ride."

"Even better. I can't ride."

"We will teach you," Rune assured her. "Unvar, you will stay here and keep things in check."

"What?" Unvar started. "I can think of several men who are vastly better suited—"

"But I have asked you," Rune said. "We will keep in touch. Should you need help, we will only be a few days away."

Unvar frowned, troubled or nervous, Lilly couldn't tell. When he met her eyes she offered an encouraging smile. His eyes darted down to Tae.

"Who is this?" He cocked his head. "Someone from Lilantami?"

"We met her on the way there," Rune said. "Tae escaped the estate of Eeris Rothar." He ducked into the building. "She will be coming with us."

"Really?" Tae gasped. "To see the ocean?" She rushed after Rune, peppering him with questions. Lilly followed them inside, laughing.

"Breathe, Tae!"

12
MAGIC BY
ANOTHER ROAD

The city of Erriath was huge and sprawling.

The days were getting warmer, and Odalys dragged Gabriel into the city to explore. The streets were wide enough for two carts side by side, with space at the edges for people on foot. Shops sold all sorts of curiosities. Some Gabriel was familiar with, others Odalys had to explain to him. His head spun. There was too much to take in, too much to see.

Two soldiers had been assigned to Gabriel. Half as many as Odalys, but still enough to ward off anyone with evil intentions. Their capes, embroidered with Emperor Yovak's three-headed flying snake, were enough to command respect. If there were any rebels in this city, they kept their distance. There were also security checkpoints at the castle wall and other critical points in the city, enough to keep suspicious characters away.

Erriath was a fortress, but Odalys saw it as her playground.

She showed Gabriel all the exciting things she thought he would like. And he seemed to like *everything*. Even the air—clean, alive, and invigorating—gave him new energy. It made him want to run and shout.

The clothes were so different than home. Men wore tall boots, with nicely tailored tunics if they were rich enough. Some wore long coats without sleeves. The lower-class men either had nothing over their shirt, or a simple vest that laced up in the front. Gabriel had the tailored shirt, but without the coat, and he felt a little bare.

The women's dresses were beautiful, though none nearly so luxurious as Odalys'. The wealthy wore soft, graceful fabrics. The clothing worn by the less wealthy women was simpler, with more muted colors, generally a dress with a second, sleeveless dress layered on top and cinched with a belt.

Gabriel took it all in. He smiled as children of the lower classes scampered alongside their parents.

"Stay right here," Odalys told him before darting off across the square. "You *have* to try the sweets from this shop." Her personal guards swept after her with surprising speed.

They probably have to be born with that reflex. Gabriel watched her until she disappeared inside the shop, leaving him alone with his guards, and the two gray-clothed slaves who attended them, Seleen and a half-elf who belonged to Odalys. Regular maids, the princess said, were too fussy.

"What's your name?" Gabriel asked the half-elf. Her eyes were a deep brown, and it made the gold slivers seem to glow.

The slave blinked, startled. Seleen's eyes darted toward them before looking away.

"Sir?"

"Your name?"

Hesitation, as if trying to discern if he was tricking her. "I... Akora, sir."

Gabriel smiled. "Well, it's nice to meet you, Akora. I've seen you a few times but never knew what to call you."

Akora looked almost frightened. "W-was there something you needed, sir?"

Gabriel froze. "No! No, sorry. I just... I like knowing names." He smiled. "Yours is pretty."

Silence, then, "...Thank you, sir."

"You're welcome." He watched her lower her eyes again, and smiled at the slight blush on her cheeks.

Watching the two slaves just stand there made Gabriel uneasy, but he pushed this aside and resumed people-watching. It was hard to imagine his father here, living in the castle, doing research, or wandering the shops like Gabriel was doing. He wouldn't have had slaves, would he? Gabriel couldn't imagine it. But maybe his father had been different in his own world, when everything was... normal.

His fingers found the hilt of his father's knife. Unbidden, his mind raced backward to catch fleeting memories, the stories he'd heard but never really listened to. He struggled to snatch and preserve the smallest details.

His jaw tensed, and a familiar, angry knot burned in his heart. *This* should have been his life. This city, or Murke, he didn't care which. Either way, this world was where they should have lived, where he and Lilly should have grown up. Not in some tiny Chicago apartment where his father was called crazy and told to shut up about his stories. Where he and Lilly were forced to ignore all the jeers at school. Where their mother was dead.

How was this fair? What had they done to deserve any of this? What had Tilas done to deserve it? He'd been hurt the most. He'd lost his whole world.

It *wasn't* fair, and the rebels were at the center of it.

Gabriel glared at nothing. His anger clawed at him, begging to be released. Guilt burned within him too. He hadn't made his father's life much easier. He hadn't believed the stories.

He couldn't fix any of that, but he could at least make sure the rebels who were responsible didn't get away with it.

Gabriel wiped at his eyes and drew a long breath, no longer interested in people. He was about to go after Odalys when a familiar face entered his periphery. The young man wore simple civilian clothes, and walked confidently, veering away from the soldiers standing outside the sweet shop.

Frowning, Gabriel watched Tesmir approach an upscale-looking tavern. He didn't go in, just stood nearby, watching patrons sweep in and out. They paid him no attention.

Gabriel was about to call to him when a woman approached Tesmir. Her face was shadowed by her cloak, but platinum blonde curls peeked out. Tesmir turned to her. They glanced once toward the sweet shop and spoke quickly to each other. The woman kept stealing glances at the royal guards. Her fidgeting made even Gabriel uneasy.

A lover? Gabriel grinned at the thought in spite of his mood. Tesmir was definitely the type of guy to know his way around the ladies. But why would they both be nervous?

Odalys' guards moved from the sweet shop. Gabriel turned to see the princess approaching him.

"These!" Odalys sat down beside him. "You have to try them. I got one of almost every flavor, and we can go back and try the others too." She paused, her eyes on Gabriel's. "Are you alright?"

Gabriel nodded, forcing a smile. "Yeah. What do you have?"

Odalys lifted the delicate lid off the box. Inside, tucked into little paper nests, were chocolates. Gabriel's stomach rumbled. When was the last time he'd had *chocolate?*

Odalys watched his face. "Try one!"

He selected one. It was smooth, and almost... heavy? He bit into it carefully. The chocolate was a shell housing a berry unlike any he'd tasted before. This one was... almost tart, but sweet enough not to pucker his face. The chocolate was the best chocolate he'd ever had. Smooth, rich, and something else he couldn't pin down but wanted more of.

Odalys peered over to see which he'd chosen. "Ooh, that's my favorite!"

Gabriel looked at his candy. Half of a glistening gold berry nestled in its chocolate shell. "What is it?"

"A sunberry. They're *so good.*" Odalys picked one out and bit into it. A string of smooth red jelly stretched from her lips before she licked it up. She looked at him. "Who were you watching earlier?"

Gabriel hesitated. "Oh, I'd seen... Tesmir."

Tesmir and the woman were gone. Gabriel shrugged. "I think he has a girlfriend."

"A girl friend?"

Gabriel let the rest of his chocolate melt in his mouth. "When a guy likes a girl, they become... attached? They like each other enough to go out together, spend a lot of time together."

With an inward jolt, Gabriel realized he was describing *exactly* what he and Odalys had been doing for the past *week.* But the princess didn't seem to notice his alarm. She smiled almost conspiratorially.

"I can think of so many people like that," she giggled. She cocked her head. "But... I have girl friends, too."

Gabriel shook his head. "That's different. A girlfriend—when a guy likes a girl and hangs out with her—is different than a girl who is a friend. Girlfriend is just one word. You have girl *friends*, that's two words."

"Oh." Odalys considered this, taking another chocolate.

"Well, we found you two at last."

Seiryu stood a few feet off, leaning on a glossy black walking cane with a silver dragon's head. By his side was a black-haired elf woman. She was tall, her posture graceful and proud. Her dress was different from the ones he'd seen in the city: form fitting, with a boldly plunging neckline. She was gorgeous, but Gabriel sensed she was older than her dress and cosmetics let on. Soldiers flanked them too.

Odalys beamed. "I was showing Gabriel our sweets."

"A fine selection." Seiryu examined the chocolates when Odalys offered him the box. He picked one. "Gabriel, I don't believe you've met my sister, Eeris."

Gabriel stood. "It's nice to meet you."

Eeris smiled brightly. "It's a pleasure. I've heard so much about you, I regret not meeting you sooner."

"Were you looking for us?" Odalys asked.

"I thought we might visit that new tea house," Eeris said. "Your mother asked for a report on it. And she gave permission to take you shopping. If!" She held up a hand before Odalys could squeal. "If you have finished your lessons."

All eyes were on Odalys. She grinned impishly. "They're close enough."

Gabriel narrowed his eyes. "You told me—"

"Shush!" Odalys snatched the box away. "Or no more for you!"

"Hey!"

Odalys gave him a cheeky grin.

"And while the ladies shop," Seiryu addressed Gabriel, "I thought I would introduce you to someone you might be interested in meeting."

"Who?"

"Her name is Entya. She is a good friend of your father, and is the weaver who healed your wounds." Seiryu smiled. "And I thought you might like to speak with her about learning magic. I haven't heard you mention it since I sent the material."

There it was. Gabriel winced inwardly. He had tried to avoid Seiryu for this very reason. Gabriel had read the books Seiryu sent, but learning magic felt too dark. Something he didn't think he wanted to get involved with.

Gabriel shrugged. "I don't think I need it. It feels... wrong. I don't think I want to be involved in it." He shifted uneasily under Seiryu's thoughtful look.

"Some people think the same," Seiryu conceded. "But that is because they are afraid of it. Fear of the thing controls you, and that is what we cannot allow."

"Magic is only as good or as evil as what you use it for," Odalys said, as if reciting from a book. She grinned at Gabriel. "Father knows the same kind of magic, and he's not evil."

Gabriel frowned. "He does? But he's an elf."

"It was a rare circumstance. He was born without magic," Eeris said. She smiled warmly. "My brother tutored both of your fathers after they learned magic. He will not steer you wrong."

"Allow me to introduce you to Entya," Seiryu offered. "She is more skilled in the art than I, and can give you answers I cannot."

Gabriel hesitated. The unease began to calm, but there remained a tiny nub of doubt. It still sounded too... strange.

Still, his simmering bitterness and anger at the rebels lingered.

They had destroyed everything.

"I guess talking to an expert wouldn't hurt."

"Good! Then let us go." Seiryu kissed his sister's cheek. "We will meet you ladies for tea." Eeris returned the kiss before turning away.

"Oh, Paetr!" Odalys bounded forward to a man who had been standing behind them in silence. "You're here too!" She handed him the box of chocolates. "You can hold these."

The man only bowed. Gabriel lifted a brow, but Odalys flounced off after Eeris with Akora and her guards in tow.

Gabriel exhaled and looked at Seiryu. "Why don't you have any servants with you?" He glanced at Seleen, who remained stoically unaffected by the events.

"I have many who could assist me," Seiryu said, "but I prefer to do things for myself. I am no invalid yet, and I will use what the gods have given me."

Seiryu limped carefully along the street. Gabriel hurried to catch up.

"So... how are elves able to rule the country?" He winced. *Oh yeah, way to phrase that one.*

Seiryu didn't seem bothered. "There is no law against it. Yovak saw the previous rule of the war lords as flawed and corrupt. They exploited the people to their own advantage, so he liberated Piensor from their grasp. I assisted him in his uprising, as did many of those who later rebelled against him. The world has been a better place for it."

"And the rebels think Yovak's just like the war lords."

Seiryu nodded. "His strictures are tightly enforced. War comes at a cost, as does recovery. The rebels accuse him of ruling for his own luxury, just as the war lords did. The fact that he is an elf becomes of little importance when he brings peace and freedom and a stronger foundation."

They stopped to let a wagon pass, laden with bright bolts of cloth. A beggar in ratty clothes approached, murmuring Seiryu's title. Instead of waving the man off, Seiryu dropped two coins into his outstretched hands. The beggar stumbled over his thank-yous and darted off.

Gabriel noted Seiryu's limping gait. "Are you sure you should be walking? Your leg is worse."

"I will be fine," Seiryu said. He cast Gabriel a look. "Don't you dare tell Raul."

"I could be bribed..."

Seiryu laughed as they reached a simple building. "Just like your father. Get in, you scamp."

The place was dimly lit. It was a tavern, and a few patrons sat around scattered tables, talking easily to one another. Seiryu seemed unconcerned, but something didn't feel right. They had left Seleen and their guards outside.

"Wait here," Seiryu murmured. He moved among the tables and approached the bar, where he spoke to a slender woman who leaned in close over the countertop. From the doorway, Gabriel glanced around the room, noting how bare it was. It smelled of alcohol and old wood.

"So, you are Tilas Faine's son."

Gabriel jumped.

A man stood far too close to him. He was rather plain, with graying hair and eyes so pale gray they were almost white. He too smelled a little like alcohol.

"Who's asking?" Gabriel asked, stepping back. His eyes flicked to the bar. Seiryu had disappeared, along with the woman. A flash of panic shot through him.

The man looked Gabriel up and down, clearly unimpressed. "I expected you to be a little more... arrogant. Your father always was."

Gabriel glared. "You must have been looking in a mirror. The only arrogance I see is yours, so..."

The man stepped closer, scowling. "Run along, boy. This is no place for you."

"Well, I'm here now, so you'll just have to deal." Gabriel's fingers curled. "Back off."

The man snarled, teeth bared. "You don't give the orders here—"

"*Thank you,* Cadrian." A woman's voice slid between them with a layer of calm. This wasn't the woman from the bar. She wore a deep red dress, and her black hair ran down her spine in a braid. Her eyes were dark but kind and curious. She looked at the man first. "Please, wait for us with the others."

Cadrian scowled at her, then looked at Gabriel, who held his gaze.

"Going to hide behind her skirts, then?" Cadrian sneered.

"Cadrian," the woman snapped. "That is enough."

One beat... two. Cadrian turned and left them. Gabriel's fists relaxed as the woman turned to him and smiled.

"Your father and Cadrian were always at odds too." She offered her hand. "I am Entya."

"Gabriel." Gabriel shook her hand. He glanced in the direction Cadrian had disappeared. "Why didn't they like each other?"

"Many differences of opinion, and just a general rivalry." Entya chuckled. "He will check his tongue in the future."

Gabriel snorted. He looked at Entya. "You're the one who taught my dad magic?"

Entya nodded. She motioned to an empty table. "Lord Rothar says you have questions. I hope to answer them and relieve your fears."

Gabriel sat as directed. A barmaid came over, but Entya waved her away with a fluid motion.

"Why did my dad learn magic?" Gabriel asked.

"Your father was a man of learning, at least when I knew him," Entya said. "He sought knowledge from all corners of the spectrum, and beyond if he could. Magic was but one area he explored. He had none of his own, and learned it so he could be better informed."

"So, he learned it for science."

"And only for the good of others. He used his magic to help Lord Rothar in his own research, and to relieve pain. In the time I knew your father, there was not a wicked bone in his body."

Entya sat back. "Magic can be a mighty thing, and it scared him once. He had doubts like you, but I taught him to harness it, to work *with* it."

"How?"

The woman only smiled. "I can only tell you if you decide to learn, too."

Gabriel bit his lip. "Why does it all sound so dark?" He waved his hand around the room. "I mean, this place is cool, but it's a bit shady."

"All magic has corners we haven't yet explored. People call this form dark magic because it has boundaries we cannot yet fathom." She smiled, amused. "And because it manipulates simple, ordinary shadows. Magic users are usually born with magic, like an elf or a seventh born, but this type is learned. We are simply reaching into the veins of magic by another road." Entya smirked. "As for the atmosphere, the social circles of this magic have eclectic tastes."

"So... you can teach me?"

"If you want it. But should you decide to learn, you cannot go back, and it will take time and energy." Entya watched him, her face so calm it settled the butterflies in Gabriel's stomach. "If that is what you want, I will help you."

Gabriel considered all Entya had said. The magic was dark because it was unknown. The books had even admitted as much.

"It's only as good or evil as you make it," Gabriel said. Entya nodded. Gabriel looked at his hands. What would they look like with fire or lightning dancing around them? What would it be like to summon walls of water? He'd seen Odalys play with her magic. It had entranced him, like a song he couldn't get enough of.

He wouldn't be useless anymore. With magic he would have the power he needed to protect the people he cared about, to make a difference. He'd never fought as Lilly did. Lilly made sure her bullies never came back. Gabriel could hold his ground against bullies, but they always came back eventually.

But with magic... *Gabriel* would be the one these new bullies feared. Being feared didn't sound ideal, but maybe it was something he'd have to get used to for a short time.

He felt the anger again. He would be the one to avenge his mother after fifteen long years. He would avenge his whole family. Give them the life that had been taken from them.

"I could protect my family with magic," Gabriel said, glaring at the table before looking up at Entya. "Like my dad did when Zal came for us."

Entya nodded. "Learning magic and training those skills is not easy, but your goals are admirable."

"I can do it." Gabriel did not hesitate. *I will do it. I have to.*

"What do I need to do?"

Entya rose. "Come with me."

She led him across the room, to a door tucked out of the way. She opened it, descending a set of stairs. When Gabriel didn't follow, she looked back.

"Where is Seiryu?" he asked. The lady at the bar had been replaced by a man who scanned the patrons with a critical eye.

"I expect he has business elsewhere," Entya said. "He cannot come with us, but I will fetch him later." She smiled. "I will not let you come to harm."

Gabriel followed Entya down the stairs. It was dim, but a lantern hung at the bottom. Noises rumbled down here, like the sound of battle.

Entya led him through a stone hallway. Doors stood at intervals. Most were closed.

"What is this place?"

"A place where we may train in peace," Entya said. "You will train here too."

They passed a set of wide double doors, propped open. Gabriel paused, his hazel eyes widening. The room within was brightly lit, a fire surrounding the stone ceiling. The huge open area was covered in sand.

Magic thrummed in this room, flung and conjured by at least a dozen men and women, most of them older than Gabriel, and all of them intently focused. Some conjured the basic elements, while others created shadow monsters, itzals, in varying sizes and shapes.

A few were locked in battle, dueling and slinging magic back and forth without pulling their punches. To the side, others were simply practicing their technique. A cluster of dummies stood while a few weavers struck them with magic.

"Whoa…"

"Emperor Yovak's dark weavers are the head of his armies." Entya was by his side. "This place was built shortly after the emperor's rise, to provide a safe space for training. It tends to make the civilians uneasy to see us train."

"Were you there? When Yovak fought the war lords?"

"Oh, aye. I was among the ones who first followed him." Entya nodded. "As was your father."

Gabriel looked up at her. "He was okay with killing those people?"

"Not entirely," Entya admitted, "but he recognized the need for change. Your father helped more in settling the new rulership." She turned away. "Come."

Gabriel took one last look at the training room before following. The hallway turned right, ending at a solid oak door. Entya ushered him into a spacious, barren room. Two men and a woman were already there. Recognizing Cadrian among them, Gabriel groaned inwardly.

"Gabriel Faine," Entya began. "This is Varta." She motioned to the woman.

The woman was old, but a youthful fire still shone in her eyes as she looked Gabriel over. "It has been a long time since I've heard the name Faine."

"He's as handsome as his father, no?" Entya teased. Varta hummed in agreement, grinning. Gabriel flushed.

Cadrian snorted. Entya locked eyes with him. "And you've met Cadrian."

The two men glared at each other, Cadrian all arrogance and superiority.

"And Phelan," Entya finished, indicating the older gentleman.

Gabriel reviewed the names before looking at Entya. "You knew I'd say yes. You all knew, didn't you?"

"Despite your doubts, Seiryu had a feeling you would want to learn," Entya said. "We saw no reason to delay."

"Do you guys always lurk underground?"

Varta cackled. "Ah, lad, when you become famous for what you do, you'll understand."

"Because you were there the day the war lords were defeated?"

"There, and fought in it," Varta said. "I'm old, so I don't see the action Cadrian and Entya do these days, hunting that seventh-born mutt Jinnet and her followers, but I like to train the younger lot and impress them."

Gabriel decided he rather liked her.

Phelan spoke next, his voice short and gruff, like Gabriel was wasting his time. "Why do you come to learn magic, Gabriel Faine?"

The mood in the room was no longer light. Gabriel exhaled and steadied his limbs. "To protect my family."

"You know what this entails?"

A chill crept up Gabriel's spine. "I can't go back once I learn."

"If you are not sure this is the path you want, do not walk it," Cadrian said. A challenge.

Gabriel stared him down. "I need to be able to fight any enemy." *I need to be able to fight the ones who ruined our lives.*

Entya smiled. "Then we may begin. Let me see your hand."

Gabriel hesitantly extended his hand, but as soon as Entya drew out a knife he pulled back. "Hold on—"

"It's alright," Entya said. "It can be healed afterward, without a mark."

This was some weird stuff, but Gabriel gave her his hand. He resisted the urge to pull back as the blade bit into his flesh. Blood welled up along the cut, smearing the knife as she withdrew it.

Gabriel's eyes were drawn to the floor, where a ring of fire crackled without burning the wood. Water encircled the fire without touching it, and in the center, a cluster of lightning sparks sizzled. An elemental target and bullseye.

Cadrian and Varta were focused on the magic. Gabriel shivered as a sudden, strong draft blew in, sweeping the other three elements into a blurred carpet. He took a step forward.

"Be still," Phelan hissed. Gabriel pulled back. Entya extended her knife to the haze of magic, letting Gabriel's blood drip from the knife tip into its center.

The shadows in the room trickled into the swirling mass of magic. Then it all went dark, turning into a foggy pit in the middle of the floor. Gabriel backed up. "Wait—"

He stopped as several small black sprites floated out of the darkness. They looked like will-o'-the-wisps, trailing smoke behind them as they meandered toward Gabriel. He shivered as they whispered and brushed over his bare skin. They felt cold, raising goosebumps along his arms.

As they explored the air around him, Gabriel focused on thoughts of his father. He had learned magic, so he too must've gone through this, and it hadn't turned him evil. He had learned it to protect the home and the family he loved.

Magic was the power of this world, and Gabriel needed it.

He *wanted* it.

He reached out to one of the sprites. It bopped against his finger and drifted away. He smiled.

"Let them know you accept them," Entya said. "They await your word."

A couple of sprites rustled through his hair. What would happen if he squished one?

They explored him up and down, as though looking for a way in. He tried not to think about that.

He took slow, deliberate breaths, letting his emotions settle. The heat of his anger was still there. That was why he was here. He could do something about it this time.

Come on then, you freaky glow balls. Let's do this.

The sprites stopped, hovering just over his skin. The whispers stopped too, and Gabriel worried he had offended them as they moved away and hovered just a few feet in front of him.

Then they hurtled forward. Gabriel yelled and backed up, but they plowed into him. The sudden impact of cold made everything go dark and silent.

When Gabriel came to, his cloak weighed him down. He winced as he sat up, his cut palm scraping over the floor.

"Easy." Entya's hand rested on his shoulder. "You are alright."

Gabriel looked around. He was on the floor, and the room was empty but for him and Entya. The magic and the little black sprites were gone.

"What happened?" Gabriel sat up carefully. "Where are the others?"

"I dismissed them. You've been unconscious for a little while." Entya smiled. "Congratulations, magic weaver."

Gabriel stared at her. "Really?"

"Try something easy. Heal your wound."

"How?"

"Focus on the wound. Imagine it closing, healing."

Gabriel frowned and looked down at the cut. He touched it, wincing as it stung. He pictured the wound sealing on its own, and the throbbing pain dissipated. Gabriel squinted at his palm in the light.

There was no wound. Gabriel gaped, feeling the area. There was leftover blood, but the skin was whole and undamaged, as if he had never been hurt. He flexed his fingers. No pain.

"Whoa..." He pinched the skin. Still no pain. "I did that?"

"Of course." Entya rose to her feet.

Gabriel grabbed his cloak and followed her back up to the tavern. There, they found Seiryu seated at a table, a small book in his hand. The elf looked up and smiled as Gabriel approached. "I hear congratulations are in order."

Gabriel shrugged. "I just stood there and got run over."

Entya laughed and patted his arm. "Take care, dear."

Gabriel turned on Seiryu when Entya left. "Where did you go?"

"I ran into a friend to whom I owed a favor. But come, the ladies will think we have abandoned them." Seiryu tucked his book away and stood. He watched Gabriel carefully. "Unless you are too tired for company. I promise I will take full blame for keeping you."

Gabriel looked at his hands. "The magic won't hurt anyone, will it? Since I can't control it yet?"

"It may react if you get overexcited, but if you are calm, you will be just fine," Seiryu assured him as they left the tavern.

Gabriel glanced up at Seiryu. "Can I help Entya and Cadrian search for the Gold Mark?"

"What?" Seiryu looked surprised.

"I keep hearing about it," Gabriel said. "Tesmir said they're causing a lot of trouble."

Seiryu looked thoughtful. "According to reports, the Gold Mark includes a great many seventh-born weavers. Earth magic is their forte." He glanced at Gabriel. "Magic that, unfortunately, can hold its own quite effectively against yours."

Gabriel wavered for a minute, then said, "I want to help. I'm not asking to jump right into battle."

"We will see," Seiryu said. "Train first, and we will discuss it after."

Seiryu led the way through the city to a lavish tea house with large windows, where a server in a crisp, cream-colored uniform escorted them to an occupied table. The smells were heavenly, ranging from sweet to tangy and everything in between.

Though Gabriel was more of a coffee person, he committed to sampling the exotic teas. For the sake of science, of course, so he could tell Lilly all about it.

Gabriel's magic stirred at the sight of Odalys. He frowned, but it wasn't an unpleasant sensation. It felt... different. An inner change he couldn't quite define. Some place inside him had been filled when the spirits had swarmed him.

Maybe this wasn't such a good idea...

No. It would be fine. It would feel normal over time. It was like putting on brand-new clothes. They never quite felt right until you wore them around for a while.

Eeris saw them first and smiled. "Well? What is the verdict?"

Odalys twisted, eyes shining. Gabriel grinned back.

"I'd show you the magic," he said, "but I don't know how yet, and I really don't want to set fire to this amazing place."

13
FRIEND OF
MY ENEMY?

The morning of their departure, Lilly found Rune arguing with Unvar again about leaving him in Murke. Kedmir stood between them in an attempt to keep things civil.

"We'll send for you when it's time to march on Erriath," Rune promised.

Unvar glowered. "Rune, I will be of more use to you in Balmarren—"

She didn't linger to listen to Kedmir's placating words, slipping outside. The city lay before her. Cold, but with the scent of spring. Not many people were about, but the rebels were still vigilant.

"Where are you going?"

Lilly turned. Jek stood by the door. His hair was damp. A bath had refreshed him, but Lilly could still see the exhaustion in his eyes. She was sure he could see it in hers, too.

"It's safer now, right?" Lilly shrugged, shoving her hands into the pockets of her new pants. The fabric felt weird, not her usual denim, but it was warm. "No soldiers?"

"There shouldn't be," Jek said, "but you still shouldn't go alone."

"I won't be long. This city is where my dad lived. I want to see what it's like." She shooed him away. "Besides, you need to rest. This place is full of rebels. What's going to happen?" She stopped. "Don't answer that."

"Just be careful," Jek laughed. "Stick to the main roads."

Lilly gave him a two-fingered salute and headed off, walking briskly to keep warm. She took in the stone-and-wood buildings, built through hard work by hands, not machines. The air smelled clean, untouched by diesel or rubber. It smelled right.

The houses hugged each other, making the alleys wide enough for only one person in most places. Lilly walked along a wider main road, paying little attention to where she was going. She let her eyes, ears, and nose guide her to whatever caught their attention. Occasionally, shops coaxed her inside for their warmth, and to rest her leg. She browsed shelves of fabric, or a display of fine quills and inks. She ventured inside a butcher's and watched the clean-shaven, scrawny boy saw the leg off of what looked like a deer.

There was even a little tea shop, where she lingered over the dried tea leaves and herbal blends for nearly half an hour. The owner was thrilled, though Lilly didn't buy anything. He gave her a tiny sample pouch of a tea—too earthy-smelling for her taste but guaranteed to promote healing.

Her father had been at home here. How hard must it have been to go from this world to one full of technology he couldn't grasp? His aversion to smartphones made sense now. Even simple kitchen appliances had remained a mystery to him. Lilly felt vibrant and, for once, not out of place.

Her mind flashed back to Nick's face, and she bit her lip. No... he was her normal. School was her normal. Chicago and shopping and TV shows and Chinese food and teasing Gabriel about his disgust for pizza were normal. Normal tea flavors were normal.

Piensor was untamed and dangerous. Too dangerous for her.

A cold wind rushed through the street, driving her into the nearest shop. It was warm and smelled strongly of something sweet. Pastries!

"Afternoon to you!"

A short, skinny old man popped in through a back doorway. His shiny, balding head contrasted sharply with magnificently bushy eyebrows.

"What can I do for you?" he asked, wiping his hands with a cloth. "Got some sunberry pastries fresh from the oven."

Lilly shook her head. "I didn't bring any money. Sorry. I just came in to get warm."

"Ah, no matter. You can help test them, and that will be payment enough while you warm your bones. Come, come!" The man waved her around the counter. "It's a new recipe. I finally managed to get the berries at a good price. With higher taxes, it's been a terrible business trying to find anything from overseas."

"Oh... sorry." The tantalizing smell of hot pastries wafted from the large oven in the back room. Lilly tingled with anticipation.

The man smiled. "Sit, sit. I'm Alphaeus. I've no tea, so milk will have to do." He set before her a steaming golden pastry with a jellied mess of berries nestled in its center. "Raw sunberries are sour, but cooked with sugar... well, see!"

Lilly bit into it, and the berries burst in her mouth, releasing a sweet, tangy flavor. Lilly moaned. "This is *amazing*."

The old man beamed. "Good! I think I'll add a bit of icing too, just a touch."

"Do it." Lilly nodded vigorously. She sipped the milk and blinked. This was sweeter milk than she was used to, and thick.

Almost too thick. She swished it around in her mouth before swallowing.

Alphaeus set to work as Lilly finished her pastry. He paused, watching her. "What's your name, girl? I like you."

"Lilly." She licked the jelly off her fingers, pinky to thumb.

"Heh." Alphaeus snickered to himself. "You look like someone I knew long ago. A little lassie then, but as fiery a redhead as you, and whenever I gave her a sticky cake, she'd do just what you did: little finger to the thumb. Told me that way she keeps her—"

"—wet fingers away from my face." Lilly's gut dropped.

Alphaeus' tornado whisking slowed. Stopped. They stared at each other.

"What is your surname, lass?" Alphaeus' tone was somber now.

Lilly wiped her fingers on her pant leg this time. "Faine."

"Your parents?"

"Um, Tilas and Hollyn?"

The baker's eyes went wide.

"Oh, my sweet stars above," he breathed. "You—you're—" He stepped back, then toward Lilly. Lilly scrambled off the chair.

"I'm sorry!" he yelped. "I'm sorry. I didn't mean to scare you. I just never thought—"

"Do we know each other?" Lilly asked cautiously.

Alphaeus set aside his bowl. "I expect you wouldn't remember... it's been a long time. You lived in this city once, many years ago, back when the first rebellion sparked."

Lilly swallowed. "Did you know my parents?"

"Hollyn, yes. She was a frequent patron." Alphaeus nodded eagerly, sitting at the thick wood table. Lilly slid back into her seat. "It was a bloody mess when the empire defeated the rebels, but your family disappeared, and nobody knew where to." He shrugged. "Those Annor boys were never the most forthcoming about details in later years."

Without warning, the baker jerked to his feet again. Lilly jumped and almost spilled her milk.

"Right!" he declared. "I near forgot!" Alphaeus hurried off through another door, and up what sounded like a creaky staircase.

For a while, the room was silent save for the crackling of the fire in the oven. Lilly stood and ventured toward the bowl of icing and ran the whisk around the bowl, trying to get the right consistency. She resisted the urge to sneak a fingerful.

"Got this right before things went bad." Alphaeus' voice called down. Lilly returned to her seat as the man reappeared, holding a small, clothbound rectangle. "I knew your mother best, and you and your brother, but your father was as elusive as the stars in the daytime. Saw him early on but then never again 'till the day all of you disappeared." He slid the parcel toward Lilly. "Where *did* you all go? Are you all back?"

Lilly swallowed. "Mom and Dad are dead... Gabe—my brother—was captured by the empire. We went... really far away, but we were found and brought back. Mom died the day we left, I think. And Dad... he was killed when we came back."

"I'm so sorry." Alphaeus' face fell. "May they rest with the Creator."

Lilly fingered the parcel. Her curiosity was almost too much to bear, but something held her back. She wasn't afraid of it, was she? Afraid of what she'd find?

"My dad brought this to you?" she asked instead.

"Aye. Came in a big hurry and asked me to keep it safe and secret. Tell no one. He wasn't sure if he'd be back for it." Alphaeus shrugged. "I live by myself, so it never took up any space. But...

well, I suppose it ought to go to you now. Don't know what's in it."

Lilly's world narrowed in on the parcel. Her fingers moved, but she barely remembered ordering them to. She watched the cloth fall back, soft with age, and reveal a simple, leather-bound book. Lilly's fingers opened it.

Her father's handwriting was like a gutpunch. Lilly forced a breath in, held it, then exhaled. His script was a little more rushed here, like he was anxious to get his thoughts down.

"I'll be around if you need me," Alphaeus said softly. "I'll get you a frosted sunberry pastry too."

Lilly mumbled a thank-you. She tucked her legs up to her chest and pulled the journal close. She scanned half a page, then flipped to one at random.

Entry 17

Eeris came back with good news: the amulet IS *real. Not just a rumor, or old records of some man long dead. She found its creator. A man named Irador. He was reluctant to tell her anything, but with a bit of persuasion...*

Lilly's stomach flipped hard. Her eyes were on the name: Eeris. Her father had known Eeris *Rothar*. Worse, it seemed like they'd been *friends*. They'd both had the amulet. She took in a slow breath. No need to panic yet. There had to be a good explanation.

...he said the amulet can be used. But Irador broke it into parts: three glass pieces from the top, and a stone. This stone, he said, was inspired by the Luminnians and their use of crystals to channel magic. I'll have to make note of this and research it further. The idea

is brilliant.

But the amulet's been scattered all over. One piece is with the amulet in Erriath's castle. It's what inspired this quest. The second is with the elves. Seir had only to send for it. The advantages of being high-born, I suppose.

The third is with the dragons. This, we know, will be a little more difficult. The dragons are an old race, not to be crossed. And I'm afraid if we ask for the glass, they'll be suspicious. They would remember Irador giving it to them, and perhaps the tragedy that drove Irador to destroy it and to exile himself. We're working on a way to win them over.

As for the stone... the Meriak have that. We're not sure yet how to proceed there.

But when put together, the amulet can do the impossible: it can hold dark magic. Outside of a body! This is what Seir needs. Yovak can only heal him so much, and Seir doesn't want to burden him with his health. Yovak is already working so hard, especially with this drastic shift in leadership now that the war lords have been removed.

Seiryu says the amulet takes the magic from another, and from Irador's account, it can kill the weaver. His first trial killed his subject, and guilt and fear drove him to Luminne. He hadn't intended that result, which led to his destroying the amulet. But the woman had been dead too long. If he had destroyed it sooner, maybe she would have lived. In the end, it only released the magic into nothingness.

I don't know how to feel about this, but Seiryu says we can run a trial on a prisoner already slated for execution. I don't think I agree with this path, but... If it can make my friend well again, I will do all I can to help.

Lilly looked up, exhaling deeply. Her fingers drifted up to the amulet around her neck. It still tingled against her skin.

Her father had been friends with Seiryu *and* Eeris. Maybe even Yovak. They had been *friends*. But Seymour had said he was a rebel all those years ago; he'd been on their side, not Yovak's. He had been a spy, so maybe this was to throw off anybody who tried to snoop around? Or was it before he became a spy?

She scanned the pages. It was more of a scientific journal, but a few other entries mentioned Seiryu and their collaborating on various experiments. She struggled to find any entry that would deny the suspicions rising in her. Seymour said her father was a rebel, but Seymour had also said he hadn't known Tilas well... what if no one had? He seemed okay with the amulet *taking the life of another*. Her father had been the most peaceable man she knew.

No. Seymour said Dad used his friendship with Seiryu. And it had taken some effort to convince him. So maybe they were friends before he was a rebel. Lilly forced in a breath. That had to be it.

Alphaeus delivered another steaming pastry, and Lilly absently bit into it as she scanned more pages, but most of them were confusing, so she skipped over them—Tilas's research on plants with strange names. Occasionally, there was an entry with an update about the amulet but nothing really helpful.

Then there was an entry she did understand.

Entry 208,

No updates on the amulet. I've come home to give Seir some space. His restlessness and pain affect his temper. Raul's medicines have helped, but they're not enough. Seir is dying, and I hate that I can do nothing for him. Not even Yovak's magic is a permanent solution. It relieves the pain and fights back the illness, but he cannot help Seir forever.

My own research has been a little more fruitful. I think I have a way to open a portal, of sorts. Not to the world where dark magic resides, like the weavers do in order to learn it, but to other worlds we never even knew existed. I haven't told anyone yet—

Lilly sat up, heart pounding. A drop of sunberry jelly nearly landed on the page, and she jerked the book aside. Lilly turned the page for the rest, but a new entry talked about some new plant her father had developed. That was it. Cut off.

She growled, flipping the pages, but there was no more word of portals or other worlds. If there had been, those pages were gone now, ripped out so no one could find them.

Or use them to follow him.

What had happened? Had Seiryu realized her father was double-crossing him? Her father ran, taking the amulet and his family to a place where he thought Seiryu would never follow. Without the amulet, Seiryu wouldn't kill anyone for their magic.

Come on, Dad... I need answers. Lilly looked down at the amulet again. How could it hold a soul? It was so small, barely two inches around.

But...

It could be the key to the war.

Lilly fingered it. If it took dark magic... it could take Yovak's magic. It could kill him, and it could end the war. The head cut off, the rest of the snake would topple.

At first the idea disgusted her. How could she think such a thing? Wasn't that the very reason her father took it away?

But then, Seiryu had had her father killed for it. And Yovak had murdered the Annors' parents, turning their sons into orphans, and forcing the older ones to become adults too soon. He'd torn apart Seymour's family, his people. He held Gabriel captive. He had sent an assassin after Lilly.

His soldiers had shot her mother in the back.

He dies. The plan settled in Lilly's mind, in the dark corner where the monster sat. *Yovak dies, and this ends. No more pain. No more losing people.*

All she had to do was fix the amulet. She would destroy it later, but for now it was hers to use. She would force them to take her and Gabriel home, too. Zal Ira knew, and most likely Seiryu did also. This wasn't her world, and she didn't belong in it. Chicago was her home. She had friends there, a life. A life that wasn't messed up by a crazy war and magic.

She would end it here and now.

"Alphaeus?" a familiar voice called from the main shop room. "Are you in?"

"Aye." Alphaeus whisked past Lilly. "Ah, the seventh son! How fare the battlelines? Come for me at last, have you?"

Jek's laugh was relaxed. "Not this time, I'm afraid. I don't think my brothers want to lose your pastries on our table."

"Ah, well, I'll take what I can get. What can I do for you?"

"I was hoping you'd seen a red-headed—oh."

Lilly stepped into the room, clutching the journal to her chest. Jek smiled. "I didn't think you'd made it far. Rune sent me to find you. It's time to go."

Lilly joined Jek and smiled at Alphaeus. "Thanks for the pastries. And the journal."

"A pleasure and an honor to host a Faine again, my dear." Alphaeus grinned. "Keep those Annors in line for me. They don't heed an old man's lectures like they once did."

Jek laid a hand to his heart. "Alphaeus, when have I ever defied you?"

Alphaeus gave him a squinty glare. "Bah! Shoo with you both. I've work to do."

Lilly giggled. She followed Jek to the door but stopped and turned. "Alphaeus?"

"Aye?"

"Do you know where my family used to live?" Lilly asked.

The baker considered the question. "Aye, I do, but it's got other residents now. Nice folks. I can give you directions."

Lilly saw Jek watching her, but he made no move to protest against a detour if she chose it. Lilly shook her head. "Next time."

She desperately wanted to see the house she'd been born in. Lived in for however short a time. But that was a quest for another day. With Gabriel, before they went home.

Jek led the way back through the chilled streets. Lilly kept pace by his side. "Have they been waiting long?"

"No. Rune just wanted to be sure you were accounted for," Jek said. "He also said he had news for you. About your brother."

Lilly's throat tightened, and she swallowed. "News?"

"I don't know what it is, only that Rune has it." Jek glanced at her. "What's the book?"

"My father's journal." Lilly involuntarily tightened her grip on it. "Alphaeus knew my family, and Dad gave this to him for safekeeping. It's mostly scientific. Lots of plants I don't recognize."

Wrong thing to say. Jek's eyes sparked with interest. "May I see?"

"Not... not yet." Lilly shook her head, tightening her grip on the book *just* a little. "I don't understand most of it, but I want to read it first." If he saw any of those damning entries...

Jek didn't seem hurt by the refusal. "Come on, before I freeze."

"You have fire magic."

"Just because I have magic doesn't mean I flaunt it."

"I would."

"Of course you would."

Back at the tavern-headquarters, Jek parted ways with Lilly to attend to his group of magic weavers. Lilly found Rune in one of the upper bedrooms that had been turned into a meeting room.

"Good, Jek found you." Rune smiled. "We've received news of Gabriel."

"Is he alright?" Lilly hurried over. Rune slid a tiny piece of paper to her. She snatched it up, tucking the journal under her arm, and unfurled it. The script was tiny but legible:

The brother in E. Safe, unhurt. Believes kin to be in danger of rebels. Advise. —J.

Lilly looked at Rune. "What the heck does this mean?" Gabriel was safe and unhurt, but... he thought *she* was in danger?

"There's only so much we can write safely," Rune said. "We may get more information later, but it sounds as if Gabriel is in less danger than we thought."

"Who is 'J'?"

"Our contact in Erriath, Jinnet. My youngest brother is there as a spy, and works with her."

Lilly reread the missive. "Why would he think I'm the one in trouble? He was the one kidnapped."

"I don't know." Rune took the note back, only to set it aflame by the candle on the table. "But if he is safe, that's as much good news as I could ask for." He watched her. "I'm sorry I can't give you more."

"No, it's alright." Lilly leaned her elbows on the table. The adrenaline surge from reading the journal had worn off, and so had the sugar from the pastries. She was tired. "I know he's safe, and he's not hurt. That's good. Whatever he's doing is keeping him alive."

She still had time. They still had time.

Just hold on, Gabe. Keep them happy with whatever it is you're doing.

14
NO LONGER A THEORY

Lilly hated horseback riding. She hated the horse. She envied Aderyn, who became one with her mount, their combined movements fluid and natural. It took Lilly a full morning just to get the hang of it. Even then, her thigh wound throbbed and she hated that too. She wasn't sure how she would survive three days of this.

During the day, the sun revealed swaths of flat, unplowed fields. Around them, farmers' homes were clustered—not quite a village, but a community of workers.

Halfway between Murke and Balmarren was an inn, but Rune led them away from it and they camped outside on their first night. When their bellies were full, and conversation started to lag, Lilly's mind strayed back to the palace balcony, where Jek had showed her how to use a weapon. How to possibly kill a man.

"Jek," she said at last, breaking the silence. He looked at her, unfocused with sleep. "I want to learn more about fighting."

This made him focus. "Should you be training on that leg?"

The others watched them now. Rune looked up from examining a small cut on his dog's paw. Lilly ignored them. "Screw my leg. I'm not going to be useless in a fight again. If somebody's coming after me, I need to fight back. I want to make sure they don't come back for round two." Lilly leaned forward. "I want to know that when I bring them down, they'll crawl away and stay away. Or, if I have to—"

Rune cleared his throat. He nodded at Tae, half-asleep in Aderyn's arms.

"You would be so willing to take a man's life?" Jek asked, lowering his voice.

"Only if I have to." She didn't add that Yovak was in the "have to" category. She peered at her leg. "If riding and bouncing on a horse hasn't made it bleed, I'll be okay."

Jek looked at his brothers. Kedmir grinned, but Rune waved them away. "Mind that you don't wake Tae."

Lilly smiled and sprang up, a groaning Jek following her. They reviewed what Jek had taught her the night on the palace overlook, then began other moves, some more complex. Many were the same techniques her father had taught her for self-defense. She smiled at this connection to him and his impossible world.

Lilly repeated the moves over and over until they felt natural. She deflected Jek's offense, twisting him around and leaving him exposed, or pushing into his space to keep him restricted and unable to fight back as she delivered a killing blow. Or a maiming one. She tried to keep her death blows to a minimum, but she didn't neglect them.

She wasn't perfect. She lost more often than she would have liked. Jek corrected her stance and approach and countless other things until she called off the training for the night, frustrated. Her leg pounded dully, and she had to hide the slight limp from Aderyn.

"You're doing well," Kedmir encouraged. "No one is perfect after one night."

The next morning, Lilly almost committed her first murder when Rune took away her blanket because she refused to get up.

But Rune was allowed to see another day, and he allowed her another night of training. This time Lilly was a little faster, and this time Kedmir was her tutor. He was taller and broader than Jek, which made overpowering him difficult.

"Use the pommel if your blade can't be used effectively," Kedmir instructed, tapping the butt of the dagger before stepping away from her most recent defeat. "It can stun a man long enough for you to get away."

She remembered this in their next match.

Kedmir was sporting a bruised jaw the next morning.

As they neared their destination, Lilly tried to still her mind as it buzzed over her lessons. She focused on the journal, safely nestled in her saddle bag. She hadn't told anyone besides Jek about it. What would they think of her father if they knew how cozy he'd been with their enemies? Before he became a rebel spy? Or she hoped it was before.

No, that didn't matter now, because he *wasn't* one of the bad guys. *Hadn't* been. Something had happened. Tilas and Seiryu had had a falling out, maybe, otherwise Seiryu's goons wouldn't have been so hostile, and her father wouldn't have been so guarded.

She wasn't sure how she would find the other pieces of the amulet. Seiryu had one of the shards, and Gabriel had the shard from their father. So either Seiryu had it now, or Gabriel had managed to keep it out of sight. Lilly wasn't sure if Seiryu had obtained the last one from the dragons, so she would start there. And then the stone, wherever that was. Once she had fixed the amulet, she would end both Yovak and Seiryu. She'd end it all and go home. Home to Nick, to Amber. Gabriel was supposed to go to college next year, and she'd have to start looking at colleges too.

"Lilly?"

Tae's voice pulled her out of herself. The half-elf girl smiled wide and pointed.

Lilly had seen the ocean once on Earth, when Amber's family had taken her to Disney World. She had splashed in the waves, tasted the salty water.

But this ocean was different. It felt foreign yet familiar. The sun reflected off its surface, spilling orange and pink and red as it descended. Something about it gave her a thrill. She breathed in the alluring, wild scent.

A big city hugged the coast, with a huge port where several ships were safely docked. The city was walled in and laid out in a circle. The harbor was safely enclosed by two arching arms of cliffs on either side, leaving a wide opening to the ocean beyond. The docks sprawled into the harbor, and ships were berthed alongside them or anchored further out.

There were no skyscrapers, only a few tall buildings about three or four stories high, but the city made up for it in width.

"Welcome to Balmarren," Rune said. "One of the finest port cities in Piensor."

"He's biased," Jek said. "We used to live here."

"Is that to mean she's not the finest?"

"No." Kedmir spurred his horse onward. "But I heard the one on the other side sits on a cliff and has a great winding ramp down to their port. This is just flat."

Rune grumbled. "More work for the sailors, I say."

Lilly grinned. She kicked her horse into action, willing to endure a little pain to race with Kedmir.

The rebel flag flew proudly on either side of open city gates. The rebel guards' faces lit up with excitement when they recognized Rune, and he had to remind them to ask for his name and business.

The city was bustling. *This* was a sensation Lilly was used to; still, her senses were fully alert as they guided their horses into the flow. Sailors swaggered by, children scampered about, women window-shopped. They left their horses at a nearby stable, and Lilly's eyes, nose, and ears tried to take it all in at once.

The tightly packed commercial area smelled of smoked fish and saltwater. She could almost taste the fish as she inhaled the breeze. Her mouth watered, and her stomach growled.

The rebels grinned and whooped when they recognized the Annors and Aderyn. Some civilians offered a friendly greeting, but others cast dirty looks at them or muttered under their breath. Some gazed vacantly. Lilly noted the barren shop fronts, and the people's tattered clothing.

Lilly shifted a fraction closer to Jek, touching the handle of the assassin's knife for reassurance. Beron growled at these people, and Rune hushed him, keeping a hand close to the dog's collar.

"What happened here?" Lilly murmured.

"War," Jek said, eyes forward. "Balmarren is Piensor's largest port, and thus able to accommodate warships. It was a few years ago, but these people—and smaller towns between here and Erriath—were forced to surrender their homes to soldiers preparing to sail, and to dark weavers. The country knows war too well, but when it comes to war beyond her waters, Piensor wasn't ready to sustain the cost. Yovak only sees it as a necessary sacrifice for his ideal kingdom."

"What about other ports?"

Jek shrugged. "Aye, they've suffered too, but when you are the biggest and richest port... it's an ideal position to funnel troops through."

"Is that why you took it for the rebels?"

"Partly." Jek smiled. "And partly because my brothers are sentimental and wanted their childhood home back."

Lilly smiled sadly. "But Balmarren hasn't recovered yet."

"No... but it's getting there. We help where we can. We pay for our food, our clothes and weapons. We hire craftsmen when we can." He shrugged. "I've helped with the harvest."

Lilly caught a hostile eye and quickly looked away. "Some people don't seem too fond of you."

Jek shrugged. "Maybe their sons are imperial soldiers, and maybe we've killed some of them. Or their sons are rebels, so their own families are divided. Not everyone in Balmarren is happy to see us." He looked ahead. "So we keep out of their way."

Rune led them through less-congested streets, where fewer people glared as they passed. Lilly walked a little easier.

As they ventured deeper into Balmarren, the city widened, the broad main road branching out into a complex pattern of smaller streets. Carts rattled over stone behind the clip of horse hooves, vendors shouted their goods to any who would listen. The tantalizing smell of foreign food hung in the air.

Lilly's rebel friends didn't slow down until they reached a barracks close to the docks. It was a two-story building with a flat roof, surrounded by a wall. The maroon banner flew there too, its stars and lilies snapping in the ocean wind.

Two rebel guards smiled with recognition, but Rune insisted they exchange the usual passcodes, a casual statement and response.

Rune smiled and nodded his approval. "Mind you keep up protocol even with those you know better than yourselves."

The guards opened the door, and Lilly stepped through into an empty space like a training arena, made of packed-down sand. The plain, two-story building stood across the field, drab and practical. Two guards at the door cheered as Rune and his brothers appeared.

"Is Isilmere here?" Rune asked, approaching them.

"He's in the war room, sir," one said. "The council has called for lunch." The guard smiled a little. "Orrun can be persuasive when it comes to his cooking."

Rune's laugh boomed. "Well, I'll see about tearing my brother from thoughts of war long enough to eat." He looked at Kedmir. "Take the others on ahead—"

"Rune."

A female voice halted him in his tracks so fast Lilly ran into his back. Around the corner of the building stood a woman with long brown hair and a dark dress, a basket at her hip. A little boy scampered around the corner next, and froze at the sight of the others.

"Lina." A smile spread over Rune's face and he hurried to her. The woman set the basket down and let him sweep her up in his arms, his large frame nearly swallowing her. The woman wrapped her arms around his neck and murmured something. Rune laughed.

"I was well aware of the time," he said.

"I'm sure you were." Lina patted his cheek before turning to greet Aderyn with a tight hug and a kiss, then surveyed the rest of them. Her eyes finally rested on Lilly and Tae. She looked at Rune.

"Who're they?" the boy piped up.

"Eliam!" Lina scolded.

"This is Lilly Faine and Tae," Rune said. "Tae we found in the forest on our way to Lilantami, and we found Lilly in Murke during the attack. She and her father and brother came from another world."

"Your world?" Lina addressed Aderyn, her eyes wide.

"No." Aderyn shook her head. "A different one."

Rune looked at the girls. "Lilly, Tae, this is Arialina, my fiancée."

"I didn't take you for a guy who could settle down and marry," Lilly teased.

Rune snorted. "I am perfectly capable." He swooped down and grabbed the little boy before he could flee, tossing him over one shoulder. "And this is Eliam."

"Put me down!" Eliam screeched, wriggling. Rune swatted Eliam's rear before setting him down.

"Rune's going to be my father in... six days!" Eliam said, puffing out his chest with pride. "My new one."

Lilly's brows rose. Lina's smile wavered, and she turned to collect her basket of laundry. Kedmir, Jek, and Aderyn looked at Rune.

"Where's Lierr?" Rune placed a hand on Eliam's head, tipping his head back.

Eliam shrugged. "I dunno. Should I go find him?"

"Nah, go on and be a help to your mother."

"Are you going to the council?" Lina asked.

"Isilmere first," Rune said. "I will find you afterward."

"Do," Lina said, walking past. She gave his brothers a warm smile and said to Lilly and Tae, "It was lovely meeting you both."

"And you!" Tae waved after her. Eliam scampered past his mother, nearly knocking the basket out of her grip and earning himself a scolding.

"He's a handful," Rune chuckled, "but he has a good heart."

Lilly cocked her head. "What did he mean by—"

"Eliam's father died almost a year ago," Jek said quietly as Kedmir herded them all inside behind Rune. "He was killed in one of the first battles."

"I promised him I would look after his family," Rune said, short and simple.

"But now you love Lina," Tae said, skipping ahead to take Rune's hand. Her smile was softer now. She understood the heaviness. The loss. Lilly swallowed, her own hurt bubbling to the surface.

Rune smiled, brighter this time. "Yes, lass. I love her and her boys very much."

The inside of the building was as drab and practical as the outside, and only slightly warmer. All bare walls, rooms and beds. Their path down the hall was brightly lit, showing other hallways leading past closed doors and ending at a mess hall.

Rune parted ways with them, heading off down another corridor, whistling as he went. Kedmir led the way into the mess hall. A cluster of men and women sat at one of the tables, hunched tiredly over their food.

"What a sorry sight you lot are!" Kedmir's voice filled the room and bounced off the bare walls, good-humored and light. Everyone jumped, then relieved smiles lit up their faces.

A young man sprang out of his seat at the sight of them. His eyes locked on Jek's as he hurried forward. Despite the lack of a scar, he could have been Jek's clone.

"Hakor!" Jek met him halfway and clutched him as if he'd just come back from the dead. He smiled like he'd been made whole again.

Hakor swatted him. "It's been a lot harder to run interference with angry civilians without you. They're more afraid of the twin with the scar than the one without."

Jek laughed. "Then the next time you get into a tavern brawl, I'll let you escape it by yourself." He moved aside to let Kedmir greet their brother.

"Who are they?" Hakor spied Lilly and Tae as he gave Aderyn a brief hug.

"Ladies with stories that will wait until after they've eaten," Kedmir said. "We were told Orrun was cooking."

Hakor nodded. "But come sit with the council for a minute? Where is Rune?"

"Prying our brother's stubborn fingers away from his war reports." Kedmir clapped his hand on Hakor's shoulder. "Now what's the matter with the council?"

He spoke loud enough for Hakor's tablemates to chuckle. Kedmir shook their hands warmly. With Rune busy elsewhere, he acted every inch a rebel leader in his own right. Lilly waved to the council when introduced, and claimed a seat beside Jek.

"Tell us everything, Kedmir," one woman said, the food forgotten. "Unvar sent word that Murke is ours, but what of the half-elves? Will they help us?"

"Prince Seymour is unable to give us aid." Kedmir tugged on his bracelet. "Emperor Yovak holds his daughter hostage, and his people are enslaved in Lilantami and in Erriath. He cannot help us without risking his people's lives."

"I told you it was useless," one man grunted.

"Yes, but your concerns were for an entirely different reason, Malamar." Kedmir cast him a glare. "You thought he was too much of a pacifist, not a monarch struggling to keep his people alive."

This silenced Malamar, and Kedmir turned to the rest of the gathering. "We will find another way to surround the capital. We can afford to wait."

"Can we?" a second woman asked. "Yovak and his soldiers grow stronger. Soon they won't care about strategy and clever maneuvers."

"We will assess the situation once Rousen returns from Luminne," Kedmir said firmly. "Hopefully his own task was successful."

"And you think his search for a weapon in that place—based on mere rumor—will make things better?" Malamar snorted. "The only warfare in Luminne is their narcissistic vanity and apathy for anything beyond fancy gowns and dance parties. Their own *High Queen* is a joke." He looked at the other council members. Some nodded in agreement. "We have all we need, right here. We're beginning to look like fools, holed up, fighting at random when the mood strikes us, instead of going straight to the capital."

Kedmir leaned back, crossing his arms and scowling at Malamar. "You are all dismissed. We will gather later tonight, and you can tell us then how we're all doomed to fail. I'm sure Rune would be happy to tell you the same things I have." He looked at each one in turn, challenging them to talk back, but one at a time they rose, taking their plates with them as they left.

Lilly watched them file out just as Rune appeared. Rune frowned at the sullen procession, then looked at the table. "What happened?"

"Kedmir didn't listen to perfectly legitimate concerns." Hakor glared at his brother.

Kedmir was unperturbed. "I'm tired of their grumbling. It's the same thing every time. It was the same thing before we left for Murke. Malamar's an old fool who just wants blood running down his blade."

Lilly shivered. Tae huddled closer to Aderyn.

"But they have a point," Hakor said. He turned back to Rune as he sat down with them. "We can't sit around until we're inspired, Rune. It doesn't work that way anymore. This war is real, not some theory, some plan."

"What do you think we did in Murke?" Kedmir snapped. "We lost a lot of good men there. Don't accuse Rune of sitting around doing nothing."

"The longer we wait, the more good men we'll lose, until we're left with the fools who don't know a sword from a butter knife," Hakor countered. "We have the manpower *now*. We could push through, surround the capital and take it, just like we have everywhere else."

"Erriath is a fortress built over many years by war lords who got sick at the thought of losing power." Kedmir rolled his eyes. "We can't just march in."

Hakor shrugged. "Then let's try my original plan."

This made Jek look up from examining the whorls in the wood table, breaking his silence for the first time. "*No.*"

"Our father did it—"

"Our father didn't offer surrender," Jek snapped.

"I'm just saying that we've been as much a thorn in Yovak's side as he is in ours. Maybe now he'll be more open to having talks."

"He won't," Kedmir said. "He'll kill the messenger and send back his head. Your plan means surrender, and we burned that bridge long ago."

"You mean *you* did." Hakor crossed his arms. "Or have you forgotten?"

Kedmir's whole body stiffened. He stood, sharply pulling away from Aderyn's hand, and disappeared through the doorway without a word.

Lilly looked at Aderyn. "What was that?"

But Aderyn was staring down Hakor. "That was far, *far* out of line."

"You don't think that death ruined our chances for peace?" Hakor turned on her now. "It was supposed to be peaceful. Nobody was supposed to be hurt. It wasn't even a proper battle, and Kedmir *killed* their top commander—"

"There were no other options that day, Hakor, and you know it," Jek cut him off. "Ked made a call, and if he hadn't, that commander would have killed more of us."

Hot silence seeped in.

"Hakor," Aderyn said quietly. "Can you let Orrun know we're here?"

Hakor didn't move. Jek stood and pulled him up. "We'll go." He pushed Hakor along before his brother could protest. The table, down to four, fell into silence for the first time in what felt like hours. Lilly slumped, her tense muscles weary.

Rune looked like he'd much rather crawl into a hole than sit there. He stared vacantly at the table.

"Sleep will help," Aderyn murmured. "They're just tired."

"We all are," Rune said. He looked at the girls. "I'm sorry you had to see that. Not quite the grand first impression I'd hoped for."

Lilly shrugged. "Sibling fights? I've seen it before. I am a *champion* at sibling fights." She winked when the others smiled.

"Where is Isilmere?" Aderyn asked quietly.

Rune groaned. "No longer in the war room, but who knows for how long. I made him leave to shave and to come eat."

Someone cleared their throat. Lilly jumped and turned. A boy with thick, dark brown hair stood awkwardly at a second door, stains on his tunic, sleeves pushed up. He looked almost like Rune but shorter, less muscular, and about ten years younger. He seemed ready to run over and greet them but stood nervously still instead. He waved to the door behind them. "I heard the fighting..."

Aderyn rose to meet him. "Orrun."

The boy smiled and embraced her. "I'm glad you're back safe." He turned to hug Rune.

"I hear you're the man to come to if a soul wants nourishment." Rune grinned.

Orrun flushed deeply and shrugged. "I usually am. I'm better at cooking than fighting on the battlefield."

"We will address that falsehood another time," Rune teased. "For now, what must we do to earn a portion of your food?"

"Good manners and no fighting." Orrun grinned this time. "And you have to tell me how you met the new arrivals."

"It shall be as you say, brother," Rune laughed.

15
LEAD AND LISTEN

Gabriel decided it was *never* a good idea to anger Entya.

Ever.

The roaring blast of fire was close enough to heat Gabriel's body before the shield of water finally closed over him. It took all his focus to hold it in place.

He waited for the fire to disintegrate before thrusting his arms forward, spearing the water straight for Entya in a horizontal rainstorm.

Entya's arms slashed through the air, and lightning cut off the water-spears in its path. Gabriel groaned.

"Come on!"

"Again!"

Gabriel growled and pulled at the shadows in the cavernous training ring, throwing up a wall of darkness. It was slow to respond, hesitating, and Gabriel cursed before forcing the magic into place just in time to protect himself from Entya's lightning. The explosive impact threw him back.

He groaned, pushing his hair from his face. Entya stood where she had been standing ever since they started the lesson. An hour ago. Dressed in dark pants and a simple tunic, with a goldenrod-colored vest over it, she hadn't even broken a sweat. Though her black hair did straggle halfway out of her braid.

"You're focusing too hard," Entya said, crossing the space between them as Gabriel sat up. He felt his body for cuts and scrapes, and let his magic heal them over.

Without warning, Gabriel swung his arm wide, and a furious bonfire launched itself at Entya. His teacher threw up her arms, water swallowing the attack whole. Gabriel scowled and tried again.

"Your magic is not like the magic someone is born with," Entya said over Gabriel's barrage of attacks. She sidestepped, and three dark spears hurtled Gabriel's way. He dove and rolled, coming up on one knee, then twisted to keep Entya in his sights as she paced.

"To the ones born with magic, it is simply a part of their body, and the instinct is already there. Dark magic is slightly different. You must work for that connection, and so there must be a process of give and take."

"Give and take what?" Gabriel snapped. "It's not giving me much of anything. I've been training for almost a week!" He stood, his hands clapping together. Lightning arced down upon Entya. Shadows enveloped her, and she reappeared behind Gabriel.

Too late. As he turned, her leg flew around and slammed into his gut. All air left him, and he doubled over.

Dark magic curled up from the training room floor and circled around his throat, pulling taut. Panic seized Gabriel and he writhed.

"You do too much at once." Entya crossed her arms, watching him. "You think too hard and ask more of yourself and the magic than you are ready for."

"Well I wouldn't if you hadn't started the fight with an attack the size of a house!" He tried to peer up at her. "Let me go. Can't we just keep practicing the elements one at a time?"

"You already know them well enough. Application in battle is a skill you must master. Practicing the elements is an exercise you can do on your own."

"I still can't summon those itzals."

The shadow noose released Gabriel, and he flailed backward a step. He turned to face Entya, but she waved her hand.

"A break. Drink and rest yourself."

"I can keep going."

"I know you can." Her smile was gentle. "But I cannot."

Gabriel squinted. "You're not even tired."

"We have been sparring for three hours, Gabriel. I am able to withstand such long battles, but our magic needs to rest. Yours most."

Entya walked to the edge of the ring, where Seiryu sat by their cloaks and waterskins. The advisor looked up from the book he'd been reading—somehow, amidst the chaos. Gabriel followed, grudgingly taking his waterskin from his teacher, and drank in silence.

"Now, why can you not summon an itzal?" Entya asked.

Gabriel let his last mouthful swish around before swallowing. "It feels... strange. It doesn't feel right. Like there's someone in my head, fighting me for control." He shook his head. "I feel like I'm being attacked from the inside, and if I use the magic—the shadows and stuff—it feels like I'm losing."

Using the shadow magic to conjure the wall had felt that way. He hadn't liked it, but it had been his only choice under pressure. His body still felt shivery. Once the magic had bent to his will, it had tried to take over. To take the steering wheel and use the magic as *it* wanted.

"You must learn to work together," Entya said. "The more complex magic you perform, the more strength it takes. So does fighting your magic. Your magic is an extension of you, but it can also try to act of its own accord. You mustn't let it, especially in a fight."

"How?"

Entya waved him back to the center of the ring. "Come, let's try."

Gabriel obeyed, eager for another fight. Entya stood close to him, instead of taking up a dueling position. "Remind the magic that you are the master. It listens to you. But do not use a heavy hand. Let it explore you as much as you explore it. It is... a partnership, with you as the leader. It obeys you, but you must be willing to listen."

"You make it sound easy."

"It will be easy in time." Entya turned him to face the far end of the cavern, where half of the area lay in darkness. Fortunately, she had arranged for them to practice alone. He didn't like getting knocked on his butt over and over in front of other people.

"Create an itzal," Entya instructed. "And let yourselves get acquainted."

Gabriel looked at the shadows that piled in the corner. He groped inward for the magic that rested there. It tingled a little, but he was getting used to it. He jumped when *something* brushed against his mind, like a cat.

"Be calm," Entya said. "You are acquaintances. Get to know each other."

Gabriel shuddered as the magic explored him. It felt like something was invading his head, yet was friendly. It invited him to explore its dark mysteries, to learn more. This time, he opened himself up to it.

The shadows in the corner shifted. Gabriel focused on them, forming a single image.

A small, black itzal emerged, like a liquid drop. Rising from the floor, it morphed and became solid, wisps of shadow swirling around it gently.

"Very good," Entya praised, smiling as Gabriel knelt by the itzal and picked it up. The creature held its shape. Gabriel felt little effort on his part, as if the creature were doing all the work.

The creature, resembling a mouse with tiny wings, scuttled up Gabriel's arm and snuffled into his hair. He laughed and clawed around for it. "How do I make it do what I want?"

"Something like mental suggestion," Entya said, examining the itzal. "Try dismissing it."

Begone, then. Gabriel squinted at the itzal. *Shoo. Go away.*

The itzal's protest brushed his mind. Gabriel scowled and tried again, forcing a little more strength into the command.

The itzal bristled but didn't go away. It grew larger and fatter, and its wings spread out to fly. Gabriel yelped as it took off, heading for the open door.

"No!" Gabriel swiped his arms together through the air, and the doors slammed shut. Seiryu jumped, and the itzal crashed into them, dropping to the floor. Gabriel glared at it. *Go away! You're done!*

The creature chattered at him, sounding hollow and deep, and it grew again. Now it was a winged pig. Gabriel blanched. "No no no—"

The itzal bashed into the doors head-first, over and over. Wood cracked. Its attempts to escape became increasingly frenzied when the doors wouldn't give.

Panic and fury rose in Gabriel's mind, and he felt the need to run, to hide. That itzal wanted out, but with Gabriel unable to control it, what damage would it do?

"Be calm, Gabriel," Entya instructed. "Do not force your will on it. Communicate with it."

"How?" Gabriel looked at her this time. He needed to get out of there. To run and find someplace safe.

Then he felt Entya's hands on his shoulders, and her voice murmured close to his ear.

"It is afraid because you are afraid. Do not fear the magic, or it will control *you*. Show yourself the master but allow it some freedoms." She looked at him. "What do you need to do?"

Gabriel looked around frantically. He couldn't let the thing run free. It was now the size of a boar. Gabriel felt its frustration turn to anger. He wanted to curl up and hide.

It wanted something dark to hide in—

Hide.

Over here! He mentally shouted over the itzal's panic. It coursed through him and he fought the urge to run to the corner himself. *The other side of the cavern!*

He summoned up a thick cloud of shadows there, thick enough for the itzal to be fully enveloped. It was a command, but also a suggestion. A possible escape. This time, he left it that way. An open-ended order, an option that he strongly requested, but he didn't try to force it.

The itzal charged into it. Calm gradually settled over Gabriel, and he tried again to dismiss it.

A grunt from the corner, and the itzal vanished, melting into its hiding place. Gabriel slumped, exhaling.

Entya nodded in approval. "Very good. You had nothing to fear from its escape—there are plenty of weavers here capable of defeating it for us—but you listened, you learned what it needed, you *felt* what it wanted."

Gabriel grunted. "That didn't feel right... none of it."

"Your father had the same difficulties," Seiryu said. His book was now closed. "Your mind must share the space with it, and that can be an adjustment in itself."

"Remember to lead, but remember to listen," Entya added. "You are skilled in using the elements as they are, but itzals can have more of their own minds."

"Lead and listen. Got it," Gabriel said, shuddering.

The large doors creaked open hesitantly. An elf entered. He was about as tall as Seiryu, with dark brown hair and a short beard and mustache. He wore a dark tunic and pants, and a gray vest embroidered with silver thread. Draped over his shoulders was a dark blue cape, giving him an air of wealth and power.

His gleaming crown gave away his identity. Though it wasn't laden with jewels, a sturdy spike at the front held an amethyst.

"Your Majesty." Entya bowed deeply. Seiryu bowed as much as he was able, and Gabriel followed suit.

"There you are." Emperor Yovak smiled warmly. "When I said I had no need of you for a couple of hours, Seir, I honestly didn't expect to have to search the whole city for you."

"I would have thought by now you'd know my haunts." Seiryu smirked. "Am I needed?"

Yovak waved him back into his chair. "Ah, not yet. Myra has found the strength to be disagreeable with Eeris, so I sent Odalys into hiding with the baby and sent myself here." He paused. "I haven't been here in a long time. I recognize none of the staff."

Entya laughed. "But you recognized the owner, surely? She must have been sent for as soon as you stepped foot inside."

"Oh yes, but I assured her I was only here to see all of you." His eyes finally settled on Gabriel. "Gabriel Faine, son of Tilas."

Gabriel suddenly felt too inferior, far too unprepared to meet royalty of Yovak's caliber. Interacting with Odalys was different. She was a princess, but beyond her luxurious clothes and occasional orders to staff, she didn't act like one. She was... normal.

Yovak was the very opposite. He carried himself with strength and power.

Then Gabriel realized he'd been staring without answering. "Yeah. Yeah, I am."

"I was sorry to hear of your family's capture," Yovak said, "but I have every confidence your father will find his own way out before any of our people can find them."

Gabriel grinned. "If my sister has anything to say about it, she might even beat our dad to it."

That had been a very legitimate fear. Lilly was known for escaping detention. Repeatedly. But with Yovak's lighthearted attitude, the idea seemed almost amusing. She *would* be the one to free herself and then free their father. Tilas would bide his time, wait patiently... Lilly would kick against the goads until something broke.

"How goes training?" Yovak addressed Gabriel still. "I'd come down just as those doors closed, and hearing what followed I deemed it better to wait, but I admit I am curious."

Gabriel flushed. "I... I'm still figuring out how to summon itzals. I can do everything else, but trying feels invasive. Like somebody else is in my head, when there's only room for me." He shrugged. "I didn't destroy the doors though."

Yovak looked at Entya. "May I?"

Entya stepped aside at once, dipping her head. Gabriel hoped he didn't look too alarmed.

Yovak strode to the center of the ring. "When I first began, I struggled as you do." He smiled over his shoulder. "Except I nearly set fire to the bedroom."

Gabriel's brows rose as he looked at Seiryu and Entya. His tutor was trying to hide a smile. Seiryu just shook his head.

Yovak looked at Gabriel and beckoned him into the ring again. "Let the magic get to know you, just like you've familiarized yourself with each of the elements. Learned magic is alive." Yovak held a hand out to his side, and a monkey-shaped itzal scampered out of the shadows and up Yovak's leg to perch on his shoulder. "You must learn to work together. It will learn from you who is friend and who is foe."

Gabriel stared in awe. Yovak grinned, as if proud of himself, and set the monkey on Gabriel's shoulder. Gabriel tensed.

Then it started rummaging through his hair.

"Hey!" Gabriel glared at Yovak.

"You think that was me?" Yovak teased. Entya laughed.

Gabriel huffed and batted away the itzal's curious paws. He took in a careful breath and summoned his own itzal. His heart thumped as the creature scampered from the shadows in the shape of a little hedgehog, and scuttled up to his other shoulder. Yovak's itzal peered over Gabriel's head at it. The hedgehog sniffed.

It felt... somehow easier. Yovak had made it look easy, and *friendly*. Not just an unknown mass of shadows that could take whatever form, whatever size, and be used to fight. The hedgehog-itzal was more docile, willing to listen to his command. Gabriel's commands remained open-ended, while willing the itzal to obey. He gave it the *choice* to heed the order.

"There!" Yovak praised. "A natural."

Gabriel beamed, reaching up to pet both. They felt cold, like the shadow armor Tilas had used to protect him and Lilly. The monkey grabbed his hand and inspected it while Gabriel brushed his other hand over the hedgehog-itzal's tiny, wispy spikes. They felt semi-solid, an elusive physicality that kept Gabriel's fingertips searching for an answer.

"Now." Yovak stepped back, and the monkey-itzal scampered to him. "Show me how you duel."

Gabriel blanched. He looked at Entya for help, but she'd already taken up a post by Seiryu's chair, watching expectantly.

Yovak laughed. "I promise, I will give you back to your teacher unharmed."

Not letting himself hesitate, Gabriel swung around, throwing out his arms as the magic rushed around him. Whips of many-tongued fire tore across the arena at Yovak.

The elf just stood there. He snapped his fingers, and a watery shield jumped up to catch the fire and splashed down, soaking into the packed sand.

"Did you feel the magic and your energy leave you?" Yovak asked. "How it drew from you to give it force and strength?"

Gabriel nodded once.

"You must track it," Yovak said. "Measure it. Don't be afraid to experiment and test it. If it feels too big, it probably is."

"How will I know?"

Yovak shrugged. "A lot of patience and practice. Now again."

Gabriel attacked again. He tried using each element one at a time, testing it. Big attacks, smaller ones, complex shields and simple ones like Yovak had done. All the while, he focused on how they felt. He sensed the energy that fueled each move, felt the drain.

It made him nervous, but when he controlled how much was

used, the magic felt focused, concentrated, rather than wildly striking at whatever attacked him.

It's like a mana meter. You use magic in a video game and the meter's depleted. You have to decide how much you can use without running out.

With this in mind, Gabriel's confidence grew. He weighed each attack quickly. Yovak, who had previously stood in place, started to move around, blocking more of Gabriel's attacks than throwing his own. He'd conjured an itzal, and Gabriel's hedgehog-itzal lunged to meet it.

Gabriel felt the tug on his mind. The itzal begging for a little more freedom. An image of the flying pig from earlier popped into his mind. A request. Asking permission.

Fine, just don't freak out.

If magic could convey indignant gratitude, his did. The hedgehog scurried under Yovak's itzal and expanded, growing wings and throwing the enemy itzal off balance.

Gabriel laughed. His "meter" wasn't empty yet, and he felt... powerful. No longer struggling to control some unknown force. He was familiar with it. He was listening, and it was obeying.

Yovak threw a thick cord of lighting in Gabriel's direction *while* his itzal was fighting.

Gabriel yelped. His magic surged in response to his alarm, and he pulled shadows around himself, his eyes on a place just behind Yovak.

He'd only practiced this part of the magic a few times, and he prayed it wouldn't leave him as dizzy as it had then. The cold sensation raised goosebumps on his arms as the blackness covered him.

A second before the lightning struck, Gabriel disappeared.

He vaguely heard the magic strike the spot he'd just been standing on. His heart racing, Gabriel moved out of the dissolving shadows to see Yovak turning in place.

Gabriel didn't give him time to act. He grabbed the shadows again, and fire sprang to life in his palms. He threw both at once, letting them morph into one funnel.

He'd seen the combination once before, in Chicago. His father had used the shadows to protect the cops from Zal's fire.

He felt the magic drain his energy more than he had anticipated. Panicked, Gabriel tried to let go of it, but the magic resisted the order. He yelped and tried to throw water after it, but none came, and his legs buckled and gave out.

Yovak flicked both hands, and a water-beast erupted from the ground, its giant maw opening wide to swallow Gabriel's magic. The contact sent water spewing everywhere. Gabriel flinched, drops of water pricking his face.

"Was that necessary?" Seiryu glowered at Yovak, holding a slightly dampened book.

Yovak chuckled, and even sounded sheepish. "Apologies. I will replace it." He looked at Gabriel. "That was very well done." He walked over and helped Gabriel up. At the sidelines, Entya gave him the waterskin.

"Drink."

"Have you used two elements at once before?" Yovak asked.

Gabriel shook his head, mouth full of water. He swallowed and pushed his wet hair from his face. "No... I underestimated how much energy it would take."

"It takes time to master that skill," Yovak said. "Building your strength in magic will be important. Transporting alone takes an immense amount of energy."

"Zal did it, across worlds." Gabriel frowned at the narrow mouth of his waterskin. "And he was still able to fight and then transport again..."

If Zal was that powerful, Gabriel had to train harder. More than he had been. He wouldn't be caught off guard again.

Yovak's brow furrowed, and he glanced at Seiryu. "Yes... but Zal was accompanied by other weavers. They may have found a way to use their collective strength to make the journey."

"Though I suspect Zal is paying dearly for it now," Seiryu said.

"Remember to carefully meter your strength," Yovak said, "and remember that your capacity will increase with time and practice."

Like leveling up. Gabriel tucked the mental note away. "Thanks. Can we rematch when I've gotten better?"

Yovak laughed. "Aye, and I look forward to it."

Gabriel smiled. His heart still pounded, and he was still breathing heavily. After he had drained his water, Entya called an end to lessons for the day, overruling his protests and ordering him to rest. He got a ride back to the castle with the two elves and stumbled into his room before his legs gave out.

Gabriel stared at the stone ceiling. His magic felt quiet, as if it too were exhausted.

The advice *had* helped. It had focused his magic, made him feel in control. Powerful.

So why was he still afraid?

He conjured the hedgehog-itzal again, watched it snuffle around his bed before looking at him.

"What do you expect me to do?" he muttered. "You're weird, and you're in my head. How am I *not* supposed to panic every time you do something?"

The itzal only watched him. Gabriel shooed it off the bed and sat up. The thing squatted on the floor, looking up at him more like an inquisitive house pet than a magical, vaguely sentient... thing.

"You're not sentient, are you?" Gabriel squinted. "Because that would suggest I've been possessed. *Then* we're gonna have problems."

No answer. Gabriel sighed, but his gaze returned to the itzal, which simply... watched. Waited. He reached out a mental hand, prodding it. He watched it morph taller, lither. More humanoid, though he couldn't tell how many fingers or toes it had. They kept shifting. A mouth took shape on its face.

Eyes! You can have eyes too! Gabriel shuddered. The itzal created a pair of narrow eyes. They were only one color, a lighter gray against the blackness of its shifting body.

Gabriel cocked his head at it. Being the only one talking was going to get weird and boring fast.

But the itzal was his magic, and his magic was just an extension of himself, right?

"Tell me what I'm thinking," Gabriel said, meeting its eyes.

He opened his mind *just* enough. The magic crept in, equally cautious.

"Bubblegum." The voice was not Gabriel's. It didn't even sound *real*. It sounded... deeper, and ethereal. Somber.

Which made "bubblegum" the worst test word. Gabriel laughed. Still freaky, but the new technique thrilled him.

"Why did I learn magic?" Gabriel asked it.

A pause. "To protect my family."

Gabriel winced. "Yeah. *My* family."

The itzal didn't move.

"Why am I still afraid of you—it—though?" Gabriel started pacing. "It doesn't feel right. It's invasive, and just... dark. Learning it required my blood!"

"But it gives you power," the itzal said. "The power you need to protect the ones you love."

It was an echo of his thoughts, but somehow... it helped to hear it out loud. Gabriel looked at it. "But then you don't listen. You just..." Gabriel hesitated. "Have a mind of your own."

"The magic reacts to your fear. Makes it manifest."

Gabriel crossed his arms. "That's the problem..."

"Magic is power."

Gabriel halted and stared. "What?"

The itzal stood in the middle of the room, still watching him. It turned to face Gabriel fully.

"It is the power of this world, and people with power have the most influence."

"Well, yeah..." Gabriel frowned. "How does that solve our problem?"

"We are a partnership," the itzal said. "You are the commander. Magic is to protect *you* as well as your family. You must trust that we will do what must be done."

Gabriel squinted. "And what is that?"

This time, the itzal bowed. "To follow your wishes. Magic must learn you as you must learn us." It straightened. "Have no fear of us. We are at your command. Your fear is ours, and that is where we both stumble. You have the power of the world. With magic, the rebels will fear *you*."

Something about the words should have made Gabriel wary, but this last statement struck a chord. Wasn't that what he needed? Something to make him strong enough to be the one to push back? To fight back danger and make an impact?

"Dad has magic," Gabriel said. "He used it to protect us."

"So there is no reason for fear. Trust his judgments if you are not yet able to trust your own."

Gabriel took a slow breath. With magic, he wouldn't be helpless. His fear had been tripping him up. But maybe he still needed more practice. That, he could do.

He *had* to. He was useless otherwise. Everyone else could do something. His father had magic and was... a warrior. Lilly would fight tooth and nail, with or without a weapon. It didn't matter to her. She had fought more than Gabriel the day everything had gone nuts.

Maybe now he would be the one to take a risk that was bigger than himself. A risk that might require his life.

The thought nagged at him. He wanted justice done. He wanted his family safe. But... what if that meant *he* wasn't safe?

His mind replayed the image of his father, full of a long-hidden ferocity, throwing himself in the path of an attack that nearly killed him. Facing danger to save Lilly. Tilas hadn't even hesitated.

If his dad could do that, Gabriel saw no reason why he shouldn't. He'd pull his weight this time. Live or die, Gabriel would have what he wanted. His father safe, Lilly safe. This world... safe, free.

The itzal disappeared into the air without hesitation when ordered, and his mind went quiet. Gabriel took a slow breath and smiled. He could do this.

A knock on his door drew him out of his musing. It was Odalys, and his heart skipped a beat. She wore a cream-colored, shimmery dress.

She lifted a delicate brow. "Who were you talking to? I heard talking, and then nobody came out."

Gabriel's cheeks flushed. "Um... I was just..." He swallowed. "Myself. Talking to myself."

Odalys smiled. "I didn't take you for someone who did *that*." She shook back her hair. "If you're done talking to yourself, I'm bored. I want to show you around the other half of the city."

Gabriel smiled weakly. "Sure. I'd like that." Entya's instructions to rest buzzed in the back of his head, but Odalys' request had a stronger pull.

He closed the door and followed the princess. "Did you do any studying today?"

"Not much. I just needed to get outside." She flashed him a cheeky smile that made him catch his breath. Her eyes dipped to his shoulder. "You have a little friend."

Gabriel glanced down. The shadowy hedgehog perched on his shoulder like a bird. Its weight was a reminder, a kind of reassurance. He smiled.

"Where are we going?"

16
CHASING A GHOST

Lilly inhaled another long, deep breath as she stood facing the ocean. This was the closest she'd been to it since she arrived three days ago, and it thrilled her.

Sailors and laborers loaded and unloaded crates and barrels, then flowed directly from work into the selection of bars that separated the docks from the rest of the city.

All the Piensoran ships were thick, brutish things, more like warships than trade ships. Some of them bore the emperor's crest above a smaller flag indicating which country it called home. The winged snake had finally taken flight, flapping in the breeze high above the heads of its subjects. But the rebel flag competed for the sky right beside it, its lilies glowing with magic to chase away the darkness.

Lilly stuck her tongue out at the nearest serpent when nobody was looking.

But the ship that summoned her, Aderyn, Tae, Rune, and Kedmir to the docks wasn't a Piensoran tradeship. This one was sleek and slender, and had a figurehead reaching for them that was vaguely humanoid.

The rest of the ship was beautiful, like a medieval version of a luxury liner. Whereas Piensoran ships were built of dark wood, this ship was made of light-colored wood, making it airy and bright.

Though it too flew the imperial flag, underneath was a bright yellow flag, with a white silhouette of what looked like a swan with a mane. It was like a fairy among goblins—though to be fair, the Piensoran ships were far from ugly. Their magnificence was just more warlike.

Auburn hair passed before her, then paced back again. Kedmir's mismatched eyes were fixed on the fairy ship being guided into port by smaller boats. When he paced one way, Lilly saw his gray eye, and when he went the other, she saw the green. Both looked equal parts anxious and excited.

"Is there anything stopping him from just jumping into the harbor?" Lilly muttered to Aderyn.

The woman smiled faintly. "I suspect only the cold water."

"Can't he take a boat?" Tae asked. Her eyes bounced to every boat, ship, and sailor, like she had to take it all in now or never.

"He could," Rune said, "but he'd be too distracted to be of use." He stepped forward a pace. "Rousen will disembark soon enough, Kedmir. You're making everyone else anxious."

Kedmir stopped pacing. His arms crossed over his chest as a gust of sea wind whipped through the harbor. Lilly shivered, thankful for the new cloak and boots.

The past three days in Balmarren had been a respite from all activity for Lilly. The Annors dove right into their work, and she had seen very little of them. Aderyn was often busy as well, but could still be convinced to sit with Lilly and Tae and have a meal.

Rune hadn't allowed Lilly to explore Balmarren yet. Their arrival had sparked some disgruntled talk, and he didn't need any trouble stirred up.

When word had come that a Luminnian ship was approaching

the city, Lilly had sprung at the chance to leave the barracks. Rousen Annor had finally returned from his trip overseas, and the rebels were alive with anticipation.

The twins were busy elsewhere, and Isilmere—the eldest of the eight brothers—was once again in the war room.

Which left the welcome committee to Rune and Kedmir. Aderyn, Tae, and Lilly tagged along. The Luminnian ship had almost reached the dock. Kedmir resumed pacing, with Tae trailing him, testing out the new boots purchased for her the day before. She took big hops, little hops, and tripped sideways to avoid Kedmir when he turned around. Kedmir didn't notice.

Other sailors and locals had stopped to watch the Luminnian ship at last drop anchor and be tied off. The gangway dropped, and rebels hurried forth to help unload. The sailors on board were sun-kissed compared to the Piensorans, and their uniforms were striking.

Kedmir finally stopped pacing, his eyes scanning each sailor that left the ship. Lilly watched as a group of them carefully unloaded a barrel into a cart that had been pulled up to receive it. A young man with two swords crisscrossed over his back pointed in the direction of the barracks, and the cart was gently wheeled away.

"Rou!"

The young sailor spun around with a joyful smile, his curly black hair windswept and in disarray. He crashed into Kedmir with a boisterous laugh.

"Ha! And here I thought I'd beat you back! Will we drink to victory?"

Kedmir laughed, clapping his brother's shoulder. "So long as we drink to yours too."

"I'll drink to anything so long as the drink isn't water." Rousen's dark blue eyes sparkled. He turned as Rune approached and hugged him too. Rune spoke low in Rousen's ear.

Rousen nodded before pulling away. "Aderyn! The lady the imperials fear only second to Isilmere and Rune!"

Aderyn's smile was bright with relief as she stepped toward him. Rousen swept her up and spun her twice. She laughed, clinging to him. "Put me down, sir! What are you doing?"

"Saying hello." Rousen smiled impishly and set her down.

"How was your trip?"

"The High Queen isn't as loyal to the empire as she wants people to believe. We have a barrel of sun powder and the recipe is under lock and key."

"You can tell us the stories over a meal," Rune laughed. "Breathe a bit."

Rousen spotted Lilly and Tae. "New recruits?" He bowed low, and Tae giggled with a curtsy.

"Lilly Faine, and Tae." Rune pushed Rousen on. "You'll hear about it later."

"Gunpowder?" Lilly looked at the men. She hadn't seen a single firearm anywhere, and she felt a bit cheated. A gun would be far better than a blade.

"Close," Rousen said. "*Sun* powder. Explosive when touched by fire. With it, the great double walls of Erriath stand no chance."

Rune cleared his throat in warning, and Rousen fell silent, though still smiling.

"Is that your ship?" Tae pointed to the fairy ship.

"Much as I wish it were, I am but a poor sailor. That belongs to the High Queen herself, and gave me passage home." He offered her his arm, and Tae latched on. "Someday after this war is over, I'll have my own ship, and I'll see the world, and all its wonders will be mine for the finding."

Tae bounced alongside him. "Can I come?"

"You will be my first passenger. Lady Tae shall grace my deck with her glory and spirit!"

Tae beamed. "What's it like there?"

"Where? The ship or Luminne?"

"Both!"

"Aww, the ship's grand," Rousen said as they left the docks. "But Luminne's even better. Up that far north, it was too warm for my winter clothes." He twirled Tae out of the way of a pair of sailors lugging a heavy crate. "It's always sunny, and the people are dressed in beautiful silks that feel so light it's like you're not wearing anything at all."

"Rou!" Aderyn chided. Tae giggled, and Kedmir laughed.

Lilly cocked her head. "Wouldn't it get colder in the north?"

"Why would it?" Rousen asked. "It never has before."

"But it's warmer in the south."

"We *are* the south," Rousen laughed. "Cold and more snow than I care to have. Up north, they drink up sunshine like the flowers. They never see a flake of snow."

Lilly was still puzzling over this as Balmarren welcomed them back into its branches of streets and side alleys.

"A detour!" Rousen announced, and pulled Tae to the side, making her squeal. He grabbed Lilly's arm too. "Come, come!"

Rune's laugh followed them. "You scamp, bring them back! We don't have time for—"

"Detour!"

"Rousen Annor!"

"Rune Annor!"

Kedmir and Aderyn were laughing too hard to be any help. Lilly followed Rousen and Tae inside a small, brightly lit shop that smelled of sugar and—

"Chocolate." Lilly gaped when the delicious, rich smell hit her. Rousen was already at the counter, speaking with the man behind it in a cheerful, excited tone. Tae stood by him, staring around at the walls and their shelves stocked with different-sized boxes tied in delicate ribbons.

Soon she was introduced to Piensoran sea-salted chocolate, and was instantly in love. It wasn't as creamy as the chocolate she knew, and a little more bitter, but still rich. The salt pierced the sweet in just the right places on her tongue.

Tae was on her fifth piece before Rune put an end to it, but Lilly sneaked her third before the swordsman shut down Rousen's sugar trip.

"Rune!" Rousen whined. "I haven't had these in months!"

"They'll be here after you've eaten something more nourishing. We've already wasted enough time. Isilmere will wonder where we've gone."

Tae skipped beside Aderyn, happily clutching her box of chocolate. She was no longer the scrawny, shy slave.

Lilly fell behind, taking in the city. Gulls screeched overhead, and she could just make out the crash of waves.

The Annor brothers' banter faded around a corner. Lilly moved faster. Maybe if she asked Rune really nicely—

A shadowed figure caught her eye, and she stopped. At the corner stood a man in dark clothing, a hood hiding his face. He disappeared when she turned his way.

It only took her a second to remember. She hadn't seen his face, but she didn't need to. Though his cloak had been wrapped around him, his height had given him away. She guessed him to be shorter than most of the men passing by.

The assassin was back. Lilly felt the cold clench in her gut. She should tell the others. She needed to get away *now*. Why he was here in broad daylight, surrounded by rebels, eluded her, but they needed to get out of here. Back within the barracks walls.

Lilly tensed as the man peered around the corner, ducking back again quickly. She hesitated. The Ghost was Yovak's attack dog. Maybe he'd seen Gabriel. If she could catch him, she could question him. Rune could even question him. He could have vital information that would give the rebels the advantage.

Taking a quick breath, Lilly started for the corner, gripping her knife.

The assassin looked out again and disappeared quickly. She hurried around the corner to see him walking away, slipping easily through the crowd. Lilly followed, her eyes locked onto him.

You're not disappearing this time. Lilly wove around crowds of people, struggling to keep track of the Ghost. One blink was enough to lose her quarry until he decided to make another attempt on her life.

The foot traffic thinned out. Lilly thought she heard someone call her name, but she didn't dare slow down or look back for even a second. Her mind was going a mile a minute just trying to keep up with her target.

Rounding another corner, Lilly crashed into a lady hunched over a small cart of vegetables. Both nearly face-planted into the fresh produce and sent half of it across the road.

"What do you think you're doing?" the woman snapped, her cane swinging at Lilly's head. Lilly ducked, backing away. The Ghost disappeared around the next bend.

"I'm sorry!" Lilly said. "I was trying to catch up to my friend—"

"I don't care!" the woman screeched. "Pick these up!"

Lilly stared. "What?"

"You heard me!" The woman jabbed her cane at Lilly again. She looked like a disgruntled harpy. "You made this mess, *you* clean it up!"

"It's not my fault your parking sucks," Lilly snapped back. "You're taking up the whole road!"

The cart was only taking about a third, but the street was narrow. The harpy glared daggers. "You, you rude, disrespectful—"

Lilly dashed off before the woman blew up into a full rage. She shrieked after her to come back, but Lilly ran faster. With her luck, the woman *would* have wings. Or superhuman speed.

Around two more corners, Lilly stopped, her sides heaving. A stitch throbbed, and she pressed a hand to her waist as she leaned against a building. The street was empty. No sign of the Ghost.

Lilly cut off a curse at the sound of footsteps behind her. She turned, ready for another go with the old hag.

But Rousen appeared instead. Lilly loosed a breath, her shoulders sagging. "You."

"What are you doing?" He hurried to her. "Are you hurt? That woman—"

"She yelled and flapped her stick at me." Lilly waved him off. "I'm fine."

"What were you thinking?" Rousen snapped, his voice rising. He grimaced and forced it lower. "It's not safe running around here alone. There's enough people here that would rather see us leave, and they'll do anything to make that happen." He frowned at her. "Why did you run off? The others were worried."

"I thought I saw the man who tried to kill me."

Rousen's slack-jawed look said more than his stammered words.

Lilly rolled her eyes and pushed past him. "But I've lost him now."

"*Why* were you chasing him?" Rousen finally got out. "And why is someone trying to kill you?!"

"I wanted answers!" Lilly whirled on him. "He works for Yovak, and Yovak has my brother." She balled up her fists. She needed to punch something. "And I'm tired of sitting around."

Rousen watched her. "I'm sorry..."

Lilly sniffed. "You didn't know." She walked past him. "Whatever. The Ghost is gone now—"

"*The Ghost?*" Rousen's voice almost cracked. "The *Ghost* is trying to kill you?" He blew out a breath. "Creator have mercy, Lilly, why does Yovak want you dead?"

"It's a long story," Lilly said.

Rousen shook his head. "Running after trouble is what my little brother does, and that landed him in Erriath." He nudged her back the way they'd come. "Come on. We'll go and tell..."

His voice trailed off. Two men stood before them, stepping out of the shadows like Zal's monsters. Lilly shifted a little closer, her hand drifting to the assassin's blade.

"Gentlemen," Rousen said, his voice now quieter, carrying a flavor of warning.

Both men drew long knives. Boots scraped the stone street behind them. Lilly spun and drew her dagger. A third man blocked off the other end.

"You're not wanted here, rebel," one man spoke.

"We don't want any trouble," Rousen said slowly.

"Well that's what you get when you start a war, son," the man said. "These are my streets. This is *our* city."

"You're Parkit," Rousen ground out. Lilly didn't dare turn away from the threat behind them. "You put two of our men in serious condition. You murdered a woman." His voice shook with barely controlled rage.

"They were snooping. That was my warning." Parkit shrugged. "Seems you didn't listen." Steel scraped across steel.

Lilly heard Rousen's twin swords slide free with a quiet hiss. "There's still time to pretend you didn't threaten me, Parkit."

But Parkit simply laughed. "Take them both. Don't be shy about roughing 'em up a bit."

His two goons advanced, one on each side. Rousen lunged at the man nearest him, swords swinging, and blocked a strike. The second man came at Lilly. His sword thrust at her gut and Lilly hopped sideways, her dagger clanging off the blade and pushing it aside. As the man stumbled forward, Lilly lunged, slashing at his side. She missed, but at least her attacker had to catch his balance against a wall.

Parkit rushed at Rousen from behind when Rousen turned to parry a blow.

"Rousen!" Lilly screamed.

The blade slashed across Rousen's side before he could turn. He cried out, and his moment of distraction gave Parkit time to pounce. One sharp strike to the jaw with the butt of a sword, and Rousen crumpled to the stone, groaning. Parkit's goon pinned Rousen down, but Rousen wasn't fighting. He clutched his side, gasping.

Parkit grinned at Lilly and pointed his sword at her. "Your turn, little lady?"

Lilly swallowed hard, gripping and regripping her dagger as Parkit and his second goon approached. Lilly stepped back, deeper into the alley.

"I hardly think that's sporting of you, mate."

Lilly pivoted, keeping Parkit and the newcomer in view. A young man stood in the narrow street, hanging his cloak on a doorknob. His dark eyes flicked to each person before him.

"Move on," Parkit snapped.

Lilly willed the man to stay. To help. Rousen groaned again.

The newcomer glanced at her dagger before meeting her eyes. There was something familiar there, but Rousen's groan drew her attention. His captor stood over him, but Rousen remained on the ground.

The stranger drew a small knife. "Now, you three can move along, and I don't have to clean up the mess, or..." He shrugged. "I can clean up the mess."

Parkit narrowed his eyes. "Who do you think you are? Mind your own business, gutter rat."

The stranger rolled his eyes, grinned, and sprang.

Parkit's goon swung his sword. The stranger jerked back only long enough for the blade to run its course, and his knife flicked into his attacker's calf. The man howled in pain, recoiling, and turned, laying down a storm of curses as he faced the stranger.

And then again, as he wobbled on his feet.

And one last curse, right before he collapsed like a rag doll, unconscious.

Parkit stared. "What the—"

The stranger lunged for Parkit and addressed Lilly, "On your left, dragonfire!"

It took her a split second to realize what he meant before she ducked under the attack of Rousen's captor. She rolled aside, her back slamming into the wall behind her.

Two things happened. First, her wounded leg buckled from the exertion and she collapsed. Then her hair fell in her face, breaking free from her last hairband and obscuring her vision. Panic choked her as she clawed it back, her fingers getting tangled in the snags for a horrifying second, as her attacker came at her again. His knife flashed down in that wasted second, and Lilly twisted, jerking to the side.

The blade cut into her cheek instead of her neck.

Her attacker staggered, the momentum carrying him too far, and Lilly sprang. Before she could think about it, she jammed her dagger into the man's shoulder. She twisted. *Bring him down. Make sure he can't get back up. Bring. Him. Down!*

The man screamed, and Lilly shoved him away, pulling out her blade and grimacing at the wet sound, at the blood that dripped down the handle. The man collapsed, whimpering and clutching his wound as she stood over him. Panic and adrenaline kept her upright. Her voice trembled as much as her body did. "Stay down."

The newcomer and Parkit were wrestling on the ground, fists flying instead of knives. Suddenly, Parkit was sidling away from the street fighter, eyes wide with horror. The newcomer stood.

"Get out," he snapped. "Take your bullies with you, and don't let me catch you laying a hand on them again."

Lilly watched as Parkit and her own attacker limped away, dragging their unconscious friend behind them.

"We're not done, rebels," Parkit swore, turning to look at them. "*I'm* not done with you."

When Parkit finally disappeared, Lilly wavered on her feet and threw an arm out to catch herself against the wall. "Oww..."

"Lilly," Rousen gasped, fighting for purchase on the ground. One eye was swollen shut, and his lip was split.

"Don't move..." Lilly turned to him. Her legs wobbled and nearly gave out.

"Wait." The newcomer approached, carefully. He was limping, and blood trickled from a cut on his neck. He looked at her. "Sit. Breathe."

Lilly did. She probably didn't have a choice: her body listened and obeyed. She watched as he assessed Rousen's injuries. Rousen held still, and spoke only to answer their rescuer's questions, but Lilly didn't listen. She tried to quell the crashing alarms in her ears. Get up, fight, fight, fight. Get up.

"Lilly."

Her name in the stranger's voice made her turn. He watched her, his eyes missing nothing. "You are safe. So is your friend."

Lilly nodded. She touched her cheek, wincing at the sting of the exposed flesh. Her blood stuck to her fingers. She was getting tired of seeing so much of it.

"Thank you." Lilly looked up at the stranger, who was using his own cloak to bind Rousen's wound. It wasn't deep, but it wasn't going to make walking any fun. She watched the stranger's blood seep from his neck. "You're hurt too."

He stood. "I'll need your help getting him back to your headquarters."

Lilly nodded and levered herself upright as their rescuer helped Rousen to his feet. He wobbled but remained standing.

The walk back was long and painful. Lilly's leg throbbed dully. Rousen winced in pain with each step, and after a short distance he was begging to rest.

"We're almost there, Rou," Lilly panted. Her limbs felt noodly and unwieldy. Her heart hadn't stopped its desperate race to pound its way out of her chest.

They reached the main roads, and it wasn't long before a handful of rebels spotted them. Lilly's rescuer surrendered Rousen to them, and he leaned to one side, favoring one leg. When she slipped under his arm, he pulled back as if stung.

"Lower the ego bar for a second," Lilly muttered. "Let me help."

The man hesitated, then leaned some of his weight on her. Lilly braced her legs and walked. Her muscles quaked, but she forced her feet to move. There was protection now. They were safe.

They reached the compound, and someone rushed ahead to deliver the passcode.

"What happened?" Rune's voice boomed over the open arena. He quickened his pace at the sight of Rousen. Aderyn and Kedmir were close behind him, with the man Lilly recognized as Isilmere Annor.

"Lilly!" Aderyn flew past Rousen to her. Kedmir hurried to his brother.

"I'm okay, I'm okay." Lilly's breath puffed. The stranger moved away when Aderyn approached. Lilly let her examine her cheek.

"Parkit attacked us," Rousen said.

Isilmere swore. "On what grounds? He knows better than to stir up trouble in the main streets."

Rousen looked at Lilly. "We... weren't in the main streets."

"Well that's where we left you both." Kedmir glared at his brother. "Where else would you be?"

Lilly hesitated. "I accidentally wandered into his territory." She glanced at Rune. "I thought I saw the Ghost."

Silence. Her rescuer's eyes were on her, though she couldn't tell if he was incredulous or impressed.

"Do you have a death wish?" Rune spluttered. Isilmere took over checking Rousen's injuries while Kedmir held him up. "What were you thinking?"

"I thought if I could catch him, I could see what he knows about

Gabriel," Lilly snapped back. She looked at Isilmere. "And maybe you guys could question him too."

The rebel leader only glanced at her, his frown set so deep in his features Lilly wondered if it was permanent.

"And you thought you could catch the Ghost alone?" Rune pressed.

"It was stupid, I know!" Lilly shrank under Rune's hard stare. "I'm sorry—"

"Mordir!"

Lilly's rescuer jolted violently, as if electrocuted. Tae rushed at them from the building, pushing past the rebels and flinging her arms around the man. He staggered back on his bad leg and nearly fell over.

Tae buried her face in his shirt. "You were dead."

Lilly stared. Realization dawned with fear. Tae's friend. The Ghost.

The *Ghost.*

Mordir met her eyes, and unease shifted in his eyes. Lilly reached for her dagger and bolted forward. She slashed at Mordir's chest, forcing him to retreat as she yanked Tae back, pushing the girl behind her.

"Rune!"

17

YOU DON'T
FIGHT ALONE

Rune spun at Lilly's call, reaching for his sword. Mordir had already retreated a few feet, hands up.

"He's the Ghost, Rune," Lilly said, keeping her eyes on the assassin.

Rune drew his sword now. Aderyn and Isilmere too. The other rebels reached for their weapons, all eyes on Mordir.

"No, he's not!" Tae protested. "He helped me!"

Mordir—the Ghost—didn't move. He stood stiffly but didn't try to escape. "To be fair, I did just save your life. I could very well have passed right on by."

"So why didn't you?" Aderyn asked. "Change of heart?"

"I don't see why I have to answer to you."

Lilly surged forward and punched him with her good arm. Mordir staggered and fell, his leg giving out. Somehow, it wasn't nearly so satisfying as it had been with Dante.

"Lilly, no!" Tae sobbed. Aderyn held her back. "Don't hurt him!"

Lilly glared at Mordir as Rune stepped between them. "I want to know why Yovak and Seiryu want me dead, and if my brother is still alive."

"Not here, Lilly," Rune said. He waved the rebels forward. "Get him inside."

For a brief moment, Mordir seemed to debate fighting, but he lifted his arms, remaining on his knees, and let two rebels disarm him. One rebel pulled a cord out from under Mordir's shirt, around his neck. A small metal ring dangled from it.

"Don't touch that," Mordir spat, showing anger for the first time. The rebel ignored him, yanking it off with a snap of the cord. Mordir snarled and writhed against his captors as they hauled him to his feet. Lilly took a step back, and Rune placed a hand on her shoulder.

"Aderyn, get Tae away from here. Lilly, find Orrun and have him tend to you. Kedmir, get Rousen to bed and find Lina." Rune looked at Mordir, his dark eyes calm with quiet anger. "Put him in one of the cells."

Lilly could hear Tae begging Rune not to hurt Mordir as Aderyn led her inside. Mordir didn't even look at the girl. Lilly's anger flared, and she turned away before she had another go at Mordir's face.

"You've barely returned from one adventure, and you couldn't wait to find more trouble?" she heard Kedmir scold Rousen. The humor was forced, like he was hiding his worry.

Rousen chuckled. "I mean, Tesmir's not here to do it, so someone had to." He yelped. "Ouch, Ked, slow down. I'm not going to die."

The humor disappeared. "Don't even tease about that..."

"Sorry."

Lilly stormed into the kitchen. Orrun cut off a startled curse when she entered. Blood from her cheek had slipped down her neck by then, and she was sure the rest of her looked no better. Orrun shoved her into a seat, apologized, then dressed her wound. His hands trembled a little.

"Hey." Lilly grabbed his arm. "It's not deep, right? I won't lose my adorable looks because of it?"

A small, nervous smile spread over his face. "Sorry," he mumbled, focusing on his work. "I should be used to seeing blood by now." His dark eyes were on the wound. "But every time somebody I care about walks in with an injury, I just..." He shrugged.

"Forget your training," Lilly finished. "Freeze up and forget what's supposed to happen next."

Orrun nodded. He glanced at her. "Don't tell the others? People already think I'm soft."

"You're not soft, you're human," Lilly snorted. "And I won't tell."

He gave her a weak smile. "How's your leg?"

"Throbs, but not bad."

After Orrun secured the bandage, he released her. Lilly made her way to the bedroom she shared with Aderyn and Tae, but she hesitated outside the door. Tae's sobs made her want to turn and run.

"He's not! Deryn, you have to tell them he's not!"

"I'm sorry, Tae..." Aderyn's voice was almost too soft to make out. "He never denied the accusation."

"But he saved Lilly and Rousen." Tae's voice was high with desperation. "He was so nice, and—and he helped me escape. Why would he hurt Lilly?"

"We will know more soon," Aderyn soothed.

Tae's whimpers became muffled, as if she'd buried her face in a pillow.

Lilly stepped away from the door, walking the opposite direction. She shoved her red hair from her face, scowling at the spike of fear that rose in her chest. She'd almost died today... she could have died. Her leg had been part of it, but if her hair hadn't come free of the rubber band...

She needed to make sure *that* didn't happen again. She had enough things trying to kill her, and her *hair* wasn't going to be one of them.

Lilly searched the compound until she found the person she needed, just leaving the main compound building with a rumpled bundle of cloths and towels. Some were stained red.

"Rousen is fine," Arialina said quickly, seeing Lilly halt midstep in horror. "It's not severe, just quite a bit of blood."

"That's not severe?"

Lina chuckled. "Not this time. He was already asking when he could get up." She walked on, and Lilly followed her hesitantly. Lina looked back. Her eyes, aged more than her years by work and strife and loss, penetrated Lilly to her core. Lilly swallowed.

"Can you cut my hair?"

Arialina deposited the soiled clothes in a basin outside one of the smaller barracks buildings, and covered them with a clean cloth. She looked back up at Lilly. "Whatever for?"

"Because it nearly got me killed today, and if I'm going to fight I need to make sure I don't die." She spat the words out without thinking. She pursed her lips. "I just... I need it out of my way."

Lina's expression softened, understanding. "Come with me."

Lilly followed her into a small apartment. Lina pointed to a chair at the table. "Sit."

Also seated there were two boys. Eliam looked up. "Hi!"

"Hi," Lilly said as she took a chair. She looked at the other boy.

"I'm Lierr," he offered, his tone much calmer than his younger brother's.

Lilly smiled. "It's nice to meet you."

"Rune rescued her in Murke," Eliam informed his brother. "And the *Ghost* tried to kill her!"

"I know."

"Eliam, enough," Lina scolded, retrieving shears from a cupboard.

"It's okay." Lilly slipped the boys a look. "I punched the Ghost in the face instead."

Eliam's jaw dropped. Lierr looked up from his writing, eyes wide. Even Lina paused. Lilly winked. "Story for later."

"Did he attack Rousen too?" Eliam breathed. "Momma had to go help him."

"Off with you both," Lina said. "She'll tell you the story soon enough."

The boys scampered. When the door closed behind them, Lina looked at Lilly. "Now, how much do you want cut?"

Lilly told her, then went on to describe what had happened. She couldn't really stop. Confiding in Lina lifted a weight from her.

When she finished, the only sound in the house was the raspy *snip* of Lina's shears. Lilly took a sharp breath, surprised. Her head felt lighter and freer.

"Better?" Lina chuckled.

"It feels so light." Lilly shook her head back and forth when Lina finished. The short ends whacked her cheek but didn't affect her vision. Lina produced a mirror. Lilly's hair just kissed the top of her shoulders.

Lilly paused, examining herself. She had only been here two

weeks, and she hardly recognized herself. She was a little thinner, and her newly shorn hair was wilder and rougher without her daily showers, shampoos, and soaps.

Her brown eyes... sadder. Older. Almost like her father's. Would Amber even recognize her? Would Nick? What would they think?

She should have attended her winter formal by now, wearing her favorite color. It would have set her hair aflame on the dance floor and kept Nick's eyes on her all night. She'd planned on giving him the longest kiss they'd ever shared, leaving him wanting more.

But the formal was over by now. The news of the Bean and missing people was probably stale to most of Chicago. Her classmates were probably getting ready for Christmas break, and here she was, in a world already approaching spring.

Lilly put the mirror away. She looked at Arialina instead, and tried not to think of the things she'd left behind, or those she might have lost forever if she'd died today.

"Thank you." Her voice was a whisper.

"You're welcome." Lina smoothed Lilly's hair and pinned one side back with a small bronze clip. "It suits you." She came around and took Lilly's chin between her fingers, lifting her eyes to meet her own. Lilly fidgeted nervously.

"You have a warrior's heart, Miss Faine," Lina said. "I see it in Rune and some of his brothers, and in Aderyn, but you... your spirit has the fire and strength to take on the world with little fear."

"I'm afraid of a lot of things," Lilly murmured.

"That's alright," Lina said. "But you try to fight the fear with everything inside you. You see it, and you look for a way to overcome." The woman's hand released Lilly's chin. "It's okay to be afraid, to fear." She smiled gently. "It's okay to be flawed. To have ghosts follow you." She tapped Lilly's forehead before smoothing her hair back again. "And I don't mean the kind with daggers."

Lina's touch ignited a wave of homesickness. Lilly swallowed, leaning into it, and Lina's arms enveloped her. She smelled like hard work and warm bread and fresh laundry wrapped all together. It made her think of another smell, one of grass clippings and sunshine.

"I thought I was going to die," Lilly whispered.

"I know," Lina said. "And in times such as these, I cannot say you won't. We don't know who we'll see at the end, or won't see." She stepped back, and Lilly didn't want to let go. Lina tipped her head back again. "But just as I have to tell Rune, and sometimes Isilmere: you don't have to be invincible, and you don't fight alone. Allies will cover where you lack."

Lilly watched her sweep the red locks into a pile. "Thanks. For cutting my hair, and for... that."

"You're welcome." Lina smiled. "Now scoot along. I'm sure Tae needs her allies right now."

Lilly slid from the chair. "Can you tell the boys I'll come back later and tell them the story?"

Arialina laughed. "Aye. Just make sure you embellish it. They enjoy it more when it's not *entirely* true."

"There were, like, eight men. And maces with spikes. And a slobbery dog."

"Better." Lina laughed again, loud and warm. Almost like Rune.

Lilly hurried back to the main building. Her feet took her toward her bedroom but she slowed. She flexed her fingers, the ones used to sock Mordir in the face. She'd do it again. But not for herself: for the little girl whose light she feared had been snuffed out by betrayal.

It didn't take Lilly long to find the holding cells, but before she could approach, a hand grabbed her arm and spun her around, pulling her away.

"What do you think you're doing?"

Lilly wrenched away from Jek. "I'm going to give the Ghost a piece of my mind."

"And what good will that do?" Jek crossed his arms. He stopped, looking her over. "You cut your hair."

"Yes. It was a hazard to my life." Lilly mimicked his posture. "You didn't see Tae, Jek. She's *crushed* because of him."

"And if she hears you beat him within an inch of his life, what will she think of *you?*"

It was really hard to stay angry when Jek spoke reason. Lilly glared, then huffed. "So why are you here?"

"Rune told me you punched the Ghost, so I wanted to make sure you didn't try to finish the job." Jek's hand lightly touched the small of her back as he led her away.

Lilly snorted. Jek's eyes strayed to her cheek. "How bad is it?"

"Hurts, but Orrun says it's not deep. How is Rou?"

"Besides the gash and a few bruises, he'll be fine." Jek's hand dropped from her back. Lilly almost wished he'd put it back. Just in case she decided that pummeling Mordir was worth the consequences. Not because she liked it.

Nick's face flashed in her head. She tried to push away the guilt in her heart. Hadn't she just been longing to kiss him? She didn't need this. He was probably worried sick, probably freaking out.

Lilly cleared her throat. "Where are you taking me?"

"To get you a cup of tea," Jek said. "We can wait there until things settle down."

"What will you do about the Ghost?" Lilly asked. "And can I talk to him?" She held up a hand. "*Not* throttle him. Just talk to him."

Jek gave her a suspicious look. "The Ghost is probably off-limits until he's been interrogated, but I can ask Isilmere."

The fire in Lilly's stomach faded. "Interrogated... they'll torture him?" As much as she despised the Ghost, the thought of torture made Lilly's lunch start a rebellion of its own.

He might have tortured you. And this way, they might learn something about Yovak and Seiryu. That makes your mission easier.

"I doubt it," was all Jek said. He fished around the pantry for tea, and soon they both had a cup. Orrun found them and made them try the cake he'd made, and Lilly inhaled three pieces before Jek had the sense to stop her.

While Orrun tried to mediate as Lilly argued for another piece, the door to the mess hall opened and Isilmere entered. His stubble had turned scruffy, and his eyes were dark-rimmed. He looked far older than his mid-thirties.

"Hi," Jek said quietly as Isilmere sat.

"Hi." Isilmere's voice was low, rough with exhaustion. He looked at Lilly, and it seemed to take a second for him to realize who she was. He smiled. "A poor first impression of our structure here, I'm afraid."

"Are you kidding? It's impressive. Parkit's ego just doesn't let him see it."

Isilmere chuckled. "From the sound of it, you helped put him in his place." He dipped his head to her. "I'm glad you're no worse for wear." He held his hand out to her. "Isilmere Annor, at your service. I'm sorry we have not been formally introduced until now."

Lilly shook it with a smile. "Lilly." Orrun set a cup of tea before his brother.

"How is it looking out there?" Jek asked after a moment of silence.

Isilmere sighed, rubbing his eyes with his thumb and index finger. "We need to do something about these imperial sympathizers..."

"We need to move on," Orrun said. He sat down again. "I know it's not my place to suggest anything—"

Isilmere gave him an exasperated look. "You have as much place to speak your mind as any of us. Tell me."

Orrun ducked his head, cheeks reddening. "We don't have anything to hold us here. We've taken control of the majority of our region, at least the places that count. We know the others have too, or will soon. We should move on now. Carefully, but..." He shrugged. "They want this war to end. That's why they fight us."

Isilmere nodded. "We'll need a few days to move out. The council will insist we leave things behind."

"You are our leader," Orrun said. "*You* decide what and who stays and goes. They want a fast victory, but that's going to get us killed. It's a week's journey to Erriath. Use the week. Don't press the troops or the horses. Close in, spread out. Striking fast after a long journey is suicidal. It's what Yovak expects. He expects us to be angry and reckless. He'll bide his time. So will we. But if we stay in one place for too long, the taxes and restrictions on food will just get worse for these people, and they won't want to deal with us, and we'll all suffer. We need to move, but not so fast that we run ourselves into the grave."

Jek smirked at his brother, his cheek propped in his hand. "I like this side of you."

Orrun flushed again. "I mean... it's just my thoughts. I don't know much about strategy. I just pick up things as I listen."

"Then you're already doing more than most people."

Lilly snickered. Isilmere smiled wearily and rubbed a hand through his blond-brown hair. "We'll have to wait for Unvar to rejoin us. And then..." He exhaled deeply. "We bring that wretch to justice."

Orrun and Jek exchanged uneasy glances. Lilly watched Isilmere. The eldest Annor looked ages older than anybody. He was a man weary of war, but he kept on fighting because it was worth the final victory. It was fight or die.

The amulet tingled against her skin, and her father's journal entries tickled her mind. She carried something powerful. If she could fix it, this war would end. Isilmere's burden of responsibility would be lifted, and his enemies would be silenced.

But first, she needed allies. Jek would probably freak if he found out, and so would Rune. Kedmir might help, and Hakor would probably volunteer to go with her. Orrun, on the other hand, would have sirens going off if he even caught wind of her scheme.

Isilmere was the one she really needed on her side. And by the look of things, Lilly suspected he would do whatever it took to win this war.

Forgotten by the boys, Lilly slipped away. She found the war room empty. There was a thick wood table, bare except for a nubby candle.

She didn't have too long to wait. Isilmere soon entered and went to a cabinet in the corner. He didn't notice her in the dim light.

"Isilmere?" The man jumped. Something banged against wood, and Isilmere cursed. Lilly winced. "Sorry."

"Sweet goddess Kaltare." Isilmere hissed a breath, rubbing his elbow. He turned to her, but his face was hidden. "What are you doing in here?" His tone was dark, but Lilly didn't flinch.

"I wanted to talk to you."

"We were both just in the mess hall..." He paused, understanding. He lit the candle before closing the door.

Lilly pulled herself up onto the edge of the table. "I want to propose something."

Isilmere approached, the light from the candle illuminating a wary sort of curiosity on his face. "And what would that be?" He leaned against the table beside her. From her seat, she was eye-level with him.

Lilly pulled the amulet into view. "Did Rune tell you about this?"

"He told me Zal Ira wants it, and possibly Seiryu Rothar too. That it's magic."

"I know what it does."

Isilmere waited.

"I found my dad's journal. Some of the entries talk about the amulet."

Isilmere looked at her, more curious now. "And?"

"It takes away a person's dark magic."

Isilmere's brows furrowed. "How did your father come upon it?"

"Sei—" She stopped herself. "Someone he worked with. A research partner, I think." She shrugged. "Yovak has dark magic, doesn't he? If I can fix this, we can use it to take away his magic. He would be helpless."

Isilmere frowned, thoughtful. His eyes suddenly had an almost hungry gleam. Unease made Lilly pull the amulet back *just* a little.

But the gleam faded. Isilmere shook his head, slowly. "No."

"No?" Lilly blinked. "But I know where the pieces are!"

"That thing is meant for dark magic," Isilmere said. He took a slow breath before lowering his voice. "I despise Yovak, but I will not take the path he has. Dark magic is not to be played with, and it's not something I will stain my hands with, even to win the war. I will not unleash something potentially more dangerous than what we already face."

"We could end this war, Isilmere. No more dying." Lilly swallowed. "No more families ripped apart."

Isilmere watched her. "This isn't just about the war, is it?"

Lilly clutched the amulet, as if Isilmere would take it away. "Yovak and Seiryu have my brother. They killed your parents and mine, and Yovak's using Seymour's people to control him." Lilly met Isilmere's eyes. *I want them to feel the same pain I do.* "This needs to end. I'll go. You don't have to be involved—"

"Absolutely not," Isilmere cut her off. "What am I to tell your brother if something happens to you? Would he want you risking your neck for his sake?"

Gabriel would do it for me. But Lilly bit back the words.

Isilmere frowned, seeing her resolve. "Just be patient. We will march on Erriath soon, and we will rescue your brother."

"Do you think he's still alive?" The words were out before Lilly could stop them. The sound of them hit her in the gut, and they squeezed her heart. If Gabriel was dead...

No. He's alive. They're keeping him alive until the Ghost shows up with my corpse. Which won't happen either.

Isilmere crossed his arms with a slow, thoughtful exhale. "If they want your amulet, they will need to get to you. Keeping your brother alive is their best chance at getting both." Isilmere straightened. He tapped the amulet. "Hide that away. It will bring only darkness."

Lilly nodded and slipped it back under her shirt. "But if we need a last resort?"

Isilmere smiled sadly. "That will be when I allow my youngest brother to lead our men." He helped her off the table. "Anything else?"

Lilly considered. "Do you remember my father? Rune said you might have known him better than the others."

The rebel leader considered the question for a minute. When he spoke, his voice was soft, as though the memories were delicate.

"What I remember of him, I see in you." Isilmere said. "I see his stubbornness, his refusal to accept defeat." He smiled softly. "But I also see your mother."

Lilly's breath caught. "You do?"

"I see her in the way you look out for the others." Isilmere chuckled. "Rousen told us how bravely you fought."

Lilly flushed. "I didn't do a good job."

"The act of doing should be lauded in and of itself. What I remember of Tilas and Hollyn Faine, I see in Lilly Faine. The blade does not scare you, and you stand before magic and roar back."

Lilly blinked back the hot wetness at the corners of her eyes. "I don't think I—"

"Reports of Murke have not passed me by." Isilmere smiled gently. "Your parents were rebels to the very core, like you."

It wasn't the information Lilly expected, but her heart buzzed with warmth and emotion. The tears slipped and she hurried to wipe them away. Her throat squeezed, and she swallowed. The words gave her a comforting strength. She didn't feel so alone. "Thanks, Isilmere."

Isilmere smiled gently. "You're welcome." He moved to the door. "Now, off with you, and stay out of trouble. I have work to do." He winked. "And we have a wedding to prepare for."

18
I WOULD HAVE YOU

The next day passed without much event. Lilly kept within the barracks walls and tried not to think about the assassin sitting in the cell in the same building where she slept. He was under heavy guard, but the Ghost made no sound, no attempt to escape. Lilly hadn't heard anything more about him and wasn't sure she wanted to.

Rousen was another story. He could be heard throughout the barracks, arguing that he was fine, and he could walk. He needed to give instructions on how the sun powder was to be handled and stored. Rune finally relented, and Kedmir stayed by Rousen's side, watching with concern when he winced, or his breath hitched.

Aderyn recruited Lilly to keep Tae occupied, but the task proved impossible. The girl's earlier grief had been deep, but now... it had gone too far this time. She wouldn't even play with Eliam, and she almost never smiled.

On the day of the wedding, Lilly managed to peel away from the preparations. She found Tae in the infirmary, rolling strips of cloth for bandages.

"Knock knock?" Lilly rapped her knuckles on the doorframe. Tae looked up.

"Hi."

"Want a hand?"

Tae shrugged, and Lilly shuffled fabric around to clear a seat. She picked up a long strip and started rolling. Tae was silent, working with swifter skill than Lilly.

"Hey," Lilly murmured, sliding her boot to nudge Tae's. "Talk to me. You're even more quiet than Jek."

The humor didn't bring a smile. Tae ducked her head, her hair veiling her face. "I'm sorry. I don't feel like talking..."

Lilly hated it. Hated to see her looking so... defeated, so gray. Her eyes had lost their sparkle, and the frown on her face didn't suit her.

"Why does he have to be bad?" Tae blurted, her voice quivering. "Why..." Her hands went still in her lap. "Why does it hurt so much to know someone I barely knew... to know he's wicked?"

"I don't know," Lilly murmured. "I don't know, and it sucks. It sucks that he lied to you..." She reached over and tucked Tae's hair behind her ear before reaching for her hand. "It sucks when someone who you thought cared doesn't. It sucks when he hurts you in ways you didn't think he ever would."

This isn't helping her. Shut up. But she couldn't. The words came and Lilly was not their master. "It super sucks that he's making you cry, and I can't make you smile. It super, super sucks that I can't hear you laugh at Kedmir's stupid jokes."

There! A tiny, sad smile twitched at Tae's lips. Lilly's other hand vaguely registered her bandage roll unraveling, but she didn't care. "And it sucks that he thought so little of you, when you deserve to be treated like a princess."

Tae's cheeks went pink. "But I'm not a princess."

"Who cares? You don't have to have a crown to be treated with respect." Lilly turned Tae's face to hers. "So don't let him make you feel this way. You're stronger than him. You are a *queen*, you hear me?"

"I thought I was a princess?"

Lilly shrugged. "Same difference. It's a figure of speech on Earth. I mean you can't let his darkness blow out your light. You're the sweetest person I've ever met, and it makes me want to throttle him."

"But he'd hurt you!"

"I punched him already." Lilly grinned. Tae frowned, but Lilly hugged her. "My point is, please don't be sad too long. It's okay to be sad, but I just hate seeing you this way."

Tae wrapped her arms around Lilly and squeezed. "Thanks... I'll try not to be very sad." She sniffed, wiping her eyes. She looked at Lilly curiously. "Did you ever have someone hurt you?"

Lilly bit her lip and started over with her bandage roll. "Once," she said. "A guy I really liked, thought I loved. But he decided he liked another girl more than me."

Tae's jaw dropped. "How awful! What did you do?"

"Well, I *wanted* to give him food poisoning the day of exams, but my best friend back home convinced me to break into his locker and booby-trap it with a disgusting amount of hot pink glitter."

Tae's eyes went wide. "What's glitter?"

Lilly grinned. "Shiny stuff that sticks to you and everything you own for a really, really long time. We did it right before he had a super important presentation at school."

Tae giggled. "Lilly, that's awful!"

Lilly shrugged, letting Tae secure the end of her roll. "But it felt really good," she said, nonchalant. "So, if you want, I'm sure we can throw a lot of flour or something on Mordir..."

"No!" Tae laughed.

Lilly laughed too, and pulled Tae into another hug and kissed her sunny hair. "A princess and a queen. Remember that." She set aside the bandage roll. "Now come on. Stop hiding and come get ready for the wedding!" She grinned. "If we're lucky, I can make Rune superstitious."

The barracks had been alive since early morning, and rebels rushed to and fro until it seemed they had forgotten about the wedding that evening.

It would be a small one, held within the barracks, but the rebels wouldn't let that stop them from decorating, despite Rune's protests. Orrun had conscripted men for his own army in the kitchen, and could be heard calling out orders from the front doors.

"You can't see the bride before the wedding," Lilly told Rune over the brief break for lunch.

Rune looked up at her from his food. "And why not?"

"Because it's bad luck," Lilly said, slicing an apple. She winked at Tae. "Superstitious stuff, but you never know…"

Rune snorted, but later, as Lilly helped set up the canopy under which the couple would be wed—similar to a Jewish chuppah— she caught him going out of his way to avoid Arialina. Tae saw it too and her smile stayed put.

There was no talk of war. Not even Isilmere entered the war room. He worked alongside the others to prepare, and even helped Lina's boys get dressed a couple of hours before the wedding.

Arialina asked Lilly and Tae to join Aderyn in standing with her, while Rune's brothers backed him on the other side. A superstition of their own, in case any pesky spirits took a fancy to the bride or the groom.

The blue sky changed to a blaze of red, pink, and orange, lighting up the ocean as rebels gathered in the cold, fresh air. Lilly stood between Aderyn and Tae, in simple trousers and a delicately embroidered shirt. Kedmir had found a decorative sword for her, and a shield for Tae. She bore it with great pride.

Isilmere officiated. His words were brief, all about Rune and Lina being each other's sword and shield in times of conflict, and each other's comfort at the end of the day. It was beautiful. A solemn hush followed as Rune took Lina's hand in both of his.

"To the ends of the earth will I fight for you," he said, his voice low. "To win you comfort and safety, and to provide for you and yours a home that fears neither darkness nor death." He offered his blade. On its flat surface were two rings. "My sword is yours, just as my heart and body are yours. Use it with me, if you will have it, to defend what we cherish?"

The last words came out like a question. Arialina smiled, tears in her eyes, as she took both rings. She held up the bigger one.

"To the ends of the earth will I fight for you," she said, her voice so soft Lilly caught herself sidling forward to listen. "To fight *with* you is my vow, to uphold your sword with you, to create for you and yours a home where death is not feared, where honor is our mantle."

Lina glanced at her boys, standing to the side. Eliam could barely contain himself.

"I will fight with you for the ones we have lost"—her voice trembled now—"and so we may not lose others." She looked at Rune. "My hearth is yours, just as my heart and body are yours. Use it with me, if you will have it... if you will have me, though I am not whole?"

Rune smiled, but Lilly could tell he was fighting not to cry, not to fold her in his arms right there. Lina held his gaze.

"I would have you whole or not," Rune said, his voice broken now, "and I would never once look back."

Arialina sobbed, and Rune bent down and kissed her after she slid the ring on his finger. She sobbed again as he slid a ring on hers, and she kissed him back.

Lilly wiped her own eyes, swallowing hard as the cheering erupted. She laughed as Tae threw her shielded arm into the air with a victory cry. Eliam flung himself at Rune, while Lierr hugged his mother tight. The newlyweds laughed and hugged the boys. The cheering got louder.

Piensorans, Lilly quickly learned, knew how to throw a party.

The compound was filled with light and laughter and music. And lots of dancing. The women twirled and were swept off their feet, the men laughing as they tried to steal each other's partner. The music was high and lively, played on instruments akin to guitars, drums, and violins. The sound was foreign and enchanting.

For one night, the war didn't exist.

Rune and Lina were at the center of it all. Sometimes an Annor would steal Lina for a spin or two before Rune reclaimed her. But that smile never left his face, just as his gaze never left his bride. Lina was fairly glowing, twirling amongst her new family as Rune and her sons chased her around.

And the food. Oh, the *food*.

Orrun had outdone himself. Everyone said it, but Lilly didn't rely on word alone. She sampled everything. And then went back for more. Meats with sauce drizzled over them, vegetables cooked in spices, and every sort of dessert Lilly could imagine.

"You're going to regret eating so much," Jek said over the noise of celebration.

"If you keep watching, you'll see I don't care," Lilly said around a mouthful of bread stuffed with chopped fruit.

Jek laughed, sitting beside her on the sidelines, looking out at the dancing. Lilly handed him her second thick slice of fruit-filled bread. "You're not dancing," she said.

He shrugged. "I've had my turn. You're not dancing either. I've seen a few young men watching you, hoping you'll stop eating long enough for them to ask."

Lilly punched his shoulder. "I don't know the dances. I'd hurt somebody." She nodded to the swarm of dancers. "Who do you think is the better dancer?"

"Oh, there's no contest." Jek pointed to Kedmir and Aderyn, swirling and dancing as if literally made of music. Lilly grinned.

"Think they'll be next?"

"Hard to say. Neither of them has said anything, but I can see it in Ked's face. The way he looks at her when she's not looking..." He shrugged. "Maybe one day." Jek looked at her. "And you? Was there anyone, in your world?"

Nick's face flashed in her mind's eye. "There was... is." Lilly looked at Jek, but the young man appeared merely curious, no sense of jealousy. A simple question.

She looked back out at the crowd, at Rune and Arialina. She knew Nick loved her, but was it an "I'll marry you even though we all might die tomorrow" kind of love?

"Why marry now?" Lilly asked, nodding to the newlyweds, avoiding the feeling of guilt she couldn't explain. Lina had broken away from the dancing to help her boys get food. Kedmir was swarmed by brothers clamoring for Aderyn.

"Why not?" Jek returned. "If you weren't sure you'd see another day, wouldn't you take the chance? Especially with someone you love more than life itself?" He watched her.

"I guess..." Lilly bit her lip. "But if something happens to him... or her—"

"Then it will happen, and they will meet again in death," Jek said, blunt and simple, but not unkind. He focused his attention on the dancers. Rune had claimed Tae's hand and was practically carrying her as they danced. Her laugh rang high and light as she clung to him. It was almost better than the music. "It helps to know you have someone who holds your heart in times like these. You don't feel so alone."

Lilly smiled. "I suppose so." She turned as Rousen approached. "Hey, how're you feeling?"

"Certainly not able to dance." Rousen winced as he eased down beside Lilly on her other side. He flashed a grin. "Unless you're desperate for one."

Lilly narrowed her eyes at him and took another—bigger—bite of her bread. Rousen laughed. His dark blue eyes gleamed with a smile that ran deep into his soul.

"You're missing out on stealing everybody's partners," Lilly told him.

"Eh, I made Lina save a dance for when I'm not walking like a stiff corpse."

Jek rolled his eyes. Lilly licked the sticky fruit juice from her fingers before leaning back. She inhaled. Smoked fish and other meats mingled with firesmoke, complimenting the music and laughter. Warm and safe.

"I remember sneaking downstairs as a child," Rousen said, his eyes still on the dancers. "I was supposed to be asleep, but some nights I would sneak down and peek into the sitting room of our old house in Murke, and see our parents dancing."

Lilly glanced at Jek, but he only watched the party, as if he didn't hear. She looked up at Rousen. "Just dancing alone?"

Rousen nodded. "Our father held our mother close, singing softly, like all that existed was the two of them." He fiddled with the silvery beads on his bracelet. "Sometimes our brothers would watch too. Our parents would usually know we were there, and then Father would chase us older ones back into bed while Mother tucked in the younger four."

Lilly smiled. "Is that how you all learned how to dance?"

"We've had the unfortunate luck of being taught by Rune and Isilmere." Rousen laughed. "And they're hopeless."

"I dunno, Rune's holding his own pretty well."

"Lina makes him look better than he is." Rousen gave a mocking scoff, and he smiled. "But it was always special to watch our parents dance. They let us watch, let us keep that intimate memory."

They lapsed into silence as they watched the dancing. Lilly turned when Rousen's hand brushed her arm. He was watching her, and she offered a weak, awkward smile. "Yeah?"

Rousen hesitated. Glanced at Jek, who wasn't paying attention, then looked back at Lilly. He opened his mouth to speak as the music wound down to a slow waltz. Everyone cheered and rushed around to find new partners.

Lilly looked back to the crowd of scrambling dancers. "What's going on?"

Jek grinned and pulled her up first, then Rousen. "Come on."

"Jek, I told you I can't dance—"

"We'll address that travesty later, but that's not what we're doing." He pushed her toward one end of the courtyard. "Go over there."

"What? Why?" Lilly turned, but Jek had already disappeared into the throng. She looked at Rousen. "What were you saying?"

Rousen shook his head, his smile almost embarrassed. "Later. You don't want to miss this."

The energy from the crowd was contagious, and Lilly found her pulse quickening as she found Lina and Aderyn at the sidelines, where several women clustered excitedly.

"What's going on?" Lilly demanded.

Lina smiled. "A special tradition." And with that, Aderyn lowered a blindfold over Lina's eyes.

"What—"

"Shh!" Aderyn waved a hand at her, smiling. Two women turned Lina in circles three times. A whistle from the other end echoed over to them. The dancing didn't stop. Aderyn gave Lina a nudge forward, into the swirl of dancers.

Lilly's heart stuttered as Lina *willingly* stepped amongst them, hands out in front of her. She heard the woman laugh every time she bumped into someone, unhurt by the slower pace of the waltz.

Movement on the other end made Lilly look up. Rune, blindfolded, also struggled to feel his way in the midst of the dancers. Any time Lina's laugh rose above the music, he redirected his course. Whenever Rune scolded his brothers for trying to trip him up, Lina redirected hers.

Looking for each other. Listening for each other.

Lilly's heart rate eased back to normal, and a smile spread over her lips as she watched the pair weave through the dancers, cheered on or distracted by unhelpful directions.

"So they always find each other," Aderyn said. "Whatever separates them, they won't be lost forever."

The excitement calmed. Lilly watched as, at last, the pair stumbled into each other, laughing. Cheers went up all around them as Rune pulled his wife close, removing her blindfold. Lina removed his and kissed him.

Eliam's loud declaration of "ewww!" set everyone laughing, and Rousen, who had taken up a seat beside the boys, hooked his new nephew in a headlock. Lierr rolled his eyes at his little brother.

Rune and Lina slid into the final waltz of the night. The music rose to the stars, to the half-moon at its zenith. It swirled into the heavens to fight back the darkness that would return tomorrow, coming to take them to the next field of swords and blood.

But not tonight.

This night would be joy. It would be hope. It would not be darkness and shadows.

Not this night.

19
THE DOG'S OFFER

Lilly didn't remember going to bed. She remembered dancing, and giving up on formal steps, and letting her soul absorb the sound and atmosphere. She'd moved and slid where the music willed. Jek had laughed. Tae had joined in.

For once, that monster in the corner didn't come out. Nothing hurt.

And Lilly felt *good*.

None of that explained how she awoke with her face smushed into the pillow or why she didn't remember actually going to bed, but she didn't care. Lilly sighed into the sheets, content. She squinted at the bed and second cot in the room. Each held one lump of blankets.

"What sorcery is this," Lilly mumbled. "Aderyn Scalestride, still in bed, when the sun..." She peered at the window. "Is probably higher than the ground?"

"Probably?" Aderyn repeated, her voice heavy.

"You think I'm getting up to see what the sun's doing?" Lilly moaned. "It's up and you're not, that's my point."

A sleepy laugh was Aderyn's only answer. Tae mumbled in her sleep, rolling over. Her shield was under her cot.

The barracks was slow to rise. Even Kedmir's knock sounded like a heavy thump, as if he had leaned his body into the door in lieu of knocking. He mumbled to the girls that Orrun had breakfast ready. Lilly opted for just tea, willing it to nurse her senses back to life.

No one saw Rune or Arialina all morning, but they reappeared that afternoon. Lina supervised the organizing of supplies, while Rune joined Isilmere in the war room with the council, preparing the move out. They'd sent a message to summon Unvar to Balmarren the day before the wedding, but the other rebels seemed reluctant to turn their attention on the battles to come. No one wanted to pick up their sword yet.

Lilly didn't either, but the tingle of her amulet reminded her that she had her own mission to attend to. She didn't leave the compound just yet. After her first foray into the city, she had no desire for round two. Over the next few days, Isilmere's messengers warned that the city was growing antsy because of the rebels' increased activity. They had to move soon.

To avoid going stir-crazy, Lilly trained. Usually with Jek, but when he was busy organizing the rebels' magic weavers, Aderyn was her teacher.

Lilly's speed improved over the few days of training. Her body reined in her wild energy and directed it into the action. It was easier to spar with Aderyn, and she learned faster that way. The exercise kept her focused, away from thoughts of Gabriel, her father, or home.

Aderyn soon upgraded Lilly's weapon to a sword. *That* took time. It was heavy and cumbersome, so Aderyn assigned light exercises for her to do after dagger practice. Until then, Lilly challenged herself to spar with her dagger against Aderyn's sword.

"Lilly wins!" Tae cheered from the sidelines as Lilly wrested

Aderyn's sword from her. Enthusiastic applause made Lilly turn. Rousen was looking at her.

"How long have you been standing there?" she panted, handing Aderyn's sword back.

He shrugged one shoulder. "Long enough to see you win a couple of times, and then to see Aderyn put you on your backside."

Lilly flushed. "Yeah, well..."

"You get hasty," Aderyn said. "Let patience be your weapon. For a woman of your size, wear your opponent's strength down, then you may move in." She took the waterskin Tae handed her.

"So she's like Tesmir," Rousen said.

"They do have several similarities," Aderyn laughed. "We'll have to keep them separated."

Lilly grinned. She caught Rousen watching her again. "What?"

"I..." He glanced at the girls, but Aderyn had begun teaching Tae how to clean a sword.

"You...?" Lilly prompted, cocking her head to the side. Rousen looked at her again. He bit his lip, as if nervous.

"I wasn't sure if I should say anything, with all that's happened to you in the past few days, but..." He shuffled his feet. "After the other day, with Parkit, I wanted to say—"

"Uncle Rousen!" Eliam flew past and crashed into Rousen, who yelped, barely able to brace himself.

"Careful!" Arialina ran to them.

Eliam shrank back. Rousen doubled over, breathing slow.

"Rou?" Aderyn stood quickly.

"M'okay," he said, straightening slowly. "It's fine."

"You don't look fine," Lilly said.

Eliam fidgeted. "I'm sorry..." he mumbled.

Rousen smiled, breathless, and laid a hand on the boy's shoulder. "I'm alright. Now what's the excitement about?"

"We're going into the city!" Eliam burst out, grinning again. "Momma and Lierr and me. We have to buy medical supplies."

Rousen looked at Lina. "Is anyone going with you?"

"We have an escort," she said, motioning to a man waiting by the wall with Lierr.

Rousen nodded, satisfied. He addressed Eliam, his tone serious. "Stay right beside your mother and whoever's with you. Mind you heed what they say."

"Yessir." Eliam saluted and scampered off after his mom.

Rousen grimaced and eased himself to the ground, holding his side, as the wall doors closed.

Lilly smacked his head. "How bad is it?"

"I was praying they would leave soon." Rousen checked the bandage. "I'd have gone with them, but..."

"There are plenty of rebels out there to keep an eye on them," Aderyn said, though she glanced at the big doors with concern.

Rousen's wound had started to bleed a little, and Aderyn helped him inside to find Orrun. Lilly joined Tae in a game involving little marbles Kedmir had given her, to keep her entertained when everyone was busy. The girls had to pop their own marble inside a ring of other marbles, *without* bumping the ring.

Lilly kept her focus on the game, and for a while, her smile felt real. Tae's giggles were infectious and soon had Lilly laughing and teasing. Lilly's head felt lighter, less cluttered. She shoved thoughts of her mission aside for now. She could do that for Tae.

Their marble ring had shrunk to a nearly impossible size when the wall doors swung open. Lilly looked up just as she flicked her marble into the ring.

She winced at the too-audible *tick* of her marble striking the others.

"I win!" Tae crowed. "What are you—" She turned as a large troop of travel-weary rebels entered. Among them was Unvar. He came forward as Isilmere, Rune, and Kedmir went to meet him.

"You made it here in good time." Isilmere grasped Unvar's hand firmly. "How is Murke?"

"Quieter and more content than this place." Unvar sniffed. "Truly, I was half-tempted to start a fight in Murke just to add excitement to the day."

Rune laughed. "You? Start a fight?"

"We are not all so skilled as you, Annor, but I can hold my own in a fistfight." Unvar chuckled. "How are things here?"

"Come inside, and we'll talk," Rune said.

Isilmere approached Lilly as Unvar followed Rune inside, and Kedmir gave the rebels their next orders.

She got up, dusting herself off. "Everything alright?"

Isilmere pulled her aside. "You can speak with him now. The assassin." His presence loomed next to her, heavy with power and strength. Lilly glanced at him. The warmth and light from the wedding had faded away. Shadows were coming back under his dark green eyes. Had he slept at all?

"Did he give you anything useful?"

"No." Isilmere didn't meet her eyes. "If he can give you anything, fine. If not, then we have no more use for him."

"So you'll just let him..." She stopped herself. They wouldn't be so stupid as to let him go. "Oh."

Isilmere gave a short nod before turning back inside. Lilly tried to ignore the knot in her gut. She was keenly aware of Tae's eyes on her. As if the girl had overheard every word. While Lilly's encouragement had helped bring Tae's smiles back, the girl still cast glances in the direction of the prison cells. But she never asked to see him.

Lilly made her way to the cells, stealthily holding her breath. What would she say when she saw him? Demand he take her to Gabriel? Show her the sneakiest ways into the castle? Would she get in trouble if she punched him again?

The rebels guarding the doorway let her pass into a room with three cells along the far wall. Two rebels sat at a table in the room. One glanced up and nodded to the only occupied cell.

The Ghost's eyes snapped to her in an instant. He leaned against the back wall and looked her up and down, as if assessing a new threat. Lilly's eyes went to the red welt on his cheek.

"Who gave you that?" Lilly tapped her own cheek. "Pretty."

The assassin watched her, his face betraying nothing. "The large one. I suspect it was for our first meeting."

Rune. Lilly winced inwardly. "You deserve it."

"I'm sure." He shifted, a wince briefly cracking his neutral features. "Come to give me a matching set?"

Lilly glanced at the guards who watched them. They might not even tell anybody if she hit him. Not that she could reach him through the bars anyway.

"Not this time." Lilly crossed her arms. "I want to know why Yovak wants me dead."

Mordir—the Ghost, whichever—angled his head to the side. "He doesn't."

"Liar."

Mordir shrugged. "I didn't receive my job from the emperor."

"But you're his attack dog."

"So I am, but he didn't send me this time."

"Seiryu, then?"

"Perhaps."

"Why kill me when they've already told me to bring the amulet to them?" Lilly pressed. She resisted the urge to touch the amulet where it rested under her shirt.

"Perhaps Lord Rothar grew tired of waiting for you."

Lilly scowled. The urge to punch him again was coming back. She took a slow breath. "Is my brother alive?"

"I don't know. I've never seen him."

Lilly scowled. "The Ghost doesn't kill women. Why am I the exception?"

This time, Mordir's silence was uneasy. "Would you disobey the orders of a man capable of taking your life in a second?" He met Lilly's gaze coolly. "The emperor knows I don't kill women, and he respects at least that. Seiryu has no time for it."

"Wouldn't the emperor step in?"

"Why? I'm his dog, not his son." Mordir shrugged. "My relationship with the crown is complicated." He dropped his gaze. "I step out of line, and I am not the only one who suffers."

Lilly's hand fidgeted with the amulet now. "You have family?"

"Does that surprise you?"

Monsters like you don't have people who love them. "Did he threaten them?"

"Not directly." Mordir let out a small breath. He looked at Lilly. "If I don't return with that amulet, I will die and the people I care about will be left with no one."

Lilly wanted to be angry with him, for being willing to kill her to save himself. But... was she any different?

No. This is different. Yovak's made a mess of everything and it's only going to get worse.

"They're going to kill you here too," she blurted. Lilly cursed herself. What kind of thing was that to say? Even to an assassin?

Mordir only nodded. "But I can be of use."

"Then you should've said so before Rune punched you."

"The rebels don't need me to fight their wars. But *you* want your brother back. I can help you get to him."

"How do I know it's not a trick?" Lilly narrowed her eyes.

"You don't. You'll just have to trust me," Mordir said. "I didn't save you for no reason."

Lilly raised a brow, and he went on. "It was in my best interests to serve the crown, but that tie will be severed sooner or later. The rebels are strong, persistent to a fault. They will wear the emperor down eventually."

"What do you want, Ghost?" Why was she still talking to him? He was just trying to save his own skin now, grasping at straws.

But he didn't seem desperate, or afraid. He was calm, sure of his words. If he was afraid, he buried it deep. He merely shrugged, like he knew something she didn't.

"I may not be useful to your rebels," he said, leaning forward almost conspiratorially. The light caught his features. He had to be younger than Rune. "But like I said, I can be useful to you and your brother. I can find him and take you to him."

Lilly laughed this time. "Or right into Seiryu's waiting arms. Do I look that stupid?"

"The rebels have enough resources and strength that they don't need me, nor are they desperate enough to believe anything I'd offer." Mordir sat back with a shrug. "Just think about it. You have your eyes set on objectives that require stealth and secrecy. I excel in both."

"I'm not desperate. I have a rebel army behind me."

He watched her. "Perhaps, but then why are you standing here now? You know who I am, so you know I have access to the castle, which is likely where your brother is." He glanced at his guards once, then at her. "Just think about it. Please," he added. "I want to help. The people under my care... I can't lose them, and they can't lose me."

"Then maybe you should have picked a better side." Lilly stepped back. She didn't want to admit he was right, and talking to him reminded her she couldn't trust him. Sure, he had what she needed, but she didn't want him to have another go at her throat. She turned to leave but stopped and looked back. Mordir watched her, giving away nothing.

"Did you even care for Tae?"

The name made the assassin stiffen. His brows twitched downward. "What?"

"Tae." Lilly faced him again. "Why did you rescue her if you were just going to dump her?"

Mordir didn't answer for a while. Lilly held his gaze, unflinching.

"Because I know what that life is like," Mordir said quietly. "And it isn't a life for Tae." He shrugged. "And Eeris Rothar is an arrogant witch who has enough underlings to satisfy her."

Lilly cocked her head. "You were a slave?"

"I'm the emperor's dog, sweetheart. I'm as much a slave as any." He smirked. "Just think about it... please." His voice went a shade softer. Not a plea, but... a request. A polite one.

Lilly turned away, leaving him alone.

20

ALMOST

Gabriel's knock was answered by a muffled, distracted "come in." He eased open the thick wooden door of Seiryu's study. The curtains were pulled back, letting in the midday sunshine. The days were getting warmer, and Gabriel wondered how Seiryu could stay cooped up inside. The room smelled like aging books and bitter ink.

"You should open those windows," he said. "Odalys keeps saying her father wants to have a servant come in and just do it for you."

Seiryu smirked, his eyes still on the scramble of papers on his desk. "A threat he's made for years. I get plenty of outdoor air on my walks." He looked up. "What can I do for you, Gabriel?" He smiled at the sight of the hedgehog-itzal perched on Gabriel's shoulder. It had become a sort of pet. A comforting weight, and a reminder.

Gabriel closed the door behind him. "I wanted to ask if you've heard anything. It's been two weeks." He watched Seiryu's face. "I know you've been busy, but... has there been *anything*?"

"I have had some news." Seiryu set aside his quill and pushed back strands of black hair that had fallen in his face. "But my contact has been... lacking, in his reports. The last was not favorable."

"What do you mean?" Gabriel wished he'd sat down first. His muscles tensed, preparing for whatever came next. Suddenly the air in the room was unbearably thick and stale with old paper and sharp ink.

"The rebels are keeping your father and sister under close watch," Seiryu said. "There was an attempt to rescue your sister—your father is under higher guard—but it was thwarted."

"What else is your guy doing?" Gabriel blurted. "Can he get a message to my dad about where Lilly is? Maybe Dad can help!"

"My contact cannot get that close, unfortunately," Seiryu said. He watched Gabriel. "Have faith. He confirmed that both were alive and seemed unhurt." He smiled gently. "We have a spy already within the rebels' secret rooms in Balmarren, where your family is now held. He will soon be providing news of a... more intense matter."

Gabriel cocked his head. "Like what?"

"We are not without our tricks." Seiryu winked. "With any luck, there will be ample opportunity for a rescue."

Gabriel tried to let that news settle peace in his heart, but his anxiety was more dominant.

"There has to be something else we can try." Gabriel approached the desk. "Why haven't the rebels asked for ransom? No message at all? What are they holding them for?"

"I don't know," Seiryu said. "That is something to consider, but while it has been an unusually long time to hold prisoners without ransom, they could have a great many reasons. Tilas Faine is a name well-known among rebels—he was a fierce warrior when he fought the war lords. The rebels have a great war-prize indeed, and they will not risk giving it up for something so simple."

"They're going to use him as a bargaining chip."

"Very possibly."

"And Lilly?"

"A means to keep your father docile and cooperative, I assume."

Gabriel considered this. He sat down across from Seiryu's desk. "What can *I* do?"

Seiryu looked at him, one brow lifted.

"Hear me out," Gabriel said quickly. "I just need to do *something*. I've been training and getting better. I beat Entya three times this past week! And I've got a five-streak win with Tesmir!"

A smile played across Seiryu's features. Gabriel forged ahead. "Let me help hunt for the Gold Mark. I can—"

"Absolutely not."

"But you said we'd talk about it after I'd trained!"

Seiryu motioned to the papers before him. "The Mark has just struck *another* of our supply stores. They left our men with the barest minimum of food, and not a scrap of clothing. We've received word that the rebels may be planning to march on Erriath. Now is not the time for you to go roaming the streets."

"Let Entya go with me!"

"Entya has her own duties."

"Then I'll join her—"

"*Gabriel*," Seiryu interrupted, his voice sharp. "I cannot risk you going out. I'm sorry. I know you want to help, and there will be a time for it. But with this recent attack, it's possible our enemies are watching the streets, waiting for us to retaliate. What would I tell your father if you were captured?"

Gabriel hesitated. His dad would be frantic... he'd turn the city over, looking for Gabriel.

"But I've been into the city before," Gabriel ventured. "Why didn't they do anything then?"

"Would you lay hands on someone surrounded by the royal family's own guard? Or in front of a member of the royal family who is *also* accompanied by guards?" Seiryu lifted both brows.

Gabriel slumped in his chair. "I'm gonna go crazy just sitting here."

"Have patience," Seiryu said gently. "War is a time where everyone must contribute. You will too, and your contribution may just be the thing to turn the tide against them. But you must be patient." He smiled. "You have much to learn yet."

The words should have been encouraging, but Gabriel didn't voice agreement. His magic stirred within him at the presence of his frustration. He didn't want to keep training. He'd trained enough. He was strong, confident he could hold his own against someone like Zal. Or even the elusive Jinnet.

Every day he waited was another day the rebels got away with more violence. Another day his family was at their mercy. Another day he was useless.

Seiryu seemed to sense his dissatisfaction. "I will discuss it with Entya. If she thinks you are ready, we will *consider* giving you something to do."

Gabriel brightened. "Really?"

"I can't promise anything, but I will talk to her." Seiryu picked up his quill. "And don't go asking her to give me a favorable report." He looked at Gabriel with a good-natured glare. "Now leave me. I have to finish organizing this mess of reports before the emperor sees them."

Gabriel stood and headed for the door. "Keep me updated?" He tilted his head. "Balmarren, right? Where is that?"

"A major port city to the northwest," Seiryu said. "It's become the rebels' stronghold in that region. And I will. Now shoo."

Gabriel slipped out, his frustrations diffused. He let fire dance around his fingertips—a trick that hardly cost him any energy—to release the pent-up emotions as he slipped into the gardens behind the castle.

At first glance, the place looked dead. But Gabriel saw tiny, fresh green buds just peeking out. Piensor's seasons were ahead of Earth's. Here, spring was coming. In Chicago it was probably snowing. Millennium Park's paths would have to be shoveled, and Tilas would have been right there, making quick work of it. He'd been as constant a figure in the park as the Bean. Locals and even tourists knew he was there to be counted on if they needed help.

Gabriel had worked the gardens once, two summers ago. He'd tanned like his father, and his fingers had earned the calluses of hard work. It had felt good, working alongside his father.

His hedgehog-itzal sprang off his shoulder and disappeared around a pile of pots. Gabriel watched it go, and his good spirits dimmed again. Seiryu had promised to talk to Entya, but how long would that take? How long could his father and sister sit in a cell? With the rebels mobilizing in different regions of the country, Seiryu was usually too busy to spare Gabriel a moment.

Gabriel scowled at the path he walked. His frustration returned. He wanted to take action.

The itzal peeked out at him. *Then do something.*

Gabriel rolled his eyes. Like what? If he snuck out, they would catch him, and *then* he'd never be free. But if he could find the Gold Mark... maybe someone there was in contact with the rebels who held his family captive. Someone must know something about what the rebels were planning to do with his family.

You can't do anything. You're just a boy trying to be a hero.
You just like to sit in your anger and sulk and feel sorry for

yourself. You've accomplished nothing.

The anger raged. No, he *was* doing something. He *would*. He just needed to find the right time—

"You look far away."

Gabriel started. He turned as Odalys closed the space between them. She smiled. "I've been following you, and you never noticed." Akora stood nearby; her eyes were to the ground, but they flicked to Gabriel's itzal curiously.

Gabriel flushed. "Sorry. Just... a lot on my mind."

The princess looked up at him, her dark eyes searching his with a gentleness he hadn't seen there before. "What's wrong?"

"Nothing."

"I don't like liars, Gabe."

Gabriel rubbed the back of his neck. "There's still no good news about my family, and I hate not doing anything. Seiryu says it's too dangerous, but I hate being useless." *Again.*

"Well, it *is* dangerous."

"I can handle myself," Gabriel grunted, turning away.

Odalys laughed and grabbed his hand, pulling him back. "Don't be mad. I'm just saying Seir has a point. That doesn't mean you can't handle yourself."

Gabriel eyed her, too aware of how soft her hand was in his. "What does it mean then?"

Odalys watched him. She smiled a little. "It means I'd hate it if you got hurt." Her eyes held his a fraction longer than usual. "And don't ever call yourself useless. Your worth isn't dependent on what you can or can't do. You're kind, and you don't need to be somebody you're not."

There was a weird kind of silence between them. Gabriel's brain caught up and realized how close they were standing. How mostly alone they were, save for Akora, who kept her distance. He couldn't even sense where the itzal had gone. Her words struck something inside him, but they dissolved in a mist. Somewhere he knew she was right... but he needed to be someone else.

Odalys' eyes flicked down. Gabriel's eyes followed, moving to her lips. Gabriel felt his temperature rise.

"I'm not sure..."

Odalys looked up at him. "What?"

Gabriel swallowed.

Well, he needed to take a plunge sometime, if he was going to do it at all.

He leaned closer to Odalys. He expected her to lean back, but she leaned *forward*. Closer. Closer still—

Then the sound of footsteps crunched over the hard, winter earth. Odalys jerked back, her breath catching. Gabriel let go of her hand just as three people rounded the corner.

A stately woman flanked by two servants paused on the path. She was dressed in a way that declared her royalty, with decorum and refinement. Her blonde hair was pulled up into a complex style, with little braids weaving through it, that revealed two pointed elf ears. She held a tiny, swaddled baby.

"Mother!" Odalys hurried over. "You're up! How are you feeling?"

The woman smiled. "I am feeling quite well, Odalys." She turned to Gabriel, and it took him a second to remember to bow. The empress looked him up and down appraisingly.

"Gabriel," Odalys said eagerly, "this is my mother, Myra." Odalys flushed under the sharp look her mother gave her and averted her eyes. "And," she peeped at the baby, "my little brother, Khaiel."

"An honor." Gabriel nodded to the baby. "I'm glad you're both doing well. Odalys said he was born early."

Myra spared a glance for the baby. "He was, but he is growing well." Her sharp gaze returned to Odalys. "Do you not have lessons today?"

Odalys' excitement deflated. "But Mother—"

"Do not argue with me, young lady. Your tutors report directly to me. Your orders of secrecy have not gone unnoticed. Go." Myra's gaze then alighted on Gabriel. It was cold. "I would like to speak to Gabriel. Alone."

Odalys started to protest, but she trudged back to the castle, her slave in tow. Gabriel almost ran after her, if only to avoid her mother's steely glare. Had she seen? How much did she guess?

Was he fidgeting? Did he have any tells that would betray him?

A shock of horror flashed through him. Akora must have seen. If Myra asked her...

Myra turned to one of the servants and passed the baby to her. "Take him inside, both of you."

Oh, he was a dead man for sure. When they were alone, Myra looked at Gabriel. "Walk with me."

Gabriel resisted the urge to walk a little behind her, and fell into step as they walked in the slowly budding gardens. He wasn't sure what to do with his hands. Should he offer the empress his arm? Was he walking too close? Close enough for her to know what he'd almost done?

You haven't done anything wrong. You're overreacting. Gabriel exhaled slowly. *You only almost kissed the princess.*

"I'm told my daughter has taken quite a fancy to you, Gabriel." Myra broke the silence and Gabriel's concentration. "That the pair of you are nearly inseparable."

"I enjoy her company," Gabriel admitted. The understatement of the century, if what almost happened meant anything.

"I'm sure." Myra didn't sound very pleased. "Gabriel, you are aware of my daughter's position, are you not?"

"That she's a princess?"

"Yes. And as such, she is expected to behave like one." Myra paused by a little pond thawed by the sunshine. Gabriel stopped beside her. "She must become knowledgeable of the world and its workings, especially her role in it as heir to the throne."

The empress turned to Gabriel. "As pleased as I am that my daughter has found your company agreeable, I do hope you are aware of how important her studies are, and that you must remember *your* place, as well."

She knew. Gabriel was in for it.

But Myra walked on. "You and my daughter are not on equal footing, Gabriel." She looked at him. "Anything between you cannot—*will not*—happen. Elves and humans together... it causes problems, and it is not what our people do. I do not want my daughter caught up in that sort of scandal and disgrace."

Gabriel stamped down the heated words he wanted to say, and restrained himself to a simple nod and said, "Yes, Your Majesty."

Stay calm. You should have known this. You're nothing compared to her. She's so far out of your league she's in a different ballpark. You're a local neighborhood park trying to get into the Major Leagues.

Myra watched him. She smiled slightly, as if amused. "I have made you angry."

Gabriel blinked, startled. He tried to school his features. "No, Your Majesty."

"I do not appreciate liars, Gabriel."

"I'm still getting used to how everything works here," Gabriel lied, hoping she wouldn't notice. "How royalty and stuff works. It's still a lot to take in." He wasn't brave enough to ask about the elf-human part.

"You will, in time. Learning is part of all life." Myra walked on from the pond and moved to a new topic. "I've heard you have been making excellent progress in learning magic." She smiled. "That you've challenged my husband."

Gabriel ducked sheepishly. "Was I out of turn?"

"I do not dictate what my husband does," the empress said. "You have as much confidence as he does."

"I do?"

"He never let people tell him what he could or could not do," Myra said. "He was told he would not amount to much, and yet here he is, more powerful than his own father." She paused again to set an empty pot upright.

"Is that why you all left? Seiryu too?"

"Life among the elves was difficult for Seiryu and Yovak." Myra's face hardened briefly. "So, they made a new life for themselves here. Reinvented themselves with hard work and hearts set on doing good. I left when Yovak asked for my hand. By then, he was king." A soft smile flickered for the briefest second. "He is worthy of all he has accomplished, yet some days he feels he must do still more."

She looked at Gabriel. "You have the same magic as my husband, and you see he does not abuse the power it gives him. He learned magic when he had no money to his name, no reputation to speak of. He patiently built this empire from the ground up and earned his place. But he did not think himself above his status."

The idea was inspiring. Yovak had come from nothing, had been nothing. But then... he'd earned power. Influence to repair the damage done.

But the silence that followed carried an unspoken message.

"You have your goals. I see your enthusiasm to train and make the difference your father saw, long ago," Myra went on. "I expect you not to let these goals fall by the wayside."

They arrived at the back doors of the castle. Myra turned to Gabriel. "I am happy you and Odalys get along so well. I do not ask that you avoid seeing her, but that you help me remind her where her place is. And that you are mindful that yours is not the same."

"I can try," Gabriel promised, quickly blowing out the angry flame that rekindled. He offered a smile. "It was nice to meet you."

A smile twitched at Myra's lips. "And you, Gabriel."

The empress disappeared into the castle, leaving him alone. The rebuke, however veiled Myra had tried to make it, stung, and left Gabriel in a worse mood than before.

He slipped inside and to his room, thankfully devoid of Seleen this time. He grabbed the sword he'd been allowed to keep to train on his own, and left the castle grounds. He knew the route by now, but still found it hard to concentrate and not get distracted by the busyness of the city. There was still so much to see.

Now, he supposed, he'd have to do some solo exploring.

His shoulders slumped. Half the fun of exploring was who he explored *with*.

No... most of it.

Gabriel spotted Tesmir near a rack of gleaming swords. "Hey."

Tesmir looked up sharply as if startled, then relaxed. "Hi."

"Have time for a spar?"

Tesmir's neck craned back as he gave a dramatic moan. "You and your training. You've run me into the ground with exhaustion, Faine. You're worse than the captain."

Gabriel smiled sheepishly. "I have a lot of catching up to do."

Tesmir considered him. Groaned again. "I'm almost done here. Claim us a ring and I'll meet you there."

Gabriel found an unused training ring and paced its circumference, swinging his sword back and forth.

Myra was right. He should know that. He *knew* that. He wasn't royalty. Whatever had almost happened with Odalys *couldn't* happen for real.

But it *had* almost happened, and Gabriel couldn't help but think about what it would have felt like.

Tesmir met him, still grinning. "Did magic lessons go bad today? You look like someone crushed your dreams."

"No," Gabriel mumbled. "Just... other stuff." He shrugged. "What's put you in such a good mood?"

"Oh, I made it through a training session without Koranos lecturing me or ordering me to run laps." He smiled. "That's enough to make anybody happy."

They took up their positions, but Tesmir didn't give the signal to start. He watched Gabriel, curious. "But why do you not look happy?"

Gabriel chewed his lip. "What would you do if... if there was something you wanted, but someone else said it would never happen? That you're not anywhere close to being... worthy of it? Would you listen, or... not?"

It was a stupid question, but Tesmir seemed to give it serious thought. "You're starting to sound like a rebel, Gabe."

Gabriel glared, lifting his sword in mock hostility. Tesmir laughed.

"Well, I'd do it anyway, but I'm not one for much rule-following."

"Now who sounds like a rebel?"

"My point," Tesmir said, "is that I probably can't be the one to decide that for you. How much are you willing to risk?"

Gabriel considered this. How much *was* he willing to risk?

He was willing to risk his life for his family. Risk everything to make the life he wanted, the life he and his family deserved.

What if that life included Odalys? Was he willing to stretch himself for her, too?

"Come on." Tesmir swept his sword around. "Let's look busy so the captain doesn't put us to work."

21

PARKIT

By dinner, Lina and her boys weren't back. Lilly tried to channel her unease into her soup. It wasn't working.

"I'm going to go looking for them." Rune broke the silence, standing and grabbing his sword from the back of his chair. His brothers cast glances around the table.

Hakor rolled his eyes. "Rune, I'm sure they're fine. They had an escort with them."

"An escort does little against a band of Parkit's men," Rune snapped. "That errand should not have taken this long."

Kedmir looked up from a small sketchbook. "You trained these men yourself, Rune. If it was unsafe, or there was trouble their escort couldn't handle, they would go to one of the safe houses. I'm sure either we'll get word that they're staying overnight, or they'll be back soon."

"Your barging through the city will only agitate the people more," Isilmere added.

Rune scowled. Lilly reached out tentatively to tug on his sleeve, nudging him to his chair. "If they're not back in a few hours, then we can worry, yeah?"

Rune's jaw clenched, and he turned to leave.

Hakor sighed. "Who wants Rune-duty?"

"I'll keep him busy," Isilmere said, pushing up from the table. "Jek, send a few eyes and ears into the city."

Lilly chewed her lip. When the others finally trickled out to whatever business called them, she snitched a map from the war room and took it outside. The light was dying into the dark of night, and the warmth of the day was gone, but Lilly didn't mind. She could keep an eye on the main entrance and Rune, who stood under the little porch awning by the main building. Isilmere's attempts to keep his brother busy hadn't worked. His eyes were locked on the big double doors, his arms crossed.

Lilly traced her finger from Balmarren northward to the mountains that concealed the coastline. The thick forest she had been in only a few days before ran right up to them. Her fingers tracked a path through the mountains, stopping at a large, circular ridge with a raised platform soaring above a valley within the ridge. It was marked with hurried handwriting: DK Territory.

"Planning a tour of the country?"

The voice accompanied the shadow that slid over the map. Lilly craned her head back to squint up at the young man standing over her. His face bore no scar.

"Kind of," Lilly said evasively. "What's a DK?"

Hakor eased to the ground next to her, looking at where her finger still rested. "Dragon Keepers. They're a group who record the history of dragons. Some of them even ride dragons."

"Really?" Lilly's jaw dropped. Actual dragon riders. "How far are they from here?"

"A week at least on horseback, longer on foot."

Lilly scowled at the map. Hakor cocked his head. "You weren't planning to go there now, were you?"

She hesitated too long, and Hakor's hand dropped on the map.

"Are you—"

"No," Lilly snapped. She pushed his hand away. "Maybe. I don't know yet. They have something I need."

"What?"

Lilly glanced around, then looked at Hakor. He raised a brow. "I won't tell anyone."

"You have to promise." Lilly jabbed a finger at him. She glanced in Rune's direction. The man hadn't moved. Made no indication he even knew they were there.

"I promise," Hakor vowed.

Lilly pulled the amulet out from under her shirt. "This is missing four pieces. Seiryu has one, my brother has the second, and the dragons have the third. There's a stone too, but I'm not sure where it is yet."

"What does it do?" Hakor reached over and took hold of it. He started. "It's magic."

"And it can take Yovak's dark magic away."

Hakor dropped the amulet. It swung down and thumped against Lilly's chest. His eyes went to the amulet, then back to her.

"Have you told Isilmere and Rune?"

"I told Isilmere..." Lilly scraped at the sandy ground. The grains burrowed under her nails.

"And?"

"I wouldn't be plotting in secret if he'd been in favor, would I?"

"Probably not," Hakor agreed. His own finger traced a path from Balmarren to the mountains. "We could go right before the others move out, when everyone's too busy to notice."

"That was my thinking," Lilly agreed. "Wait, *we?*"

"You thought you could manage this all on your own?" Hakor smirked. "If you're right, that amulet could be a powerful weapon.

So why shouldn't we use it?" He looked at the map, then back up at her. "How do you plan on getting the piece Rothar has?"

Lilly stared at him, then shrugged. "I don't know yet. It's a work in progress." Her eyes strayed to the other Annor man outside. "Will he be alright?"

Hakor looked. "I'm sure he will... though it's not like Lina to be gone this long without sending word." He shook his head. "We'll either hear from them soon, or they'll walk right through those doors."

As if on cue, the doors opened.

Lilly scrambled to collect the map as Rune's arms unfolded. A lone messenger slipped in.

"Commander!" He held up a note. Rune stormed forward, and Lilly was impressed the messenger didn't flinch. She and Hakor stood, silent and unseen, as Rune tore the note open.

Barely two seconds lapsed before Rune seized the messenger by his shirtfront. "Where were they last seen?" he roared.

"Who?" *Now* the messenger looked scared.

"Rune!" Hakor reached them and pulled the messenger free. "What's wrong?"

"He has them," Rune said, his fingers curling around the paper. "Parkit has Lina and the boys." His voice almost broke. Lilly couldn't breathe.

Hakor took a step back, stunned. "How? How did he—"

"I don't know, Hakor!" Rune's voice rose again. Hakor flinched. "He has them now, and wants us to leave the city."

Lilly frowned. "Well, that won't be a problem. We're already leaving."

"Not fast enough," Rune growled. "He wants us to leave by dawn. We're not ready."

Hakor pushed him toward the main building. "We need to find Isilmere."

They found him with the council, going over plans. Lilly and Hakor followed behind Rune as he moved to the table and slammed the note down.

"This is on your head, Isilmere!" he roared. The council all backed away. Isilmere looked at the note.

"We all thought the errand was safe," Isilmere said carefully. "I didn't think—"

"No, you didn't," Rune cut him off. "You were too busy in here to think that Balmarren might still be dangerous."

Isilmere's face twisted in anger, but Rune wasn't finished. "I follow your orders, you know I do. But telling me to stay when my *family* could be in danger is one order I will not obey. I should not have obeyed!" Rune's voice was almost feral. "Gather the best fighters. I will be collecting my family."

Isilmere frowned. "Rune, it's too dangerous. Parkit knows the slums better than we do, and that's likely where he's keeping them. If you go, he'll be waiting. It's a trap."

"Then what do you suggest we do?" Rune snapped. "I know we can't leave tonight. We can't leave for another two days! Either we leave behind vital supplies, or we burn the bastard down now."

Isilmere said nothing. It took Lilly a second to realize what the silence meant, and she felt sick. Rune's body went completely still, the way it did right before he attacked in a spar.

"Rune," Isilmere said slowly, "we can't risk it either way. We can't leave this soon, and we're going to lose more men than we can afford if we try to find them. We don't know where they are—"

"So you would just let them die?" Rune's voice shook with fury now. "Tell me, Isilmere, if it was one of us, would you leave us to

Parkit's mercy? Let us die?"

Isilmere stiffened, but his voice was still calm. "If we go after him, we will start a war in the city, and innocent people will die."

"And if we don't, innocent people will die," Rune snarled. "My wife and sons will die. We can find them. Send out people to ask around, people who know the streets, who know Parkit."

"Anyone who knows Parkit will be too scared to help us," Isilmere snapped, his calm finally breaking. "He expects us to rescue them, Rune. Parkit is no fool. He knows we can't leave yet. The only option left to us would be to rescue them. He will be waiting, and men and women will die. If it gets into the main streets, all of Balmarren will suffer."

Isilmere met Rune's eyes without flinching. "Think, Rune. Use your head. Parkit expects us to come to him. If we don't, he may try something else. More demands, perhaps ransom. He knows if he hurts Lina or the boys, you will rain hell down until there is nothing left of him. And you're the one with the army. He likes to strike in the dark, in secret. He won't act unless he knows he has the upper hand. He wants the advantage. Don't give it to him."

"He has it." Rune's tone suggested he was ready to lash out at anyone who got too close. Lilly guessed the council knew it. They kept well beyond arm's reach.

"He thinks he does," Isilmere corrected. "He thinks that with your family, he'll have you under his thumb. He wants us to come to him."

Rune ran his hands through his dark hair. Lilly saw his anger crumble a little. "Isilmere, I can't lose them."

Isilmere didn't answer. Lilly hated that and wished he would. He couldn't promise anything. All they could do was wait.

No. We can't wait. I won't. Lilly's hand went to her hair, short and light now. Lina's voice echoed her words from that day. *Look for a way to fight the next battle without weakness.*

They were at the disadvantage now. Parkit thought he had them cornered, but he'd given them the ball, and Lilly wasn't about to make the weaker play. She'd never been good at waiting anyway.

Isilmere dismissed the council, leaving him and his brothers alone. Lilly left too, striding out of the room. If Parkit wasn't bluffing, she had tonight to act. She had seen the man's violence, his desire to make Rousen suffer. She snarled at the floor as she paced a few corridors over.

He wasn't bluffing. Parkit didn't look like the kind of guy who bluffed. Sure, he was looking for Rune to come running, but he would hurt Lina and the boys if that didn't happen. He knew *that* would bring Rune, and no number of rebels could stop him. Parkit wanted them crippled. Taking out Rune Annor would do just that.

Lilly rubbed her face. The panic and the looming clock counting down made it hard to think of a plan.

There had to be something... The rebels couldn't approach without Parkit knowing. They needed someone who knew the streets, the dark alleys Parkit and his cronies skulked in, well enough to sneak in without being seen.

And she knew just the man. Someone who could lose a tail in the streets and come right back to whip Parkit's butt.

She pivoted around and ran. She bolted past Kedmir, ignoring him as he called after her, and hurtled to the holding cells.

The guards were busy at a game of cards, and Lilly forced herself to slow down, to breathe. She had to look calm. She was just here to talk to the prisoner again.

Mordir's eyes tracked her movement as she entered, as if he'd been waiting for her. He sat on the floor, a tray of half-eaten food pushed to the side. He glanced at the guards and lowered his voice. "You look as if a ghost is after you."

"Parkit has Rune's wife and kids," Lilly said, ignoring the jest. "If we don't leave the city by tonight, he's going to hurt them."

"That does sound problematic. Is my execution moved up?"

"You were able to lose me in the city," Lilly said, stepping closer to the bars. She heard the guards laugh over their game. "You know these streets. You disappeared right before Parkit came." She watched him. "Have you had assignments in this city before?"

"That's a dangerous question to ask," Mordir said. "Why is that important?"

"Because you would know where to lie low," Lilly said. "You would know the best places somebody like Parkit would skulk around."

Mordir tilted his head back. "And what if I do? What good would my just knowing do you?"

Lilly balled up her fists. "Please, help me. Help us."

"Parkit's going to expect an attack," Mordir warned.

"I know," Lilly snapped. "But not if we have someone who knows the streets as well as he does. Use his advantage for our own gain."

Mordir lifted a brow. "You can't sneak a large company of rebels around the slums of Balmarren, love."

Lilly rolled her eyes. "No, but *you* can get a small team through."

"He's going to have men lying in wait," Mordir said. He stood and approached the bars. Lilly remained rooted in place. "If you're caught, he will do worse things to you than to Rune Annor's family. He knows your face."

"I'm not scared." A lie. A huge, fat one that Mordir saw the second it flew out of her mouth.

"Yes, you are, but I admire your bravado." He leaned a shoulder against the wall. He watched her. "Alright, here's our deal, dragonfire. I help you rescue Rune Annor's family, and you help me get something I want."

Lilly hesitated, eyeing him warily. The guards were still focused on their game. "What?"

"Help me kill the emperor," Mordir said, his tone slipping into a dark whisper. "Hang him, stab his heart. I don't care. Use magic if you have it."

Lilly resisted the urge to touch the amulet under her shirt.

"But he *dies*," Mordir finished, "one way or another."

Lilly pursed her lips. The way Mordir said it made it sound heartless, dark. But wasn't that what she wanted, too? Get rid of the man who had destroyed her family? She would have someone on her side who actually knew how to kill.

"And if you think about it," Mordir said, "you get even more out of this too." He smirked. "Your rebels win, and you rescue your brother."

"Done." Lilly said the word before she could reconsider.

Mordir's shoulders relaxed, and he nodded. "You'll need to bring my things." His eyes darted over her shoulder, then back to her eyes. "And if you need to, the small leather flask mixes well in wine, but I usually use it for my knives."

Lilly stared at him. "Is that supposed to make sense to me?"

Mordir shrugged and stepped away from her. "Don't take too long. Parkit won't."

Lilly turned to go but looked back. "Parkit knew who you were. That's why he ran, isn't it?"

"He knew because I told him." Mordir settled back, as if this were a casual conversation. "He wasn't about to give up that fight, so I gave him incentive. He decided his life was worth more than two rebels."

Good. He's a coward. The guards barely glanced her way as Lilly left, and she exhaled a long breath.

Now all she had to do was find a way to free a dangerous assassin from under the noses of the Annors.

22

INTO THE DARK

It didn't take long for word to get out about Parkit. Isilmere was nearly outnumbered by his brothers, but his order held. The twins were the only ones who seemed to side with their older brother, and even then, Lilly knew they hated doing nothing.

Lilly went about her mission quietly. She avoided the dining hall, where Rune and his brothers sat. They were keeping an eye on him, but it was only a matter of time before their brother snapped. His tone spoke violence, and the arguing escalated to shouting. Aderyn removed Tae from the scene almost immediately.

Lilly crept into the empty war room and found Mordir's things stored in a cupboard. She pocketed the ring and stuffed the assassin's weapons into a pack.

His words ran circles in her head. She found the flask and sniffed it. It was pungent, and she sneezed and nearly sloshed the stuff out.

It mixes well in wine? How was that supposed to help her with the guards? She needed them distracted. Putting them to sleep would be better, but she didn't have—

Lilly grinned wide. She glanced at the set of knives.

Of *course.*

Stealing a bottle of wine wasn't very hard, but opening it to pour the sedative into it was a hassle. She almost lost the whole bottle, but the wine did effectively mask the smell of the sedative. Once she accomplished this mission, she made a detour to the armory.

The sun had set long ago, which only made Rune more difficult to contain. Lilly found herself hating Isilmere for keeping him here.

She crept back to the cells, gripping the wine bottle tightly, and breathed slow. This would be easy. They wouldn't suspect a thing. She didn't know how long it would take, but if it worked as fast as it had when Mordir drugged Kedmir and Parkit's goon...

The guards looked up expectantly as she entered. Hopeful.

"I wanted to pass this along." Lilly pasted on a bright smile. She tried not to look at Mordir. "With all the excitement, no one's probably remembered to change your shift."

Lilly guessed right. The hope in their eyes dimmed, but they accepted the bottle. She strode back out, listening to the guards laugh and even offer a toast to late shifts.

Seconds later, she came back to find them slumped over the table. One had fallen to the floor.

Mordir stood by his cell door. "That was one of the most amusing things I've seen in a long time."

Lilly fished out the keys. It took her two tries before she got the door open. She tensed, expecting the Ghost to lunge for her. No one would even know. No one would find her body until the guards woke up or someone remembered to change the shift.

But Mordir walked out toward the guards instead.

"We're not killing them!" Lilly hissed.

Mordir rolled his eyes. "I'm not killing them. I'm buying us time. Help me."

After stuffing the guards into the cell, Mordir walked away without looking back. Lilly fished through her pack for his equipment and handed it over. Mordir slid the multiple knives into his strange harness, along with objects she didn't want to know the use for. He took his dagger and looked at her.

"Mine," Lilly said, gripping the handle of the dagger's twin at her side. "You left it."

Mordir glowered. "There was a ring, too."

Lilly handed it over. "Is it a wedding ring?"

He tucked it under his shirt. "If Parkit hasn't hurt your friend's family, he will soon, or send a final warning. We need to get moving."

They kept to the shadows. Outside, three rebels stood watch in the courtyard, illumined by a few torches set into the walls of the compound.

"Ideas, dragonfire?" Mordir's voice came close to her ear. She resisted the urge to swat him away.

"Distract them, or knock them out," Lilly murmured. "*Not* kill them."

"Contrary to popular belief, I don't kill people on a whim."

"Oh, of course not. You take the blood money first."

Mordir didn't answer that. "Wait here." He brushed past her and slipped into the deeper shadows.

For several long seconds there was silence. Two rebels turned their backs on the main gates, where the third stood watch. Lilly gaped as Mordir grabbed the third, hauling him into the darkness with barely a sound. Her heart leapt into her throat.

He's not gonna kill them. This is gonna be fine.

A couple heartbeats later, Mordir sprang out of the shadows again, silent as a ghost. Lilly flinched back, waiting for the alarmed cries, but none came. Both rebels crumpled at Mordir's feet. He dragged one into the dark as Lilly hurried over to help.

"You don't have to be so violent," she said.

"Would you prefer I lure them into the dark like a street prostitute?" Mordir countered.

Lilly rolled her eyes and turned to the compound doors to unlock and open one.

"Who's there?"

Lilly grabbed Mordir's arm as he reached for a weapon. Unvar appeared in the light of the torches. He took a step back when he recognized her. "Miss Faine? What are you doing out here? Who is—"

Mordir moved faster than Lilly could react. Unvar's confusion turned to horror as the Ghost lunged for him. The councilman scrambled for his sword, but Mordir got to him first, pushing Unvar into the wall and grabbing his throat.

"Mordir!" Lilly winced when her voice rose. She yanked at his arm and received a hard shove in return. Lilly snarled and swung her palm against the cut on Mordir's neck.

The Ghost recoiled from the blow, hissing in pain. He released Unvar, and the councilman slumped against the wall, hacking and sucking in air. The Ghost's face was contorted with furious hate.

He lunged again. Lilly darted to intercept, but another figure beat her there. He hooked an arm around Mordir to hold him back.

"That's enough!" Rousen grunted. "What is going on here?"

"What are you doing?" Lilly snapped, planting herself between the men. She prayed Rousen could keep Mordir restrained. "We're not killing anyone here! That's what I said!"

"Lilly, what is going on?" Rousen interrupted.

Lilly hesitated. "I'm going to rescue Lina and the boys."

"You—with *him?* Are you insa—"

"I can't sit around and do nothing," Lilly snapped. "Mordir knows the streets. He can get me in and out."

"And you trust him?" Rousen gave them both an incredulous look. "After what he just did?"

Not in the slightest. "For now, I have to." Lilly glared at Mordir. "Though the jury's still out." Mordir glared back.

Rousen looked at Unvar. "Do you know him?"

"No!" Unvar blurted. "I found them sneaking off, and this madman attacked me!" He stood, shaken and careful to keep Lilly between him and the assassin. "I don't know who he is or what he wants."

"Mordir?" Lilly prompted.

"We don't have the time," Mordir hissed. "We have to go."

Rousen turned to Lilly. "I can't stop you, can I?"

"Not really," Lilly said. "I don't think Parkit's bluffing. We can't wait."

"Isilmere has forbidden anyone to go out!" Unvar said, indignant.

"Yeah, well, I don't do orders well." Lilly looked at him. "So, if you'd be so kind, shut up and—"

Mordir wrenched free. Lilly yelped as he shoved her aside, his other arm bringing the end of his dagger down on Unvar with a *crack.* The councilman crumpled at their feet.

Lilly dropped to her knees by Unvar. "Mordir!"

"We were wasting time," Mordir said, his voice cold as he sheathed his dagger. The look he gave her was ice and exasperation.

Rousen rounded on Lilly next. "Lilly, this is insane. Do you even know where you're going?"

"Mordir does." Lilly looked at him as Mordir pulled Unvar into the shadows. "Rou, we can't sit around and hope Parkit's bluffing. He could have killed us just for stepping into his territory. As strong as Rune is, Parkit's angry enough not to care."

Rousen's jaw worked. He sighed, scanning the courtyard.

"Isilmere's going to kill us."

Lilly stopped halfway to the doors. "Wait, you're coming?"

"Either he comes, or I knock him out too," Mordir said. Lilly threw him a dirty look, which he ignored. He looked at Rousen. "You're still healing. If we get into trouble, you will die."

"If it means getting Lina and the boys back to Rune, that's fine with me." Rousen set a hand on his side. "I'm healed enough."

"How heroic of you." Mordir helped Lilly open the door. "I hope it's worth it."

The street was empty as they slipped outside. Lilly glanced around, making sure they were alone, and followed Mordir deeper into the city. It was eerie with silence, and Lilly didn't like the way her footsteps seemed to echo.

Mordir led them along the main road for a while, then veered down a narrower street. This one contained doors to a few taverns, where the lights were on and laughing voices thrummed within. The smell of liquor was heavy enough to reach the street. One even had music and singing. Its sign was so rotten all Lilly could read was "The Boar's Fart."

Outside, men and women loitered. Mostly women, who purred sensual words in Rousen and Mordir's direction. Lilly glowered at them. They gave her nasty sneers in return.

They walked on until they were completely alone, leaving the lights and noise of the taverns behind.

"Wait here," Mordir said. "Keep your backs to the wall, and your eyes on the road. If you hear anything, *don't* investigate." He looked at Lilly as he said this.

"What are you going to do?" she countered, but he slipped away, melting into the darkness.

"Report to Parkit, most likely," Rousen muttered, hunching

against the cold.

"He won't," Lilly replied. "He has too much to lose."

Rousen scoffed. "What does a man like him have to lose? Other than his life?"

"Is your life not enough to lose?" She didn't tell him about the deal she'd made. Rousen would have called off this mission in a heartbeat.

The assassin came back a few minutes later. His voice held a trace of deadly quiet that made Lilly shiver. "This way. I found your quarry."

They followed Mordir deeper into the slums. It smelled of waste and liquor and other things Lilly didn't want to identify. It made her head spin, and her throat choked on her own breaths. She grimaced and fought to keep her dinner.

Mordir stopped them a few turns later. "Parkit is just ahead. Now would be a good time to have a plan."

Rousen looked at Lilly. She dug around in her pack and pulled out the small, thick sack she'd stolen from the armory. "We'll spread this around. Either as a distraction, or a way to end his bullying for good."

Rousen spluttered for words and reached for the bag, feeling the bulge. "You *stole* some of the sun powder?"

"Yes, because if it works the way I think it does, it's going to come in handy." Lilly replaced the sack.

"We're *not* using it!" Rousen snapped. "That much could bring down the entire block. When I saw it used in Luminne we were in an *empty field*."

"I'm not going to use all of it," Lilly huffed. "Just enough to keep Parkit busy."

"That's not..." Rousen glowered at the sack, then at Mordir, like it was his fault.

"She's right," the Ghost said. "You two are going to need a big distraction to spirit away three people unnoticed."

"What about you?" Rousen asked warily.

"I can set the powder for you," he said. "Parkit knows who I am. He might even think I really *am* sent by Death."

Rousen snorted. Lilly nodded. "Let's do it."

After giving Mordir a small amount of sun powder, Rousen drilled them with instructions on how to light it, and Mordir led the way. Lilly followed, Rousen behind her. Lilly peered at the saggy house. The wood was old, support beams bowing under the years of weight. It creaked and popped in the wind, making Lilly jump.

The inside was no better. They entered a dirty, smelly kitchen. Lilly gagged, and Mordir gave her an unimpressed look.

The room was unnervingly empty. Lilly glared at Mordir. "Did you kill anyone?" she whispered.

"That's a rather broad question."

Lilly punched his arm, but he knocked the blow away. "*No*, I didn't. I kill only at your command, *Highness*."

Lilly was about to punch him again, but Mordir continued. "Parkit is just ahead. Your friends will likely be up those stairs."

Raucous laughter behind a door at the end of a long, dark hall made Lilly's skin crawl. She nodded. "Keep him busy. We might need a few minutes." *Because if any of them are hurt...*

"Don't take too long," the assassin said. Lilly turned to the stairs, Rousen's hand on hers to follow her. She *just* caught the sound of a door opening and closing, and prayed Mordir wouldn't screw them over. She wasn't so sure anymore.

Upstairs wasn't much better. The floor was carpeted, and Lilly tried to ignore the condition it was in. She crept along the narrow hall, trying all the doors they found. Most of them were empty.

"We'll never find them at this rate," Rousen said. "We're taking too much time."

Lilly frowned at the hall. "I'll go around the corner to try those, and you keep trying here. If we meet in the middle—"

A scream erupted up ahead. Lilly's feet were moving before she realized it, and she shoved her weight into a door already partially open.

It slammed into someone big and thick. A man cursed, stumbling, and Lilly reached around the door to bring the butt of her dagger where she thought a face would be.

A howl of pain, more curses, and something heavy thumped to the floor. There was lantern light here, and Lilly saw the large man cupping his ear, trying to catch the blood flowing from it.

"Lilly?"

She turned. Arialina and Eliam were bound hand and foot in the corner. Lierr lay at Lilly's feet, also bound, eyes wide with terror.

Lilly's breath whooshed out as Rousen barreled in. He hurried to knock out the incapacitated man groaning on the floor.

Lilly knelt to untie Lierr. When she'd freed his arms, he scrambled backward away from the man.

"Is Papa here?" Eliam whispered as Rousen untied him and Lina.

"No, but he's waiting for you," Rousen said, helping Lina up. She gathered her boys in her arms. Kissed Lierr's head. Eliam hugged his brother.

"We need to go," Rousen said. "Mordir can't keep Parkit busy much longer."

"I'm afraid I missed that appointment." Parkit's voice came from the door. Lilly whirled, and the man's hand closed around her throat.

23

CONTINGENCY PLAN

"Where is this 'Mordir'?" Parkit snarled, his grip tightening as his other hand wrenched away Lilly's dagger. Lilly choked, clawing at his arm when she couldn't reach his face. He looked at Rousen. "You're not the Annor I wanted."

Rousen held his swords in front of him, keeping between Parkit and Lina and the boys. "Let her go."

Parkit observed Lilly's attempts to free herself. "I was prepared to bring down the great Rune Annor himself. The emperor would have given me a handsome sum for his head. And yet all I get are the rebel necks I neglected to slit the last time."

Lilly grimaced as his grip tightened. "Too... bad."

She wrenched the bronze hair clip from her hair and jammed the edge of it down into Parkit's forearm.

Her aim was true, and Lilly yanked it the rest of the way, the gash running deep. Parkit howled and released her, staggering backward and clutching his arm. Blood already leaked over his hand, dripping onto the floor. Lilly rubbed her throat, wiping the clip clean on her pants.

Rousen cut between them, both swords out and pressed into Parkit's neck, keeping him against the wall.

"You touch my family again," he snarled, "and I will make you bleed until you have *nothing* left."

"A rousing speech, but we have to go."

Lilly stood and glared. "Where the hell were you?"

Mordir rolled his eyes. "Doing what you asked. All I found were a few of Parkit's cronies getting drunk and gambling away their fortunes." He looked at Parkit, eyes narrowing. "Was my warning not enough?"

Parkit's face paled. "Y-You work for them?"

"I work for whoever pays the highest, but that's not your concern."

Rousen looked at Mordir. "Did you set the powder?"

"No, because I couldn't find him." Mordir motioned to Parkit. "I wasn't about to set it for a bunch of drunks." He looked Parkit over. "But here we are... already defeated, and bleeding out, by the look of it."

Parkit's terror slowly twisted back into a sneer. "Maybe, but I won't be the only one who dies tonight." He laughed, loud and grating. "You invaded my house, but you've invited the enemy into yours." Parkit cocked his head, as if listening. "You should run along home, or the emperor will have your friends' heads before they can roll out of bed."

Horror hit Lilly in the gut. "An ambush?"

"He's lying, Lilly," Rousen growled.

"Am I?" Parkit laughed. "You'll hear the screaming soon enough—"

Lilly yelped as Rousen's sword swung at Parkit. The butt of the weapon cracked into the man's skull, and he crumpled, blood now leaching freely into the old wood floor.

Rousen silently stepped forward, tore off a strip of Parkit's shirt, and bound it tight over the gash. The fabric was quickly stained dark.

"Will he live?" Lilly asked.

"If his followers find him in time," Mordir said. "We have to go. If he's not lying, the rebels won't know what's coming."

The Ghost led them out of the building. The city bells controlled by the rebels were ringing, deep and thrumming and rippling over the rooftops of the city. They went back the way they'd come, but faster. Lilly struggled not to burst into a full run until they reached the main road, passing confused rebels on watch duty as they staggered out of her path.

"Lilly, wait!" Rousen yelled after her. "We need to be—"

The bells stopped. Lilly saw a red glow cresting the rooftops in the direction of the bell tower.

Lilly looked at Rousen. "They're setting the city on fire?"

"Probably just the tower," Mordir said. "Keep moving."

Rebels staggered out into the streets, eyes wide with alarm and confusion. Lilly ran faster. She had to warn the others, get them up.

A man burst out from a dark alley, grabbing her and bringing her down. Lilly cried out as she kicked and fought. Rousen was at her side, and threw a punch into the man's jaw, knocking him off her. An imperial.

"Go!" Lilly stopped Rousen from finishing the job. "He's out cold, leave it! Back to the barracks!"

But more and more imperials were coming out of their rat holes as more confused rebels stumbled from their beds. Many left their houses without weapons.

They didn't have time to realize their mistake.

How many soldiers were there? How had they gotten inside?

"This way!" Mordir yelled, pulling Lina and her boys down a side street. Lilly pushed Rousen after them, the war cries of the rebels roaring around them as they realized the danger.

A stitch in Lilly's side pulsed with every stride. They had to reach the compound. How many imperials were inside already?

The deeper they went into the city, the more imperials they found. Mordir had to take them around, closer to the harbor, to avoid the fighting. Lilly glimpsed rebels with no armor fighting ferociously against men *with* armor. They clustered around the imperials to pen them in.

Some succeeded. But Lilly saw many others cut down. Her heart filled with dread and her stomach twisted. They wouldn't make it.

Just a few blocks from Balmarren's harbor, they came upon another fight. Imperials had two rebels on their knees. A woman and a young man. The woman screamed for mercy as a soldier raised his sword to the neck of the young man, who glared up defiantly.

Lilly's terror exploded in her scream. "No!"

The imperials whirled. Mordir whipped past Lilly, her scream summoning him from the shadows. His dagger stuck into the throat of the would be executioner with an awful sucking sound. The young rebel grabbed the soldier's sword and sprang at the men holding the woman. Rousen joined them a second later as Mordir pulled the rebel woman out of the way. More imperials were running to them.

Lilly pushed Lina and her sons down another street. Getting to the barracks without the help of trained fighters would be too dangerous. "We'll hide in the docks. Go!"

They rushed through the streets without Rousen or Mordir, Lilly slightly ahead, peeking around corners before they ran on. Blood pounded in her ears, keeping time with her heart. Adrenaline fought the monster threatening to paralyze her at the sounds of battle, at the screams that rent the air.

Eliam cried out behind them. Lilly spun around to see him on his hands and knees, tripped by the body of a rebel. He stared at it, horrified.

"Go." Lilly stopped Lina. "I'll get him. Get to the docks, find a ship and hide in it."

Lilly ran back to Eliam. She squeezed between him and the body, ignoring how it felt against her leg.

"Hey," she said, taking Eliam's shoulders and shaking him. The boy looked at her numbly. "Eliam, you're okay. It's gonna be okay."

"I'm scared," he said. "He's dead, isn't he?"

"Yeah." Lilly swallowed the lump in her throat. "He's dead. But you're not. So you need to get up and *run*." Lilly forced his gaze back to her. "I'm scared too." She pointed back the way they'd come. "I hear sounds of fighting, and I remember my first battle. I came to this world in the middle of a fight, and I saw people die too. I saw my dad die."

Eliam's eyes were on her now. Lilly ignored the tightness in her chest. "There's something inside me that wants me to freeze and give up. But I don't. You know why?"

"Why?" His voice was so soft she almost didn't hear it.

"Because I can't," Lilly said. "I have people who need me. My brother's out there somewhere, and he needs my help." She pulled Eliam to his feet and turned him away from the body. "You've got your brother and mom to take care of now. I know you're scared, and that's okay. But you've gotta be brave too, and being brave means doing stuff that scares the living hell out of you."

Eliam nodded, wiping his eyes. "Lierr's older than me, though."

"So? My brother's older than me." Lilly pulled Eliam forward. "Even big brothers need help. Now come on. We'll find your mom and brother and then your dad."

"I don't think so, sweetheart."

The slimy, greasy voice froze Lilly in her tracks. She pulled Eliam close as Zal stepped from the shadows. He held a sword, and by his side was a six-legged itzal, the shadows forming jagged spikes along its spine. It morphed and swirled, its body never quite solid. It had a tail like a scorpion, and sometimes it split into two.

"That was a beautiful speech," Zal said. "Truly, I was touched."

"Didn't your mom ever tell you it's rude to eavesdrop?" Lilly spat, backing up as Zal advanced.

The man laughed. "I do love your fire." Zal inspected his blade. "Now come along nicely and give me the amulet. I don't have time to draw things out, unfortunately."

Lilly's hand almost went for her neck. The familiar weight was missing. She hadn't risked bringing it with her, and had left it in the barracks. Now, she wished she had it. If a soldier found it...

Lilly scrambled for a solution. The only place to run was back, and they would only find more fighting there. The street was too narrow.

"Give me the amulet!" Zal snarled.

"Come and get it then!" Lilly shot back, pushing Eliam toward a dark corner and drawing her dagger. If she could keep Zal busy, Eliam could run.

The itzal lunged for her.

A long, slender vine pierced right through its body, holding it in midair for a second before the shadows dissipated into nothing. Its hissing shriek vanished.

Zal swore. He and Lilly spotted Jek in the same moment, standing in a patch of lantern light. Zal frowned. "Was that supposed to scare me?" More shadow monsters emerged from the shadows, hunched, with long, wiry limbs and scythes jutting from their joints.

Jek said nothing. He stood in the middle of the street, and his hands twitched up. Vines burst from the stone, cracking it, and others slithered out from planter boxes under windows.

The itzals lunged, and Jek flung his arms forward; the vines charged in a storm of green and lashed among the monsters.

Lilly grabbed Eliam's arm. "Go!"

They darted past the weavers. Zal bellowed angrily, and sent an arc of lightning their way. Lilly recoiled, the magic light illuminating the street. Her skin prickled.

Another bolt pierced Zal's and redirected both into the wall. Lilly realized the shriek was her own when the stone exploded.

"You will die, seventh!" Zal roared.

Lilly hurtled for the docks, watching Eliam's back as he raced ahead of her. They broke out of the confines of the streets, into the open air. Fish and ocean struck her nostrils, and she scanned the dark ships.

"There, Eliam!" Aboard the Luminnian ship, Arialina's and Lierr's silhouettes leaned over the rail.

In the moonlight, shadows billowed up, twisting and expanding. Lilly skidded to a halt, memories flooding her. Fear nearly clogged her throat as she screamed, "Eliam, stop!"

The stupid kid didn't stop until the shadows dissipated. Zal laughed as he grabbed Eliam's arms, twisting him around. Lina screamed.

"Let him go, Zal!" Lilly snapped.

"Then give me what I want," Zal replied coolly. "And the boy won't take a swim."

"What did you do to Jek?" Lilly stalled.

"I don't leave sevenths alive." Zal sneered. "Surrender, Faine's daughter. You don't want an innocent child hurt, do you?"

Lilly's lips twisted back in a snarl, but she slowly bent down to drop her weapon. Her hand felt uncomfortably empty. She prayed he was lying, but her heart stung. If Jek was dead...

"There's a good girl..." Zal encouraged. "Now, give me the amulet, and we can go see your brother."

Lilly looked up. "Is he alright?"

Zal shrugged. "Last I saw he was alive." He grinned wickedly. "Can't say for how long, though." He gave Eliam a rough shake when the boy struggled again.

Lilly nodded, lifting her hands. "Let my friends go free."

"Of course."

"Lilly, get down!"

Relief had never felt so sweet. She dropped to one knee, bending low as long arrows of fire crackled overhead, flying for Zal's head. Jek stalked toward them, fury in his eyes illuminated by his fire.

One sweep of his arm, and Zal pulled water from the harbor onto the docks, shielding himself. The arrows fizzled out.

Zal snarled. "You hurt me, you hurt the boy."

The shadows began to move. Lilly stared as more hunched-over monsters with long limbs peeled away from the night shadows. They snarled and prowled toward Jek, their hands turning into needlepoints and sword blades. Their jaws curled back, and the shrieks they loosed made Lilly's heart falter.

Jek swept his arms up, and more vines shot out of the cobbles like rockets. The vines sliced through the itzals like swords, and a few of them disappeared. The rest screeched and backed off. Zal swore as red lilies bloomed on the vines, surrounding the itzals and releasing pollen that seemed to glow. Lilly stared, open-mouthed.

"I will kill you like I've killed your brethren," Zal roared. "And I've killed many over the years."

Jek roared. The pollen came faster. The itzals shrieked and tried to claw their way out, then they disappeared. The vines turned to Zal just as he summoned more itzals. Eliam let out a squeak of terror.

Lilly turned to him. She had to separate them.

With Zal struggling to fend off Jek, Lilly snatched her dagger again and ran for him.

"Lilly, no!" Jek's voice was filled with fear. Lilly didn't stop. Zal was too tall for her to reach his face, but she slashed at his arm just as he turned, startled out of his concentration.

The dagger bit into his flesh, cutting an angled gash down his arm to his hand. Zal howled, releasing Eliam and clutching his wound. Lilly pulled Eliam away and pushed him behind her. He clutched her backpack.

"You will die with the rest of them," Zal snarled. Fire burst in his hands, pulsing bigger and bigger—

With two swings, fireballs the size of exercise balls soared toward Lilly and Eliam. Lilly couldn't move. Her heart hammered. She was going to die.

Water arced up from the harbor, slamming into the fireballs with a piercing hiss. Lilly winced, holding Eliam close. Salt water splashed in their faces.

Vines burst up in a ring around them. Zal growled. "I want that amulet!"

Itzals shrieked and slashed with abandon. Others targeted Jek. Eliam sobbed, and Lilly gripped her dagger as the shadow monsters struggled to reach them. She slashed at any long, twisted limbs that broke through, but Jek's magic got to them first.

Eliam screamed, and Lilly whirled around. One of the shadow monsters had him by the ankle and dragged him to the edge of the ring, where the monsters had overtaken the vines.

"No!" Lilly darted forward. She grabbed Eliam's arms and pulled him to her chest, swiping her dagger across the monster's limb. The creature let go and snatched her wrist in the space of a heartbeat, jaws clacking. Lilly stabbed at it, but her knife went through it harmlessly. The beast pulled her out of the ring and pinned her down, while its friends fought off the vines.

"There now, was that so hard?" Zal smiled as itzals surrounded Jek. Two monsters had grabbed his arms and pulled him down to his knees, holding him there. One itzal had long, bony fingers around his throat. His sides heaved, and his body flinched with every blow to the vines.

Zal approached Lilly, blood dripping from his wound as it closed up before her eyes. Healed. "Now give me that trinket, love, and we can all go home."

"Let go of me!" Lilly demanded, struggling. Panic knifed through her. What would he do when he found out she didn't have it?

Zal ignored the order. "Just hold still—"

Jek roared. Lilly jerked her head around as the itzals caught fire. Startled, the monsters let go of him and tried to recover, but Jek was already running. He slammed into Zal as a vine pierced the monster holding Lilly. She rolled to her feet and sprang toward Eliam. Jek jumped into the vine ring with her.

The vines arced over their heads and plunged into the ground on the other side. They wove a dome over them, interlocking and twisting around each other, forming many deeply rooted layers. The space inside was tiny, and Lilly felt Jek's warm breath on her neck.

Zal laughed. "You think your magic can save you? I know your weakness just like you know mine, seventh!"

Lilly looked at Jek, fear rising in her throat. He smiled tiredly. "I've still got a few tricks." He nodded to the vines, and Lilly watched as a thin film of water thoroughly soaked them to a dewy sheen.

Eliam reached out and touched the thick wall of green. "They're all wet." His voice trembled with tears. "They can't burn now."

"Not right away, no." Jek shook his head. He winced as the dome shook, but it held firm under the barrage of fire that crackled and hissed outside. Lilly's heart pounded.

Jek started to speak, but a cry escaped his lips instead, and he doubled over, writhing and shaking with the effort to fight back. Lilly heard snarling and scratching on the other side. She heard more vines coming alive and snapping at the monsters, trying to replace the broken ones. "Jek, we need a new plan. You can't do this much longer."

"I can." Jek's voice was strained. "It's alright." He grimaced. He was too pale, and sweat dripped from his brow as he fought the pain. The little space grew warm, and Lilly could smell fire. Against dark magic and fire magic, Jek would die.

A second later Jek faltered. Water drops spattered on Lilly's head. "I'm sorry, I can't hold two at once anymore—"

"Hey, hey." Lilly supported him. "Just hang in there. The fighting is all over the place. Somebody's bound to find us, right?"

Jek nodded, eyes closed.

Zal's laugh came muffled. "Running out of strength, seventh? Hand over the girl, and maybe I won't make your death a slow agony."

The green dome shuddered as the shadow monsters attacked

again. Jek let out another cry. He was shaking. Losing consciousness.

Think, think, think. Lilly caught herself looking around, as if there were something she could use. But there was nothing. All she had was a useless dagger and a pack full of—

"Jek!" Lilly twisted, her nose bumping into his chin. "I have a really, *really* stupid idea that might get us killed, but if it works, it'll save our butts."

Jek frowned, then flinched at another wave of pain. "What... do you have in mind?"

She told him. Eliam's jaw went slack. Jek only looked resigned.

"We have to time it just right," he rasped.

"We're not far from the water. We can dive in." Lilly looked at Eliam. "Can you swim?"

"Yeah," Eliam squeaked. "What about Momma and Lierr?"

"Can they swim?"

"Uh-huh."

Lilly shimmied out of her pack and pulled the sack of sun powder out. "Then you've gotta run as *fast* as you can. Tell Lierr and your mom to jump in the water. Don't stop. You run, and you dive."

Eliam nodded, his eyes wide as he stared at the sack. Lilly turned to Jek. "On my count."

Eliam wiggled around so he faced the harbor. Jek did too. Lilly drew in a warm breath. Sweat dripped down her neck.

"Jek!" a voice cried. Lilly's heart skipped at least ten beats. Rousen.

"Who are you?" Zal snarled. "Another—"

"Now!" Lilly gasped. Jek roared as he forced the vines apart. They unraveled, swinging outward and lashing at imperials and rebels, just as they burst onto the docks.

Eliam shot for the water, Jek behind him, bellowing to the rebels to find cover. Lilly threw the sack in the air, as high as she could. Relieved that she didn't see Rousen, she ran for the water.

"Jek!" Lilly screeched, her feet pounding the weathered stone and wood planks. She saw Jek spin, seconds before his feet left dry land. He threw a flaming arrow at the sack while Zal watched in confusion.

Lilly reached the edge of the water when the world exploded.

24
THE BOY WHO
WANTED TO SEE
THE WORLD

A wall of heat and power shoved Lilly into cold darkness.

For a minute, Lilly drifted below the surface, her head throbbing in pain and her ears ringing. But the water was still and quiet. It was a comforting sensation. Dark silence.

Then her lungs reminded her she was not a mermaid. The cold tore through her, and the salt water stung her eyes when she opened them just long enough to locate the fractured light at the surface.

Lilly hacked up part of the ocean when she came up for air, flailing blindly for something to grab.

But instead of something solid, her limbs got tangled in a large sheet of fabric. She gasped and tried to push away the waterlogged flag, sinking briefly as she writhed around. One kick and flail later she resurfaced, coughing out salty water that made her tongue and throat shrivel. She just glimpsed a maroon banner as it bobbed and sank.

Someone grabbed her, and she twisted and slapped.

"It's me! It's me!"

Lilly gasped and choked, struggling to swim with Jek toward one of the support beams of the dock. Wood splinters dug into her fingers as she clutched it. Her breaths heaved.

"Eliam," Lilly gasped.

Jek's body shook hard, his arms straining to hold him up. He scanned the water and sighed with relief. "There."

Lilly looked and let out an unrestrained sob of relief. Arialina and her boys floated on thick pieces of wreckage. Lilly craned her head back to try to assess the damage. But all she could see was the fire's glow and occasional sparks lighting up the night sky.

"Hey!" The voice belonged to a stubbly-faced man looking down at them. "Hold on, we'll get you all up!"

A handful of rebels swiftly fished them out. They lugged Jek's limp body onto the dock. Lilly crumpled beside him, shivering despite the heat pulsing nearby. Lina came up next, hugging her boys and crying with them.

Lilly forced herself to survey her handiwork. The port was in ruins. Buildings were leveled, and fire spread to the ones beyond. Half the dock was gone, and several of the nearby ships were burning into their watery graves. Including Rousen's Luminnian ship.

Bodies lay scattered, imperial and rebel alike. It was too much like Murke, and Lilly squeezed her eyes shut against the scene.

Jek coughed and rolled onto his side, groaning. Lilly moaned and sat up, turning away from the destruction to lean over him. Jek didn't have the strength to avoid the water dripping from Lilly's hair, but his eyelids flickered open for a second. Lilly swallowed a sob, and a half-crazed laugh came out instead. "We're alive."

He grunted, eyes closing again. Lilly looked back. Rebels rushed to douse the flames, and others picked their way through the debris, checking bodies for life.

None.

"What happened here?" a rebel asked, awed.

Another shook his head. "Didn't see. Was almost to the dock when it happened."

Lilly hung her head, sucking in smoky air. She didn't feel like explaining herself.

Zal. Her head shot back up, but it was impossible to discern his body from the rest.

Or he escaped. Lilly scowled. How could he have? He'd been dumbfounded by their actions. He wouldn't have had time to escape, would he? Or had he raced for the water too?

More voices shouted across the dock. Rune and Kedmir burst into view, leading a squad of rebels. They halted in shock, taking in the damage. Rune's eyes scanned the dock until he saw Arialina. His cry was hoarse when he yelled her name, and Lina stood to let him hold her tightly to him and stroke her hair as she cried into his shoulder. Rune knelt and took his stepsons into his arms next, tears in the big warrior's eyes.

"Creator be praised," he kept saying as he pressed kisses to their heads. He then moved to Jek and Lilly. He looked Lilly over, a hand going to her cheek.

"Are you hurt?" he whispered.

Lilly could only shake her head, her hand still on Jek's shoulder. Rune turned to his brother, feeling for a pulse and relaxing when he found it. "What happened here?"

"Lilly and Jek saved us, Papa," Eliam said. He shivered in Lina's arms. "They used the sun powder."

Rune stared. Lilly ducked her head. For once there was no fight in her to be defensive. "Zal was here. I didn't know what else to do—"

Rune pulled her close. Lilly buried her face in his shirt, her sobs escaping when her body registered the safety there. Rune let her, rubbing her arm. "You're all alive. That's what matters."

More shouting erupted. Lilly peeked up to see Hakor, sword drawn, eyes wide and feral. But when he saw Jek, he dropped his sword with a panicked cry.

"He's alive," Rune said as Hakor slammed to his knees beside his twin. Roused by the noise, Jek stirred as Hakor cradled him to his chest. He mumbled something, reaching for his twin's hand. Kedmir's cry came next.

But his was one of terror and grief. It was more a wail. Kedmir had fallen on his knees beside one of the bodies. A young man with curly black hair.

Two swords lay nearby.

"Rousen!" Lilly's scream brought everyone's attention. She pushed to her feet, shaking, and tripped over her jellified limbs twice before reaching Kedmir.

"Is he alive?" Lilly gasped, falling again. Debris ground into her knees and palms. She hissed when a hot ember burned her. "Ked?"

Kedmir didn't answer. Tears welled up in his eyes. Lilly looked at Rousen and saw the wound.

Thick, jagged pieces of wood, like spears, lanced through Rousen's torso in two places. He grimaced, choking on his next breath.

"Rousen." Kedmir's eyes flicked over the wounds before locking onto his brother's face as Rousen slowly came to. "Stay with us,

Rou—"

Rousen's eyes fluttered; he looked at Kedmir and Lilly, fearful. He winced as Kedmir cradled his head on his lap. Lilly sobbed.

"You'll be okay," she promised. "You'll be okay."

Rune was there in seconds, followed by Lina. A rebel held Lierr and Eliam back. Hakor was protesting as Jek wavered on his feet, hurrying to them.

Rune knelt down next to Rousen, giving him a gentle smile before examining his wounds. His face fell. Lilly felt her chest constrict.

Kedmir saw it. "No, no. He'll be alright. He'll—"

A sob choked him off, and Rousen's shaking hand reached for Kedmir's. Rousen opened his mouth to speak but only flinched and coughed.

"Easy, easy," Rune said, his trembling voice softer than Lilly had ever heard it. "Keep still..."

Hakor let Jek sink to the ground before dropping too. He shook his head, panic in his eyes. Jek's eyes filled and he gripped Hakor's shoulder.

"Rou, please don't go." Kedmir's whisper cracked, tears rolling down his cheeks.

Lilly hated the helpless panic that clutched her. Hated how familiar it all felt. Hated the firelight playing cruel shadows over Rousen's face, making him look already dead. He tried to speak, but with each attempt he coughed, blood trickling from the corner of his mouth.

Jek laid a hand on Rousen's shoulder. "Shh..."

Rousen seemed to understand what was coming. He held the gaze of each of his brothers, communicating love with only small, trembling smiles. Hakor protested, and Jek held him. Rune wrapped an arm around Lina as she buried her face against him. Kedmir's tears fell freely as he begged his brother to hold on.

Panic welled in Lilly's chest, cutting off her air, urging her to save him. To do anything.

But she didn't move. She ignored the rubble digging into her knees. Her own pain meant nothing. She had seen Rune's hand slide away from examining the wounds. He hadn't tried to fix them. Rousen was dying. He was going to die. Lilly choked on a sob, on the panic that strangled her.

Rousen's body quivered as he made an effort to speak, but a spasm of pain cut off the first word, and a small whimper escaped him. He looked terrified but did his best to hide it with a weak smile. As if to say, "It doesn't hurt near as much as it looks."

"Shh," Rune murmured. "It's alright, Rou."

"There has to be something." Lilly's voice cracked. She turned to Rune. "He can't die."

Rune looked at her, his eyes dull and sad, as helpless as she felt. Hot tears trickled steadily down Lilly's cheeks.

Rousen looked up at Kedmir, then again at each of his brothers, as if committing them to memory one last time. His gaze faltered, skipping around as if looking for others. Lilly choked on a breath. Isilmere, Orrun. They weren't here. They should have been here. And the youngest, Tesmir. They should all have been here.

He looked at Lilly. A tear slipped down his cheek, and he gave her a shaky smile.

Lilly sobbed. There was more than friendship in that smile. Something he hadn't said at the wedding, and at the barracks before Eliam ran into him. Something he'd never get to say. And it killed her.

But he took a breath that made him wince, and spoke in a voice that was barely a whisper.

"Maybe..." he gasped, then tried again. He gave a tiny, tiny smile. "Maybe they'll be dancing..."

Rousen's body gave a small spasm of pain. His dark blue eyes drifted closed, and his grasp on Kedmir's hand slipped. Kedmir's sobbing plea went unheard as his brother's shaky breaths slowed and faded.

"No, no, no," Kedmir sobbed. His voice rose to a scream. "Rousen, please!"

Rune held Lina as she sobbed. Jek pulled Hakor close. Kedmir bowed over Rousen's body, his grief tearing his world apart. His body quaked with each shattering cry.

Lilly choked on a sob of her own, pressing a hand to her mouth. She inhaled a sharp gasp and raked her fingers through her hair, trying not to lose it. It wasn't working.

He can't die. Panic wrapped around her like a vise. *He can't. Not now. Not him. He can't be dead.*

Lilly couldn't stop the cry that escaped her, both hands pressed over her mouth. This couldn't be happening. Rousen couldn't be gone. That young man with the bright, friendly smile. Who would see the world and would take Tae with him. The young man whose smile had told Lilly what he hadn't been able to say. And she couldn't tell him anything in return. Because he was gone.

It was all gone. Just like that.

"We need to get back to the compound," Rune said quietly, his voice hoarse, as he pulled Lina up with him. She returned to her sons while Rune approached Kedmir. His younger brother resisted at first but gave in and let Rune guide him to his feet. Kedmir's green eye looked dull against the gray one. As if his life had left with Rousen's.

The twins had to help each other up. Jek's eyes met Lilly's, full of pain and anguish. Lilly bit her lip and started up, but he turned away.

I did this. Lilly looked at Rousen's body, more peaceful than he had been just minutes ago, without the unbearable pain. *I didn't give him time to run. He was still healing, he didn't have time.* Jek's words in Lilantami countered these thoughts. She shouldn't blame herself. How could she have known? Nobody had been prepared for any of it.

It didn't help much, but it did quiet the accusing voice in her head.

Someone touched Lilly's arm as the Annors made their way through the rubble and the burning. She drew in a breath and looked up to see a stranger. His eyes were soft, sad, as he offered something to her. A maroon-colored cord braided with a green one, and threaded through three silvery metal beads with strange symbols. The maroon matched Rousen's dark blood.

Her breath caught, but she took Rousen's bracelet. The one that was supposed to mean strength, the reminder for him and his brothers as they fought. She looked up to call Kedmir, but saw him already watching her. He glanced at the rebels collecting their dead, at the ones quietly moving Rousen. His dead, grieving eyes looked at Lilly again, then he turned and left.

Lilly clutched the bracelet. She tore her eyes away from Rousen's body and looked ahead, trying not to see the numerous other bodies they passed by the harbor. Too many. She hadn't meant for there to be this many, or this much blood. She hadn't meant for any of them to die.

But they had.

The walk back was slow and silent under the gray of dawn, and far too similar to another city, another trail of death. The metallic stench followed them. The perfume of war.

Rebels called to each other, yelling whenever they found a survivor. Lilly's gut clenched with the keening of a woman somewhere nearby. How many more wails would rise from the city?

How could this have happened? Who had let the enemy in?

Lilly wanted to find someone to blame. Someone to blame for Rousen's death, the deaths of countless others. The city was huge. The fighting was probably everywhere, was maybe still going on. She needed to find someone else at fault. Someone other than herself.

Yet there was no one else. Not that she knew of. Parkit, maybe, but she found no satisfaction in being angry with a corpse. If he was dead.

Death surrounded and trapped her. Each turn brought her face-to-face with more dead. Her father's face flashed before her, and Lilly grimaced. She fought to block it all out, letting herself shut down to avoid it.

She just wanted it all to *stop*.

25

A REMINDER OF WHAT IS LOST

The rebels opened the compound doors, not bothering with a password. The inside was chaotic, and blood stained the packed earth. Rebels hurried their wounded inside.

Rune separated from them to find Isilmere and any surviving council members, and Lina shepherded the others inside to get warm. Jek had fallen unconscious halfway to the compound.

The tables and chairs in the dining hall had either been shoved against the walls or piled in broken pieces, and the room had been transformed into a hospital. Rebels lay in the long room, bloody and hurt. Some looked too still.

"Kedmir!" Aderyn's cry drew her attention. Aderyn ran to them but stopped, looking at them each in turn. "What happened?" Her eyes locked on Jek's limp form.

Kedmir only shook his head, coming forward and hugging Aderyn as if she were the last thing death could take from him. Aderyn held him, eyes wide, and whispered gently as his shoulders shook. Lilly looked away. Hakor stayed close to his twin as Jek was lowered to an empty space on the floor. Jek was too pale, his body working too hard to breathe. How much had all of that magic cost him?

Aderyn hurried to Jek, looking him over, and Lilly found herself hug-attacked by a small girl with sunshine hair.

"Lilly, are you okay?" Tae demanded. She scanned the room, counting. "Rou and Isilmere and Orrun. Where are they?"

Dead, Lilly thought, but the word didn't make it to her voice. *Rou is dead. I killed him.* Isilmere and Orrun... were they dead too?

Does it matter? the voice asked. It was cruel, and it hurt, but Lilly didn't have the strength to fight it. *Everything is ruined. The rebels are in shambles because of the ambush. And you basically demolished part of their headquarters. You killed some of them.*

Lilly sensed people moving around her but not what they did or said. She didn't want to. She didn't *care.*

Someone helped her to bed. Aderyn. The numbness melted then, and Lilly told Aderyn everything. Her voice came in a rush, to race the grief that closed in.

She ended up sobbing as Aderyn held her.

But then everything was dark, and silent. Like the water. Only this time, Lilly couldn't escape the feeling of drowning.

Lilly awoke to her minor burns and old wounds in fresh bandages, and found a bath and clean clothes waiting for her. The bath didn't wash away the hollow feeling in her heart, but it did help her to focus.

"Afternoon." Aderyn smiled gently. Her gray eyes were rimmed with red, and her voice was soft with pain and exhaustion.

"Morn—what?" Lilly pulled up short, frowning.

Aderyn nodded to the window in the makeshift infirmary. "Long past morning."

Lilly could only nod. "Where can I help?"

I need to do something. To work and not think.

Aderyn pointed. "You can help me by checking on Jek. But mind you don't wake Hakor—he's been sitting up for hours with no sleep."

Lilly looked over where Aderyn pointed. Hakor lay curled on the floor, a blanket draped over him. Jek was awake beside him, sitting on a bedroll. He looked up as Lilly approached.

"Hi," she whispered. She nodded to Hakor. "How is he?"

"Tired, like all of us," Jek said, his voice flat, toneless.

"And you?" Should she sit by him? He didn't look like he wanted company.

Jek's face pinched, and he said nothing. He scratched at a spot on his chest.

They remained like that for a minute. Lilly picked at her bandage. She pulled in a breath and said, "Jek, I'm sorry—"

"We shouldn't have done it," Jek cut her off.

"I know. I should have waited. Given everyone a chance to run—"

"No, we shouldn't have done it *at all*." Jek's eyes met hers. Anger simmered behind the grief. "It was foolish. Why..." He looked away.

Lilly bit her lip. "I'm sorry."

"Sorry doesn't bring him back," Jek spat, glaring. "Go away."

Lilly started. "Jek—"

"Please." Jek's voice sharpened. "Please just go..."

Lilly backed up, guilt slamming into her, wave after wave. She left, ignoring Aderyn and Tae when they called to her. She found her way outside, where rebels were trying to patch up the barracks.

The walls were like jagged teeth in places, and piles of stone and wood supports had been stuffed between them. Buildings were patched with rough wood. There were no permanent fixes, she realized. They wouldn't be staying.

Rune stood overseeing the work and the packing. He looked more tired than ever, though his voice held steady.

Lilly moved to him, and he turned as she approached. He offered a small smile. "I wasn't sure if we would see you until we moved out."

She had no smile to return. "I need to be busy. Where can I help?"

"There isn't much to do." Rune sighed. "The last of the fighting ended a few hours ago, so I'm still receiving reports."

Lilly didn't want to ask her next question. "Isilmere and Orrun?"

"Captured," Rune said, his voice tight. His face had the same pinched look Jek's had. "A dark weaver took them ahead of the retreating troops by magic."

Zal. It had to be. Lilly bit her lip, mostly to keep from swearing, and also to keep down the monster rising in her chest, threatening to squeeze everything inside her. Rousen, dead. Isilmere and Orrun, as good as. Yovak would not be kind.

"I'm sorry, Rune," she whispered. *For everything.* "The dock. How many did I—"

"Don't." Rune stepped forward, wrapping his arms around her. Lilly clutched his dirty tunic, and her breaths hitched as she struggled not to cry. Rune stroked her short hair. "Don't think it, lass. You did what you had to."

"I could have found another way."

"There was no other way," he said softly. "In war, those choices are the hardest to make, because often they demand the greatest sacrifice in order to claim the battle."

"I didn't win anything. I killed him." A sob broke through her voice. Rune's arms tightened.

His voice hardened. "You saved Jek and Eliam, and Lina and Lierr. Rou wouldn't want you to blame yourself."

Lilly pushed her face against the rough fabric to hide her tears. "I'm sorry for going against orders."

"I know," Rune said. "I would have done the very same thing. I do not blame you." He tilted her head up. "Know that, and do not blame yourself."

Lilly nodded, but it was a lie. She did blame herself. She'd messed up *big time*. This was different than wishing she had done more. This time, she had done too much. The city might have been saved, but what had happened at the docks... That hadn't been a victory.

She hated herself for it. And hated that nothing she could do would fix it.

The city was now clear of bodies, but the streets still held the blood. Though rain would wash its presence away, Lilly wasn't sure if it would ever leave. Not really.

It was a chilly day, and Lilly hugged her cloak about herself as she stood with her friends and several of the rebels on the beach just outside the city. The sun was setting, blazing through the water in its daily finale. Lilly didn't see the beauty or awe in it like she had at other times. She didn't bend down to feel the coarse sand beneath her feet. She didn't care.

Some distance from the shore lay one of the wrecked ships, towed out by one that had survived the blast.

Lilly fought the lump rising in her throat. It looked eerie by itself, empty. The only movement came from the flag affixed to its highest point, the growing dark hiding the rebel stars and lilies. But Lilly knew the bodies of the dead rebels and imperials had been laid on its decks. This time, nobody argued against Rune's decision. Everyone was too tired to care. Too full of grief and shock.

The battle had just barely been won. Balmarren's natives had rallied with the rebels where they could, but a solid third of the rebel forces had been killed. Lilly didn't know how many civilian lives had been claimed, and she didn't ask. She had heard the grieving wails. That was answer enough.

On a small cliff nearby, Kedmir stood with a handful of archers, bowstrings drawn back. Rune gave the signal, and burning arrows flew to the ship, nearly all meeting the mark. The blaze was almost instantaneous, finding flammable materials and what oil the rebels could spare.

Lilly felt a sob stick in her throat and swallowed painfully, raking her fingers through her windswept hair and forcing herself to watch, to remember every second like a brand. She heard Tae crying somewhere behind her.

It wasn't fair. Rousen shouldn't have been dead. Isilmere and Orrun shouldn't have been gone. They should have been here. Did they know? They probably heard the explosion but couldn't know what happened, or who survived. Or who didn't.

I'm sorry, Rou... Lilly's chin quivered, and she bit her lip as the flames climbed.

Then Rune's deep baritone thrummed to life. The melody he sang was soothing. Lilly tried to focus on his words, letting his voice sink into her heart. He sang about going off to find fame and fortune, confronting all obstacles with courage. Even when facing death.

The last lines made Lilly's breath catch in her throat as she watched the fire slowly consume the ship of the dead:

"But wherever I may roam," Rune sang softly, "I will always return home..."

Lilly's heart twisted with the sudden urge to go home. She wanted normal things. Safe things. She wanted school, she wanted to hug Amber and feel her realness, to hear her jabber on about how cute Gabriel was, and whether Lilly could at least drop hints for her.

She wanted to smell car exhaust and greasy food. To taste nasty cafeteria food, and to listen to Gabriel express his distaste for pizza. Heck, she'd even be happy to see Dante again. Maybe she'd even apologize to him.

She wanted Nick. Lilly's breath caught again, his face swirling in the smoke of the burning ship. She wanted to feel *his* realness, to hug him and tell him she loved him more than life, to make him kiss her until she couldn't remember all of *this.*

She wanted a world that didn't feel as cruel as this one.

Lilly pulled in another breath, letting the smoky smell linger in her nostrils. She looked at Rousen's braided maroon bracelet in her hand.

She secured it around her wrist. The beads rolled over her skin, cold and uncaring.

A different reminder. A reminder of what was lost, of what she'd done.

The next day, the rebels split their time between packing and assisting the city in repairs, especially at the docks. They offered their help quietly, working with heads down. Anyone with a grudge was either in hiding or too nervous to pick a fight—the rebels had found Parkit's body, and that seemed enough of a warning to anyone else.

Lilly put distance between herself and Jek wherever she worked. He never spoke to anyone, and she didn't try to speak to him. Trying took too much energy. She needed it focused elsewhere.

The rebels would be marching southeast on Erriath in two days, but Lilly would go north. The amulet was the only way to make this end. She wasn't going to lose anyone else.

It didn't take much effort to find out if Hakor was still on board. He found her first, and asked when she planned on leaving. The plan was the same: they would leave right before the rebels did.

"Any sign of the assassin?" Hakor asked. He'd found her on the flat rooftop of the main building, a place she'd come to use for its privacy.

Lilly stared ahead. Mordir had disappeared. She'd noticed a while ago. The last she had seen of him, he was fighting alongside Rousen. But after that... no sign. Maybe he was gone.

No. He wasn't gone. She'd bargained with the devil. He would come back.

"How is Jek?" Lilly asked instead. She didn't feel like admitting another mistake. Rune had been furious when he'd found out about Mordir, but he hadn't given her a lecture. Yet.

Hakor shrugged noncommittally. "I don't know. He's distant even from me, and I'm not sure if that should scare me." He chewed his thumbnail, glancing at her wrist, at Rousen's bracelet. "I don't know."

"How are you doing?" Lilly looked at him. His dirty-blond hair looked unwashed, and his gray eyes dull. Without a scar, he looked younger than his twin.

"Like I could cut down a dozen imperials." His voice turned bitter. He shook his head. "So, we're going north, to the dragons?"

"Yeah," Lilly said. "Dragons. They have one of the amulet pieces."

"You think they'll agree to help us fight too?"

Lilly shrugged. "Can't hurt to ask."

Hakor nodded. "Rune says Erriath has catapults at the walls. We have people on the inside who will help, but if we have dragons too..."

The idea warmed. If they had dragons on their side, they could deal so much more damage. Lilly figured the fictional information she possessed about dragons came pretty close to being accurate. *Really big, strong, breathes fire, flies.*

Ahead of them, the rebel flag still fluttered. The stars winked in and out from its folds, and the lilies almost matched their brightness. A banner under which the rebels stood fast. Their reason to fight.

She exchanged a look with Hakor. He gave a slight nod. He was ready whenever she was.

26

TOO LATE

The tendril of shadow snapped toward him like a live whip. Gabriel swept his arm around, summoning an itzal and sending it forward. The creature's smoky mouth clamped down on the whip, jerking it away from Gabriel. He twisted his wrist and bowled a fireball at Entya.

His mentor dodged it only by a hair. Gabriel's magic sang with glee. Entya was becoming exhausted. So was Gabriel, but he was confident. This would be his victory, and his blood roared. He was getting stronger, powerful enough to keep up with Entya.

It felt... *great*. He was frustrated he had nowhere to use it, but that day was coming. He would find a way. For now, he reveled in the strength. His itzal leapt onto the battlefield, and Gabriel let it. Entya summoned her own to meet it.

The breeze picked up, and his focus wavered as a honeyed smell wafted to him. Gabriel blinked. He recognized the smell, but the subtler one, the one that smelled like springtime, he knew better.

Odalys and Eeris came around the corner of the gardens, stopping quickly to avoid walking into the sparring area. Entya had moved their training to the yet-untended gardens the past three sessions, to take advantage of the warmer days and fresh air.

Odalys' excited grin spread warmth through Gabriel's heart to the rest of his body, and a smile twitched at his lips. In her light yellow, flowy gown, she was just beautiful.

Oh man, was she—

His itzal shrieked at him. Gabriel whirled just in time to receive a faceful of shadow monster as Entya hurled it back at him. Gabriel yelped and landed on his back with the itzal on top.

"C'mon man," he wheezed. "Faster warning next time."

The itzal glowered accusingly and disappeared.

Real mature.

Cheeks burning, Gabriel sat up. Odalys giggled and waved as she and Eeris walked on.

He watched them leave, his duel forgotten as the springtime scent faded.

He had tried to follow Myra's warning. He encouraged Odalys to pay attention to her studies. He offered to help her—in the presence of a chaperone—when he wasn't busy.

But it did nothing to deter Gabriel's heart from pounding faster each time Odalys laughed, or smiled at him. They both remembered the day they'd almost taken that next step. They never spoke of it—too many listening ears—and from what Gabriel could gather, Odalys wasn't embarrassed by it.

And then there were days where he found himself wondering what it would have been like if it had happened. And his heart beat faster.

"You must let her go, Gabriel." Entya's voice stabbed his thoughts.

It took Gabriel a second to come back to himself. "What?"

Entya nodded in the direction Odalys and Eeris had gone. "You know it is not possible. She is heir to the empire."

"I know," Gabriel said, sharper than he intended. "I'm not... I'm not *courting* her or whatever."

"No, but your feelings are becoming more obvious," Entya said. "Should a suitor sense you are competition, it would make Yovak's position difficult."

Gabriel wanted to argue but pursed his lips. He'd hoped it wasn't *that* obvious. If Entya could see it, Myra would.

"Humans and elves were not meant to intermingle," Entya said as he picked himself up. "The elves forbid elf and human unions. Her suitor will come from her people, and you—"

"I *know*," Gabriel growled. "I don't know what their problem is, but I would *never*—"

"I know you would not," Entya said, her voice calm. "The servants and the court know you are an honorable young man. But the world does not know you. Yovak cannot have the empire soiled with scandal." Her expression softened. "Odalys must marry within her caste, and her people."

His heart squeezed. It hurt. "Yeah," Gabriel muttered. "And I'm in neither."

Still, anytime thoughts of Odalys threw off his focus, Entya would start in on why it wasn't right. Heaven forbid a human and an elf found love. They could do everything else around each other: talk, explore, be friends. Elves could *rule* the country.

But love? Out of the question. Disgusting.

"You are her friend," Entya went on, though Gabriel wished she wouldn't. "But do not let friendship be mistaken for love."

Too late. His mind replayed Tesmir's advice: How much was he willing to risk? He hadn't taken that next step. His heart wanted to say "everything," but common sense...

Well, common sense told him he'd be slowly murdered by Odalys' mother if he even breathed the wrong way in Odalys' direction.

Gabriel looked at Entya. "Fine. Can we keep sparring now?"

Entya watched him, obviously not believing him, but she didn't press it. "I have other business I must attend to. You've kept me here an hour later than I planned."

Gabriel didn't feel up to arguing with her. He collected his sword and waterskin from Seleen. Gabriel took a heavy swig as he walked. Entya followed behind.

While his tutor had become a welcome constant in Gabriel's life, a source of support and counsel, she sometimes harped on this stuff enough to test his temper.

But she was right. It wouldn't work between him and Odalys, even if they both wanted it. And while that day in the gardens had seemed like a pretty strong indicator, he wasn't sure if Odalys *did* want it. He wasn't sure he was brave enough to ask.

"Ah." Entya's voice interrupted his thoughts again. "Your other teacher has come for you."

Gabriel looked up to see Tesmir ahead of them in the main hall. Entya put a hand on Gabriel's shoulder. "Go on. I must make sure Cadrian is behaving himself."

Gabriel watched her retreating form before approaching Tesmir. "Did Koranos finally ease up on all the work he's been giving you?"

Tesmir's eyes had a far away look. After a moment, he answered, "Oh, no. Well, yes, but—"

"There you are!" Seiryu's voice changed Tesmir's open expression to that of a blank-faced soldier. Gabriel turned as Seiryu approached. The elf stopped, looking at Tesmir thoughtfully. "Annor, isn't it? What are you doing here?"

"I came to find Gabriel for our lessons, my lord."

"Lessons will have to be rescheduled," Seiryu said. He turned to

Gabriel as if that were his final word. "I have news."

Gabriel's heart thumped hard. His breathing stalled. His vision narrowed on Seiryu. Nothing else mattered. It had been two days, and there had been no word.

"Did they find Lilly?" Gabriel didn't miss Tesmir's gaze watching them. "My dad?"

"Our forces staged an ambush in the rebels' headquarters in Balmarren. Your family was there, but guarded by a seventh weaver. He overpowered our own."

Gabriel tried to ignore the way his gut twisted into unnatural knots. "The way you started talking, I thought it would be good news."

Seiryu glanced at Tesmir. "I was coming to that. We've taken two of their leaders hostage. They are on their way to their sentence, but if you have questions of your own, you may ask."

Gabriel felt an uneasy tingle in his spine. "Their sentence?"

"Forty lashes," Seiryu replied without any hint of pity. He looked at Tesmir again. "I believe, Annor, you will also find interest in these captives."

Gabriel looked at Tesmir. The soldier held very still as a cluster of armed soldiers came around the corner. There was a crack in his stony features. Something... worried?

It was gone in a breath. In the midst of the soldiers walked two men in dirty clothes. Captain Koranos stood at their head, and frowned when he spotted Tesmir.

Seiryu held up a hand and spoke first. "Annor," he said, watching the young soldier carefully, "I believe you know these rebels."

Gabriel turned to Tesmir, mind whirling. Tesmir's eyes had locked onto the prisoners, though his expression was hard to read. He recalled the conversation long ago. Tesmir was at odds with his brothers. His brothers were rebel leaders.

The taller and older of the prisoners had the same blond-brown hair as Tesmir, and held Tesmir's gaze steadily. The younger, with dark brown hair and dark blue eyes, just looked scared. He looked from one to the other, lips parted.

"Annor," Koranos growled.

Tesmir blinked and shifted. Took a breath. "Yes, sir. I know them."

Seiryu addressed the prisoners now. "Your brother has become a fine soldier of the empire. His progress has impressed even me." He smiled. "But come and greet them, Tesmir. I think it has been many months since you last saw each other." The elf watched Tesmir like a hawk.

Gabriel's magic stirred, excited. This was the enemy, the leaders. That was good, right? Without leaders, the rebels would collapse. It would be over.

"Hello," Tesmir said. His voice was steady, and he watched his brothers.

"Hello," the older man said. He looked Tesmir up and down. "You haven't been sleeping well. Is your conscience finally eating away at you?"

Tesmir's previously neutral expression shifted into anger. "I see yours hasn't. You dragged everybody else into an ambush that could have killed them all."

"At least I didn't abandon them."

Tesmir snorted. "Abandon? Is that what we're calling it now?"

Gabriel studied the prisoners, his hedgehog-itzal sniffing the air like it sensed the tension. The taller one's expression was stoic, his posture steady and confident. The younger man seemed to be trying to make himself disappear.

"These are the ones who have taken your sister, Gabriel," Seiryu said, turning to Gabriel. He motioned to the older, then the younger. "Isilmere and Orrun Annor. The mightiest of the rebels." He looked at Orrun and smirked. "Or, one of them is." He glanced at Isilmere. Isilmere held his gaze without flinching.

Gabriel's anger heated, his magic thrumming against his fingertips, begging to be used. He hadn't thought he'd be so angry, so... ready for a fight. But here, standing so close to the ones who *held his family prisoner*... restitution had to be paid.

"Why did you take them?" Gabriel asked. He waited until Isilmere looked at him. "What do you want with my family?"

Isilmere watched Gabriel, his expression exhausted but resolute. "We protected your sister from our *emperor's* henchmen." He glanced once at Seiryu. "She is safe, I swear to you."

Gabriel forgot to breathe for a second. "Just... just my sister? What about my father?"

Isilmere frowned. "Your father?" He looked at Tesmir, then Seiryu, then back at Gabriel. "Gabriel... your father is dead."

Gabriel stared at him. "No... you're—you're lying."

"I'm sorry." Isilmere's voice dropped, almost gentle. "He died the day you arrived in Murke."

Gabriel's gut twisted until he thought he'd be sick. He took an uneasy step back. This wasn't true, it couldn't be true. He would have heard about it. It had been *three* weeks. Three. He would have known. Would have felt it, wouldn't he?

"No, he's not." Gabriel shook his head. "I would know. I would have been told." He looked at Seiryu for confirmation, but the elf wasn't looking at him.

Seiryu looked almost... pained. But not in a way that suggested this was news to him. There was no shock, no great sadness at first hearing his best friend was dead.

"You knew," Gabriel said. "Seiryu, why didn't you tell me?" His magic stirred louder, and Gabriel realized he was shaking.

"I didn't know until I first received the report of the Balmarren attack," Seiryu said quietly. "I didn't know how to tell you—"

"So you let these people tell me?" Gabriel pointed at Isilmere. "I deserved to *know*! You had no right to keep that from me!"

Something was building in the back of his throat, and it was painful to swallow. Gabriel's breaths were shaking, threatening to overwhelm him with the thing now growing in his heart. He didn't want it. Didn't want it. No. This wasn't true.

Gabriel turned his glare on Isilmere. "How did he die?"

"Gabriel—"

"Shut up!" Gabriel snapped at Seiryu. He glared at Isilmere. "How did he die?"

Isilmere's eyes were sorrowful, pitying, and it only made Gabriel angrier. He didn't want a rebel's pity.

"It happened right before they took you," Isilmere said quietly. "He was protecting your sister."

Gabriel hated how he knew what Isilmere spoke of. He remembered it too well. It had been a nightmare for a few nights after arriving in Erriath. Nightmares that ended in a grave. A grave Gabriel found himself buried in too.

His father hadn't been dead when Gabriel attacked Zal, but how long had he lived after that? Gabriel's heart squeezed. Tilas had been dying, and Gabriel had left his side out of anger.

"We didn't kill him, Gabriel," Isilmere said. "Those weavers who took you were not ours. They were the emperor's."

Gabriel glared. "They were stupid defectors. I already know."

"Gabriel—"

"Did you even try to save him?" Gabriel choked out. "Did you even try to keep him alive? Or did you drag my sister away and leave him to die in the street?"

Isilmere stared. "No, no... we did all we could, but his wounds were too severe. He died minutes after we got them to safety."

"Safety." Gabriel scoffed, more to hide the gasping cry that almost escaped. "You call imprisonment safety? Tell me, do you feel safe now?!"

He wasn't even sure what he was saying at this point. He just needed to hold back the thing that was coming. That would come, though he didn't want to believe it.

This couldn't be real. This world... *this* was his father's home. It couldn't be this cruel and twisted. This wasn't how things were supposed to happen. Tilas was supposed to be alive, and safe. He would have the life he deserved. They *all* deserved.

Isilmere said nothing, and Gabriel wished he would. Wished he had someone to direct this anguish toward, someone who would talk back. Otherwise he might start swinging.

He swallowed hard. He heard Seiryu's order to take the prisoners outside. He jerked away when Seiryu tried to lay a hand on his shoulder.

"Gabriel—"

"What?" Gabriel glared at him. "You were too late, Seiryu!"

He was late? What about you? You left Dad to die, alone, while you ran at Zal like an idiot. You left Lilly unprotected in a strange world just because you were angry and thought you could be the hero.

He was no hero. He'd been too late. His magic couldn't bring back the dead as far as he knew. And he'd just *left* Lilly alone, to protect herself when the rebels came for her.

"Where is she?" Gabriel whispered. "Where is my sister now?"

Seiryu's voice was softer. "As far as we know, she is still in Balmarren."

Gabriel nodded, unwilling to risk arguing. The looming *thing* would crash down on him and he wouldn't be able to control it. It would be his first days with his magic all over again. Something big, something he feared.

He looked at his hands. He had good control over his magic now, but it simmered below the surface, ready to react to his slightest command. His emotions would drive it if he wasn't careful.

Seiryu watched him. "You don't have to watch—"

"I do," Gabriel cut him off. "I'll come."

"Are you sure?"

Gabriel was already walking, ignoring the question. Maybe he wasn't sure. But he needed to see justice done. Something to tell him his father's death wouldn't be left unavenged.

Tesmir fell into step beside him. "Gabe, I'm so sorry—"

"Don't," Gabriel growled. "I'm not in the mood for pity."

His magic growled at Tesmir, but Gabriel held it in check. It wasn't Tesmir's fault. If anything, Tesmir was a victim of this stupid war too.

In the half-square just outside the gates of the castle wall, men and women had already crowded around. Unease slid down Gabriel's spine when he saw two wooden posts on a metal base, an iron ring on each for the shackles on Tesmir's brothers. But it was replaced by anger, and something... different.

Justice will be dealt. A taste of what you can accomplish once you find Lilly.

Seiryu waved a man over. He wasn't a large fellow, but the coiled whip made Gabriel's stomach flip.

"Gabriel." Seiryu's voice was almost careful, as if he expected to be shut down again. "Would you like the honor?"

Gabriel started. "What?"

"These men left your father to die," Seiryu said. "I think it's only fitting that you deliver vengeance."

Gabriel glanced at Tesmir. His friend wasn't looking. He stared at his brothers. But his expression wasn't angry. It was... sad?

"Gabriel?" Seiryu prompted.

Gabriel looked at the proffered whip, a little uneasy.

But something whispered in the back of his mind. *Do it.*

27
SETTING AN EXAMPLE

The whip was still held out to him. Gabriel hesitated but reached for it. His magic thrummed: *Justice. Justice.*

They left your father to die, and they dragged Lilly away. You wanted to protect her, and make a difference in a world that leaves an innocent man to die in the street? This is where you must begin. Set the example.

The rebels were bullies, and it was time Gabriel started doing something more about bullies than he had before. Stop waiting for somebody else to put them in their place for him.

No more would he be useless to the ones he loved.

Set an example. His magic brushed against his mind, a soothing balm against the grief that he was struggling to fight, to deny. *They will be your first example. Lilly is still out there, but who knows what state she's in? Isilmere may have been lying. Set the example now, display your power, and word will get back: the rebels who hold your sister captive will not be spared, just as they didn't spare your father.*

Gabriel's jaw clenched, and his fingers tightened around the whip's handle. He stepped past the man, walking toward the shackled rebels. The crowd around them whispered and pointed, looking at Seiryu, then back at Gabriel.

Let them talk. Let them speak of Gabriel Faine, who delivered a message this day: he was coming. And he would be a storm of his own making.

Isilmere glanced over his shoulder at Gabriel. If he was alarmed, he didn't show it.

"Gabriel," he said softly, "please. Does any of this make sense?"

No, it didn't. It was cruel and confusing and Gabriel hated it.

And Isilmere was part of the problem.

His magic stirred, but Gabriel ordered it to heel. No magic this time.

"Please, don't do this," Orrun begged, watching Gabriel move behind Isilmere. "Gabriel, don't, don't—"

The whip cracked faster than Gabriel thought he could make it. It landed as solidly, and Isilmere jerked, groaning.

Gabriel froze, horror sluicing over the rage and grief. His whip hand seemed to reverberate with the blow.

The strike tore clean across Isilmere's back, and the blood seeped from the long line. Isilmere's breaths turned ragged as he righted himself. Orrun was curling in on himself, not watching.

Gabriel couldn't move. Couldn't raise the whip for a second blow. He could only stare, horrified.

No. This wasn't what he wanted.

He wanted justice. He wanted to squash the rebellion just like Yovak had done.

But not like this. He would set an example in other ways. Not by whipping a helpless man chained to a post in the middle of the city.

"I can't..." Gabriel whispered, taking a step back. He looked at Seiryu almost nervously, but the advisor's eyes had softened, as if he understood. He beckoned Gabriel to him. Gabriel's feet obeyed, and he returned the whip to its owner when prompted.

"I can't." His voice refused to go above a whisper.

"It's alright," Seiryu murmured. "It's alright... go back inside."

Gabriel nodded numbly and turned his back on the scene. His mouth felt dry, and he couldn't move fast enough to avoid hearing the whipmaster continue. The crack, the following groan.

He glanced once at Tesmir. His friend and teacher didn't look at him, his eyes on his brothers.

You wanted justice. This is how justice is dealt.

Maybe, but this wasn't how Gabriel wanted it. His mind replayed the last time he'd seen his father. Lying in the snow, his coat smoking and burnt, his body wracked with wounds and pain. Gabriel didn't remember a lot of blood, but it had been three weeks since that day.

Three weeks... Tilas had been dead for three weeks. And Gabriel never knew. Believed he was alive, healthy. Believed Tilas would heal his wounds and wait for the right time to escape with Lilly.

Gabriel barely heard the whip cracking over and over, and his breathing heaved as the castle guard closed the doors behind him. Silence settled over him on the outside, but inside his mind and heart were screaming. He hurried to an empty hall as he gasped and struggled not to fall apart.

Those were just dreams now. Ideas he could only wish were true. Ideas that finally made the tears squeeze out, blurring his vision.

Ideas of his father training him in magic, helping him understand it more and more. Ideas of seeing him and Seiryu reunited and introducing him to Tesmir and Odalys. Or asking him for all the stories he had told, and then all the ones he'd never told.

Gabriel choked on a breath. He'd never hear those stories now. He'd forgotten most of them, and now he found himself clawing at whatever scraps of memory he could find.

Dead. His father was dead.

Gabriel loosed a roar, unable to hold it in anymore. He ignored the guards that came running. Ignored Seleen. The tears fell fast, unstoppable. He wasn't supposed to lose both of his parents. That wasn't how this was supposed to be!

"No..." Gabriel pressed his forehead into the cool stone wall. But it didn't help. The tears came anyway. Faster, faster—

"Gabe."

He choked on a cry and looked up. Odalys stood before him, still in her yellow gown. She looked ethereal. The guards were still there, but at a wave of the princess's hand, they withdrew out of sight. Seleen left too, casting Gabriel a worried look before disappearing.

"What happened?" Odalys hurried to Gabriel, closing him in her arms. He hugged her tight, squeezing his eyes shut as if he didn't want to see the world anymore.

Her hand stroked his hair. "Hey... what happened? What's wrong? Are you hurt?" She pulled back, searching his face. "Gabe?"

He shook his head, letting her press her forehead to his. He opened his mouth to speak, but a small sob escaped him.

"Shhh..." Her fingers traced over his face. He had stubble there. He'd forgotten to shave that morning. But her fingers hovered over the stubble, *just* lightly grazing it.

"What happened?" she whispered.

Gabriel started to speak, but his lip quivered. He shook his head just as Odalys pulled him close again.

"He's dead." He hated how small, childlike, his voice sounded. "He died that day we came. I didn't know. I don't know—" He sobbed, and Odalys hugged him tighter. It was comforting and safe. It kept him from falling apart entirely.

Lilly's still out there. The thought skipped through the suffocating grief. *She's out there, and now she doesn't have anybody. We're all we have left.*

Fear struck him, and his magic hummed in response. Gabriel pulled back, taking a deep breath.

"I'm so sorry..." Odalys whispered. "Your father?"

Gabriel could only manage one tight nod. He wiped his eyes on his sleeve, but the tears still fell. "I saw rebels, the ones from the ambush. They said he'd died—"

Another sob choked him, and Gabriel scowled, pacing away to regain his composure. It wasn't working.

Odalys took his hand again and turned him around to face her. Gabriel hiccupped on a sob as her hands cradled his face, and her forehead rested once more against his.

"Shhh..." she whispered. She peered up at him, catching his gaze. Gabriel's heart, for all the pain that threatened to crush it to dust, beat a little faster. Her breath was warm against his face, making his skin tingle.

Entya's warning whispered into his mind. They shouldn't be alone like this. It would ruin Odalys, and it would cause more problems. And Gabriel would probably be murdered by Myra. Brutally.

This was crossing a line he had promised not to cross.

Gabriel started to pull back. "Lyss, we can't..."

"Can't what?"

"This..." His face felt suddenly bare without her hands there. "It won't end well. Humans and elves..."

Odalys considered him. "What if I don't care?" Her eyes searched his. "What if I don't care... and we can figure it out as we go?"

He stared at her. She didn't *care*? Didn't care that just standing this close, alone, would be enough to condemn them both?

You don't care either, though.

Odalys made him feel anchored, focused. She brought order to his mind when everything was flying in disarray, falling apart.

No, he didn't care. He really, really didn't care. His world was falling apart with no way to stop it, but Odalys was one of the last threads still intact.

One step was all it took to close the space between them, and he kissed her. Kissed her before he could second-guess himself.

Warmth raced through him, up to his face and his ears. His lips tingled. At first he forgot to breathe, but then it came back to him, and he kissed her. Her lips were as soft as her fingers, and tasted like... he wasn't sure. But they were nice. He stepped closer and felt her breathing quicken.

He felt her smile against his lips, and she kissed him deeper. Gabriel's spine tingled as his hands touched her waist, his mind racing with pleasure that blanketed the pain, just for a little while.

They pulled away a moment later, though Gabriel's breathing didn't slow. He watched Odalys.

She smiled at him. "About time. I'd started to wonder if I would have to order you to kiss me."

Gabriel smiled. "It wasn't... bad?"

"I don't have anything to compare it to." She kissed his cheek. "So, it was perfect."

Gabriel's skin tingled, and he stepped back. His breath shuddered out, and he wiped his eyes. "Sorry... that might've been poorly timed."

"You needed it." Odalys reached for his hand, squeezing it. "I should go... Mother's expecting me for lessons, and if I'm late she'll be suspicious." She hesitated. "Will you be alright...?"

Gabriel tried to smile. "I don't know..." He withdrew his hand from hers. "Three weeks... and I didn't know..."

"You couldn't have known," Odalys whispered. "The rebels probably kept that information closely guarded. The ambush made them vulnerable."

Gabriel nodded quietly, and this time forced a smile. "I'll be okay by myself. You can't get in trouble, and neither can I."

Odalys nodded and started to walk away, but she stopped and looked back. "Gabe?"

"Yeah?"

"Are we really doing this?"

His lips still tingled. "I want to." He left it open to her, to back out if she wanted.

"I want to," Odalys repeated. And she disappeared.

Alone again, Gabriel reached the safe confines of his room and curled up in bed, still fully dressed.

But Odalys wasn't there to help hold the dam, and it burst.

He prayed the pillow was enough to muffle his sobs. By itself the thrill of the kiss wasn't enough to help him control it.

Had Gabriel looked up from his grief, he would have seen his magic, pulling at the shadows to cover him in blackness. A cocoon to hold out the rest of the darkness that was rebels and death and a world that didn't care.

The kitchen had seemed like a pretty safe hiding place. Somewhere he would be left in peace.

But there he was, sitting with a dish of spiced meat wrapped in pastry dough, when Seiryu limped carefully down the steps and into the room.

"Your slave told me you were down here," was all Seiryu gave for explanation.

"Seleen probably thinks I'm a wreck who needs watching." Gabriel pulled off a piece of the meat-pastry and popped it into his mouth. He didn't look at Seiryu.

Seiryu glanced around the kitchen. It was spotless, ready for the morning's work. "How long have you been in here?"

Gabriel shrugged. "An hour, maybe." An hour after his tears had finally dried up, and his pillow was thoroughly soaked. Somehow, he'd blasted straight past crying himself to sleep to being too emotional *to* sleep. Eating had seemed the only logical thing to do. It worked for Lilly, so he didn't see the harm in trying.

"I need to apologize to you, Gabriel," Seiryu began. "I should have told you about your father, and I am sorry I withheld it. I will not offer excuses again, only my apology."

"It's fine." Gabriel shrugged. "I would have found out either way."

Seiryu frowned but seemed satisfied by the answer. He sat down at the table with a small sigh. "I've spoken to Entya..."

Gabriel looked at him mid-bite.

"She has agreed to let you accompany her as she hunts for the Gold Mark."

"Really?"

"If you still want to."

Gabriel nodded. "I do. What will I be doing?"

Anything. Anything but standing around remembering I failed.

"You will stay close to Entya," Seiryu warned. "Most of the work is simple investigation. We have yet to engage them in battle of any kind, or even discover their favorite haunts."

Gabriel nodded. "I'll do it."

Seiryu smiled. "Good. I will let Entya know. It will be good practice for you, I think." He watched Gabriel, his smile slipping. "How are you doing?"

Gabriel ducked his face to his plate. He exhaled shakily. "I really don't want to start crying again... I don't want this to hurt so much."

He heard Seiryu stand, and the elf's steady hand on his shoulder was comforting. Neither spoke, and Seiryu left him to his thoughts and food.

Seiryu's offer only helped a little. It tempered the self-pity Gabriel had fallen into. Gave him a point to focus on, to work toward.

He would find these rebels that lurked in Erriath, and he'd make them all pay. They might not have been there in Murke, but they were on the side of the war that left Tilas to die, and that was enough.

Gabriel let his magic wrap around him, a reminder of how far he was willing to go. His father had died for them, died trying to keep them safe. Gabriel would live or die fighting for Lilly, but either way...

Those rebels had messed with the wrong family for the last time.

28

LEAVING

Balmarren was growing more and more agitated, everyone frantic with preparations for their departure. It felt like the fuse had been lit for another sun powder explosion. The rebels didn't have much time to get out before it went off.

Lilly and Hakor worked quietly to prepare for their own mission, but nobody seemed to notice. Rune hadn't been able to flush out the spy who had let in so many imperial soldiers—there had to be one. No one knew where to start looking, and it put everyone on edge. Who could you trust when you weren't sure where the threat was coming from?

After directing the rebels to pack, Rune would stay in the war room long after dark, poring over maps and plans, safe from suspicious eyes. No one said why, and it wasn't necessary: if Isilmere and Orrun were tortured, their old plans could be revealed.

The rebels needed the amulet as bad as she did now. Jek still avoided her and everyone else, and Rune's and Kedmir's tempers were short as they rushed to make new plans. Desperation was rampant, and they needed a stroke of good luck.

Still, every time Lilly thought about her own plans, she hesitated. Did she really want to kill someone? Add another name to the list?

Parkit had been different. She hadn't given herself time to think. It had been in self-defense, and in defense of Arialina and the boys.

This time, it would be purposeful. A conscious and planned act.

He's killed hundreds, the monster whispered from its corner. *His death will save hundreds more lives.*

Making fresh plans and preparing to move out took a day longer than Rune and Kedmir had hoped. As they worked out new routes and strategies, Lilly helped Aderyn and Tae load their smaller carts with supplies. The loaded carts were kept clustered behind the main compound building.

Someone grabbed Lilly's arm as she turned from her cart. She spun around. Her eyes widened in shock.

"Mordir!"

"Shh," Mordir hissed, his face nearly hidden in his cowl, and glanced behind her at Aderyn and Tae, who were busy working with Lina on their next round of Cart Tetris. He pulled Lilly behind her cart, and she jerked away, punching his arm. Mordir flinched. "Ow! What was that for?"

"For leaving." Lilly glared at him. "Where have you been?"

"Lying low." Mordir crossed his arms.

Lilly narrowed her eyes at him. "You sure took your time coming back. The imperials have been gone a few days now."

"You can be suspicious all you like. I've come to make sure you hold up your end of the bargain."

"Yeah, yeah." Lilly shoved another crate into the cart she was working on. "I'm going north."

"Erriath isn't north."

"Is it not?" Lilly huffed. "I *know,* but if we're doing this, I have to go north."

"For what?"

Lilly flicked her amulet into view for a brief second. "This can take his dark magic. His life goes along with it."

Mordir lifted a brow. "You sound like you've made up your mind on the matter."

"Yep." Lilly climbed into the cart and shoved things around to avoid looking at him. Something deep down compared her to the assassin, and she shoved that aside too. She wasn't doing this for money.

Mordir watched her in silence, hidden by the cart. Lilly looked over to the others. No one had noticed Lilly's slowed pace. Yet.

"Killing someone changes you," Mordir said. "I won't make you help me if you don't want to."

"Where's this coming from?" Lilly cocked her head. "Are you backing out?"

"No." Mordir shook his head. "But I'm giving you the chance to. I know what happened at the docks. You're in shock, you're grieving—"

"I'd be doing this even if the docks hadn't happened," Lilly snapped, her voice dropping into a snarl. "Whether or not I made a deal with you."

Because it already has changed me. Her heart ached, and she took a minute to breathe before speaking again. "And since when do you care? You kill for a living."

Mordir pursed his lips, but said nothing. Lilly turned to him. "Yovak has to go, or more people will die. People I care about. He has my brother, and he killed my father. He's the reason Rousen is dead." She stood. This time, she didn't care if he saw her tears. "So I'm going. You can come if you like."

Mordir watched her, his own expression closed off. "You're going alone? You'd never come back."

"I have someone coming with me." Lilly paused. "How did you even get in here?"

Mordir smirked. "Trade secrets. When do you leave?"

"Tonight," Lilly said. "Hakor and I are leaving tonight. The rebels are leaving in the morning." She glanced back. "Wait by those little buildings over there, and I'll have you meet Hakor now."

Mordir slipped away, avoiding other rebels hard at work. They didn't take any notice of him. No wonder he'd been able to sneak in. Rune would have a fit.

Lilly found Hakor with Jek, packing tents into another wagon. "Hakor!"

Hakor turned and lifted a hand in greeting. Jek didn't look up. Hakor finished tying his knot and jogged over. "Everything alright?"

"Can I talk to you?" Lilly glanced at Jek. "Alone?"

Hakor followed Lilly to the small buildings against the back wall of the compound, used mostly for storage. She stopped when they were out of sight and frowned. "Well, he *was* supposed to be here."

Someone moved out from behind one of the buildings. Hakor went for his sword. Mordir reached inside his cloak.

"No, wait!" Lilly stepped between them. "Hakor, this is Mordir."

"The *assassin*?"

"...Yes."

"The one who tried to *kill you twice*, then saved you, and who you freed—"

"I know how this looks." Lilly glared at him. "But he can help us."

"Absolutely not!"

"He helped rescue your rebels in the fight, and he helped rescue

Lina and the kids," Lilly hissed. She crossed her arms. "He's coming."

Mordir watched Hakor, easing his hand from his cloak. "I am sorry about your brother."

Hakor's jaw clenched. He stepped around Lilly and right up to Mordir. The assassin watched him calmly. He was a little shorter than Hakor, and had to look up.

"Why do you want to help us?"

"Yovak threatened people I care about," Mordir said. "Just as he has yours."

"If you make one wrong move—"

"I'm sure you will try." Mordir was still but not tense.

"We leave tonight," Hakor said. "Be here by—"

"Please tell me you aren't serious."

Jek's voice was cold and almost accusing. Lilly whirled around, startled. Hakor's twin stood behind them all, his gray eyes dark under bent brows.

"You're leaving?" Jek looked at Hakor. "Why?"

"Lilly asked me to," Hakor said.

"With the emperor's dog?" Jek looked at Mordir, his hostility growing.

Lilly stepped between him and Jek. "He's coming with us."

Jek scoffed. "And where exactly are you going? Rune's not going to let you go off by yourselves with an *assassin*."

"I'm going to stop Yovak." Lilly crossed her arms. "And fix the amulet to take Yovak's dark magic."

Jek stared at her. "Are you *crazy*? That is the most fool thing I have ever heard!"

Lilly started to speak, but Hakor cut in. "Lilly's right, Jek. This dark magic is quickly becoming our only chance at winning this war. Taking Yovak's greatest strength will either kill him, or cripple him enough to be captured."

Jek stared at him, then at Lilly. "Then I'm coming with you."

Lilly forgot her next line of argument. "What?"

"If you're going dark magic hunting, you need someone who can fight it," Jek said. His features softened when he looked at Hakor. "I can't lose anybody else..."

"If we play this right," Lilly said, "we won't."

Jek held Lilly's eyes steadily. "Revenge won't bring anyone back."

The pain in Lilly's heart flared. "This isn't about revenge. This is about stopping a monster who's hurt us both, before he can hurt anyone else." A half-truth. Lilly held Jek's gaze when he said nothing.

"So," Mordir said, breaking the silence, "that will be four making up this party? Should we invite anyone else, just in case?"

Lilly glared at him. "We'll meet at the north gate of the city tonight. Can you find us horses?"

Mordir nodded. "I can. You're going north?"

"To the Dragon Keepers." Lilly ignored Jek's incredulous stare. Mordir lifted both brows but didn't protest. Lilly forced an uncertain smile. "I've never seen a dragon up close. Gabriel will be so jealous."

The preparation had left Lilly bone-tired, but the adrenaline at the thought of leaving surged through her.

Dinner was a silent affair. Aderyn joined forces with Lina to drag Rune out of the war room so he could eat and sleep before they left Balmarren in the morning. Kedmir's eyes were dull, and he responded very little to anything Aderyn or Tae said.

Tae's smiles weren't really sincere, though she tried her best. Aderyn walked as if she'd lost her purpose. Lilly hadn't seen any of them cry since Rousen's death, but she saw the sleepless emptiness. Saw the red around Hakor's eyes. Heard the dry sound in Rune's throat.

It hurt to watch. It hurt knowing *she* had done this to them.

She left the table early, and no one stopped her. She rechecked her pack, filled with supplies she had filched throughout the day. The amulet was tucked safely under her shirt, and her father's journal was bundled in an extra set of clothes.

She crawled into her cot fully clothed, her back to the room, and waited for Aderyn and Tae to go to sleep. It felt like hours before their breathing slowed to the steady pace of sleep.

Lilly waited a few minutes longer before slowly creeping out of bed, wincing every time her cot creaked. The girls didn't stir. Lilly pulled her pack out and slipped into the hall. She crept past the empty war room and through the kitchen door.

She tried to ignore the painful squeeze in her chest at the sight of Orrun's workspace.

Out the back, Lilly darted across the cart-packed space and to the far wall, where a small door stood unguarded. Or it would be, after the twins left their guard posts.

"Ready to go?" Lilly whispered when she joined the Annor twins at the door.

Hakor nodded. Jek watched her, his face... closed off. He looked away before she could speak.

The city was dark, silent, tense. Jek led them through the streets to the northern gate unchallenged.

It was closed.

"Someone's coming," Hakor whispered.

The cloaked figure glanced around before slipping around the corner to the gatehouse with four horses.

"Did you kill anyone?" Lilly emerged from hiding.

Mordir jolted and spun around. He cursed.

"I could have killed *you!*" He wrenched his hood back. "I've got the gates unlocked, but I'll need help working the winch."

Lilly turned to the gate tower. "We can do that."

Mordir showed her and Hakor the gate's winch, and they set to work. Lilly tried to ignore the unconscious bodies draped over a table, cards strewn across its surface and on the floor.

The gate groaned, its gears and pulleys squealing against each other beside Lilly's ears. She winced at each sound until they had the gate just open enough to let them out.

Lilly hurried back outside only to skid to a stop. Someone else stood beside Jek. Someone small, with sunny hair.

"*Tae?*"

Tae turned at Lilly's voice. "Lilly? What are you all doing?"

"What are you doing here?" Lilly demanded. "Go back to bed!"

"I followed you," Tae said. "You left your bed and I thought I would keep you company, like you did for me on Rune's wedding." She paused, her voice dipping into a soft quiver. "Are you leaving?"

Lilly knelt by Tae. She took a slow, calming breath. "For a little while, but we'll be back as soon as we can."

"Lilly, you don't have to go. It's not your fault, what happened."

Lilly's next words clogged in her throat, and she hugged Tae. "I know..." *Lie.* "But this will help everyone."

"We need to go," Mordir said as he untied the horses.

Tae whirled. "Mordir."

The assassin visibly cringed. Tae stared at Mordir, then Lilly.

"Why is he going?"

"He's going to help me," Lilly said.

Tae looked at Mordir again. "Are you?"

Mordir hesitated. "I am..."

"You tried to kill her."

"I know."

"Are you going to again?" Tae's voice became a *fraction* harder. Lilly wasn't sure what scared her more: that tone, or the fact that Tae had turned to completely face the assassin.

"We don't have time for this," Jek hissed. "Tae, go home."

"No." Her voice steadied, and she squared her shoulders. "I want to come too."

"No!" Lilly, Jek, and Mordir blurted. Lilly turned Tae to face her. "You're not coming!"

"I can help," Tae said. Her voice dropped to a whisper. "I can help with Mordir. I know him better than you do. He won't hurt you when I'm with you."

Lilly couldn't find an argument. She remembered how he'd reacted when she asked him why he'd rescued Tae. It had been only for a second, but his mask of sarcasm and arrogance had slipped. For whatever reason in his murderous brain, he cared about Tae. Cared about her innocence. Or so it had seemed. Something inside him was soft to her.

And if Lilly said no, Tae would probably tell Rune. Or Aderyn. Lilly wasn't sure which would be worse.

"Alright," Lilly said. "You can come."

"Are you insane?" Jek asked. "When Rune finds out—"

"We'll be long gone before he does," Lilly said. "And what would you do, just send her back? Then Rune *will* find out."

Tae grinned. The little brat.

Mordir swung up into his saddle. "She'll have to ride with someone, if she's coming."

"She'll ride with me," Lilly said. She smiled at Tae. "Sisters stay together, yeah?"

Tae's lips parted in an O, then spread into a wide smile. The half-elf scampered to the horse, and Hakor boosted her up first, and then Lilly behind her.

"Hold her tight," Hakor told Lilly.

Lilly was beginning to regret volunteering. Horseback was bad enough by herself, but now she was in charge of a horse *and* Tae?

When everyone was mounted, Mordir and the twins looked at Lilly expectantly. This was her mission. It was her call.

"North," Lilly said. "To the dragons." She turned her horse to the darkness outside, and the beast surged forward. The sound echoed through the city streets for only a breath before the horses' hooves were muffled on grass and soil. She heard the boys follow, and after Jek's magic vines had eased the gates shut again—with far too much squealing—they left the faint glow of Balmarren and rushed headlong into the dark open country. Only the ocean wind followed them.

Please let this journey be boring and full of petty arguments. Just this once, nothing exciting.

They kept off the main roads to avoid imperial tolls, and tried to avoid any little villages or towns along the way. The less they saw of people, the better, so they rode along the coast. The sea breeze blew in sharp and clear night and day, and the waves were a welcome noise at night when conversation was lacking. It was lacking a lot. The Annor twins and Mordir kept out of each other's way, only speaking when they had to. Not even Tae could coax a conversation out of them.

Lilly fingered the beads on Rousen's bracelet, watching Jek's frequent glances in Mordir's direction as the assassin sharpened his dagger. If Mordir noticed, he pretended not to.

When it started to rain three days into the quest, Lilly and Tae won out in the argument for sheltering in the next town or village. A place that had civilization, hot food, and dry rooms.

No way was Lilly camping out in the *rain*. It tasted mildly salty, and made her hair feel stringy.

The village they found was just a few hours from the mountains, a few miles away from the coast. Despite how quiet and empty it seemed, Mordir was agitated. His eyes darted to any and all movement, and he was more preoccupied than Lilly had ever seen him.

He barely seemed to register Tae's hand slipping into his after they dismounted.

The spring rain was cold and harsh. Lilly shivered and cursed at it as they walked through the mucky street.

"Keep your heads down," Mordir said.

Lilly soon saw what he did: soldiers. Their armor gave them away as they too hurried to find shelter from the rain.

When they reached the inn, the group hustled inside. Lilly was the last to enter, but she stopped just shy of the door, under the stoop. She turned, looking at the rain.

Rain.

Her first rain in Piensor.

"Lilly." Jek emerged from the warmth inside. "What are you doing?"

Lilly held out her hand to the rain, the drops plinking off her fingertips.

"When I was little," she said, "I'd go outside in the first rain of the year. I wouldn't wear a coat or anything. And the first thing I'd do was look up and open my mouth to as many drops as I could fit."

Lilly was alone in the street besides Jek, so she took a step out from under the stoop. She lifted both arms wide, tilted back her head, and drank of her first Piensoran rain. The faint bitterness lingered, but she didn't care. She savored the flavor.

When she'd taken her first swallow, she *smiled*. She shook her hair back and turned to Jek.

"Then I'd jump in puddles until I was soaked," she said, "but to heck with that, I want fire and food and sleep."

Jek chuckled as she barreled past him inside. Lilly sighed with relief at the little communal fire in the corner of the main room. Hakor, Mordir, and Tae were already sitting by it.

Hakor paid an exorbitant amount of money for rooms for themselves and stalls for the horses, but nobody complained—it came with meals.

While Jek went back out to tend the horses in the adjoining stable, Lilly wrung the rainwater out of Tae's hair, then scrunched her own hair like a sponge. The rain made her hair look more dark auburn than red.

The fire itself smelled smoky and thick, but it was warmth and Lilly wasn't going to complain.

"It's cold," Tae chattered.

"I know." Lilly wrapped her arms around her. "You'll warm up soon. And food will help."

The boys returned with dinner, and there was silence while the hot meal was consumed. It definitely wasn't Orrun's cooking, rather tasteless and a bit tough, but it was hot. Lilly was keenly aware of the innkeeper watching them, specifically Mordir, but when they calmly ate their meals, the man wandered off to a back room. The other patrons had been curious at first, but now the dining room buzzed with conversation.

Lilly glanced at Mordir. "Does he know you?"

"Doubt it." Mordir sipped his broth. "I try not to leave familiar faces in my wake."

Jek gave him a warning glare. Tae was busy watching Hakor carve eyes and a nose into her crusty bread. It made her giggle, and the sound brought a smile to Lilly's face. Laughter had been minimal during the trip, and it sounded so... normal. Something that hadn't been tainted by war or shadows. Not yet.

The food eaten and their bodies warmed, Lilly's party went to their rooms. They were tiny, with only two beds each. Lilly left the boys to figure out who didn't get a bed and pulled Tae into their room. It was drafty, so the girls ended up sharing a bed.

Tae was asleep in seconds, her breathing steady and soft. Perhaps having been a slave had taught her to fall asleep in any conditions. Lilly almost envied the skill. She tried not to move around too much, but sleep didn't come as easily as it had for Tae. The rain pounded against the walls and the little window, a rhythmic lullaby; but the cold, and the dark and unknown future drove the peace away.

Lilly stared at the ceiling. What would she do if she found the dragons? Asking them for the piece of the amulet was risky. They might know what it did. Or, worse, they'd lost track of it. After all, it was a tiny piece of glass, and dragons were supposed to be huge, weren't they? Big enough for people to ride, at least.

This scenario was far from comforting. Lilly scowled and rubbed her face. *Stop thinking about it and sleep, you idiot. Worrying won't make things better. You'll just be a miserable, sleep-deprived brat—*

The soft click of a door and creaking floorboards cut into her self-lecture. Lilly frowned at her door, but the creaking walked away from her room. The sound had come from right next door, from the boys' room.

At first, Lilly figured it was one of the boys in search of a toilet, but the way the innkeeper had looked at Mordir, and the assassin's nervous behavior the whole way to the inn...

It was stupid. So incredibly stupid. *Again.* But Lilly eased herself out from Tae's snuggle, soothed her when she stirred, and crept to the door.

29

THE GOLD MARK

Gabriel groaned, smushing his face into his mattress. He shifted slightly when he heard the crinkle of the parchment. Groaned again.

When he felt sufficiently woebegone, he peered up at the map again, sitting in the late evening light that filtered into his room.

It was as detailed a map as he could get. Gabriel hadn't explored all of Erriath yet, and seeing the entirety of it on a map... there was still so much more to see. The city was surrounded by two walls: the outer wall, which admitted people from the outside to a thin strip of land that seemed to house the stables, smiths, and tanneries. The inner wall was next, and that led into the city proper.

And the Gold Mark could be *anywhere*.

It had been three days since he'd started searching. And he had no idea how many hours of sleep he'd had since. He needed to keep busy, avoid thinking about...

Gabriel ground his palms against his eyes, breathing slowly. He'd lost track of how many times he'd cried, how many times he'd had to escape people to be alone.

Three days without a breakthrough was taking its toll. Gabriel was starting to wonder if this network of rebels had decided to simply... disappear.

He'd visited every site where the Gold Mark had attacked, but not even the places where the network hit provided clues. The only similarity was they all had a connection with the military. Beyond that, the attacks were random.

The search team consisted of Entya and Cadrian as the leaders, with a motley of other dark weavers and a few soldiers. All the dark weavers Gabriel worked with wore black metal armguards, engraved with Yovak's crest: a three-headed snake with wings, a sign of power, strength, and ferocity. Gabriel made a mental note to find a pair for himself.

Cadrian's mood had darkened when he found out Gabriel would be assisting them, and he made sure everyone knew it. Gabriel fell for the bait a few times, and they bickered until Entya threatened to take them both off the team. Gabriel ignored Cadrian's subtle jabs after that.

Gabriel scanned the map again and had started looking for something to write with when a light knock on the door drew his attention. Before he could get up, Seleen answered it.

The slave looked at Gabriel. "Her Highness, sir."

Gabriel motioned for him to move aside, and stood to greet Odalys.

"Hi." Odalys smiled up at him. "I promise, on my honor as a princess, that I, Odalys Zilfanden, have finished *all* of my work, and Mother has given permission to explore the city again." She glanced at the map on his bed, then at him. "If you want. There's still a bit of light left to go out." She started to reach for his hand, but stopped herself.

"Thanks," Gabriel said, "but I'm busy."

Odalys' face fell. "Busy? But you just got back from searching with Entya all day. What are you doing?"

"I'm just busy, Lyss." Gabriel ran a hand through his brown hair. "I'm not searching now, but I'm trying to figure out where else to search."

"Oh." Odalys frowned, then her smile returned. "I can help."

"How?"

"I don't know, but you look like you could use it." She started to walk past him to the map.

"Odalys." Gabriel caught her waist but quickly moved to her arm when he remembered Seleen standing by the door. "I don't need help."

Odalys stepped back. "Are you upset with me?"

"No," Gabriel sighed, slumping onto the bed. "Sorry, I just... I don't need help. And I can't go out today."

Odalys narrowed her eyes at him. "You've been busy for three days. I barely see you anymore."

"Well, we're both supposed to be busy." The sting wasn't entirely intentional, but Odalys looked a little hurt.

"You're acting different," she said quietly. "You act... I don't know."

"Well, my father died and I didn't know until recently, so I'm gonna act a little different." Irritation started to rise in him. "Sorry, Lyss. I need to get back to work."

Odalys crossed her arms. "Have you been sleeping?"

"What?"

"Sleep. It's a healthy thing to do. Wasn't sure if you were aware."

Gabriel frowned. "I'm *fine*."

"Are you? Because I've never seen you this short-tempered with *anybody*, let alone me. Not even with the slaves."

"Sorry."

Odalys glared. "You know, a 'sorry' is usually supposed to *sound* sorry."

"What do you want from me, Odalys?" Gabriel snapped. "The rebels killed my father, and they have my sister hostage. The Gold Mark is a menace, and they could have information about Lilly. Did you expect me to just sit around and wait for somebody else to find the solutions I need?"

Odalys blinked. She approached him and sat beside him. "No, I'm just worried about you. You're... not you. You're obsessing over this more than anyone else is, and I'm worried it's changing you." She looked up at him. "Changing you in ways that will cause you to lose the best parts of yourself."

I feel like I already have. "This is why I learned magic," Gabriel said. "And I can finally do something about all of this. I can finally fight, and I can finally be useful to my family. So I don't have time to explore right now."

"Alright, fine." Odalys stood and primly smoothed back her dark hair. Her lips were set tight. "I'll leave you to it, then."

Guilt poked him. "Lyss, I'm sorry—"

But the princess was walking away. She didn't look back at him as she shut the door behind her before Seleen could do it.

Gabriel groaned, falling back on the mattress. He stared at the ceiling. "Did I mess that one up, Seleen?"

"I'm... it isn't my place to say, sir."

Gabriel scrubbed at his face. His mind was no longer on the task at hand.

He needed fresh air. A quick walk before he made the show of going to bed for Seleen's sake. He'd been inside only a couple of hours since returning from the search, but it already felt stuffy.

Maybe it would wipe away the guilty feeling, too. He *didn't* have time for exploring or any of that. Not right now, not when he felt so close to finally doing some good.

He was also a little annoyed that Odalys had guessed he hadn't been sleeping well, but that was beside the point.

The gardens put him at risk of running into people now that it was warmer and getting greener, so Gabriel paced the front courtyard in the fading daylight. Servants glanced at him curiously, sometimes warily, but he ignored them.

Short of tearing this whole city apart, we have nothing to go on. Nothing to track. No prisoners to question. Gabriel had hoped a rebel would be drawn out at Isilmere's and Orrun's whippings—an attempted rescue or something—but not even a whisper. Isilmere and Orrun knew nothing, or so Seiryu had said.

Gabriel glared at the ground until he heard footsteps that didn't sound like the quick, purposeful steps of a servant or slave.

Tesmir pulled up short when he saw Gabriel, his light-hearted expression waning a little. Gabriel swallowed.

"Hi."

"Hello." The young soldier's voice was cooler than usual.

Gabriel chewed the inside of his cheek. "What brings you out here?"

Tesmir pointed behind him. "I was just delivering an order to the cook. With the attacks on supplies, we have to have our supplies delivered to the castle kitchens. Better security, I guess."

"Oh."

Awkward silence was something Lilly was better at fixing. Gabriel cleared his throat. "Are you upset with me?"

Tesmir frowned. "Upset? No. Why?"

"We haven't had lessons in a while, and I haven't seen you around." Gabriel shrugged.

"We've both been busy."

There was something else to it. Gabriel could see it in Tesmir's face. But his friend didn't offer it, and Gabriel didn't ask. Tesmir started to walk away.

"Oh, hey!"

Tesmir stopped and let Gabriel close the distance.

"Would you want to help me search for the network?" Gabriel asked. "We have no leads, but I think what we need is somebody who knows the city."

His hypocritical attitude turned his stomach, but Gabriel smothered his conscience. Tesmir had resources in the city, whereas Odalys had a terrifying mother who would sooner have him fed to a dragon than let her daughter help him.

"I don't know it *that* well." Tesmir shrugged. "I stick to the main roads."

Gabriel frowned. "Well... would you know anybody who might help? Or know anybody who might know someone?" He snapped his fingers. "Like that girl you met with a while ago."

Tesmir's eyes snapped up to Gabriel's. "What?"

"Weeks ago I was in the city with Odalys, and while I was waiting for her I saw you talking to a girl." He grinned. "Is she your girlfriend?"

Tesmir stared. Gabriel frowned. "Hey, what's wrong?"

"Nothing." Tesmir shook his head. "Sorry, it's nothing. I just... didn't think anybody I knew saw us."

"Could she help?"

"I don't think so. She keeps to herself. Even I can hardly find time to see her." Tesmir shook his head again and stepped back. "Sorry, I don't think she can help. I need to get back."

Gabriel blinked. "Oh. Yeah, sure. See you around."

"Mmhmm."

Gabriel watched Tesmir leave the courtyard, frowning. Maybe his friend was just in a mood—

"You don't really believe he's got nothing to do with any of this, right?"

Gabriel whipped around, his magic singing through him. Cadrian stepped into view. Gabriel bristled.

"What do you want?"

"I was just passing through." Cadrian sauntered over. "Couldn't help but overhear that sorry excuse for, well... an excuse."

"What are you talking about?"

Cadrian lifted a brow. "Think about it, Faine. Tesmir *Annor*. His kin are the most well-known rebels in their whole bloody army. The *son* of the infamous Ranson Annor, the man who started the rebellion the first time." He smirked. "You really think his loyalties are exclusively to the crown?"

Gabriel glared. "Mind your own business, Cadrian. Tesmir isn't a traitor."

"All gods, you are disgustingly loyal." Cadrian rolled his eyes. "I haven't trusted that boy since he came here. No one with that kind of rebel history is ever entirely unsympathetic to their cause."

"What proof do you have?" Gabriel snapped. "Unless you can show me proof, shut up and leave."

"I'm free to come and go in the castle just like you." Cadrian sneered. "But wait, you're not allowed, are you? Entya's precious little student needs to be kept so safe."

Gabriel's magic flared, and his fingers crackled with lightning. Cadrian smirked.

"I'm not here to pick a fight with you. I have better things to do with my time." He jerked his chin in the direction Tesmir had gone. "You spend so much time training with him, so think about it. How *loyal* has Annor really seemed? He didn't even jump at the chance to whip his rebel brothers. Rothar offered him the chance. I would've taken it."

"Because you're a jerk," Gabriel muttered. "So what? They're still family..." He swallowed hard. "You only have so many of them."

"Family who will all hang anyway." Cadrian said. "Can you honestly tell me, with absolute certainty, that Tesmir Annor shouldn't be on the top of our list of people to investigate?"

Gabriel hated how, unbidden, his mind considered the possibility. Tesmir hadn't really given the impression of being a traitor. He shared the empire's sentiments toward the rebels, and Gabriel had seen how he spoke to Isilmere. He wasn't cruel, but he didn't seem to care, either.

But that day his brothers had been whipped, Gabriel had also seen that crack in Tesmir's resolve. Sadness. Worry.

Then he remembered watching Tesmir in the city, with the girl. The frequent glances at the royal guards, and the way they disappeared when Odalys came out of the sweet shop.

Gabriel wasn't sure he liked the doubt that started to seep in. He let out a breath. "Do you think it's worth following him?"

The dark weaver grinned. "I already am."

"What?"

"I sent an itzal ahead. Tracking him right now."

"You can do that?"

"Had to. I knew it would take half my lifetime just debating with you about it."

Gabriel glared at him. "If this is just a trick to get me in trouble—"

"Hardly, Faine." Cadrian started walking. "I don't like you much, but right now you and I are the same: Not in the mood to joke around about this. We're both tired of this useless running in circles and pretending like we have something to go on. This is the best lead I've seen in weeks."

Gabriel swallowed, but he followed the weaver. He hoped Cadrian was wrong. "Should we tell Entya?"

"And have her stop us because we don't have any proof? All gods, Faine, you're a bore."

"I'm just saying—"

"And I'm saying grow your own spine," Cadrian hissed. "Stop running to Entya and stand on your own feet for once. Make your own choices." He smirked. "I would never jeopardize Lord Rothar's prized protégé."

Gabriel almost punched him. He walked a little faster, trying to ignore the sting. Ignore how close that hit.

They caught up to Tesmir easily but kept a safe distance. The young soldier seemed... wary. He kept glancing around, stopping at random vendors and forcing Gabriel and Cadrian to slow their pace or stop on a corner.

"Where's your itzal?" Gabriel asked.

"Gone. No reason to keep it around once we had eyes on him."

"What do we do if he leads us someplace useful?"

"We scout it out, and *then* you can tell Entya."

They walked on. Tesmir left the main road and started down another, one mostly lined with smaller shops and bakeries.

"This isn't the way back to the barracks," Gabriel murmured.

"It took you this long to figure that out?" Cadrian rolled his eyes. "What is he doing?"

Gabriel turned. Tesmir had stopped at the corner of a little shop front with books in the display windows. He was no longer scanning his surroundings. His attention was on a woman with curly, platinum blonde hair.

Tesmir gesticulated with urgency, and the woman, several years his elder, frowned darkly and grabbed his arms to still him.

"Cadrian," Gabriel breathed.

"I see it," Cadrian said. "Seems a little suspect, don't you think?"

"I think I've seen her before." Gabriel shook his head. "I recognize her hair. She and Tesmir met up when I was in the city with Odalys."

Gabriel's mind whirled. He didn't want to believe it.

Cadrian grinned. "Well... so much for returning to his barracks like a good soldier."

Gabriel pulled out of his dismay and tried to grab Cadrian's sleeve. "Wait, don't—"

But Cadrian pushed past him, fire bursting to life in his hands. Civillians yelped and scattered. Tesmir spun around, and the woman lifted her arms, as if readying to attack.

Cursing, Gabriel ran to catch up.

The first sensation felt like a bunch of tingly needles lightly pressing into him, beneath his skin. Then his magic stirred, louder and louder—

Green vines broke through the stone street with a monstrous crack, sending chunks of rock flying. Gabriel recoiled, and yelped when a chunk clipped his temple, knocking him off his feet.

Cadrian was laughing. "Your greenery isn't fireproof, my dear!"

Heat blazed in the narrow street, and the vines blackened and crumbled. The woman cried out, doubling over.

"Jinnet!" Tesmir sprang to her side before she fell.

Gabriel rocked to his feet, blood trickling down his temple, and stared. Jinnet. The leader of the Gold Mark.

And Tesmir was by her side, *helping* her.

But Jinnet pushed Tesmir behind her. Her arms moved in a fluid dance, summoning more vines to try to grapple Cadrian's arms and legs. They burned as quickly as she summoned them, and with every blaze, she cried out in pain.

Gabriel's skin prickled, his magic stirring into a frenzy. Before he could second guess himself he dove aside just as a torrent of water magic crashed past him. Cadrian spun in place, and a wave of shadows lifted from the street, shoving the water into the shops. Gabriel heard people scream from within.

"Cadrian, the people!" Gabriel snapped.

But Cadrian's focus was on the five new fighters that now flanked Tesmir's companion. Arms outstretched, ready.

Rebels. The Gold Mark.

More vines erupted from the stone, and civilians started running, panic and terror setting in.

Fire scorched them to ash, Cadrian directing the flames, his lips curled in a wicked smile. A couple of the fighters jerked as if punched. Jinnet staggered again, and Tesmir caught her.

Water crashed down on the fire, dousing the blaze with a loud hiss. Gabriel's magic sparked at his fingertips, but Cadrian beat him to the attack. The dark weaver pulled from the shadows until they created a bulky, ogre-type creature that almost didn't fit in the street. Its meaty arms swung down at the nearest rebels, bellowing like a deep drum.

Vines exploded forth, rising up and up to wrap around the ogre's forearms. They tugged the limbs down. The ogre snarled, fighting back. More fire licked up the lengths of the vines, breaking them. Jinnet had eyes only for Cadrian. Vines speared through stone to grab the dark weaver, but Cadrian burned them off in seconds. He was *laughing*.

Gabriel felt frozen, a little bit afraid. What could he do? Anything he tried would only be countered. He wasn't ready for this. Wasn't ready for an actual fight where he could actually die.

But as the ogre thrashed and struggled against the vines that kept trying to lash its arms down, it was ramming into the shops and houses. Wood and stone cracked on impact, and some of the smaller ones collapsed entirely.

Civilians screamed and started running, shaken from their terrified stupor. But with the ogre's clumsy stomping and struggling, Gabriel spied a few civilians who were trapped.

His father jumping in front of Lilly flashed in his mind. Giving his life to protect someone else.

How could Gabriel do anything less?

"Faine! *Gabriel!*"

He sprinted forward, flinging itzals in all directions. They sprang to obey his orders, claiming civilians and getting them far away from Cadrian's destructive monster.

His own target was a pair of young guys who looked eager for a fight. They had knives out, and Gabriel wasn't sure who they planned on fighting, but one jumped into the street *just* as the ogre-itzal tripped over a taut vine.

Gabriel pulled up the shadows, throwing them toward the boy. The itzal took shape: a mini dragon, and it grabbed the boy *right* before the ogre-foot came down.

"Get out of here!" Gabriel yelled. "Go find Entya! Get more help!"

The two boys fled, and Gabriel turned to help the others. The rebel weavers didn't seem to even notice him, or if they did, they didn't assume he was with Cadrian. They never tried to attack. All their focus was on Cadrian, and it was taking its toll. Cadrian cursed, his ogre-itzal writhing as he threw flame and crackling lightning one at a time, only to be countered.

Tesmir stood behind the line of rebels, eyes round in horror. Gabriel's fear churned into anger. His friend was a rebel. A *traitor*. How long had he been informing the enemy? He must've been why Gabriel's searching had been so fruitless.

Why Tesmir said no when Gabriel asked for his help.

This was a mistake. They should have brought backup, brought the whole team. Gabriel turned from the last group of civilians to see *more* weavers spring out of hiding, all attacking Cadrian and his itzal. Cadrian still stood, but the ogre was now decidedly smaller, and tripping over its own feet.

Gabriel wasn't sure how many seventh weavers were there, but there was a lot of earth magic flying around. He pressed to the wall, a thrill racing through him as he tried to find an opening. His magic thrummed with eager anticipation. Wasn't this what he'd trained for? Fighting the rebels, finding his sister. Finding... his father.

They killed him. And Tesmir was on their side. Gabriel remembered the sympathy Tesmir had offered. Had it even been real?

Gabriel's fists clenched. He pulled at shadows and broke into a run. The magic filled him, ready to be used. Ready to attack. Maybe some days you didn't have backup and just had to do whatever you could. And right now, he needed to get out of here alive.

Cadrian was on his knees, and his ogre was now just a little taller than a man, and both itzal and weaver were easily subdued by the vines. Gabriel stared as actual *lilies* bloomed on the vines, the color of dark blood, and a glowing pollen poured out, floating on and around the ogre-itzal and Cadrian.

The itzal shrieked and writhed, and Cadrian cried out, struggling to escape. Fire flared once, burning the vines just enough for him to tear free, but the magic followed him, the pollen landing on his arms, his face.

Cadrian screamed.

"Let him go!" Gabriel roared, throwing his strength into his magic. It roared alongside him, surging up in the form of a fiery serpent. He heard the flames crackle and hiss as the magic lunged for the ogre, snapping it up and burning the vines.

The less magic Cadrian had to focus away from him, the better. The dark weaver looked ill. He still writhed as the pollen nearly covered him.

They were *torturing him.* Cadrian cried out in pain, struggling to escape the vines that kept tangling in his legs. Whatever the pollen was, it was harmless to his outside body. It was doing something deep inside. Deeper than muscle tissue and blood vessels.

Gabriel turned his magic to every rebel he could see, anger boiling over. A few well-aimed hits—

"Gabriel!"

Tesmir stepped into view. His sword remained at his belt, but Gabriel redirected his magic. He held it close, a trigger taut and ready.

"You're a spy," Gabriel spat. "Aren't you?"

"Gabe." Tesmir held up his hands. "Just wait."

30

THE ONE THEY FEAR

"Why should I wait?" Gabriel snapped. "You've sided with the enemy."

He was never really your friend, was he?

"We're not the enemy," Tesmir pleaded. "*They* are the enemy." He pointed to a limp Cadrian, who moaned weakly as the pollen settled, motionless, around him.

"Lilly's safe," Tesmir went on. "She's alright."

"Tesmir, not now!" Jinnet barked, her voice hoarse. She stood shoulder-to-shoulder with another man, whose water magic splashed Cadrian in the face, disorienting him. Jinnet's earth magic was indistinguishable among the rest, but she didn't seem to have a problem dividing her focus between it and Tesmir.

"How do I know that's not a lie?" Gabriel asked. "How could you work for them?"

"I've always worked with them," Tesmir said, his voice not angry, but... sad? "I'm a rebel in more ways than the empire thinks." He grinned weakly. "Let us explain."

"No!" Gabriel's magic whipped back to life, spitting fire and electricity at the nearest weavers. They yelped, and their magic shielded them just in time. "Tell them to back off! They're hurting him!"

"Gabriel, stop!" Tesmir stepped forward. Jinnet grabbed his arm. "Gabe, listen to me!" He waited for Gabriel to look back at him. "I'm not the enemy! I'm your friend, I always have been."

"My friend wouldn't turn traitor." Gabriel's anger bubbled over. "My friend wouldn't be allies with the people who let my dad die, or torture a man in cold blood."

A chilling thought shuddered through Gabriel. How quickly the street had filled with rebels. Magic weavers with earth magic to trump the shadows.

A trap. Tesmir had known. A trap to catch one of the emperor's strongest weavers. Gabriel was just an unfortunate witness.

"They tried to save your father, Gabe," Tesmir pressed. "I swear it. And your sister is *safe*. She's not a prisoner." The soldier-spy held Gabriel's eyes. "She's safe, Gabe. Rothar and the others have been lying to you."

"Kill them, Faine!" Cadrian gasped, chest heaving for air. "Stop letting them fill your head with lies and kill them!" He winced, slumping when he tried to escape. He was losing consciousness.

They killed your father, the magic whispered against his mind. *They left him to die in the street. In the cold and snow.*

Gabriel roared, his anger rising again. He wasn't ready to kill. He didn't *want* to kill.

But oh, he'd make a statement for sure. He and Lilly shared blood. He had to have some of that statement-making ability too, right?

He was here, and very much able to fight. Finally able to push back. And now he'd finally found his quarry.

Fire erupted around him, burning warm against his skin and charring anything else it touched. It contrasted with the cold shadows he drew to himself. He let them both grow, pouring his strength into them. He felt the magic drain his imagined "mana meter," but he was willing to take the risk.

Jinnet yelled at the other rebels to retreat, and they darted away into the narrow tangle of alleys.

Not this time.

Gabriel thrust his hands forward, and the shadow-fire combo hurtled toward the rebels, a many-headed serpent. Gabriel heard alarmed cries but didn't check to see if anything hit. He focused on the pair in front of him, the pair that had yet to run away.

"Gabe, stop!" Tesmir yelled, resisting Jinnet's pull. "We're not the enemy!"

"Yes, you are," Gabriel growled under his breath. He willed the magic to grow, to hunt all rebel weavers.

The man who kept close to Jinnet's side shoved Tesmir into a retreat.

Rebels cried out in alarm as they threw magic behind them in their flight, fighting the fire and the darkness that became an inferno. But Gabriel didn't feel any more drained. He frowned, risking a glance behind him.

Entya stood, arms outstretched, as she glared at Jinnet. One hand flicked toward Cadrian, and the vines burned, the pollen burning away too. Jinnet cried out, staggering to her knees. Entya sneered.

Gabriel wasted no time throwing a fireball, but it was met by a gaping, watery jaw that swallowed it with a piercing hiss. The water dropped, splashing in Gabriel's eyes. The man who'd shoved Tesmir glared at Gabriel before twisting his hand, sending another rush of water at Entya before turning to Jinnet.

Entya's shadows sliced through the magic, but the Gold Mark was well into their retreat. Tesmir hesitated and looked back. Gabriel snarled and rushed after them.

"Gabriel!"

Entya's sharp voice brought his feet to a halt, and he looked back. "They're getting away—"

"Let them," Entya said, her voice cold as steel. "We are not enough to face them, and Cadrian requires medical attention. I cannot go with both of you."

Gabriel wanted to argue. Entya glowered, and he stepped back toward her and Cadrian. His magic stirred, brushing against him eagerly. He sensed the itzal before he saw it, peeking out from a shadowed corner.

Follow them. Keep me posted on where they're going.

If Entya saw the itzal dart off after the rebels, she made no comment on it.

"What in the name of the great gods were you both thinking?" she snapped instead.

Gabriel looked at Cadrian, but the man, though conscious, seemed in no hurry to answer.

Fine. Gabriel had no problem throwing him under the bus.

"Cadrian suspected Tesmir to be a rebel," Gabriel said. "He thought we could follow him to the network. We saw him talking to the Gold Mark leader, and Cadrian attacked them."

Entya stared. "Without any backup?"

"Cadrian thought you'd say no."

"And rightly so!" Entya looked at Cadrian. "You utter fool! What were you thinking, attacking them without help? And bringing *Gabriel* into it?"

Gabriel bristled but said nothing. Cadrian rolled his pale eyes, defiant even in weakness. "Don't act so superior. Fifteen years ago you would have done the same thing with another Faine."

Gabriel blinked. Entya, if the jab affected her, didn't react. "Then perhaps you need another fifteen years to learn what I did. Going alone is as good as walking to your death. How many times have I warned you against taking premature action? How many times has Emperor Yovak—"

"Woman, you're not my mother, so lay off," Cadrian snapped.

Entya's stare was so icy Gabriel didn't dare speak up. Finally, his tutor sighed slowly before glancing at him. "Were any civilians harmed?"

"I don't think so. I got them all away while Cadrian fought the rebels."

"Good. At least one of you had some sense." She looked up at Gabriel and beckoned him over.

He took one step and his legs nearly gave out from under him. Something shadowed and dark caught him, and he looked into the eyeless face of Entya's itzal.

"Fool boy." Her tone was a fraction softer. "Used too much energy, didn't you?"

Gabriel flushed, letting the itzal help him walk to the veteran weavers. "I was angry... they kept saying things about Lilly, how she's safe, and how the rebels aren't the enemy."

"A common tactic. They will use your emotions to sway you," Entya said. Gabriel nodded, looking at his feet. He was too tired to look her in the eyes.

Entya's hand rested on his shoulder, and he felt her magic stir around all three of them, the itzal dissolving into the smoky pillar of shadow that took them from the destroyed street to a couple of blocks from the castle. There, they had to walk to the gates and be let in. No weaver was permitted to transport into the castle itself.

In the main hall of the castle, the staff rushed forward, some dropping their armload of bed linens in their haste.

"Run ahead and tell Raul we are coming," Entya snapped at a half-elf slave. Gabriel hurried to help support Cadrian when he moaned and sank in Entya's grip.

But his tutor pushed him away. "No. You must go to His Majesty. He will require a report." Entya held Gabriel's eyes just long enough for the words to sink in, then she turned away, ordering another servant to her side.

Gabriel remained in the middle of the hall. He realized his breaths still came in great heaving gasps. The adrenaline surged and sparked around him, begging to be released but finding no safe way to do it.

And his itzal... it was somewhere in the city, lurking. Following.

And he was tired. His energy was drained, and he wanted to sleep.

Tesmir's words were running circles in Gabriel's head, only adding to the pounding headache the battle had brought on. But the anger and betrayal hurt worse.

Gabriel started walking. So many days of training with Tesmir. They hadn't been very close, but Tesmir had been one of the only two friends his age Gabriel had.

Now he'd made one friend angry with him and been betrayed by the other.

He found a servant, who directed him to Yovak's private study. The doors were closed and seemingly unguarded from the outside. Gabriel didn't have time to knock.

Of course, there *were* guards inside the room. Dark weavers, or at least one was. Gabriel was met with a crackling blade of lightning, the sparks jumping to his exposed neck and making him flinch.

Yovak and Seiryu both stood in the room. They looked up in alarm.

"Gabriel?" Seiryu's brows furrowed.

"An attack," Gabriel said, "by the Mark."

Yovak waved his hand, and the guards withdrew. Gabriel resisted the urge to rub his throat and stepped forward.

"Where?" The emperor's voice was cold.

Gabriel shrugged. "I don't know streets. Cadrian and I were following Tesmir, and Cadrian attacked him and the leader of the Mark."

"Tesmir?"

"That Annor boy," Seiryu supplied. "The one Gurdrin recommended to us out of Murke."

Yovak's eyes narrowed. "And on what grounds did you do this?"

Gabriel flushed. "We... Cadrian suspected him. Since his brothers are rebels, and his father was one."

"No other evidence?"

"No, sir. Your Majesty, I mean."

Yovak's frown deepened. Seiryu beckoned to Gabriel.

"Sit down and tell us everything."

Gabriel obeyed willingly. He related the scene as he could remember it. But he left out Tesmir's pleas.

Yovak's eyes were on Gabriel as he spoke, his features drawn in concern. Seiryu claimed the seat near the table, easing weight off his bad leg.

"Can you still sense your itzal?" Yovak asked when Gabriel finished his report.

"Yes sir."

"Can you give it orders? Ask it to show you what it sees."

His magic almost seemed to respond before Gabriel asked. In his mind's eye he saw darkness at first but then torchlight. Tunnels. Humanoid shapes hurrying back and forth. The itzal relayed a location: just on the outskirts of Erriath, to the west.

"West side of Erriath," Gabriel said. "Tunnels, I think. Not much detail."

Seiryu looked at Yovak. "Tunnels? Those old smuggler routes?"

"Likely," Yovak growled. "Cursed be their blood. I thought we closed those off."

"Earth magic."

Yovak glared at his advisor, then looked up at Gabriel. "While your behavior was foolish, you have given us an advantage. But one we will have to act on quickly."

"Why?"

"Because you will need to remain awake in order for us to accurately find them." Seiryu's smile was pitying.

"But they will not move now," Yovak said. "They are not stupid rats, either. They will think they escaped danger. Let them rest easy tonight, and think themselves the victors of the day. We attack at dawn."

Gabriel's heart sank. "I have to stay awake all night?"

Yovak only nodded, looking at him like he was a soldier expected to follow orders. Gabriel supposed he was.

"Did they say anything to you?" Seiryu asked. "The soldier boy, or any of the weavers?"

Gabriel chewed his lip uneasily. "They... yeah. Tesmir said my sister was safe, and that they weren't the enemy." He looked at Seiryu. "But Entya told me they say that a lot."

Seiryu glanced at Yovak. Then he stood, careful to leave weight off his leg. "I will send orders to Koranos, Your Majesty, and to the dark weavers to be ready for dawn."

Yovak nodded, distracted. "Do not let him send out searches for the Annor boy, nor tell the other men. I don't need their grumbling to get around and spook the rebels too soon."

Seiryu bowed. Gabriel stood, forcing his muscles to stop spasming long enough to bow, and followed Seiryu out. Seiryu grasped Gabriel's shoulder, leading him down the hall.

"The rebels will often use such words to recruit," Seiryu said carefully. "But, in your case... it is different."

"Why? What would they want with me?"

Seiryu watched Gabriel carefully, as if weighing his next words. Gabriel stopped walking, dread creeping up and eating away the last traces of adrenaline. "Seiryu?"

"I suspect they want you as leverage," Seiryu said. "You would be a powerful bargaining chip."

"But they already have Lilly. Why would they want me too?"

Seiryu's face morphed into pity and something like grief. Fear and dread clutched at him. "Seiryu—"

"We received a report from the team we sent to rescue your sister," Seiryu said quietly.

"No, no." Gabriel shook his head, backing up. "Seiryu, no—"

"They found her body, left behind." Seiryu's voice was so soft Gabriel barely heard it over the roaring panic in his ears. The magic that writhed with the pain. "Her throat slit. The rebels have been marching toward Erriath, and the team intended to rescue her on the road."

He was going to be sick. Everything he'd eaten today was coming back in waves. Gabriel staggered back, catching the wall. "No. No, that's not true. Why would they do that? She was their leverage. She was their bargaining chip. That doesn't make any sense."

Gabriel looked up at Seiryu. His breaths shook, and each inhale hurt. "Seir, no, no—"

The elf's eyes were dark. "I'm so sorry, Gabriel. I'd sent Entya to look for you as soon as I heard."

Gabriel stared at the floor and willed himself *not* to be sick. No, this wasn't possible. This *was not possible*. She couldn't be dead. She was way too stubborn to die. She would have fought tooth and nail and—and everything—everything else—

Seiryu's hand grasped his shoulder. Gabriel choked on a sob.

"She can't be dead," he gasped. "Not Lilly. Not Lilly. She can't— she wouldn't die. She wouldn't let them—"

"No one is invincible," Seiryu said softly. "But you must be strong, Gabriel."

I can't. I can't be. Gabriel pulled away, running his hands through his hair as his throat and chest and heart squeezed and squeezed. A cry escaped him and seemed to echo through the hall. He pressed his sleeve against his mouth. He tasted smoke and the remains of the fight.

Gabriel looked at Seiryu. His figure was blurry and watery. Gabriel gasped. "Seiryu—"

The elf's strong arm came around him, holding him so tight Gabriel almost couldn't breathe, but it kept him together. Something tighter than the pain and agony suffocating him.

Seiryu said nothing as Gabriel sobbed, only gripped him tightly. If staff encountered them in the hall, Gabriel didn't know. He didn't care. He didn't care about anything anymore. Lilly was gone. There would be no rescue. No seeing her brought within the safety of the city, to the safe, secure walls of the castle. To Gabriel.

He'd been too late. Too late again. He'd left them alone. Been an idiot and rushed into danger he hadn't been halfway prepared for, and he'd left them at the mercy of rebels.

You would have been captured too.

But maybe he would have been able to keep them alive.

Gabriel sucked in a breath, and his body shuddered. Seiryu's grip tightened.

"You must be strong, Gabriel," he murmured. "Be strong for them both... you have been hurt, but you are also the one to lead us to one of the rebels' strongest roots and remove it."

Gabriel shook his head. "I can't. I can't—"

"Yes, you can." Seiryu stepped back, still gripping Gabriel's shoulder, and looked him in the eyes. "I have no doubt you are as strong as your sister. This organization of rebels here is as much at fault for her and your father's deaths as the ones out there. And we have the opportunity to bring them down." He searched Gabriel's eyes. "But we're going to need your magic to do it."

Gabriel wanted to be as confident in himself as Seiryu was. He wanted to do something. But everything inside him was frozen in time. Frozen, numb. Dying.

He looked at his hands. His magic. What was the point of it anymore? He'd learned magic to protect his family, to save them. And he'd done *nothing*. He felt it in his veins even now, roiling with the agony that wanted to break him. But what was he to do with it now? Where was that power he had felt before? What good had it done him?

There wasn't any use for it, but he couldn't get rid of it.

"I don't want this anymore," Gabriel whispered. He looked up at Seiryu, panic building. "I can't do this. I don't want it—"

"Shh, shh..." Seiryu held him again. "Breathe. Think."

"I don't want it anymore." Gabriel's voice was muffled against the elf's shirt. "I can't use this. What's the point?"

"The point?" Seiryu looked at him. "Gabriel, everything is the *point*. You chose magic to protect, to bring justice, did you not?"

"Yeah."

"You learned magic to fight back, to become the change you

wanted to see, did you not?"

Gabriel looked at him. Sniffed. "Yeah?"

"Then that is the point," Seiryu said. "These rebels have hurt you far more than they have hurt many of us. But you, my boy, can fight back. You have a strength your father had, a will to see things changed for the better." He smiled sadly. "You have a power many can only dream of."

"Some good that's done." Gabriel pulled away. "What am I supposed to do now, Seiryu? I can't... I can't trust myself to use magic like this." His fingers curled into fists, yet they still shook. He looked at Seiryu. "How do I fight like this?"

Seiryu watched him for a time. He sighed. "You use it. Take that pain... that grief. Let it be not a noose, but a reminder. Remember them, and you will remember what you fight for."

"What I fought for is gone, Seir!" Gabriel snapped. "They're both dead!"

"Aye, but you still fight for freedom," Seiryu said, his voice calm. "You fought to free them. You fight to free your father's home, do you not?" He smiled faintly. "Remember this pain, and remember that you fight so no one else may feel it too. Use it to be strong, remember the strength of your father, the strength of your sister. Remember that, and the strength they lend you—the strength that burns in your shared blood—will be all the stronger. The strength that makes you more than you believe yourself to be."

"How?" Gabriel's voice cracked. "I don't know how."

"We will start with the dawn," Seiryu said. "And start with the ones who would see your family's killers enter this city and tear down the throne you help defend, the throne that means peace."

Gabriel looked at his hands again. His magic had quieted some, though he still felt the pull of the itzal in the city.

He wasn't sure he wanted any of this anymore, but the truth soothed the pain a little. He didn't know what he'd do, but he could, at least, do this... he could still fight. There wouldn't be anyone coming around the corner to fight for him. Lilly wouldn't be the one the bullies feared this time. He would be the one they feared. The one whose name they knew. The one who pushed back and held his ground.

Fought for the ones being bullied.

Gabriel nodded, taking a long breath.

This last thing he could do. For Lilly. For their father.

Make them burn. Make them fear.

Justice.

31
MADE OF FIRE

The hall was empty, but Lilly moved swiftly, ignoring the creaking that betrayed her. She didn't care. Let Mordir know she was following. The cool hilt of the dagger at her belt reassured her.

The front room still held a few patrons. Men who'd had a late work shift and sought shelter before the trek home. They laughed amongst themselves, happy and seemingly ignorant of the two figures slipping out into the rain, one after the other. The tavern master wiped the scarred tables without looking up.

It was dark, wet, and cold. Lilly glimpsed Mordir's figure walking away, only vaguely illuminated by the random lanterns that lit up the street. Lilly hurried after him, keeping close enough not to lose him but far enough away to evade his notice. Or she hoped.

Her first rain in Piensor was no longer a marvel. It soaked through every layer she wore, and then, it seemed, through her skin to her bones. It turned the bare earth to squelching mud under her feet, sucking at them with every step. She shivered as she walked but didn't turn back. Her mind wouldn't rest now. Mordir had too much mystery surrounding him. No way was she giving him a chance to stab them in the back. He walked with too much surety between the muck puddles, as if he knew just which street he wanted—

As if he'd been here before.

Lilly cursed, grabbed a tin cup from a trash mound by a wall, and threw it. In spite of the dark, the rain, and the cold, the cup pinged off Mordir's back between his shoulders.

The Ghost whirled with such speed Lilly backed up despite the several yards already between them. His dagger was drawn.

"Hi." Lilly announced herself before he had a chance to throw the blade.

Mordir's curse was worse than hers. "Silver stars above, Faine! What are you doing?" He stalked toward her.

Lilly held her ground and crossed her arms. "Kinda late to be wandering the streets, isn't it?"

"So you decided to follow me? Again? Do you want me to kill you?"

"You seem pretty familiar with a village you've never been to," Lilly said.

"I never said I'd never been here. It's a small village, but I know how to avoid people when I want to." Mordir glared. "Except you, it seems."

"The Ghost can't run from everyone." Lilly said. "I don't know what Tae sees in you, but I—"

Mordir's hand whipped out, grabbing her shirt and pushing her against the wall. His other hand clamped over her mouth. Lilly thrashed.

"Stop it!" Mordir hissed. "Look."

Lilly looked. Her heart thudded as two figures walked past the narrow street they stood in. Lilly only needed to see the gleam of armor from their lantern light. She heard them laugh and step down the street across from them, the rain falling behind them like a veil.

Lilly pushed his hand away. "Why are soldiers here? A tiny place like this isn't worth much to Yovak, is it?"

"This village is the closest to the mountains," Mordir murmured, "so it would be the first to receive traders. Trade tax—" He stopped, looking at where his hand clenched her shirt. "You brought that amulet with you?"

Lilly frowned and shrugged. "I didn't take it off when I went to bed."

Mordir cursed. "Fool girl. Get back inside!" He grabbed her arm, pulling her back the way they'd come. They stuck to the shadows, larger now with rain clouds sulking overhead.

"Why are you worried?" Lilly tried to pull away, but this time Mordir didn't let her. "Mordir, let go of me before I stab you in the neck."

"I didn't come all this way to see you get robbed in the streets of the one thing that will help us both, or caught by soldiers and searched," Mordir snarled, whirling on her. His dark hair flung droplets into her face. "You don't think before you act. Maybe you were born in this world, Faine, but you don't know how to live in it. This world is no friend to you, and will sooner leave you dying in its streets than offer you comfort."

He jabbed a finger at the amulet hidden under Lilly's shirt. "Sooner or later Seiryu will get desperate and send more than just an assassin to bring him what he wants."

Lilly bared her teeth and yanked away, not caring that it hurt. Mordir let go anyway. "You mean like Zal? Yeah, he already did that. And I beat him too."

"Along with some of your own people, if I remember."

Lilly froze. She cursed and shoved him away. "Shut up. You don't know what happened."

"I know enough."

"No, you don't!" Lilly spun on her heel, remembering just in time to keep her voice down. "You weren't there, Mordir. You disappeared when it was convenient for you. So no, you *don't* know what happened. I had to make a call I'll regret every second I'm alive and Rousen Annor isn't." She swallowed the pressure building in her throat. "This world has already been unkind to me, but I'm not some delicate princess. I know how to handle myself when people are jerks and are out to hurt me and the people I love. This place is just more deadly."

The assassin stood quietly. Lilly wanted him to argue back, give her a reason to throw another tin cup. Maybe a rock. At his head.

But he didn't, and she didn't throw anything at him. He walked back the way they'd come. "Come on."

Lilly frowned. "Come where?"

"I'm taking you back to the inn. I'm not going anywhere now that I've been reminded how nosy you are."

Lilly glared at his back, but when he didn't stop or turn around, she followed him. "Where *were* you going?"

"It amuses me that you still think you're entitled to know things about me."

"So you were going somewhere."

Silence.

"I'm just curious."

"Then you must live with your curiosity."

They turned the corner and Lilly stopped, reaching out to grab Mordir's arm. He started to speak, but Lilly held a finger to her lips.

The inn stood before them, dark and quiet. Empty. Even in the rain Lilly had been able to hear the conversation and laughter within when she and the others first arrived. But now, all she heard was the rain.

Was the inn closed already? Lilly hadn't been gone that long. The patrons had looked far too settled into their meals and drinks to be ready to leave at closing.

Lilly shivered and approached the door. If she was locked out—

The door opened as easily as it had before. Lilly found her other hand wrapping around her dagger as she stepped inside, cautious. The room was totally dark, but hints of the warmth remained. The smell of hot food lingered in the air.

"Lilly," Mordir whispered. "Wait."

Lilly waited only long enough for her eyes to adjust. She saw dark shapes of plates on tables, and upon further inspection, found them still full of food. Still warm.

She shivered again, and not from the cold. She turned to the stairs. Tae. She was alone. Lilly had left her alone—

Someone—some*thing*—stood on the bottom step. Lilly nearly screamed, drawing her dagger and grabbing a meat knife. Mordir stood by her, his dagger drawn too. But the thing just squatted on the stairs, a hunched-over, spindly-limbed beastie. It wasn't quite solid, but like shifting shadows. An itzal.

"Faine'sss daughterrr," it rasped, its grin unnaturally crooked. Lilly stiffened, taking a step back. The thing didn't follow, and instead turned and pointed up the stairs. "Come innn... your friendsss are waiting..."

Fear grabbed her throat, but Lilly held her ground. "What did you do to them?" She could have sworn the thing grinned. The itzals she'd seen before hadn't had faces. This one did, a jagged maw that kept grinning at her, narrow eyes watching her. A sickly tingle crawled down her spine and settled in her stomach.

"*Lilly*," Mordir whispered, "just wait."

But the itzal only ascended the stairs, climbing on all fours. Lilly looked at the assassin, unable to hide her fear. "The others."

"Jek is a seventh. He can deal with a dark weaver."

Lilly's gut twisted. It should have reassured her, but somewhere inside, she knew Jek hadn't defeated whatever waited up there.

Ignoring Mordir's protests, Lilly ascended the stairs, fists tight around both weapons. The itzal waited for her midway, and carried on up the stairs. They only creaked under her weight, and she glanced back. Mordir wasn't following.

At the top, the itzal stopped beside the door to the twins' room. It was open. The itzal gave a mocking bow, motioning to the door, and was swallowed into the shadows. Lilly crept forward, hardly daring to breathe.

There was light in the twins' room. Fire magic, hovering in one corner. Just enough to illuminate three figures kneeling on the floor, and a fourth standing over them, gloating like he'd just won a battle by himself.

"There you are." Zal grinned. He held a blade of shadows in one hand and played it over his other hand, like he was trying to decide how to use it. He stood behind Jek, whose sides heaved for air as if he were drowning. His shirt was torn, and blood dripped from a wound on his chest. Jek could barely look at her. Hakor was to the left of his twin, with Tae between them.

Lilly glimpsed two hunched shadow monsters lurking in the far corners, but she didn't risk looking closer at them. "What did you do to him?"

"What, this one?" Zal's knife lowered to graze Jek's jawline. Hakor snarled and wrenched against the shadows anchoring him. Tae flinched, tears streaming. Zal ignored both. "You weren't here, so I had my fun with him. It's been just lovely having the whole building to myself." His grin looked maniacal. "The screaming doesn't bother anybody."

Lilly's blood ran cold. "Let them go, you sadistic, cowardly son of a—"

"Then make this easy," Zal cut her off. "You know what I want."

"Don't you dare," Jek choked out, his voice hoarse, raw. "Don't give it to him—"

Zal flicked his wrist, and shadows slithered over Jek's mouth, gagging him. He writhed, and the burnt vines and lilies sprawling through the window and over the floor tried to make a comeback.

They went up in flames. Lilly yelped and flinched back, and Jek screamed into the gag. Hakor roared profanity and thrashed until one of the itzals came forward and struck him, stunning him.

Tae sobbed. "No, please! Please!"

Before Lilly could act, the fire went out. The plants were ash, and Jek slumped forward, held up only by the shadows. Zal tsked and looked at Lilly.

"The amulet, if you please." He played with the shadow knife again. "Or we can watch the seventh scream some more."

Lilly chewed her lip, resisting the urge to reach for it. That amulet was her only chance at getting Gabriel back. Maybe even her only chance to go home.

Where was Mordir? He must have heard the yelling.

"You told me to bring the amulet to Erriath," Lilly said, stalling. "The amulet for my brother. That's what you said."

"Yes, but you're going in the opposite direction." Zal rolled his eyes. "Surely you've looked at a map since you got here." He spread his arms wide. "But now you have others to think about, no?" He smirked. "And your brother is no longer part of the deal, anyway."

Everything came to a screeching halt in Lilly's head. Her breathing, her heartbeat, the adrenaline. She stared at Zal, trying to pick out the lie.

"What did you do to him?" Lilly's voice came out like a breath, not nearly as strong as she'd intended. "What are you talking about?"

"Yes, Ira." A new voice joined them. Lilly jumped away from the door as Mordir appeared, his eyes dark and angry. "Tell her what exactly you mean."

"You know each other?" Lilly gaped.

"We tolerate each other," Mordir said. "Now tell the lady what you're talking about."

Zal laughed. "Faine's boy was never part of a deal. I imagine if he's not dead yet, he will be soon."

Lilly looked at Mordir for explanation. Mordir met her eyes. They were still dark and angry, but not at her.

"Don't give him what he wants," he said. "He's baiting you. And besides, it's best not to take everything he says seriously." Mordir looked back at Zal. "He usually talks out the other end."

Zal's sneer melted into offended fury. Mordir reached for his dagger, but a figure shot from the corner, a figure Lilly had failed to see. Tae screamed.

A second man swung Mordir into the wall, slamming his head against it and letting him crumple, moaning. Zal watched, amused, as he curled up and clutched his head. The second man stepped over him to block the doorway. Lilly recognized him as one of the weavers Zal had brought to Chicago. The only one who had survived the trip.

Zal sniffed. "Some dog of the empire you are, Jaeranys."

"Stop it!" Lilly snarled at Zal. "Leave them all alone!"

Zal bared his teeth. "Then give me what I want."

Panic began to fill her, drown her. Think, she had to think. Gabriel couldn't be dead. Wasn't there some sibling-sense that told you when your brother was in danger? Wasn't that how it worked? She'd have sensed it, right?

Lilly looked back at Jek, who'd managed to straighten a little. He watched her, eyes intense. He gave the subtlest shake of his head.

Seiryu couldn't get hold of the amulet. It could hold dark magic, but what else could it do? Her father's journal said that Seiryu was a scientist. Who knew what else he'd come up with? He'd already found a way to Earth. If he went back with more magic than anybody should have...

The Bean might not be the only thing blasted apart. Yovak's conquest could expand even further.

Zal scowled. "Why don't I give you something more to think about?" He moved from behind Jek to his right. To Tae. Lilly's breath caught, and Tae shrank back as Zal's hand closed over her throat. The other, still holding the knife, stroked her hair.

"No!" Lilly's voice was joined by Mordir's this time. The assassin had managed to find his hands and knees.

"Zal," Mordir growled, "don't you *dare*—"

"Is this one your favorite, Ghost?" Zal crooned. He stroked Tae's hair, ignoring her sobs. "Your new pet—" He paused, genuine surprise replacing his malice as he looked down at Tae. He moved her hair back from her ear, revealing the half-elven tip. "What's this now?"

Tae trembled violently in his grip, and squeaked when he twisted her around and gripped her jaw. She could only twist so far, and she whimpered in pain. Zal frowned. "You're half-elf." He looked at Mordir, frowning deeper. "Isn't Eeris Rothar's estate where the little princess runt was?"

Mordir glared. "Let her go."

Zal cocked his head as if in thought. "Funny, you were there too... and now here you both are."

Mordir didn't respond. Lilly looked at him, then Zal. A princess? Tae?

Despite the panic and terror, something in Lilly's mind clicked, and her eyes flew wide. Seymour's daughter had been taken fifteen years ago. Tae was about fifteen. A half-elf girl, taken as a baby. Unsure where she came from...

Lilly looked at the boys, hoping someone else had realized it too. But Mordir only glared at Zal, and Jek still struggled to breathe and recover. Hakor lay limp on the floor but was coming to, groaning. The itzal towered over him, waiting.

"I wager I'd get a handsome sum for bringing her *and* that amulet back," Zal mused. Tae squirmed.

Lilly gritted her teeth. Seymour's daughter had been with them the whole time. Tae, the girl who'd been told she was just some unwanted product of lust, abandoned or secreted away to hide scandal.

The empire had taken this little girl to force her father to his knees.

Lilly looked at the Annor twins again. The empire had taken parents from them too. Yovak had made orphans of them all, and for his own gains. For his own twisted utopia.

How am I any different? This amulet was hurting people. It had gotten Rousen killed. It had killed her father. Now it was killing her friends. It had killed rebels.

No. *She* was hurting people. Because she was hurting and wanted others to hurt.

She just hadn't meant for those others to be innocent people. There were people already hurting without Lilly throwing in her own grievances. But they were fighting for what they still had, not over what they'd lost.

What was Lilly fighting for? Her own revenge? To rescue Gabriel, but that wasn't what her anger wanted. Her anger wanted Yovak to suffer. Somewhere along the line it had stopped being about Gabriel and more about her.

She wasn't helping anybody. Her fight was only for herself, and it was more harmful than good.

What did she have to fight for? Gabriel, sure, but was that all?

Friends who've taken me in like family, who knew me when I was so small. A world my parents fought for. A world that was mine once.

Zal huffed in feigned impatience. "Perhaps you need a different sort of incentive."

Lilly stiffened, her hand hurrying to her neck. Zal didn't move, but the other weaver did.

The blade slid into her side before she could react. Lilly jerked with a gasp, grabbing the man's sleeve to steady herself. The weaver's face was stony as he pulled the knife out, the blade dripped with her own blood.

"Lilly!" Mordir yelled, struggling to rise. Lilly gasped and staggered against the wall, dropping the meat knife and clutching the wound. The pain wasn't too bad at first, but then it started to burn.

Mordir lunged for the weaver, his own dagger slashing down and piercing the man's own side. The weaver screamed, and Mordir shoved him down, letting him slam into the bedpost.

Zal growled, lifting his hand toward Mordir. But before a single spark of magic left him, Jek roared to life, the shadows dissolving around him as another batch of vines tore through the window and lashed around in a crazed fashion. Like angry octopus tentacles.

She hiccupped on another gasp, and pain spasmed. *So not the time.*

Zal snapped his fingers, and the room was ablaze with fiery vine whips. Jek screamed again, slumping. He gasped, heaving, as the ash rained into his damp hair.

"Think carefully about your next move, seventh," Zal hissed. "Your precious lady doesn't have a lot of time. That wound won't kill her, but the dragonleaf will."

Jek froze, eyes going wide. Even Mordir stopped, his eyes on Lilly now.

"Stop," Lilly rasped. She coughed and tried again. "Jek, Mordir, stand down." She didn't know what dragonleaf was, but she didn't have time to ask. Tae and Hakor didn't have time. The itzal now clutched a handful of Hakor's hair, and a sharp, needle-like arm was at his heart.

The men hesitated, glancing at her. Lilly pushed off the wall, despite the pain that fogged her vision.

"Stop," she gasped again, struggling to stay upright. Gosh it hurt. Was being stabbed supposed to hurt this bad?

"The amulet for your own cure," Zal told her. "And your friends, I suppose."

Lilly staggered. Jek moved away from Zal and wrapped an arm around her. She wasn't sure how he held her up, but she appreciated the support. Lilly held Zal's gaze, as if looking away might make him notice the others again.

"Let them *all* go." Lilly pulled the amulet from around her neck. Zal's eyes tracked her hand like a hungry wolf. She clutched the amulet. It was too dangerous a weapon for Seiryu to have, and it was her one shot at Gabriel's safety. Maybe even their chance to go home to everything they knew. Everything normal.

But it wouldn't be normal. Crazy Tilas's kids would be crazy too. Even if they found a way to go home, it wouldn't be the same. It would never feel normal again.

Somehow, this world *did* feel normal. Holding a dagger, fighting with it. Breathing the air—even if that was hard right now— touching magic, seeing it with her own eyes. It freaked her out, but this world was hers, like it had been her father's. The place where all of his stories lived.

She wasn't going to ignore them a second time.

"Fine," Zal said. "Hand it over."

Last chance. Lilly's thumb ran over the metal of the amulet. *You might be making an even bigger mistake than the harbor. You won't be able to go home.*

Lilly looked at Jek. His eyes were on Zal, then his twin, and Tae, still in Zal's grasp. Exhaustion mixed with fear, with anger. His body shuddered beside Lilly. Mordir stood somewhere behind them, unmoving. Hakor was awake, watching them with wide eyes, trying to understand. His eyes jumped from Lilly's face to her bleeding side, to Jek and Zal and back to Lilly.

Tae's whimper snapped Lilly back into focus. She shut down the thought and threw the amulet at the window, wincing as the movement stretched her side.

Doesn't matter. Nothing is worth losing more family. She didn't care about any "cure." That wasn't why she'd done it.

Her friends mattered more, and that was that. Gabriel mattered. If Rune's message so many days ago was still true... maybe Gabriel was doing alright. He could hold on a little longer for her.

Instead of scrambling for the window, Zal only smirked and let his itzal snatch the amulet out of the air just before it went sailing into the night. Zal took it from the itzal with a grin and pocketed it.

"A wise choice." Zal dismissed his itzals and hauled Hakor and Tae to their feet. He held their arms tight, and neither dared move.

"When I find you, I'll kill you," Lilly snarled. "This time I'll do it right."

"You won't be alive long enough to try," Zal laughed. The shadows rose around him, Tae, and Hakor.

"*NO!*" Lilly screamed, shoving Jek away and staggering forward. She forgot the pain. Forgot the burning that had begun to crawl through her veins. Tae was sobbing, struggling against the dark weaver. Hakor tried to twist away.

"Lilly!" Tae screamed.

An arm scooped around Lilly's waist. She twisted, jamming an elbow into Mordir's face. She caught his temple, and it was enough to release her. Lilly ignored the burning pain that stabbed her side and lunged for the smoke pillar, but she stumbled right through it and collided with the opposite wall. Zal and Tae and Hakor were gone.

Lilly screamed in frustration as pain tightened in her chest. Maybe Zal would change his mind. Maybe he would come back. Take her instead of them.

The pain held her to the wall, roaring with the panic. Lilly couldn't think, couldn't calm her breathing. She heard footsteps and whirled, dagger out, but dropped it when the pain seized her limbs. She cried out, nearly collapsing.

Mordir hurried to her, but Jek pushed past him and got to her first. Lilly felt her voice break. She hardly noticed Jek's support. "He took them."

Everything was all wrong. This shouldn't have happened. She'd given up the amulet, so Tae and Hakor should still be here. Lilly should have known. She should have acted faster, should have known he'd trick her.

But Tae was gone. Back to that wretched woman who might hurt her, treat her like property, feed her lies again. Had Tae realized the truth? Had she made the connection too?

And Hakor... she hadn't thought about what Yovak would do to Isilmere and Orrun. But with three Annors in his grasp? There was no guarantee Hakor would survive the night.

"He took them to Erriath, didn't he?" Lilly gasped, grabbing her side again. She looked up at Mordir. There was a cut somewhere on his head where he'd been shoved against the wall: blood trickled down his temple. "You know him. That's where they went, isn't it?"

She saw pain in Mordir's eyes. Lilly pushed away from Jek, making Mordir retreat a step. Her head spun, and her gut convulsed. "Answer me! This is your fault—"

Lilly's body spasmed, pain ricocheting through her veins like thousands of little grenades. She shuddered, barely suppressing a scream.

"Lilly!" Jek crawled to her as the rest of her sank to the floor. The pain still raged, twisting her insides over like... noodles? Like something, anyway.

Lilly whimpered. "Why's it hurt..." She jerked, curling up to fight another scream.

Mordir stalked to the dark magic weaver still on the floor, partway through using his magic to heal his wound. The weaver shrank back, but Mordir's boot landed squarely on the wound. The man howled.

"Mordir!" Jek snapped.

Mordir knelt, his foot still pressing into the wound as he grabbed the weaver's shirt and yanked him closer. "Did Zal have anything for the dragonleaf? Do you?"

The weaver laughed breathlessly. "You're the assassin. You tell me."

Without Zal's fire magic lighting the room, Lilly didn't see what Mordir did, but she heard the sickening slice of steel across flesh. She would have thrown up if the agony hadn't overwhelmed her.

"Mordir, enough!" Jek barked. "Leave it!"

Mordir's silhouette rose, dropping a now limp body. Lilly's breaths shuddered. Every inhale hurt. Her limbs shook, burning, burning. Her lungs started to burn too.

"What do we do?" Jek demanded. "She's dying!"

"I know." Mordir turned to them. "I'm aware of what dragonleaf is."

"S-someone tell me-e, then?" Lilly choked on the words. Talking didn't help, but she needed to focus on something other than the feeling of everything burning away inside her. She tried to push herself up, but the pain held her in place.

"The worst of poisonous plants," Mordir said.

"Su-uper." Lilly's body spasmed again, and a cry escaped her. "Where's the cure?"

"There isn't any." Mordir knelt beside her.

Lilly stared at him. "I can't die."

Mordir held her gaze. "I didn't say you would."

"Stop talking riddles and help her!" Jek roared.

Lilly clutched Jek's shirt, her sides heaving, as he gathered her in his arms. The wound stung, but it was nothing compared to her veins. They were turning against her.

"Mordir, there has to be something we can do!" Jek held Lilly close, as if the pressure would help. It didn't. Lilly cried out, the pain circling through her, attacking again and again and again...

"Give her to me." Mordir reached for Lilly. She shrank away, but another wave of pain made her gag, and her resistance was pathetically feeble. She grimaced at the dampness of his shirt. She wasn't sure she wanted to know if it was rain or blood.

"Where are you taking her?" Jek's voice shook.

Mordir stood. "To the only chance she has."

Pain shot through her, coursing through every vein she possessed. Lilly's fingernails dug into her arms, trying to claw out the pain. Find the source, find those burning little grenades...

"I can't breathe," Lilly gasped. "Like it's all—"

"I know," Mordir said after her cries subsided. "Just hold on." He turned. "Keep up, Annor. It's not far."

Lilly lost all sense of time. The rain, though cold, was only a mockery of relief. Touching her but just out of reach. Her fingers scratched at her arms, trying to relieve the pain in between her agonized screams.

The burning only got worse. Lilly's spine arched, and Mordir almost dropped her. He had to set her down until the worst of it passed. Lilly gagged, choking. Her throat felt inflamed, swollen.

They stopped walking after what felt like an eternity. The burning still smoldered under the surface, but the spasms had slowed. Lilly huddled against Mordir's chest as he directed Jek to pound on the door.

The pounding synced with that in Lilly's head. She yelped at another spasm, gripping Mordir's shoulder. He grunted.

Jek's pounding stopped abruptly when the door opened. Light from a single candle illuminated a woman's hardened expression.

"What in the name of—"

Mordir pushed past her. "Dragonleaf, Iluna. Hurry."

"*Mordir?* Dear gods, what are you doing here—"

"*Dragonleaf,* Iluna!" Mordir barked. "Where can I put her?"

The hard surface of a table supported her. Lilly gulped in air and offered weakly, "S'not so bad now. I can get up."

Mordir held her down. "Don't."

Lilly shook her head, tears pricking her eyes. "Tae and Hakor, I have to get them back—"

The burning flared. Lilly arched her back, a scream choking her last words. It was worse now. So much worse. Like it was burning its way out of her.

"Iluna!" Mordir roared, holding Lilly down. Lilly screamed, the grenades going off all over. She tensed, struggling to fight it. Her wound stung, and Lilly jerked.

"Hold her still!"

More hands held her down. Lilly struggled. "No, no. Let me go—"

"Help her!" Jek's voice broke through the fire. It sounded shattered. So, so afraid.

The burning slowed, but now her heart burned too. Lilly choked on every other breath, and she clawed at the table, trying to steady herself.

This wasn't how it was supposed to end. She couldn't die. She had to find Gabriel, because he *wasn't* dead. She had to rescue Tae and Hakor... had to help the rebels win... had to make her dad proud...

"There's nothing I can do." The woman's voice floated through Lilly's thoughts. "It's moving too fast. If I'd caught it right away, maybe, but it's been—hey!"

"Move!" Jek snarled. "Just hold her down!"

"Annor, what are you doing?"

"Not losing her." Jek's face appeared in Lilly's hazy vision. His scar stood out in the pale light, his dirty-blond hair plastered around it, but his eyes held hers. A stubborn gray.

"Hold on," he said.

Lilly coughed, choking on a breath. Tears slipped down, fear roaring with the pain. "I can't..."

"Yes you can," Jek urged. "You're made of fire. Fight it."

His hands pressed against her wounded side. Lilly jerked, yelping. The burning in her veins flared, but something else did too. Something... she wasn't sure. Not hot, but comfortably warm.

Warmer. Warmer. Hot.

Lilly screamed, arching off the table. The new heat raced through her veins, catching all the grenades and containing them right before they went off, shoving them back the way they'd come. One by one.

The fire dulled to an ache, but everything still burned. It burned and burned—

But then everything went very dark, and very still, and very quiet.

32

JUSTICE

Dawn arrived, and Gabriel was almost relieved. It had started to feel like it would never come. Like it had forgotten.

When everyone was asleep, the castle was eerie, and he wasn't sure how much of what he remembered had been real. He'd wandered through most of it, he thought. Maybe. He hadn't risked the castle's library, despite desperately wanting to explore the pages of books found nowhere on Earth.

He vaguely remembered guards redirecting him when he wandered into places he shouldn't. He remembered venturing outside, where the night air was on the cusp of getting warmer. Smelling wetter. Seleen had been with him for a little while, but Gabriel had sent him to bed.

His orders had been to stay awake, to hold the connection with his itzal until he could lead a group right to the rebel hideout. Before, he'd seen it as a daunting task.

But it had been the easiest thing in the world, and he'd hardly noticed until the final hour or two.

In the dark, empty halls and gardens, his tears had been shed until he was dry. He grieved alone. Only the stone was witness.

Lilly... how many jokes had they made that she'd be the last to go, the last Faine to die, because she'd fight Death to the death? How many times had she boldly claimed she'd probably defeat Death and get to live another hundred years before he had the courage to try again?

But now she was dead... and he wasn't.

He didn't remember when the tears had stopped, and the numbness in his chest had replaced his heart. But it was better than feeling.

He'd lost his family in less than a week. Barely time to mourn the one before the other left him too.

It hurt, and he wanted it to stop hurting.

Gabriel passed a familiar servant in the hall. A middle-aged man Odalys had once called Paetr, Eeris' servant, bowed as he and a wisp of a girl passed Gabriel. Dressed in the gray uniform of a slave, the girl appeared hardly more than nine or ten, and looked utterly petrified and miserable. She only glanced up at him before bowing her head, her messy blonde hair hanging in her face. Half-elven ears peeked out.

I feel you, kid. Gabriel left the confines of the castle. Today, it seemed, was not a day for smiles.

Entya waited for him in the courtyard alone. She was dressed in light armor, as was he, and her dark hair was pulled up at the nape of her neck in a secure bun.

"Are you ready?" she murmured. Her eyes asked another question, one Gabriel didn't want to answer.

He turned to the gates. "Let's go."

They left the castle, slipping to the barracks, where Captain Koranos waited with two dozen soldiers, sixteen dark weavers, and a dozen normal magic weavers.

For a while, the imperials would have the upper hand. They would be a force to be reckoned with. This time, Gabriel was ready.

This time, he wouldn't lose.

He was too aware of the eyes that watched him guide the group with Entya and Koranos. He would be literally leading them into battle. A boy with only a few weeks of sword and magic training to his name. Gabriel didn't want to think about what he must look like, with exhausted eyes that spoke of shed tears.

His magic brushed against him, whispering assurance. Victory would come with the dawn.

Then they were moving. Gabriel reached for his itzal, feeling it out. The creature reached for him. It was weaker, a mirror of his own strength. He wouldn't be much help in this fight, but he would try. He didn't have much else to lose, right?

Dad would have your hide for that thinking. Gabriel scowled ahead. *And Lilly would beat to a pulp whatever was left. You have everything to lose, and you're going to fight for it.*

They made good time in reaching the west side of Erriath. Gabriel had no doubt they had already been spotted. No doubt the same thing had happened yesterday. He was grateful Erriath still slept, unaware of the battle that would soon be waged in her belly.

The taut feeling between Gabriel and his itzal eased, and it was better able to give them directions down to massive tunnels just inside Erriath's inner wall. The entrance was in the home of a gatekeeper and his family.

They were arrested when they denied knowing of the entrance when it was found in the gatekeeper's own larder. The underside of the trapdoor had green vines painted on it, with golden lilies and five stars.

Gabriel's hurried walk turned into a sprint. His heartbeat quickened, pulse thumping as adrenaline rushed alongside his magic, making it sing. He felt whole again with his magic all in one place.

The tunnel was one long path to their quarry, and it didn't take long to find the main rebel camp. The imperials exploded upon a cavernous space with ramshackle little cloth huts or tents. The Gold Mark had been in the middle of packing up, fleeing. The space smelled of unwashed bodies and utter fear.

Rebels spun around as soldiers charged, and weavers stood back, letting their magic do the work. Gabriel lost sight of Entya as he came down upon his first opponent, a man with matted black hair. Gabriel didn't reach for his sword. He pulled at the shadows, wrapping them around him and throwing them out like so many little shards of glass. Matted-Hair Man lunged aside, but his leg was peppered with wounds.

The sounds of fighting echoed in the cavern, so piercing that Gabriel's head throbbed. His magic whipped around, looking for another enemy to consume.

No. Gabriel paused long enough to check the magic. *We don't kill.*

But they killed your family.

"I know..." Gabriel whispered. "But I'm not like them."

The magic felt disgruntled, but Gabriel was confident it would obey. He thrust out a hand, and fire licked up the lengths of a cluster of vines that had begun to weave around him. An older woman cried out, staggering back.

The soldiers were mostly there to make arrests or handle any non-magic rebels there, but the place was in so much chaos Gabriel had no idea who did or didn't have magic. It was flying everywhere, striking stone or people or cloth. People were screaming, rushing to escape while the rebel weavers covered them. Entya and the other dark weavers shook their wall, and soldiers without magic rammed through it.

Gabriel threw himself into the battle. His strength was limited, but he was able to hold his own and, at least, help watch the backs of his comrades. He was grateful the rebels didn't have much of the same armor as the imperials. It made them easier to pick out.

Remember this pain. Remember the strength of your father, the strength of your sister. Remember that, and the strength they lend you—the strength that burns in your very veins—will be all the stronger.

Gabriel roared, letting his grief and pain bubble over. It hurt, but it fueled his magic in ways that burned, that made him feel stronger. Powerful.

The cold shadow magic slid into his hand. A whip of darkness coiled at his feet, the magic a pulsing song of power, of purpose.

He wasn't going to kill anyone. But that didn't mean he wouldn't make them feel his pain.

The whip struck true wherever he directed it. It snapped against the side of a seventh weaver who tried to ambush Entya, and wrapped around the ankle of another who tried to run at him. Gabriel yanked on the whip, and the rebel flew into a pile of tent canvas.

He was mindful of his energy, but he fought any weaver that came at him, though all seemed hesitant to attack him. Cowards. Gabriel snapped his whip, letting the sound be his war cry.

Gabriel slashed his arm outward, and fire ripped across the space between him and a seventh weaver. There were a surprising number of these, and even though their vines could counter dark magic, the sevenths weren't trained like imperials were. The dark weavers knew what to expect. News of Cadrian had put them even more on edge. Earth magic was dangerous, maybe even deadly.

A sharp pain slammed into his side. Gabriel yelped, tumbling across the ground. A boot clipped his skull as someone ran by, and he lost the shadow whip. He twisted to his feet, barely avoiding another boot, to face a *child*.

Gabriel hesitated. The kid couldn't have been more than ten, with mousy brown hair that flopped in his eyes. Angry, scared eyes.

"Go away!" the kid yelled. Vines grew up around him, a protective force rather than an offensive one. The lightning blast must have been a lucky shot. Gabriel grimaced, pressing his hand into his side. The healing magic did its work quickly, but he felt his strength drain.

"Leave us alone!" the boy cried. "You're bullies!"

Gabriel almost laughed.

"You think we're the bullies?" He stepped forward, his hands flickering with fire. "Bullies are the ones who leave innocent people to die in the street!"

A snap of his fingers, and fire magic peppered the kid's vines, burning them up hungrily. The boy cried out, collapsing and struggling to escape. Gabriel kept walking, his anger and grief rising.

Kill them.

He squeezed his eyes shut. He wouldn't kill. He wouldn't take a life. Not a *child*.

Gabriel glared at the kid before him, trembling in pain and terror as he approached. He lifted his hand. No death, but he didn't need this brat getting in his way.

"No!"

Someone ran in front of the blast of wind magic, grabbing the kid and throwing him out of the brunt of the force. Both tumbled a short distance, unharmed.

But Gabriel's mind saw something else. A day so long ago, but a day that was burned in his memory.

Lilly, trapped in place while Zal's magic hurtled to her. A killing blow.

Tilas, shielding her with his body and taking the full force of the magic. Enough to kill him. Enough that it *did* kill him.

Gabriel gasped, his throat too tight. Tesmir groaned on the ground, the little boy pinned under him, shielded from the attack. Tesmir pushed up, looking at Gabriel. Anger and betrayal and desperation all vying for a place in his pale green eyes.

Gabriel glared back. *You're the traitor. Not me.*

He lifted his hands again for another round. Vines shot up and wrapped around his wrists.

"No!" He twisted, yanking hard. The vines didn't budge, and Gabriel saw Jinnet walking toward him, arms outstretched.

"We don't want to hurt you, Gabriel," she said. "We can help you."

"Your people murdered my sister!" Gabriel screamed. "Murdered my father! Tortured Cadrian! I don't care what you have to say!"

Fire raged under his skin, burning and burning. He released it, searing the vines until they were nothing but ash. The woman flinched back but held steady.

"Jinnet!" Tesmir yelped as he pulled the kid away.

Gabriel's dark magic shifted in the shadows, ready. Gabriel thrust his hands forward, and itzals sprang forth from all around him. Mostly humanoid, but one looked like a cheetah. They converged on Jinnet, their limbs long, some jointed like a praying mantis, and sharp as blades.

More vines burst up, cracking like whips into the itzals. All were sliced neatly in two. Gabriel swore.

"Gabriel, you need to listen," Jinnet tried again. "Your sister is—"

His magic roared up again, and Gabriel let it run rampant. His chest heaved for air, but it wouldn't stop. Didn't want to stop.

"You're what's wrong with this world," he spat. "You're the bullies, the ones hurting other people. You're not going to hurt anyone else!"

Gabriel's magic nearly filled the cavern, shadows coming to life and lashing out at any enemy it could reach. The rebel weavers started to run, and Gabriel's magic hunted them down. A few shadows caught the ankles of fleeing rebels, tripping them up for other dark weavers or soldiers to take prisoner.

Jinnet stood before him, unafraid. She watched him, and he glared back. He gathered his magic to himself and pushed it toward Jinnet. Her vines burst out of the ground again, and this time they blossomed with the same red lilies.

Fire blazed between them. Gabriel jerked back, his shadow magic fading so the water magic could hold back the fire. He cursed his inability to use two elements at once.

"Quall, no!" Jinnet yelled. "Get the others out of here!"

Gabriel spun around. A man stood a few feet away, glaring at Gabriel in challenge. The same man who'd hovered so close to Jinnet the day before.

Gabriel flicked his wrist, and a tongue of fire zipped toward him.

Quall smirked as water fell upon it like a guillotine, leaving him unharmed.

"Is that the best you have, dark weaver?" Quall mocked. "I haven't seen you kill a single man. Too afraid to face that guilt?"

Gabriel snarled. The fire had been growing behind Quall. Jinnet screamed, but Gabriel yanked his fist back, and the fire magic blasted toward Quall full-throttle.

Quall leapt clear, but the fire struck him in the side and threw him several feet before he hit the ground.

"No!"

Gabriel twisted and threw out his arm. Lightning sparked along his arm like an arrow, flying for Jinnet's stomach.

Tesmir jumped in front of the magic *again*, yanking Jinnet to the ground. He screamed when it struck his leg. Gabriel snarled, turning to them and ignoring the searing memories.

Burning fire licked up his back. Gabriel screamed, staggering forward and collapsing when his legs gave up. He glimpsed Tesmir limping and pulling Jinnet along, toward an exit the rebel weavers were barely holding. The imperials were crowding around, nearly there.

Pain paralyzed Gabriel. He gasped, tears stinging his eyes as he turned on his hands and knees. Quall wasn't even sitting up. He glared at Gabriel, defiant and ruthless.

Gabriel snarled, letting an itzal tower over Quall. The weaver scrambled back, but the itzal was faster. It sprang on Quall, pinning him down and hissing in his face. He struggled, and the itzal's arm morphed into a scythe and pierced Quall's shoulder. The man screamed.

Quall writhed as Gabriel eased to his feet, limping over. The sounds of battle were distant, though they were only yards away, on the far side of the cavern. Gabriel didn't care. He had no strength for that.

For this, however...

He looked down at Quall. The weaver's sides heaved, and his temple was bleeding, standing out against a streak of gray hair. But he still glared up at Gabriel.

"Going to kill me now?" Quall panted. "Do it. Let me see how monstrous you imperials really are."

Gabriel frowned at him. His adrenaline was calming, giving way to the pain that had once been a fire to his fight.

Now, he was only tired. He was done. He felt nowhere near fulfilled, but he didn't care.

"No," Gabriel said. "You're more useful alive."

The itzal cracked its other hand into Quall's head, knocking the weaver unconscious.

Dawn did bring victory, though Gabriel didn't feel victorious.

He stood among the destruction he and others had wrought. The rebel camp was a ruin. Huts and food stores were scattered across the floor. Bodies had been scattered too, but those had been cleaned up a while ago. There wasn't any point cleaning up the rest.

Without a fight, his anger and rage cooled. He gazed around and let the silence of the place envelop him. It was better than facing the empty feeling in his heart, the feeling of purposelessness.

What now? A question he'd asked a lot during the hours of recovering from the fight. He'd watched rebels be taken away to the cells, almost two-thirds of the Gold Mark. Including Quall, still unconscious. Jinnet and Tesmir hadn't been among the dead or the captured. That defeat stung.

Footsteps made him turn, and the movement triggered exhaustion levels he'd never experienced, and suddenly his legs couldn't hold his weight. His vision flickered. Someone gathered him into their arms.

"Rest now." Entya's voice murmured softer than a whisper. "You did well."

Gabriel wasn't sure he agreed. His bones quaked at the thought of moving, of using any magic at all. His burned back throbbed where Entya touched it, but he was too tired to tell her that either.

Using his magic to heal it felt like too much work, and... he wasn't sure he wanted to. He'd done things with his magic he hadn't done before. He'd attacked a *child*, and tortured Quall. He'd attacked women.

If this was power, Gabriel wasn't sure he wanted it anymore. But what choice did he have? What choice did he have but to move forward? To keep advancing, growing, training?

"I felt like the bully," Gabriel mumbled. He rested his head against Entya's shoulder, too tired to hold it up himself.

"Sometimes it may well feel that way," Entya said, her voice still gentle. Understanding. "But the difference is how we use the power given to us. Bullies use it for their own gain, to feel stronger and superior. To exploit the weaker." She looked him in the eyes. "Were you any of those things?"

Gabriel considered. "No... I don't think so." He grimaced. "I did use it to make them feel like I did. To hurt."

Entya's features faltered, and he felt her kiss his head.

"Ahh, my boy... that is no fault when you grieve. We have asked more of you than we deserved to ask, when you have experienced more loss than any."

She stroked his hair, and Gabriel's eyelids began to droop.

"No, Gabriel." Entya's voice floated to him. "You are no bully. You are a fighter. You fought for your country, just as your father did."

Gabriel felt her magic close around them both for the second time in the span of just a handful of hours, cold but safe.

"Now rest. You did well. You did well."

Gabriel's mind slipped into silence, her words a lullaby that soothed the guilt.

He slept, and did not feel pain.

33

NORTH

Lilly woke to the sound of soft voices. Her eyes drifted open lazily, her vision focusing on a room she didn't recognize. It was a nice room. Clean, tidy, more like an adult's bedroom than her own back home.

Her fingers slowly spread over the heavy quilt that hugged her snugly against the mattress. It was scratchy, but somehow she didn't mind.

The rest of the room was sparse, but cozy: a wardrobe in the corner, a chest under a curtained window, and a small desk in the other corner. It looked a little like Tilas's old room.

The familiar squeeze in her heart throbbed, and Lilly took stock of the rest of the room. Not much decoration. The bed was situated against the back wall, and the door was to her left, along with a figure half lying on the bed—

Lilly started, and pain twinged in her right side. She drew in a sharp breath, wiggling a hand to her side. It felt... thick? Like something stiff was stuffed there.

Bandages. That was the word she wanted. But what interested her more was the person dozing next to her. He sat in a chair pulled up to the bed, but his top half rested on the bed, just within reach.

Lilly smiled a little, watching him. It was creepy, yes, but... she'd never seen Jek so still. Even when still, he looked... solemn. He didn't look restful like Gabe did when he napped or something.

She slid her left hand over to him, smoothing back his hair from his forehead. The scarred side of his face was hidden against the mattress, and he had a softer look without it, in spite of the somber expression.

Jek stirred at her touch, and Lilly pulled back. He blinked sleepily, his eyes drifting up to her face.

His eyes widened. "Lilly?" His voice was so quiet she almost didn't catch her name. It trembled, too.

"Me," Lilly confirmed. "Wanna—hey, hey." She grabbed his hand. "Why are you crying? Don't cry. What happened?"

Memories flitted in...

"Blessed Creator," Jek whispered, his grip tightening. "We almost lost you..."

Lilly swallowed. "But you didn't, yeah? I'm not dead. Somebody's gotta keep you and Mordir out of trouble." Talking hurt, but she needed to keep her own voice steady, and talking helped find solid ground.

Jek tried to laugh and wiped at the tears. Lilly squeezed his hand gently. "Hey, don't cry... I'm not dead."

"I know." Jek nodded. "I know, but... you almost were."

Lilly shuddered. The memories were coming back into place. The pain, the terror...

"Come here." Lilly tugged him closer. Jek obliged, and Lilly grasped his shirt in a hug, anchoring herself to something as alive as she was. Tears pricked her eyes, and she loosed a breath. *Don't think about it. You're alive. You are not dead.*

"I'm not going anywhere," she whispered. She felt him reply with a small nod, and she pulled back and searched his face. "Are you hurt? What did he do to you?"

Jek's hand strayed to his chest before he could stop himself. "Zal hasn't quite forgiven me for what happened in Balmarren."

"I'm sorry..." Lilly whispered. "If I hadn't left the inn—"

"If you hadn't left, he would have captured all of us," Jek cut her off. "And you would have been taken to Erriath too."

Lilly bit her lip. Tae, Hakor...

"I'm getting up now," Lilly announced, "so either help me or have me ignore you when you try to protest."

Jek's brows raised, but Lilly was already pushing the quilts off with one hand and trying to lever herself up.

"Alright, alright, hold on." Jek hurried to support her. "But Iluna's going to be the one you have to worry about, not me."

"Who's Iluna?"

Jek smirked. "Mordir's wife."

Lilly's jaw dropped. "He's *married*?"

"She's nice," Jek said. "Though I should warn you, their children are energetic."

"Mordir has *kids*?"

How? How could someone like the Ghost... a family? Why was this so shocking?

Because monsters don't usually have families like that.

Jek watched her carefully. "Please stay in bed."

"Mm-mm." Lilly inched her legs to the edge of the bed. "I want all the way up."

"Lilly, you're still recovering, just take it easy—oh for the love of Allare, hold on."

Lilly smiled, smug, as Jek assisted when she ignored his protests. Her legs wobbled, and she clutched at Jek's shoulder until they steadied. Deep, slow breaths.

She wasn't dead. She wasn't going to die. Not this time.

Taking steps felt like trying to remember how to walk. Her side twinged, but the pain was nothing compared to what she'd felt before. She could deal with this.

When they reached the door, Lilly glimpsed a cot in the corner of the bedroom. "Whose is that?"

Jek glanced over. "Usually Iluna's."

The door opened. Lilly grabbed the doorframe and hobbled out by herself for a few steps into a tiny dining room.

Two people sat at a table, mere feet from the door. Mordir, facing the door, stared.

"Lilly."

The woman sitting across from him turned in her seat. She had thick, black hair tied back, with dark eyes like Mordir's. She was very pregnant but still moved with grace. Her eyes went wide.

"I'm not dead?" Lilly offered.

"Aye, we can see that." Mordir sat back, as if trying to take in what he saw. "But I didn't expect you to be walking this soon."

"She refused to stay in bed," Jek said as the woman stood and helped settle Lilly into a chair. Sitting felt wonderful, but Lilly tried to hide the gasp of relief.

"My wife, Iluna." Mordir motioned to the woman. "Best healer in the village."

Iluna tsked at him, her cheeks going a little pink before she turned to Lilly again. "How are you feeling, love?" Iluna felt her forehead, then her pulse.

"A little weird, but okay otherwise?" Lilly submitted to the check up.

Iluna nodded, satisfied. "How about your side?"

"Dull pain, but really only if I move too much."

"Like walking mere minutes after waking up." Jek slid into a seat beside her. "I expected you to be willing to stay in bed."

Lilly shrugged one shoulder. "Normally, you'd be right."

But she'd almost died. She didn't want to lie around. She needed to be upright, talking. Breathing. Not feeling like an invalid. Her hand drifted to her wounded side. It throbbed from the exertion but nothing more. The rest of her, though, ached. Like it was still shaking from the aftershock of all those grenades.

The burning, bursting grenades...

Lilly shivered and pushed the memory away. "So, why *aren't* I dead?"

Mordir nodded to Jek. "The poison had progressed too far for us to do anything, but Jek..." He shook his head. "It was a miracle."

Lilly looked at Jek for a better answer. Jek still watched her. He cleared his throat. "Remember I told you my magic can cleanse plants of disease and such?"

"Yeah?"

"Well, dragonleaf is plant-based." Jek shrugged a little. "It was all I had to go on, and I thought, if I could draw it out of you like I can other plants... at first I didn't think it was working, but I felt the difference. Your pain seemed to ease, and I just kept going."

Lilly smiled. "Thank you." She looked him up and down. "It didn't hurt you, did it?"

Jek shook his head. Lilly searched his face for a hint of a lie but found none. She leaned against him and felt him relax. "Thanks." Leaning against a boy who wasn't Nick like that made her feel a twinge of guilt, but she didn't move. At the moment, she didn't much care.

"You're welcome."

A sharp, childish cry erupted from another room, and a little girl with blonde hair came running out, tears streaming down her face.

"Zye took my blocks!" The girl pointed to a little boy lurking by the doorway. His hair was the same dark shade as Mordir's. Almost as black as Iluna's.

"Hush." Iluna wrapped an arm around the little girl and looked at the boy. "Zinaan?"

"I wanted to play with them too!"

"But your mother's told you to ask first, has she not?" Mordir turned in his chair to face the child. Zinaan didn't meet his eyes.

"Yeah..."

"Did you ask?"

"No..."

Iluna nudged the little girl toward her brother. "Then you must ask."

Silence for a second. Zinaan glanced up. "Ivy, can I play with blocks too?"

Ivy, still looking a little offended, wiped her eyes with her palms. "You can play with *some* of them."

Zinaan grinned. He looked at Mordir for approval, but his eyes caught on Lilly. He froze. "Who's she?"

Lilly managed an uncertain smile. "I'm a friend of..." She took a stab in the dark. "Your father?"

Mordir smiled. "Lilly, meet Zinaan and Ivy." He motioned to the boy and girl in turn. "They were instructed to play *quietly*." He gave them both firm looks, but neither seemed too chastised.

"Were you sleeping in Momma and Papa's room?" Zinaan asked. "Momma said we couldn't go in there to play."

"I was," Lilly said. "But I'm awake now." She looked at Iluna. "Sorry for putting you out of your room."

"Nonsense." Iluna waved her hand dismissively.

"You screamed a lot," Zinaan said. "Ivy cried."

"*Zinaan.*" Mordir's voice was sharp. Zinaan flinched.

Lilly flushed. She looked at Ivy. "Sorry if I scared you, girl friend."

Ivy watched her, part shy and part curious. "Are you better now?"

"Yeah." Lilly offered her a bright smile and poked Jek. "His magic saved me."

"Mister Jek's magic is amazing!" Zinaan blurted. "He showed us some last night during supper, and he made Ivy a flower crown!"

Lilly feigned a shocked jaw-drop and looked at Jek. "How come I never get a flower crown?"

Jek rolled his eyes. "If you want one, you just need to ask."

"You can have mine," Ivy offered.

Lilly turned to her. "Nah, you keep it. It means he likes you." She winked. Ivy giggled.

"Go play, now." Mordir stood and herded his children into the other room. "And mind you play *quietly* this time."

When the children were safely occupied with their toys, Lilly rounded on Jek and slapped his arm.

"Ow!" Jek recoiled. "What was that for!?"

"A *flower* crown?" Lilly hissed.

"Would you believe me if I said I didn't use magic?"

"No, because it's winter, and flowers don't grow in winter!"

Jek watched her warily but offered a soft smile. "I'm alright, Lilly. Honest. Picking flowers doesn't hurt much. And if it makes a little girl smile..." He shrugged sheepishly. "She really wanted one."

Lilly huffed. "Well, when this whole war is over, I expect my own flower crown. Like, maybe three of them."

"Of course, Your Highness."

Mordir cleared his throat. "Speaking of war, we should discuss plans to get you both back to your rebels."

Lilly whipped her head to him so fast it made her side twinge. "Back? Why?"

"Because we set off on this quest for that amulet, didn't we?" Mordir lifted a brow as his wife stood and left the room through another doorway that led into a kitchen. "And now, we don't have that."

Lilly bit her lip. No, they didn't have the amulet. They had nothing. Lilly wasn't even sure they still had their supplies.

But giving up felt wrong. Going back with nothing to show for it except almost dying seemed pathetic. Rune and the others wouldn't see it that way, but Lilly would.

"No."

"No?" Both men looked at her.

"I'm not going back." Lilly met their eyes in turn. "You two can do what you want, but I'm still going up those mountains. I'll send Rune a message, let him know what happened."

"I sent one to him," Jek said. He frowned at her, as if trying to find an argument she couldn't refute. "I told him what happened, and that Hakor and Tae are in Erriath."

Lilly gave him a grateful nod. It must not have been easy for Jek, telling his brother that Hakor and Tae were now captive, and that they'd lost the very thing they'd tried to keep out of the empire's hands.

But he'd done it for her. He'd saved her life and relayed the news that would probably send Rune into a rage.

Mordir crossed his arms. "Lilly, you were almost killed. The mountains hold a lot of unfriendly things."

"So like, the rest of this bloody, violent country? Shocking." Lilly leaned forward. "I'm going because this fight isn't just about me anymore. I have people in Erriath who could really use the dragons' help. My brother. Jek's brothers." She held the Ghost's eyes. "And Tae."

The assassin's irritated expression fell. Jek said nothing. Lilly dug her fingernail into the grain of the wood table. "She's the half-elf princess, isn't she?"

Jek gaped. Mordir nodded slowly. "That's what I gathered... I didn't know it when I first met her. I thought she was just a slave."

"I need to bring those dragons back with me. I'm a rebel, even before I met all of you. Turning back isn't in my blood."

Mordir sighed. "I don't know why I expected it to be."

"The dragons can give us a major advantage," Lilly pressed. "Yovak has catapults. If we have dragons, we can destroy those before they touch our lines." She tilted her head in thought. "I'll ask them for the other shard of the amulet too. Seiryu has the amulet now, and he has at least two other pieces. That leaves the dragons' shard, and the stone. It sounds like the stone is tricky to get to, so maybe we can beat Seiryu to it."

Mordir groaned. "You'll be the death of us all, Faine."

Iluna glared at him.

Lilly looked at Jek. "And maybe we can cut through the forest and hit up Lilantami on the way back down. If Seymour knows where Tae is, maybe he'll be convinced to help us too. Somehow."

"The half-elves haven't trained in years," Jek reminded her. "And there are the ones at risk in Erriath."

"We'll burn that bridge when we get to it." Lilly shook her head. "No more dark magic. We'll find another way to win." She touched her side and tried to smile to lighten the mood she'd darkened. "But I have dibs on Zal. Y'all can have Yovak and Seiryu to yourselves now."

Mordir laughed. "You're something else, dragonfire." He stood. "But while I won't fight you on this plan, there's still the matter of your own health." He held her eyes. "You are in no condition to go anywhere."

"We can't wait!"

"We also can't almost lose you again," Jek said quietly. "Mordir is right... those mountains aren't tame ones. We can't just leave now."

Lilly pursed her lips and was casting about for a counter argument when Iluna spoke.

"A compromise." The woman set a plate of food before Lilly. "You need to let your wound heal anyway, and walking will only make it worse. Stay here another three days. I won't let you leave until I'm certain you won't relapse." Iluna looked at Mordir. "All of you will need more rest if you're going up those mountains."

Mordir nodded, something unspoken passing between them. Iluna passed to the other room where her children played. Lilly glimpsed Mordir grasping her hand briefly as she brushed by him.

"That's fair," Jek said. He looked at Lilly. "We'll need fresh supplies anyway."

"And lie low until the village has settled down," Mordir added. "No one else was hurt, but Zal's arrival scared the ones he chased out of the inn. We're lucky we haven't been found out yet."

Lilly huffed, poking at her food. "Finnnne." She looked up. "Wait, 'another three days'? I was out for *three days*?"

With a plan in place, the rest of the day moved agonizingly slowly. Lilly and Jek remained indoors, babysitting while Mordir accompanied Iluna into the village to get a feel for the overall mood, and to find a few supplies they would need.

Mordir's kids knew nothing of their father's occupation, and he warned her not to breathe a word. They—and the village—thought he was an imperial soldier. Just a simple, unimportant soldier currently on brief leave to make sure the rebels hadn't bothered his family.

Lilly had withdrawn from playing with the kids, to catch her breath, when Mordir and Iluna returned.

"These taxes are highway robbery," Iluna was growling. "So high, and people can barely feed themselves, let alone their babes. And I can't find a good supply of herbs and medicines for a decent price anywhere to restock my own stores! And if I hear one more merchant tell me about limitations on how much I can buy, and what I can and can't buy because *His Majesty* has declared it not useful to his grand plans of recovery—"

Mordir juggled more packages behind her, and Lilly stood. "Can I help?"

"Sit, sit." Iluna flapped a hand at her. "This is why I have him. I won't have you reopening that wound."

"No ma'am."

Mordir gave her a "good answer" look as he helped Iluna sort and organize the packages. Lilly eased back down and watched. "What is all this?"

"Supplies for us, mostly," Mordir said. "But others are for Iluna's healing arts."

Lilly watched Iluna set out small jars and paper packets that smelled both pungent and sweet. "Why is it all so expensive?"

"Because the emperor believes it best," Iluna muttered. "Bloody man apparently doesn't realize not all healers have as luxurious an allowance as his own physicians. Taxes to fund his wars, taxes to 'recover' the country. Limits on what can and cannot be purchased."

Mordir smirked. "Your time will come when you outrank even the royal healer."

"I don't want your flattery."

"Yes you do."

"Go put those in a corner of the kitchen out of my way." Iluna flapped a hand at the heavier packages, the supplies for the journey. She accepted only a brief kiss before shooing Mordir away. She glanced at Lilly. "Have the children tired you out?"

"They have more energy than I do. It's not a fair match."

Iluna laughed. "So you left Jek to their mercy?"

"He has magic, he'll survive."

Shaking her head and smiling, Iluna resumed her organizing. "We couldn't buy as much as you would need for a journey up the mountains and back, so either you will have to ask the Dragon Keepers for more, or hunt along the way."

The night was peaceful. Lilly tried to bully Iluna into taking her bed back, but the woman bullied Lilly into staying in it. Iluna was a force not to be crossed. Mordir stood behind his wife during the debate, motioning for Lilly to surrender and submit.

Lilly only did so after Iluna picked up a knife to chop vegetables for supper.

The night brought too much time to think. Lilly was alone in the bedroom this time, which didn't help.

She worked the numbers in her head. A month. She had been here a month. How could so much happen in so short a time? She'd gone from causing school disruptions one day to almost dying from an incurable poison and being healed by a boy with magic. She'd fought with a dagger, she'd cheated death more times than was probably healthy...

She'd watched people die. Lilly bit her lip, the pain sinking in as fresh as it had been the first time. Loss didn't get easier. That pain didn't seem to be leaving anytime soon.

Her hand skimmed over the bandage, freshly changed with a poultice that helped dull the pain. Her body had finally stopped trembling, as if realizing that the danger was gone. No more poison. No more burning.

Lilly inhaled slowly, then exhaled. She refused to dwell on any of it. Get up and keep moving. She would take the phrase "walk it off" literally. She needed to face forward, not back.

The beads of Rousen's bracelet rolled against her wrist. She fingered it as sleep slowly overcame her.

It would be a new reminder. She had bigger things to fight for. Fight to make sure the deaths had not been in vain.

I'm coming, Gabe.

The next two days passed without incident. The village seemed to have calmed after the other night's events, and no one seemed inclined to investigate. The soldiers did minimal work, but without any witnesses or any missing bodies, it wasn't a case that held their attention. The rain had washed away any blood trails that might have led them to Iluna's house.

They departed a little after noon, when Iluna finally pronounced Lilly well enough to travel. *After* Lilly proved to them that she could walk without tripping over herself or collapsing. And on condition that she remember to change the bandages regularly.

"I'll send you a full report," Lilly promised.

"Don't die again, and that will be enough," Iluna said. "Just... be careful."

"We will." Lilly hugged the woman. "Thank you for all your help."

Iluna hugged her back. "Make sure my husband doesn't go off riding dragons."

Mordir, who crouched by his children to say goodbye, glared good-naturedly. Lilly and Jek stepped back to let the couple have a few moments alone.

"Are you ready?" Jek murmured.

"Hope so," Lilly breathed. "Things hurt, but we can't afford to take more time."

Jek chuckled. "You're impossible."

"One of my many charms."

The kids squealed. Lilly looked up to see Mordir pull back from kissing Iluna, grinning. Iluna swatted him.

"Off with you!" she ordered. "And mind you stay out of trouble!"

"Bye Papa!" Zinaan and Ivy waved. "Bye Mister Jek!"

Jek sketched a bow, making them giggle.

"No goodbye for me?" Lilly teased. Ivy rushed to her and hugged her legs. The impact jarred Lilly's wound, but she lowered herself down to hug the girl. "Be good, okay? And maybe I'll see you again, and we can make flower crowns."

"Yes!" Ivy giggled. "And see dragons!"

"And see dragons," Lilly laughed, using a simple walking staff to pull herself back up. Ivy scampered back to Iluna, and the Jaeranys family waved as Lilly and the boys struck off down the street.

Lilly hadn't realized how close they were to the mountains until she left the village. They loomed, high and intimidating, warning away those considering hiking through them. Lilly almost wished they could ride—*almost*—but they had left the horses behind at the local stable. Dragons would spook them too much, and they'd be cutting back through the forest where there would be no room for a horse.

Adrenaline fueled Lilly's steps as they began their walk. The throbbing in her side gradually waned until she barely noticed it. So much depended on this trip. Without the amulet, Lilly needed *something* to bring back. Her actions had gotten Tae and Hakor kidnapped. She couldn't go back empty-handed now.

She didn't know what she'd say. Didn't know what she'd do if the dragons and the people with them said no. But she had to try, and one way or another she'd make sure she descended those mountains with an aerial army at her back.

"Lilly?" Jek stood beside her, and Lilly realized she'd stopped walking. Mordir turned a few feet ahead, questioning.

Lilly shook her head and adjusted her pack. This would work. She would pull Gabriel from the wolves' lair using every advantage she could find. She would save the world her father had given up everything for. The world her parents had once fought for together.

She'd been a storm for her own anger and hatred. Now she'd be a storm for others.

"Come on. Let's find ourselves a dragon army."

ACKNOWLEDGEMENTS

Spoiler: Writing a book is HARD.

Like, I could not have done all of this by myself. And I didn't. I have been so incredibly blessed by so many people. *Empire of Blood* has been a *beast* to write, from its days as just one mammoth book to the later stages of it becoming a duology.

It's been a *journey* with this novel. It's been a work in progress for years, and it's so weird finally seeing it finished. Done. Or mostly. The other half is still to come.

But I've grown with this novel. My writing has improved through each revision and edit. Through every infuriating brainstorm session, I learned new things.

And through it all, I've only kept my sanity with the help of these amazing people:

To my family: You've all been so supportive and loving, and have given me all I needed to grow in my writing, my faith. Mom and Dad, you guys most of all. I love you both, and all of your love and support have meant everything to me.

To my incredible writing squad, the Sparkly Space Wrimos: Kate, Anna, Jameson... you girls are epic. You all have stuck with me through my rants and rambles and helped me when I was stuck, and offered amazing advice. I've grown in my writing because of you guys.

To my alpha and beta readers: Jameson, Kate, Anna, Abigail, Peggy, Sarah, Nate, and Kyle. Y'all rock, and EoB is vastly better because of your feedback and advice.

To my editors: RaeAnne of Lavender Prose, thank you for helping *Empire of Blood* improve in its story and characters and world. Nicole Shultz of Confident Creations, thank you for helping me put grammar in its place, and slaying the many commas I use. xD And Kate, for being an absolute *boss* at proofreading and catching mistakes I've stared at for months and never saw.

To Julia: You have been so supportive and always excited for anything *Empire of Blood* related. You're so sweet and always willing to help and I love you.

To (the other ;)) Nicole, and to Stephanie: Thank you for being there for EoB's baby years, and the years of character role-plays that helped define the characters and the world.

Especial gratitude to Stephanie, for Aderyn Scalestride. Thank you for giving her into my care, and for always being willing to help me out with figuring out her dialogue or actions. And, by extension, all of the character development Kedmir got out of those conversations.

To Laura Hollingsworth, for giving EoB a GORGEOUS cover that I can't stop staring at even months after I saw it the first time. To Anna, for the AMAZING character cards for preorder goodies. To Mary Weber, for helping me make sense of this craziness that happens with launching a book (you've saved my sanity more than you know). And to Susie Poole, whose formatting prowess has done so much better than I could have (you too are a lifesaver).

To my cover reveal team and my launch team: You guys rock and I am beyond grateful. Thanks for making this journey so awesome.

To you, dear reader. For picking up this humble story that's grown into what it is today. For (I hope) enjoying reading it as much as I enjoyed writing it. For loving the characters as much as I do. You're amazing, and you're why I write.

And to the One who gave me the gift of story. Thank you for giving me all of these amazing people, and the resources to become a storyteller for Your glory. And for keeping me from throwing in the towel and deleting all the files.

And to Spotify, for (hopefully) not worrying when I played that Titanic song a lot during that one particular chapter.

Thank you, and I hope you've enjoyed reading *Empire of Blood*!

PRONUNCIATION GUIDE

Faine – Fayne
Lilly
Gabriel
Tilas – Tie-lass

Rebels
Annor – Ah-nor
Isilmere – Iss-sill-meer
Rune – Roon
Kedmir – Ked-meer
Rousen – Roo-sen
Orrun – Orr-run
Hakor – Hay-kor
Jek – Jeck
Tesmir – Tess-meer

Aderyn Scalestride – Ah-derr-in Scale-stride (OR: Ah-dare-rin)
Tae – Tay
Mordir Jaeranys – Mor-deer Jay-ran-iss
Iluna – I-loo-nuh
Zynaan – Zy-nan
Unvar – Oon-var

Imperial
Zilfanden – Zill-fan-den
Yovak – Yoh-vack
Myra – My-ruh
Odalys – Oh-dal-iss

Khaiel – Ky-ell

Rothar – Roth-ar
Seiryu – Sare-yoo
Eeris – Eer-iss

Entya – En-tee-yah
Zal Ira – Zal Eer-uh
Cadrian – Cad-dree-ahn
Raul – Rawl
Seleen – Sell-een
Akora – Ah-kor-uh
Phelan – Fell-an
Varta – Var-tah

ABOUT THE AUTHOR

Olivia Cornwell is a storyteller with a love of dragons and magical worlds. She writes stories of hope and redemption and familial relationships, and far too many sarcastic characters. She writes to entertain her readers (and may or may not collect their tears along the way) and share the truth of her Creator. At least when she isn't struggling to control her characters, drinking a lot of coffee, or hoarding chocolate.

She hides out in Ohio, and in her spare time Olivia cuddles her niece and nephews, and yowls back at her cat (who is most likely her familiar). She also enjoys adopting the characters from her friends' novels and keeping them safe from their own dangers.

You can find her on the usual socials: Instagram (@livvy_cornwell), Twitter (@livvycornwell), and sometimes Facebook (Olivia Cornwell – Author). She also has a few stories to read for free on Wattpad (@livvycornwell).

You can also find more information on her website: orcornwell.wixsite.com/oliviacornwellauthor

Made in the USA
Columbia, SC
18 July 2022

63613741R00262